1787

Flowerdust

Tor books by Gwyneth Jones

Divine Endurance
Flowerdust
White Queen

FLOWERDUST

Gwyneth Jones

TOR®

A TOM DOHERTY ASSOCIATES BOOK
NEW YORK

FLOWERDUST

Copyright © 1993 by Gwyneth Jones

This book is printed on acid-free paper.

A Tor Book
Published by Tom Doherty Associates, Inc.
175 Fifth Avenue
New York, NY 10010

Tor ® is a registered trademark of Tom Doherty Associates, Inc.

Design by Nancy Resnick

Library of Congress Cataloging-in-Publication Data
Jones, Gwyneth A.
    Flowerdust   /   Gwyneth Jones.
      p. cm.
    "A Tom Doherty Associates book."
    ISBN 0-312-85894-9
    I. Title.
    PR6060.05163F57   1995
    823'.914—dc20   95-15454
                                         CIP

First Tor edition: July 1995

Printed in the United States of America

0 9 8 7 6 5 4 3 2 1

Wayang

Oh Lord let me be a *wayang* in Thy hands
Whether I be hero or demon, king or commoner,
animal or plant or tree. Let me be still a
wayang in Thy hands. Then shall I speak your
tongue, whether I be valiant in the turmoil of battle
or small as a child at play amongst the waringins

This life of mine on earth is filled with toil
and strife, and my enemies who are many, mock me.
Their ridicule flies to its target swifter than
plumed arrows; their words strike deeper than
krisses. My struggle is not yet at an end.
And soon Thou wilt take me and I shall lie
amongst the others whose plays are over.
I shall be amongst the thousands in darkness.
And my struggle was not yet at an end:
Still my enemies dance.
Lord, let me be a *wayang* in Thy hands
Then after a hundred or a thousand years, Thy hand
will bestow upon me life and movement once more.
Then, one day when my time has come for Thy eternity,
Thou wilt call me to Thee again, and I shall speak
and contend anew.
And one day my enemies will be silenced, and the demon
will lie prostrate on the ground.
Oh Lord, let me be a *wayang* in Thy hands

Noto Suroto, *Wayang Liederen*
(translated from the Dutch)

FLOWERDUST

1

ON A DAY of baking sunlight in the middle of the third month, a small person in white clothes presented herself at the Cold Storage building, on the causeway side of the city of Ranganar. The Butcher volunteers recognized her and let her in as soon as she asked. The cat, Divine Endurance, slipped under the gate. She never felt the need to ask permission to do anything.

Inside the building it was stuffy and dim. Harassed young Samsui hurried about, the sleeves of their blue cotton jackets rolled and trousers tucked up to the knee for coolness. Their rosy, earnest faces were crumpled with worry. The Koperasi had made a delivery of supplies yesterday. The men were being very generous. No one knew where this food came from; but there was heaps of it, and not in good condition. The Kops had simply driven their treader into the yard and dumped its contents, in no kind of order. It was a struggle merely to sort out the perishable from the nonperishable—and by the time you'd done that, of course the perishable had perished!

"Silly fools," commented the cat. "They collect all this food, leave it to feed the rats, then they don't eat the rats. Humans are absurd."

"It's meant for the people from across the causeway."

"Meant to be wasted? Now that makes a kind of sense."

Cho looked at the cat sidelong, and pattered on through the ranks of torn cartons and oozing bales of grain. She stopped, and crouched to peer into the innards of the defunct ice plant. "Poor thing."

The doll called Chosen Among the Beautiful and the toy cat called Divine Endurance had traveled far, in time— it seemed—as well as space, to reach Ranganar. In the city where they were created, time had been standing still for who knows how long. Since the mysterious catastrophe when the toymakers vanished, the machines in the factory had labored on alone in a desolation: tireless, faultless, helplessly obedient. When they finally ran down, the cat, who had been the factory mascot, set out with Cho, the last of the machines' creations, in search of the toymakers and of the third remaining doll, Cho's "brother," who had made this journey long before.

They had found the human race, or at least a ragged and divided remnant thereof. One division lived here, on the fertile Peninsula jutting down from the Asian landmass into the ocean—with this island of Ranganar lying off the southern tip. The other people, who ruled the Peninsula, lived at sea on artificial islands.

The dead ice plant was an uncomfortable reminder for the two survivors from another age. They were machines themselves, however marvelous, and machines were not wanted here. True Peninsulans had learned to do without them. Even in Ranganar, where machinery was supposed to be acceptable, mechanical things were somehow neglected and falling into final decay.

Out on the Rulers' Islands, things were different. Something of the toymakers' civilization survived there, clear, simple, clean. Divine Endurance admired the Rulers. She found the Peninsulans messy and muddled, and their attitude to machines insulting. In her opinion, Cho's place was out at sea.

But Cho had been made to be the perfect companion of

one special human. On the Peninsula she had found her *person*. Her loyalty was settled; her journey was over.

"Come on," grumbled the cat. "I thought you had an errand with these particular smelly degenerates."

The camp was for refugees. A long causeway joined Ranganar Island to the mainland of the Peninsula. People had fled across it because of an outbreak of rebellion in the north, against the Rulers' occupying army. Cho gave Divine Endurance another mistrustful glance. She knew that the cat could twist the inbuilt rules that bound them both to serve and protect all humans. And she knew how much Divine Endurance resented having been abandoned. When the cat started *encouraging* her to help her human friends, Cho was suspicious.

"Why are you following me around? I thought you were on the other people's side."

She squatted, slim arms folded on her knees, watching the cat narrowly. Divine Endurance did things that were *not allowed*. It was Divine Endurance who'd insisted they could leave the factory by themselves. Cho knew that special artpersons, *geisha*, like herself, were not supposed to do that. You ought to be taken, by the person you were going to belong to . . . The thought of that disobedience still troubled her.

The cat's diamond-blue eyes slitted smugly.

"I am looking after the Rulers' interests. Don't worry."

Cho decided it didn't matter. She didn't mind if somehow she was helping the Rulers as well as her own side. She made no distinctions. Her purpose in life was to make humans happy: first her dear companion, then all the rest. Her joy was the certainty deep within her that she had the power to do so. However complicated or strangely simple their needs might be, Cho could do anything that was required. *An angel doll can grant, will grant, every wish of the human heart . . .* She had heard that said of herself, and she knew it was true.

"The Samsui women are having trouble with the refugees. Something bad is happening."

The doors on the other side of the huge shed stood ajar. The miasma of the camp drifted through: laden with woodsmoke and the stink of urine, shit, ripe garbage. "Something bad?" The cat's whiskers twitched derisively.

"Derveet says we have to find out what it is. Urgently. Otherwise the Samsui will let the Kops take over the camp."

The Koperasi, the Rulers' occupying army, were themselves Peninsulans: renegades and collaborators. They were hated up and down the Peninsula. But on Ranganar island their presence was accepted, if not welcomed. They shared the running of the city with the Samsui women.

"Derveet! Pah!"

The cat glowered over this name, tail twitching sourly—the name of the insolent human who had stolen Cho's loyalty and interfered with Divine Endurance's plans. A figure, a skeletal shadow, blocked the bar of sunlight that fell between the shed doors.

"Who are you?"

It was a woman, a Peninsulan. Cho looked up uncertainly. The Samsui, the city women, were heretics. The refugees were orthodox Peninsulans, who shouldn't use machines. Cho wondered if she was welcome in the camp. If she was not, it would be difficult to do as Derveet had asked. Derveet would not want her to defy the *dapur*, the women's rule that was law in the Peninsulan states.

"I'm Cho."

The woman came up. She was unveiled, which was unusual. Her step was wandering and loose-jointed, as if she were half-asleep. She crouched and touched Cho, who quietly let herself be examined. Skinny hands pinched her flesh, wobbled her wrists, traced the whorls of her ears. She saw that the woman's pupils were hugely dilated. The whites of her eyes glistened silvery-blue. Cho recognized these signs. She knew about the "medicines" that humans used. But the drugged eyes saw more clearly than most.

"What are you? Some kind of doll? Some kind of device? You've come to the right place. This camp is a machine. Most of it is invisible. Whatever you do, you are part of its works."

Cho was astonished. But it was a relief, for once, simply to be herself. Most humans—in this strangely changed world—didn't allow her that. They knew what she was, or they soon guessed. But they didn't want to think about it.

"I am a product of the Tumbling Dice Toy Factory. Our humans died long ago. Divine Endurance says that means we can do what we like, but I don't believe her. I know I'm still meant to belong to someone, and to do what I'm told, and never to do harm."

The woman laughed loudly. "How can you do anything but harm? You belong to the Rulers."

"I don't!"

"You must. We all do. Oh, God, if this were over. Death by slow torture, why endure it, the end is certain." She grabbed with bony hands at her spiky cropped hair, as if her head were likely to fly off if she didn't hold it. "I've heard of the magic doll. You are famous. Is it true you can grant wishes?"

Cho was delighted: she nodded. "Anything you like."

"Is the scholar awake?"

Ramli the stud rolled over in the slack webbing of his bed. Endang heard the jingle of his rings and chains, the animal susurration of a man-length sheaf of braided hair. He lay still in the hot, sweaty gloom, in the miasma of the night's terrible visions, trying to breathe evenly. Ramli replied, propped on one elbow, his gleaming V-shaped back to Endang's mat: "He's quiet, at least. He keeps me up half the night, whining and flinging about. He has bad dreams."

"There's a job for him. No, don't wake him," as Ramli shifted on his bed. "Call me when his eyes are sane. I don't want to waste my breath on a gibbering lunatic."

At home in the hills of the Timur border, this family was

rich for their kind. The stud had a house of his own in the main courtyard. Here in the camp he had to share his pen, in the back portion of a shambling makeshift shack. Ramli had no need to fear the "extra male." None of the family's women would touch Endang, the polluted. But his malice didn't need that excuse. He hated the interloper. They all did: the stud, the boys, the women, too.

Endang lay curled on his side listening fearfully, his eyes open a sliver. What kind of job? He could see the outline of the speaking boy, through a drift of dirty gauze that modestly veiled the stud's quarters. These Timur peasants had pretensions, and wealth. Their matting mansion was the size of ten of the ordinary refugee huts. It was cluttered with the screens and veils of orthodox custom, to keep the women and the stud and the neuter boys decorously apart.

He couldn't hear what the two were saying. Something about the Garuda dam? They were muttering about a "he" who was not Endang: a "he" who was being talked about everywhere in this heretic city of Ranganar. Endang realized that they were discussing not a man but a woman. A *failed woman*, one who had been proved infertile, was known as "he" in the Peninsula. "The man-woman Garuda—" he heard, and a dismissive snigger. They were talking about the lone survivor of the Peninsula's greatest royal family: a woman who had been fighting long and secretly for the lost cause of Peninsulan independence . . . lost until this very year, when the last Garuda's fortunes had suddenly changed. Endang could have laughed. Times really must be changing if Ramli the stud was taking an interest in politics!

Peninsulan women, who ruled society from the *dapur*, the sacred hearth, made boys of most of their male children. Civilized people did it with drugs or meditation. Less refined folk used the knife. The chosen few, the studs, were kept whole: enclosed, petted, ignorant. In the worst case, they were little more than prize animals. This family called

Endang "the scholar" (with a sneer) because his fate had been different. Once, he had been to college at Sepaa, the big Koperasi base town on the south coast of the Peninsula. And before that . . . He closed his eyes, mouth twisting bitterly.

Once, I was a gentleman . . .

The Timurese would have hated him without his education if he was as mindless as a Timur stud should be. He was not one of their own. He had been born in Gamartha, a northern state, into a devout, traditional family of small landowners. They were, in their way, liberal, and kind to their young consort-to-be. But when he was fourteen he was left an orphan. His mother-sisters, the fertile women of his immediate family, were dead. His "uncle," the man Endang should one day have supplanted, dutifully took the traditional route for a gentleman who has outlived his use. Endang didn't want to die. He ran away, and flung himself on the mercy of distant connections in the neighboring state of Timur.

They were very different from his own people, that household in the rich base town on the coast of Timur. They were enlightened Peninsulans who admired the Rulers, and accepted the ever-present Koperasi pragmatically. Endang was an "extra male." He was too old to be made a boy, and they didn't need him as a stud. When he pestered them, they saw no harm in his having an education.

The Koperasi, the collaborators, had become a nation on their own account after generations of foreign rule. They were not governed by women. They were an army of *men*. They had no *dapur*. They increased their numbers by buying, stealing, trading. There were plenty of unwanted male children in the traditional states. In the occupied territories, which had once belonged to the Garudas, there was a population of plantation workers—slaves, Endang had unwisely learned to call them. The army recruited from their ranks too. There were boys among the Kops, but few in the higher ranks . . . It was exhilarating—a whole world of studs, *men like himself,* walking around free: with cropped hair, with authority, with strange fancy gadgets that gave them powers the *dapur* denied to the orthodox.

But the Koperasi college had been Endang's downfall. He started out with heartfelt gratitude towards the Kops, and to the Rulers, whose benign influence had saved him from death. He began to read, he began to think. He began to think a little too much, he became involved in politics.

For a subject people there is only one kind of politics, that of resistance. His guardians caught him expressing dangerous opinions. They sent him away into the country—for his own safety, they said. So Endang the scholar became a domestic animal.

He had escaped, three times. He didn't go back to his relatives. They knew what fate they had condemned him to. They would not interfere. He had tried to survive in the underworld of the coastal towns, with the other outcasts: the failed women, and the extra men, who had been reared as insurance alongside the chosen stud and then thrown out by their families. But Endang had too little courage or too much imagination for that world, and he didn't know how to hide. Each time, he had been tracked down by the husky boys his "ladies" sent after him. The peasants of Timur are known for their avarice. Endang was *property;* they wouldn't let him go. Besides, the women were afraid of his relatives, who had paid them to keep Endang off the streets.

Each time, when he was brought back, it was worse.

He wondered what was happening in Timur now. He was kept enclosed, but he was sure there had been no violence around that squalid village in the border hills. The rising against the Koperasi was in the north, in Gamartha, Endang's old country. But there was such a general feeling of unrest and uncertainty this year, it didn't take much to get people moving. The inland Timurese had fled from rumors, by instinct, like the slaves on the run from their plantations—and they had all converged on the causeway, and arrived in Ranganar.

Endang's "guardians" were not so innocent. They had come to Ranganar for their own reasons, content to leave their farm untended for a season. They wouldn't lose by it. Their wealth wasn't in the land. They were moneylenders, these women: not ashamed to handle the Koperasi currency that was pollution to the truly orthodox. Hateful creatures, parasites! That a gentleman of Gamartha should have fallen so low . . . He almost groaned aloud at the miserable humor of the thought.

The muttering stopped. The speaking boy had gone from behind the gauze. Endang's heart thumped. Now he'd missed his chance to be forewarned. *What job?* The women had started using him as an errand boy since they'd arrived in the refugee camp. Their errands were alarming. But the pay was good. He swallowed the taste of nightmare in his mouth, thought longingly of peace and escape: *what job?*

Ramli sat up and kicked. He was a powerful young man. He was allowed space for physical exercise at home, and he kept his body in beautiful shape. Endang grunted in pain and pulled himself away. He was chained by one wrist to a staple hammered into the floor. He could probably pull it out, but there was no point. He had nowhere to go. The stud stretched against the matting wall behind his bed, smoothing his pierced foreskin back from a stalwart erection. Ramli always woke like that, and he eased himself, which strictly he should not do. Endang looked away.

"Want some? There's plenty!"

Penned in this corner, he had nowhere to go. He had seen the older women, no longer fertile, straddle that jutting horn as casually as they would take a drink of water. The childbearers used a little more ceremony, but not much. Nothing was sacred to these ladies—except money.

"What does it take to get you hard, scholar? A Kop uniform?"

Endang shrugged, unmoved by the insult. It had been

agony at first, to be chained here beside a beast in rut, in the reek of sweat and oil and semen, through the heat of the day and the stifling closeness of the night. But Ramli's company didn't bother him anymore. The real world had become the lesser evil. What went on in his mind was so much worse.

"Don't go back to sleep. You're wanted. They have a plan to recover the stuff."

Somewhere between the hills of Timur and the refugee camp, the peasant usurers had found a new source of profit. They had become drug dealers. In itself this was not surprising. The blessed weed, acar, though illegal by the Rulers' law, was cultivated openly everywhere in the hills. Bandits ran the traffic and supplied—naturally!— the best weed to the Koperasi. Someone must supply the refugees . . . But it wasn't acar that the women had. It was something else: something that made your mouth dry, your eyes blue, and gave your soul wings.

Escape, escape . . . How he wished he'd never touched the stuff. Acar was not addictive, so Endang had not known his danger. Nobody had warned him—of course not!—what would happen to him when there was no more of this infinitely stronger comfort.

He tried not to react to Ramli's news. He didn't know how the women got hold of their supply of the strange drug, but he knew that the flow had stopped. The "ladies," who didn't touch the stuff themselves, were furious. Endang was in torment.

Ramli, still casually nursing his erect member, leaned out of the murky curtains and called: "Parangtriti! He's awake!"

The speaking boy returned. The ladies were orthodox in this: they would never speak to their males. Or to a heretic, or a Kop, or any other polluting inferior. Parangtriti was their grand vizier, who dealt for them with the world outside the *dapur*.

"Your task," he said, squatting against the gauze, his

bald head nodding, "is to entrap the failed woman, the notorious bandit who has gone to earth in Ranganar since the uprising began in the north. The heretics have brought him to the camp today, thinking he will help them with their behavior problem. You are to speak to him, gain his confidence and then arrange things that will be explained to you. We have learned that he will know where to find the dust. He will secure it, and we will then take it from him."

"Derveet!"

Through the gauze, the old boy's wizened face screwed up as if at an unpleasant taste. "The bandit," he agreed. "Sometimes known as Anakmati, sometimes as 'the last Garuda.' "

Endang felt as if someone had punched him in the belly. He grasped at once the purpose behind these bland directions: a purpose of which the boy seemed oblivious. "This isn't your idea! We've been set up! We're being ordered to betray her!"

Ramli chuckled. Parangtriti bridled primly. "Him," he corrected. "All we want is the return of our property." He raised himself into the back-bent hobble of a respectful boy in the presence of his *dapur*. The women were there, at the far end of the earth-floored room, hearing everything: their sly, stony eyes glittering within their dark veils.

"I won't do it! You're crazy!"

"Huh." The speaking boy snorted contemptuously, and shuffled away. Ramli lay back, grinning broadly. He wound a hank of gleaming black braid, thick as his forearm, around one wrist, and stroked his ringed and decorated naked breast with the tassled ends. "Then you'll have bad dre-ee-ams!" he crooned. "The scholar will have more bad dreeeeeams!"

Two large boys, Parangtriti's minions, came and put Endang out in the alley behind the mat mansion, to think things over.

He thought of his own fall through the ranks of Peninsulan society: from the young gentleman of Gamartha to the debased slave of Timurese peasant criminals. He thought how it mirrored the collapse of the Peninsula. How the traditional way of life had become rigid and brutal under the pressure of foreign rule. How the *dapurs* had turned inward, becoming corrupt or simply refusing to see what was happening . . .

The Peninsula was a federation of small states, each with its figurehead prince and traditional government by the royal *dapur*: each princedom controlled more or less directly by the Koperasi, who answered in turn to the invincible Rulers. That was the way it had been, while the Peninsulan people decayed and their resources were plundered . . . until a few months ago. But the foreign power that had ruled the Peninsula with increasing despotism suddenly seemed to be crumbling. Their power was collapsing, and there was nothing to take its place. The rising in Gamartha was for the Gamarthans. It was commonly accepted that they would turn on the Timurese, whom they detested, as soon as they'd dealt with their own Kops. There was no one who could unite the states, who could save the Peninsula from chaos, except for Derveet.

To the native rulers of the Peninsula, she meant legitimacy. She was a Garuda. Her family had been paramount among the royals for fifteen hundred years, before the Rulers appeared out of the southern ocean. To the underworld of extra men and failed women—to the brigands and the whores and the Koperasi who dealt with them—she was Anakmati the wily, fearless bandit with friends in the strangest of places. To the Samsui, the heretics who had built a city of polluting machines here on Ranganar, she was Derveet: the only Peninsulan leader who would speak to them rationally, who respected their choices.

If you'd met her, you did not forget her.

Endang had met her once, while he was a college student. That was long before she became a credible partisan leader. But she was already at work on the hearts and minds of the Peninsulans. He had guessed her identity— she let him guess—while struggling to resist her charm. She had changed his life.

He laughed: a little cracked, crazy sound, startling the boy on guard. Changed his life? Destroyed it! But he would not betray her. She was the last dream of hope.

The Timurese peasants didn't know that he had met Derveet, and she might even remember him. They knew very little about Endang's past . . . They didn't know what they were asking. They wanted to secure their supply of the wonder drug. They had been told how they could achieve this. What could be more simple? It was crystal clear to Endang that his ladies were being used by some malign hand with interests far beyond drug dealing. But they wouldn't listen to him. If they understood, they wouldn't care. They didn't give a damn for the fate of the Peninsula.

He found that he was crying, sweat mingling with his tears. It was a burning morning to be staked out in the sun. His joints ached, his mouth tasted of poison, the world seemed unreal. The ladies had a little dust in reserve, he knew that. If he did what they wanted, or maybe (he grew blurrily cunning) *pretended* to do it, he could sleep tonight.

I won't. I won't, he whimpered. *They can't make me . . .*

Around noon, the boys came and took him to their own part of the big hut. At the stud's curtains, Parangtriti and Ramli were playing cards, through the decorum gauze. They heard a heavy, low, repeated thudding, like a rice pestle in the distance: small animal noises quivered between the strokes. Ramli grinned.

"Bad dreams in the daytime!"

"The scholar will see reason," agreed the grand vizier.

Derveet walked away from the shack-mansion of a numerous and almost certainly criminal tribe of Timurese. It was the end of a long, hot day of fruitless negotiation. Beside her, Atoon paced sedately. Miss Cycler Jhonni, their self-appointed Samsui escort, rushed around them like an overgrown kitten, practicing her *pencak silat*—Peninsulan unarmed combat—on the air.

The Butchers, of all the trade clans the most sympathetic to the Peninsulan cause, had given the refugees a campground by the old Cold Storage buildings, out on the causeway road. At first this had been tolerable. The Samsui city had retreated from the Peninsulan side of the island, where the water table was rising and the land sinking into a maze of brackish creeks. Out beyond Cold Storage there were only Ranganarese kampongs. But there were more refugees than anyone had bargained for, and they began to misbehave. There were murders, rumored orgies. Volunteer helpers were threatened; donated supplies disappeared from the Cold Storage sheds. The other Samsui, in council, warned the Butchers that something must be done—or the Kops would be brought in.

The Butchers possibly had a better grip on present realities than their sisters. They could imagine the consequences if the Koperasi troops based in Ranganar attempted to impose law and order by force out at Cold Storage. The refugees were not the only Peninsulans on the island. There were the Ranganarese themselves, whose boys were the Samsui laborers and coolies. And there was the West Bank—a no-go area for Ranganar's Kops, and a bolt hole for the most desperate of Peninsulan criminals, right beside the commercial center of the Samsui city. How would these Peninsulans react to a Koperasi action against the defenseless refugees?

But the Butchers didn't argue. They knew the state of mind of the Samsui majority. In frightening times, frightened people will do crazy things. They had begged for time, and consulted with their own radical fringe: Peninsulan sympathizers who were in contact with actual known rebels. They had asked for help.

Derveet was dressed as a man, in her most drop-dead

bandit finery: silk brocade jacket and breeches tailored close as skin. The prince of Jagdana was attired more soberly. He was posing as a simple Peninsulan gentleman, in the city on family business, trapped here by the unrest. Atoon's spectacular looks were not much dampened by a dull suit. Luckily (there was something to be said for the practice of enclosure) the risk of the Hanoman prince's being recognized was small. Few outsiders had ever seen him.

He was with Derveet in Ranganar because his family had sent him to support her cause—an astonishing gesture of confidence which still amazed her. This was the first time she had brought him across the river, away from the relative safety of the West Bank. It was necessary. The Inland Timurese would have nothing to do with a failed woman with black skin, no matter what his reputed rank and calling. But though they kept their own studs in chains, they would let their speaking boys converse with a modest gentleman from a different dispensation—while the gentleman's villainous bodyguard lurked in the background.

They'd talked, but they'd told nothing. She felt eyes on her from the dark tumbledown doorways as she walked. She wondered if they had heard of her; if they recognized Garuda? Most probably they did. They'd surely heard of the blowing up of the Garuda dam, and the raising of the Eagle. It would make no difference. Peninsulans revered beauty and order . . . which meant the deformed, the wrong-colored, the infertile were outcast. Without a sign from the ruling women of Timur, these peasants had no reason to respect a black failed woman. And who were the ruling women of Timur now? It was hard to say: it had always been the state most influenced by the Rulers, and the royal court was governed by a Koperasi regency.

In fact, it probably gave these ladies great pleasure to have the chance of snubbing the upstart, infertile Garuda. It was something, she supposed, to have brought a little happiness into this depressing place.

Jhonni prowled the mud boulevard. Her curly hair was

bound back with a red-and-white bandanna. Instead of Samsui trousers she wore a sarong of painted cloth. A jangle of amulets festooned her jacket. Most Peninsulan sympathizers were Butchers, or else Pabrikers: poor women with a long history of radical ideals. Jhonni was a Cycler, child of the richest, smartest clan in the city. But her enthusiasm for the Cause was unbounded.

She paused in her air-punching and ran up to Derveet, breathing hard. "Mama says the Gamarthans are on the point of taking Nor." This was the biggest of the northern Koperasi towns. "They'll hold the whole Gulf! Mama says—" She danced from foot to foot, puzzled by Derveet's indifference. "Aren't you interested?"

Atoon answered for them both. "Nationalism is a running sore," he explained, in his habitual tone of gentle calm. "The only good news we can hear from the north is that the Gamarthans have come to their senses, sued for peace, and embraced their local Kops as fellow Peninsulans."

They had reached a crossroads of two wide alleys. Miss Butcher Handai, who was supposed to be here to meet them, was nowhere in sight. Atoon and Derveet patiently sat down on the ground, in the shade of the last hut in the row. Jhonni hovered over them, crushed by Atoon's rebuff and Derveet's silence.

Derveet was the Samsui girl's idol. Jhonni would die for a smiling glance from those dark, imperious eyes. She dreamed of adventures in which she saved Derveet's life, or fell bleeding at her feet, martyred for the Cause . . .

"What do you want me to do?"

Vanish, thought Derveet. *Before you ruin this charade.* But the girl's naive excitement was so innocent. It was hard to be harsh with Jhonni, even when the child was at her most maddening.

"Don't you have work to go to?" she suggested hopefully.

Jhonni grimaced. "We're fixing the desalter. It's acting up again. Mama says she needs more hands."

The production of fresh water, always important on the water-hungry island, became crucial whenever the piped supply from the Peninsula was interrupted—as it was now.

"Fixing the desalination plant. My, how tedious. However, if you could bring yourself to endure—"

"But I'm a volunteer," countered Jhonni. She pointed to the official armband, which she'd converted into her bandanna. "Mama can't stop me doing charity work. I'm *supposed* to be here."

Derveet sighed. "Then sit by us and wait for Handai. Quietly."

The sky overhead was a flat blue as if it had been painted. Jhonni squatted on her heels, a trick that came naturally to native Peninsulans. It was agony for Jhonni's inflexible tendons. The heat of the day had not yet begun to fade, and the camp was very quiet. A Timurese girl came by, too young to wear the veil, slender as a reed in her sarong and high, binding sash. She laid an offering of rice and flower petals before a shrine that someone had put up at the crossroads. Jhonni saw the silver cloud-and-mountain icon that represented Bu Awan, the great mother: in front of it a figure of Naga the Serpent, patron of Timur. The girl lit two incense sticks, dropped the match, and stamped on it with her heel. The next passerby would scatter petals, rice, and incense in the dirt. It didn't matter. Gifts to the gods had meaning only in the moment of giving.

Jhonni breathed the atmosphere of the traditional Peninsula. She felt close to some wonderful revelation, and grateful to the Gamarthans for having driven this magic into prosaic Ranganar. She gazed with chagrin at her feet, in their canvas slippers. Proper Peninsulans went barefoot. She had not been able to bring herself to copy them in here, where every step was going to land your foot in something disgusting.

Jhonni was unused to boredom, didn't know how to wait.

"What would you do, Derveet, if it was the end of the world?"

Derveet was rolling herself a tobacco cigarette. Supplies of all kinds were disrupted. The blessed weed, acar, had vanished from the city. She sprinkled a little crumbled resin on the foul-smelling brown fragments, with a grudging hand.

"Me? Die, I suppose."

"No, I mean if you had warning. I'd go . . . I'd take my padded jacket, and dried food, and a water bottle, and a rubber sheet to sleep on . . . and some string, and a mending kit. I'd go north, up into the landmass, and wait it out. Oh, and a knife. And my book of cutout opera pictures . . ."

"What would you be waiting for? I don't quite understand."

"It's just my game." Jhonni blushed.

It was the trait she most hated in herself. That and her red-and-white skin, so ugly beside the true Peninsulan gold. And her thick ankles. She searched in vain for another conversational gambit. If she crouched here staring dumbly, she would seem—hideous thought—like a schoolgirl with a crush.

Derveet lit her cigarette, coughed, and passed it to Atoon.

The Koperasi had closed the causeway. They did nothing to stop the refugees coming in, but traffic north was tightly watched. The straits were thick with patrol boats, and Derveet's channels of news had dried. She and Atoon had hoped that they would find out something of the true situation in the north from the refugees. It was no use. If they knew, they wouldn't say.

The stockyards stood on a rise of ground. Derveet could see over the tents and shacks, back towards the city. In Cold Storage Park, where the Samsui used to gather after work, drinking tea and eating ices while their children ran about in the cool shade, a team of Koperasi were at work with heavy machinery. They were cutting down trees and scorching undergrowth: clearing the ground. For what? As she watched, a group of camp volunteers appeared on the road, marched to the park gates and accosted one of the men in uniform. There was a brief parley. The women retreated. The yell of saws and the whine of weedcutters started up again.

"Do the Kops know something we don't know?" murmured Atoon.

"Undoubtedly."

A group of boys sidled up, each of them with a toddler to mind and a baby on his hip. They were fascinated by Derveet's black face. In their families *aneh*—the deformed, misshapen, or wrong-colored—were abandoned or sold to the Koperasi. A black failed woman in fancy tailoring was a new experience. Jhonni wondered about the boys. Had these ones been changed by meditation, or was it done the way you castrate an animal? They were kids. The thought of them under the butcher's knife made her shudder. She struggled: she wanted to believe that the Peninsulan way of life was beautiful and perfect. Of course, the boys accepted their fate. They were content.

If I were a Peninsulan, she wondered, would my mama have thrown me out because my skin is red? It was a disquieting thought.

In the last of the shacks where Atoon had gone in to parley with a peasant speaking boy, she had glimpsed the stud. He was lying on a string bed behind a curtain, but someone had carelessly pushed the gauze aside. He was naked, except for his chains and rings. His hair, uncut and loose, trailed over his ornaments in thick black skeins. He wore a headband of dark and shiny material, and was painting his toenails. A tinny sound of music had come from somewhere around him . . .

In front of her the prince, sober and elegant, with his hair dressed low in gleaming coils at his nape, took a hard pull on the cigarette and grimaced.

"Have you ever tried alcohol?" he asked gloomily.

"Once," said Derveet. "Can't say I'd recommend it.

There are plenty of good reasons to burst into tears and run around trying to knife people. Who needs chemical assistance for that?"

"We won't find out anything this way. All I hear is that the Samsui are trying to make them send their girls to school, where heretic teachers will corrupt them. The Samsui are trying to kill sick people, with dirty knives and disgusting potions. And the Samsui are stealing their nightsoil, under a ridiculous pretext known as 'hygienic latrines' . . . Worst of all, the heretics insist on giving food to the *aneh* slaves, which is a wicked waste. How I hate peasants! Pedigree long as your arm, no thought or feeling for anything beyond their own patch of dirt."

Derveet grinned at the bitterness of his tone.

"Atoon, you *are* a peasant."

He frowned, ignoring this sally. "What was that thing on the young gentleman's head?"

"It's a sort of musical box. A Koperasi toy. You can buy that kind of gadget on the open market up in Timur. It doesn't mean anything. Doesn't mean they have to be dealing with the Kops."

"A machine!" It was ironic. "These Timurese studs. They get everything their own way."

Timur was a state of startling contrasts: fierce orthodoxy up in the hills; Koperasi rule; manic court intrigues around a puppet prince . . . and on the coast, native Peninsulan towns more Koperasi-ridden than Ranganar. Atoon pondered in silence. Derveet wondered if he was thinking about the musical box, or about the stud himself. She was a liberal, or so she believed. She was in favor of social reform, a gradual end to enclosure, education for men. But to sit here beside Atoon, having seen that sleek male animal, pierced and chained . . . it was a curious challenge. It seemed one must do something *at once*, about either one or the other.

"And yet," he said at last, "the Samsui are right. There's

something going on: more dangerous than the problems natural to the situation. One can taste it in the air . . . I wonder what happened to the mad clown?"

The Samsui volunteers spoke of a mysterious figure, dressed—disguised—like a clown in a puppet show. He wandered the camp like a harmless crazy, but he'd turned up in various suspicious circumstances. Though they couldn't catch him to question him, they'd become sure he was involved in the sudden crime wave.

"Saw us coming, obviously." Derveet grimaced, tossed the end of the vile cigarette onto a moist pile of refuse. "Maybe Cho will have better luck."

"She's here?"

"Oh, yes . . . somewhere about. Making people happy, you know."

They smiled. Cho always wanted to make people happy. And her sweet nature made everybody love her. It was no wonder her arrival on the Peninsula had been taken as a good omen by everyone who met her, even before they knew what a strange treasure had fallen into their hands.

It was Atoon who had first encountered the doll-who-was-a-person, at the end of her journey out of the desert landmass. But he'd been convinced, for reasons that satisfied him at the time, that she was Derveet's agent: come to call him from his comfortable prison in the Hanoman palace of Jagdana, to join his friend in the last battle for the Peninsula. He had sent the courageous girl (as he thought her) on to Derveet. And so Derveet became Cho's *person*, whom the angel doll was bound to serve.

The angel dolls were barely remembered in the records of the Peninsula, a footnote to ancient history. Derveet had only recently discovered the truth of her doubtful, incredulous suspicions about this perfect young girl. There was still a lot about Cho that she didn't understand. Maybe Cho's makers themselves had never wholly understood the angel dolls. But Cho was so gentle. If you couldn't understand her, you could trust her goodwill. And God knows, this camp could use some goodwill.

Derveet was not surprised that she and Atoon had failed to discover what was wrong. She hoped the visit itself might have some effect afterwards. If the Timurese weren't impressed by a black Garuda, their criminal element would have recognized the notorious Anakmati. They might think twice about making trouble, knowing the Samsui volunteers had a famous bandit backing them.

The best answer would be for the rising in the north to burn itself out, so the refugees could leave. She doubted that the solution would be so simple. Nothing was ever simple! But Derveet had a charm against disaster now. She smiled again, thinking of Cho: her lucky angel. After the years of useless struggle, the tide of the battle had turned. Surely it had turned!

The Peninsulans had been speaking, out of politeness to the Samsui girl, not in their native language but in High Inggris, the language of the Rulers and the common tongue of Ranganar. But Jhonni wasn't paying attention. Before silence fell between Atoon and Derveet she had drifted off into a dream of adventure and noble sacrifice in the mountains of Gamartha. It was Derveet who suddenly stirred. "Here come our friends," she remarked dryly.

Miss Butcher Handai was approaching the rendezvous, but she was not alone. A troop of young Samsui volunteers marched with her, at their head a large, square-built woman in the white clothes of the Physician clan. Handai was making faces of frantic apology. Derveet and Atoon rose to their feet. The Physician surveyed them with dislike. "So these are our interpreters. Mr. Ardjuna and Mrs.—or is it Mr.?—Krisna?"

Atoon bowed gracefully. "Delayed in your beautiful city by the closing of the causeway," he explained. "Very glad to be of any assistance—"

Derveet, in her role as bandit bodyguard, merely grinned.

"They look like a couple of criminals to me," said the Physician bluntly, unmoved by the fact that the Peninsulans clearly understood her words. "You'd better pay them off and get them out of the way."

The bandit turned to Miss Butcher.

"Is something wrong, Miss?" The words were mild. Mrs. Physician couldn't see the expression in the bandit's large dark eyes. But she saw, indignantly, how Miss Butcher seemed to quail before the flashy Peninsulan criminal.

"What's the matter, Butcher Handai? Don't tell me you're *afraid* of the creature! Let me deal with her . . . him, whatever—" She scowled, irritated by the paradoxes of Peninsulan custom.

At that moment, an uproar burst out. A mass of people came tearing towards them, shouting and dragging what seemed to be a dead body in their midst. The crowd boiled into the open space of the crossroads like a swarm of angry bees, forming a thick ring. Jhonni was surrounded by jostling bodies. She had lost sight of Derveet, and the prince, and the Samsui party. She pushed and shoved frantically. The wall of bodies gave way—as if they wanted the Samsui girl to see—until she was in the front row. A body lay in the dust. It wasn't dead. An emaciated young woman crawled to her knees and stood swaying, half-naked, her *dapur* robe trailing on the ground. Her hair was growing raggedly out of the customary *dapur* crop. Her eyes rolled back in her head, sightless. She spoke: loudly, insistently. There was white spittle at the corners of her mouth.

"They are in gold. Everywhere there is light, light, light. They do not eat the way we do. They drink and piss and eat and shit but not the way we do; they have special ways. They are imprisoned in glass and they sleep in their coffins, which is right because they wake in the Bright Land!"

A sweet scent flooded the air; a light seemed to rim the woman's body. She was doing magic. It was wonderful. Jhonni had never dreamed she would see anything like this in the refugee camp. The rites of the *dapur* were secret. No

Peninsulan, not even Derveet, would tell you about them clearly. Jhonni was enraptured. But she knew that this was wrong, something had gone terribly wrong . . . Suddenly, she knew what she must do.

"Don't be afraid! I'll calm her—"

At the sound of the loud Samsui voice, the crowd grew still. The people around Jhonni pushed her forward. She held up an amulet of Bu Awan, the sky mother. Light caught on the plaque of crudely engraved silver. Jhonni began to chant.

> "Bu Awan, Bu Awan,
> Awan, Awan, Awan.
> Bu Awan, Bu Awan,
> Bu Awan, Awan, Awan, Awan . . ."

Atoon, on the far side of the circle, started forward with a muttered exclamation. Derveet touched his arm and shook her head. The refugees stirred maliciously. Jhonni was within arm's reach of the medium. Like a snake striking, the stick-limbed Peninsulan grabbed the sturdy Samsui by the throat, by the shoulders: lifted her clear into the air. She shook Jhonni and threw her, the way a big house cat will shake and fling a rat.

Jhonni landed in a heap. The visionary ranted on.

"They come to shore as moving images, as sound moving through the air to be caught in boxes. Their skin is dry and cool. They are waiting for the day when they depart from the world. They have made a promise; they will not leave us behind."

"She sees the Rulers' floating islands!" cried someone in the crowd. "She reads their minds! She will tell us what becomes of the Gamarthan rising!"

The Samsui Physician suddenly burst into the ring, her white jacket rumpled and showing blossoming patches of sweat. She'd got hold of a long stave of wood, which she brandished frantically. *Dapur* magic filled the most skeptical Samsui with unreasoning dread. "Stop this! How dare you! I'll set the Kops on you!"

And then in a rush, in a moment, the crowd was gone, the crossroads as quiet as before. The mad girl had vanished too. The doctor dropped her pole, suddenly bewildered and defensive.

"Why didn't someone hold on to her?" she demanded. "I don't believe in *dapur* magic. It was some kind of fake . . . Is the kid all right?" Physician assistants had hurried to Cycler Jhonni. But Jhonni, on her feet again, answered for herself.

"She didn't hurt me. She didn't mean to hurt me—"

The doctor had turned on Miss Butcher. "Actually, I'm glad this happened. You can't argue now. This thing has to be contained! It's a seeping reservoir of crime, disease, evil orgies! They're not refugees, they're economic migrants. They don't ever mean to go home. The way things are, what's to stop them walking out, spreading into our city?"

"What if they do?" cried Jhonni. "There's streets of houses standing empty in Peninsula Side. We're supposed to be reformers. We could reform them!"

Mrs. Physician glared at the Samsui girl in a sarong, and did not trouble to reply to this degenerate child's raving.

"I'm going back to the gates, Miss Butcher, to meet the Koperasi. You'd better get rid of your gangsters." The Physician and her volunteers marched away. There was not a refugee in sight, boy or woman or child: but the black doorways listened.

"The Koperasi?" repeated Derveet.

"Yes," said Handai. "They changed their minds. I didn't have a chance to get in touch with you. I'm *sorry*, 'Veet. I can't tell the clans what to do. I'm just a crazy radical . . ."

Miss Butcher Handai was the center of Peninsulan sympathy among the Samsui. She and Derveet had worked together, serving the same Cause, though Miss Butcher, despite her sympathy with the oppressed, was a republican, and an atheist, and had stern ideas about the evils of traditional culture. "What *was* that?" she demanded. "It couldn't have happened at a worse moment . . . I mean, it could, it could have happened in front of the Kops. Was that m-magic? Or what?"

"The Koperasi!" Derveet seemed stunned by this news.

"Oh, shit. That's right. You two have to get out. The Kops are on their way. Tour of inspection, frighten the criminals, bully the peasants. The men didn't want to come but the damned Physicians insisted: you know how they *won't* believe that the *dapurs* have their own medicine . . ." Handai was babbling, on the point of running after Mrs. Physician. "*Please* go. I've got to be there . . . minimize the damage. Can't let Physician Mersin do all the talking." With an agonized glance at the prince and the rebel leader, she ran to face a military invasion. Derveet and Atoon were left with the failed exorcist.

Jhonni wished she could disappear.

"I'm sorry, I'm sorry. I behaved like an idiot."

Derveet picked up the Bu Awan amulet and handed it to her.

"Nonsense. You were possibly a little hasty. Now, Jhonni, Cho is in the camp somewhere. Could you find her for me? Ask her to join us. We'll be by the road into town."

The Koperasi had been busy. There were two new notices nailed up on raw posts at the edge of the camp, carrying the same graphic warning that greeted travelers arriving at the Ranganar end of the causeway. A stick person, the Eagle badge of the former premier royal family over its head, flailed its limbs, zapped by a Koperasi lightning bolt. For the literate, the message was elaborated in basic High Inggris.

Campground only for innocent victim of rebel action.
Princedom of Jagdana people—not allowed.

Princedom of Gamartha people—not allowed.

Member of Proscribed House—not allowed.

Servant or connection of Proscribed House—not
  allowed.

Criminals, migrants, traders—not allowed.

Persons of these kind must report to Administration
  Compound.

A ditch ran at the foot of the causeway bank. The refugees were washing clothes, bathing, grubbing for roots,
hunting dragonflies. As Derveet watched, an elderly
Timurese boy came down with a bucket. He picked about,
trying to find a spot unpolluted by the presence of the
aneh. He abandoned the attempt, filled his bucket anyway,
and for a moment crouched on the sticky bank. His once
good-quality clothing was the color of dirt. He sobbed,
rocking on his haunches. "Oh, God, help me bear this
pain. Oh, God, please help me bear this pain . . ."

Derveet turned away, ashamed to witness the misery she
couldn't alleviate.

It was ironic that the Samsui, and the Kops too, were so
terrified of *dapur* magic. When the Rulers first arrived, it
was the other way around. They came like the risen dead,
carrying the weird sorceries of a world the Peninsula had
left far behind. No one dreamed of *envying* them, in those
days . . . How Derveet wished she could feel herself unaffected by the medium's vision of that shining world out at
sea. It was nonsense. The Rulers were a dying race. There
was no numinous power in them. For generations they'd
been losing their grip, leaving the Peninsula to the helpless
Kops, who spread ruin more from incompetence than malice.

Derveet had been struggling for years to convince her
people that this was the truth, that they only had to stand
together and the Rulers' power would crumble. Now at last
she seemed to be proved right. The Gamarthan rising

looked bad, but the other signs were so good. If only she could keep her nerve . . .

But a pall of depression had fallen over her. She pitied Miss Butcher: poor Handai, caught between her respectable fellow citizens and the incomprehensible wiles of the Peninsula. Derveet was not as horrified by the threat of coming face-to-face with a troop of Ranganar's Kops as she'd made out. She was better known to the Kops than to the Clan Council, and had more friends in the Admin Compound than she had among the respectable Samsui. But it was of a piece: the obstinate stupidity of the city women, the brute force of the Koperasi, the sly cunning of the refugee criminals . . .

Everything looked worse. Each tattered sheet of canvas had grown a new film of desolation. A bedraggled chicken, scratching in the slime that ran from a midden of human excrement, possessed fewer feathers. The hot sky bent lower. Sweat on every surface of flesh trickled and formed greasy pools. Her clothes chafed her. She longed to go back to the crossroads of the Naga shrine, to see if that scent still lingered, like a promise of lost paradise.

"Dust," she remarked. "I wonder where she got it."

Atoon looked at her wryly.

"Well. If you don't know, my dear bandit Garuda, who does?"

"No wonder the Samsui find their visitors hard to handle. Flowerdust is a delightful thing. But it has a way of making the rest of the world look worthless . . . Damn. I'd dearly love to know where she got hold of it. I want some!"

"Me too," agreed Atoon, with such fervor that they both laughed.

Derveet pondered. "It's a pity we couldn't find the clown. A Timurese, they said, but he can speak classy High Inggris with a northern accent: an unusual combination. You know, that reminds me of a young gentleman I once met."

"A young gentleman of Timur?" Atoon was skeptical.

"Yes, and I met him. How could this be? Well, he was no ordinary young gentleman. I met him at a political debate. I'm afraid I did him a bad turn."

"Ah. You converted him to the cause of independence?"

Derveet laughed. "You're right, another of my victims. I wonder if he has ever forgiven me. Have you, Atoon?"

A vision of the palace of Jagdana vanished from his inner eye, like a fading dream. The scent of flowerdust had told him that he would never see that lovely place again.

"I am eternally in your debt," he told her solemnly.

The camp bustled. Girl children flitted about, placing their palm-mat offerings. Aristocratic banners stood on poles outside matting huts: the serpent of Timur, the monkey-badge of the Hanomans of Jagdana, the goat of Kambing Negara, the tiger of the Singhas of Gamartha. It seemed as if every other peasant family was related to royalty. In the back quarters good women went half-naked, shadowy figures with well-used breasts and seamy muscled shoulders. In the alleys boys carried open buckets of shit to newly dug vegetable plots. Young women went visiting and gossiped on the corners, silent and shrouded but for their flickering eyes.

Jhonni stormed along, trying to stop herself from crying. She remembered the bandanna, tore it off and threw it away. The shame of what she'd done enveloped her: the silly chanting, the amulet. How Derveet must hate this stupid, ugly Samsui girl who kept hanging around her. It was over. Never again would Derveet have to tolerate and humor Jhonni.

She saw a pair of blue cotton suits and red-and-white armbands ahead, and blindly turned aside. She couldn't bear the company of her fellow volunteers. They were nearly all Butchers: virtuous dissenters, good-for-you as pork fat. They had no romance. They thought about nothing but shit and medicine, cleaning things and feeding people. *These people*, they always said, talking kindly about the Peninsulans as if they were idiot children.

Her pace slowed. She was the idiot, never thinking of anyone but herself: *notice me, smile at me*. She would start a new life. She would clean out latrines with quiet dedication. If Derveet came by, Jhonni would say hello and have no time for more. She would work night and day, grow thin and frail. Her wrists and ankles would become delicate, her cheeks curve inward instead of bulging out . . .

Quite by chance, she came upon the Cold Storage building. She stared at this huge, blocky structure, unable for a moment to identify it. In front of the big shed, adult volunteers were clustered around a troop of enormous, red-faced men in dark red uniforms. The Kops didn't consider pigment deficiency a deformity. Jhonni woke up with a start and beat a quick retreat. And there was Cho, right in front of her. Jhonni remembered her errand.

It was an odd scene. Cho was sitting, eyes on the ground and arms curled around her knees, in a narrow gap between the backs of two rows of refugee shacks. Opposite her, in exactly the same pose, there squatted a strange-looking creature dressed in grimy colored rags. Jhonni had the impression that she had interrupted something, but she didn't think she'd heard voices. Cho's brown cat was sitting on top of one of the huts, licking itself. Nobody else was about.

"Oh, hello. I was looking for you. Derveet wants—"

The doll-who-was-a-person came from a ruined city deep in the landmass, where the earth was poisoned and nobody had lived for thousands of years. She had reached the Peninsula all on her own, and Derveet and Atoon had found her. Although Cho was important to the Cause, no one seemed to know quite how; or at least they didn't tell Jhonni. It was strange, because Peninsulans weren't supposed to approve of machines. Perhaps it was the fact that

Cho was such an *incredible* machine that made her a good omen. And she didn't belong to the Rulers. She was on the rebels' side.

Cycler Jhonni had never possessed a doll. Samsui children are given only useful toys. If Jhonni wanted to play babies, she could help with her little sisters and cousins. She had no experience of huggable toys, something special and lovable and your own. But when Cho was there, your arms wanted to reach out. You longed to pick her up, cuddle her. Cho smiled with her whole face, like a light breaking.

"Derveet. Where is she?"

"Down by the road. Be careful, Cho. There are Kops about." Jhonni cleared her throat, trying to behave naturally, afraid Cho could tell she'd been crying. "Did you find out anything?"

Cho frowned. "Yes and no. It's confusing." She looked gravely at the clown. "Endang found me."

This was a problem for Cho. Endang was miserable, but he didn't *want* her to remove his pain. It was a puzzle that she kept meeting. Making humans happy was a conundrum so prolix—though it looked so simple—that she could almost lose her way in its absorbing mazes.

"Will you come and talk to Derveet?" she asked him.

The clown started and recoiled.

"Keep her away from me . . ."

Cho sighed, accepting another puzzle, smiled good-bye to Jhonni and trotted away.

Divine Endurance was tempted to stay. Feline intuition told her that the meeting between the particularly stupid human, Cycler Jhonni, and this particularly miserable human, Endang, held promise in terms of the downfall of her enemy Derveet.

Downfall? Divine Endurance was governed by the same rules as Cho. But she had made terms with those immutable laws a long time ago. She corrected herself complacently.

The meeting might be important in Derveet's progress towards true freedom, eternal bliss, and riches beyond the dreams of avarice.

But she had been Cho's guardian for a long time. Contrary to human opinion, habit in a cat is stronger, and at least as pleasurable, as the satisfaction of curiosity. She followed Cho.

The skinny creature wore layered shreds of bright and dirty rags; his hair was a matted forest. Jhonni recognized the costume of a *wayang* character, a puppet from a traditional puppet show—the wise fool, the clown-servant who accompanies the hero.

Sometimes the clown is the mouthpiece of the *dapur*, telling secrets that the ladies have decided to share. Jhonni felt she ought to do something. This heap of rags might be important. She sat down, keeping her distance so as not to alarm him.

"Where are you from, Endang?" (*Darimana?* she said, assuming she had to use the Peninsulan language.)

A shake of the matted head.

"Did you see any fighting where you come from?"

Another shake.

"Do you know who's causing trouble in the camp?"

No response. But she had a strong feeling that the grotesque object wanted to tell her something. "I know you're not a woman, but are you a man or a boy? Cho didn't say. I'm sorry, I suppose that's not polite."

Endang shrugged. "It's not important."

Jhonni was startled. The voice was normal, totally unlike the mad snarl when he had yelled at Cho. The face he lifted was the face of a human being—thin, and hollow around the eyes, but not crazy-looking. And, she suddenly realized, he was speaking High Inggris.

"Who are you?" he asked. "What's your name?"

"My name's Jhonni. I'm a volunteer. A relief worker."

She pronounced her name the way she'd decided it was pronounced: *Dj-honni.*

"Joni," he repeated.

"No, Dj-honni."

"Where did you find a name like that?"

"In a book. It's very ancient. I chose it for myself."

"It's a Rulers' name," said Endang, with a cold smile.

"It is not!"

"It's pronounced *Joni.*"

He drew in the dirt with a filthy, clawlike fingernail. Jhonni saw with amazement that he was *writing*, with practiced economy. He had spelled her name wrong. He looked up, making sure he had her attention, and wrote something else. *Bungadebu* . . . He saw her frown and scrawled again, swiftly, but the letters were clear as print.

FLOWERDUST

It meant nothing. Endang obviously thought it was very important. Elation leapt into Jhonni's mind. Perhaps there was a way to redeem herself, after all!

"Endang, do you know something Derveet should know? When you heard her name you seemed frightened—"

"I know she's in terrible danger."

The narrow alley was still empty. No one had passed the entrance. Jhonni had heard the Koperasi moving away into the camp. She wondered if Physician Mersin was telling them about the *dapur* magic. She wondered where she'd left her hat. Lost hats were the bane of Jhonni's life. Her skin was so poorly pigmented, and sunburn hurt. But to wear a sun hat made her feel such an ugly cripple. She rarely kept one in her possession more than a day.

What odd things come into your head when something exciting happens. Jhonni gazed at Endang, unable to believe her luck. And after making such a fool of herself!

"Danger?" she repeated softly. "What kind of danger?"

But he shook his head. He wouldn't say more. Not here, she guessed, where Derveet's mysterious new enemies might be nearby.

"Can you write it?" Another shake. She frowned, thinking of ways and means. "Can you get out?"

"Of the camp?" She could see he was trembling, and felt a shiver of vicarious fear. "We are not fenced in. Not yet."

"Good. Now listen, Endang. If you want to help Derveet, I'll tell you what we'll do . . ."

When she'd gone, Endang stood and looked down. Quite a good hand, neat and educated. You could see that, though the letters were scrawled in dirt. He smeared them away.

The clown pranced out towards the Cold Storage building, dipping and whirling to send his rags flying, and keening as he danced, a tuneless, crazy song. The meaningless wail disturbed no one. His ladies heard it, and knew that all was well.

2

IN THE COOL of early morning, Derveet climbed a crumbling stone spiral staircase, skipping the gaps and ducking under lumps of shifted masonry. Cho and the cat came behind.

On the roof a boy with a raddled, wicked old face squatted in front of a line of wooden hutches, his sarong tucked around his knees. The squalor of the West Bank was hidden from this angle. The rooftop looked out on a riot of greenery and flowers: flame of the forest, frangipani, mango, and raintree. There were trays of rice cakes drying on red tiled roofs, washing spread on the worn limbs of giant stone demons; pools of mist, tumbling cisterns. In places slabs of worked stone jutted through the leaves. The sea was very near: the smell of it was in the air.

Ranganar Island had been a famous pleasure resort, before the Samsui bought the island from the Garudas to found their reformers' colony. (Or leased it . . . There was a legal wrangle over that point which had never been resolved. It had become irrelevant as the Rulers' power grew.) Here on the West Bank, where the heretics had never penetrated, fragments of splendor survived. Derveet lived in what had been the Garuda water palace. One L-shaped bathhouse remained standing, over a colonnade of bluestone pillars beside a square bathing pool. The short arm of the L was taller. The rooms below were unusable, but its roof housed the pigeons.

"Selamat pagi, madam!" Semar greeted his mistress with a broad leer. His teeth were remarkable for such an old man: a full set, large and square cut and yellow as a horse's. He delved into a cage and brought out a gray pigeon, with slate wings and a silver-toned head. Derveet spread a handful of tiny paper rolls on the top of a coop, selected one, and slid it into the message carrier on the bird's leg.

The ruin was called Rumah Merpati, Dove House. This flat roof was surrounded by a balustrade of carved stone feathers. They might be dove's or eagle's wings. The paramount royalty had used both badges. Derveet liked to think she was carrying on an ancient tradition in keeping the pigeons up here. Except that the Garudas probably did not use the gentlemen's bathhouse of their seaside villa as a post office.

The royal family of the south had been systematically murdered at the end of the Great Rebellion, that desperate fight for independence which had ended in catastrophic defeat nearly a century ago. The valley in which their palace stood was flooded to make a reservoir for Ranganar City; the Kops did their best to obliterate every trace of their existence. But an infant prince-elect had been smuggled away before the end, to the caldera of the Mother Mountain, Bu Awan. The *aneh,* the deformed outcasts, had a kind of sanctuary there. The prince grew up with them, and eventually sired a child, who became the legendary, doomed Merpati, the Dove of Bu Awan. When she was barely more than a child herself, Merpati tried to raise a new rebellion. But it was too late. The Peninsula's forces were exhausted. The rising collapsed; Merpati was captured. Her father made a deal with the Koperasi, binding them both to permanent exile in return for his daughter's life. Whether Merpati would have accepted that fate would never be known. She died far away on the Black Islands, giving birth to the child she conceived under Koperasi torture.

After her grandfather died, Derveet had returned to the princedoms. The old man had told her a secret, and she

knew there was hope for the Peninsula. She presented herself at the palace of Jagdana. The Hanomans of Jagdana
were always the Garuda family's faithful allies. But though
the women of the royal *dapur* acknowledged her legitimacy,
they refused to listen to her plans. *It's too late, you will only do
harm,* was their only answer. *Submit, and wait for the wheel to
turn . . .* The first and last law of the hearth is the protection
of life, of human lives.

The young Derveet, undaunted, had gone from Jagdana
to the *aneh* of Bu Awan, her mother's people. When she realized that she could not forge them into an army, she became
a bandit: dealing in acar and spreading her message of hope
and resistance through the Peninsular underworld. When
the fame of Anakmati became a danger to her friends in Jagdana and on the Mother Mountain, Derveet removed herself to the heretic city of Ranganar.

She refused to give up. But she remembered what the ex-
iled prince, her grandfather, had taught her. She knew that
nothing was any good unless she could win over the *dapur*.
She *must* have the women on her side. She had been raised
in exile, outside the sacred hearth; and now she was a failed
woman. It seemed they would never listen to her. She could
never prove herself to them, never discover their secrets.
But in Ranganar, where she least expected it, she had found
a way.

Derveet had met plenty of failed women in the underworld. They were no use to her: they were lost in despair.
Their support—even if you could have relied on it!—was
worthless. But in Ranganar, there was a group of exiles who
were different. The heretic Samsui, ironically, revered the
classical dance, the Peninsula's greatest art. Their dance
theater was renowned throughout the princedoms, and
the artists were Peninsulan women: failed women, of
course, but not ruined and dishonored. Derveet met them
through Butcher Handai and found at last the metal that
she could forge into the core of her new rebellion.

Thereafter began a daring campaign against the Koperasi

in the south: raids on property, destruction of equipment, general harassment. The "terrorists"—who took curious pains to avoid any loss of life—remained unpunished, untraceable. But rumors started flying secretly of the astonishing nature of this band . . . It was the dancers who had helped Derveet to blow up the Garuda dam, just before the year's end. That was done for show. The Kops soon repaired the damage and restored the water level in the reservoir. But not before the whole Peninsula knew that the Garuda palace had risen from the flood: that the Eagle had taken flight again.

Then Derveet had retreated to the West Bank, and the terrorist campaign had halted. She knew that the women of the Peninsula understood what she had done, why the Koperasi had been helpless against these mysterious raiders. She waited for their verdict. Atoon's arrival in Ranganar was proof that the ruling women of Jagdana had come over to her cause. Jagdana was one state: still, it was an immense improvement on none.

"This is a dangerous moment," she said to Cho. "The Rulers are losing their grip, but chaos is encroaching. Nothing must go wrong. Handai was right to be horrified by that magic show in the refugee camp."

"It wasn't real magic."

"What's the difference? The Kops wouldn't have known that."

"But they didn't see it."

"That's right, they didn't." Eyes meeting, they considered the timing of that incident. It was puzzling. "Maybe it was a coincidence: the young lady just *happened* to run amok in my path, a few minutes ahead of a Koperasi inspection?" Cho shook her head firmly. "No. I don't think so either."

She took another bird from Semar, a black cock with white wingtips; inserted the message. "The Ranganar Kops don't want any trouble," she said to Cho. "They know who

I am, they know where I live. They'd probably be as grateful as the Samsui if I could keep those refugees quiet. I'm not afraid of them, for myself. But I'm afraid of what they might do if they were to panic about women's magic. Which terrifies them now, when they still believe it isn't real. I think the show we were given was a warning. Another time, a performance could be arranged for the Kops. Someone is encouraging me to get involved in this affair. Why so keen?"

The bird leapt from her hands, its first wingbeat an audible, soft crack. It stooped as if it was falling, and then rose high, effortless, to become a cutout bird shape against the bright sky. Derveet followed its lovely flight, over Ranganar's fetid little river, over the Samsui city, forgetting her anxiety in simple pleasure.

"Where's that one going?"

"To Jagdana, eventually. If he gets that far . . ." She gazed northwards. "Our world is shrinking. You know that, don't you, Cho? Slowly but surely, surely and not so slowly. In the first decades of the last century, the court of Jagdana was in correspondence with a city on the edge of the landmass: I've seen the letters. The end of that story's lost. Now, even the Black Islands are empty. And no word from any other land for generations."

"Except me and the cat."

"Except you." Derveet smiled. But Divine Endurance, who detested to hear this degenerate woman speak of the real world, the lost civilization, laid back her ears and growled softly.

Semar hadn't noticed that the cat was so near his birds.

"Pah!" His shout had no effect. He raised a threatening hand. The cat glared, affronted.

"Oh . . ." murmured the doll-who-was-a-person, uneasily.

Derveet laughed. "You'd better leave Divine Endurance alone, Semar. Or she'll turn you into something unpleasant."

"She wouldn't do that!" protested Cho.

"No?"

Derveet noticed that Cho's tone was serious, as if turning Semar into something unpleasant was within the cat's power. She could believe it . . . almost. Sometimes when she looked into those blue eyes, Derveet felt the presence of a mind: neither animal nor marvelous machine, but utterly hostile. But Cho loved her, so the cat must be tolerated. Possibly she was simply jealous.

"Just stay away from my pigeons."

Divine Endurance sat up on her haunches and gazed at Derveet, not so much defiant as contemptuous. She seemed to come to a decision, for her own reasons. She leapt from the coop, and jumped to curl up beside Cho. Semar said "Pah!" again, and thrust a gold-bloomed, mauve bird into his mistress's hands.

"*Masih, dua.*" Still two more.

Derveet thought of the vertigo she had felt—in the library of Jagdana palace, years ago—when she first grasped the scale of the ancient past, of the vast tracts of loss that surrounded the world she knew. She was falling in emptiness, tumbling like the black pigeon. Then—crack—her wings opened and she soared into the empty sky.

"There must be other human communities scattered over the earth," she said. "Getting on with life in their own ways. But we can't reach them, nor they us. So, we are alone. That's what's at the back of the *dapur*'s determination not to risk lives."

The birds went north to Jagdana, and to Derveet's friends in the hills of the occupied territory: bandit country. Since the outbreak in Gamartha no word had returned. Only a few pigeons had come back, exhausted, her own messages untouched. There was no news from the north, except for the Koperasi bulletins pasted up on the walls of the Administration Compound, which no one with any sense took at face value.

The rising in Gamartha was not the response she was

looking for. It was not directed by *dapur* women; it involved only men and boys. Limited violence was an outlet the women of the Peninsula allowed their volatile menfolk from time to time, knowing it would achieve nothing. She hoped that it was a minor affair, a brushfire that would flare and die. But as the days went by, her disquiet grew.

If Derveet had her way, there would be no glorious fight for freedom this time. The Rulers might be failing, but *that* was still a contest the Peninsula had to lose. There would be no open war. Precisely what happened next was up to the women. She did not know how they would act if they took up her Cause—only that there would be great changes.

She had to wait, and hope that the ruling women of Gamartha would still answer her, once the fire had died down. And Timur, the other great princedom? She hardly expected anything from the Koperasi-dominated court. But there were certain families she had hoped to hear from, some way, by now.

"Boys, I'm going to run out of birds."

Semar grinned his bad-horse grin. "Nah, madam. Plenty of pigeons in Ranganar."

"Thief! I don't want you to steal. Besides, you fool, they won't know the way to Jagdana."

"Ah." Petruk, the second in rank of the Dove House boys, had appeared with the morning offering tray. "But we know. Can tell them!" His grimace of cunning idiocy was a practiced marvel.

"What shining intelligence! You'll draw them a little map, I suppose. I am privileged to know you two.

"Nobody seems to realize," she grumbled, scowling into the north, "that I could have started a romantic uprising of my own. I may be black, I may be a failed woman. But I have my admirers. I could have raised a little hell: burned out a few towns, ruined a few rice harvests, caused thousands of Peninsulans of all persuasions—some in Kop uniform, some not—to be slaughtered . . ."

It was ridiculous to resent the excitement that the Gamartha rising had aroused. "I must keep out of it," she said. "If the dancers are straining at the leash, if Cycler Jhonni—poor child—is disappointed in me, it's too bad."

The boys lowered their eyes, pretending not to hear. It was their usual response when they felt she was burdening them with troubles above their station. Cho, perched on the balustrade of stone wings, looked on with grave understanding.

Derveet returned to present affairs.

"This Endang in the camp. I think he must be the same Endang I met in Timur a few years ago. You say he knew me?"

Cho nodded. "But he said"—she reproduced, faithfully, the agonized snarl of the clown—"'*Keep her away from me!*'"

"Mmm." Derveet frowned. "Interesting . . ."

She finished setting off the pigeons. Semar fed the rest. Petruk presented her with a fringed purple sash. She lifted it from his arm and tied it casually, took the offering tray. Petruk ignited incense with her cigarette lighter, fanned, then squeezed the burning tips between his fingers until they just smoldered.

She carried the tray to Bu Awan, who was carved in a niche in the northern balustrade, delivered the Sky Lady's breakfast briskly. Folded hands and knelt and rose, crossed the roof to the goggle-eyed relief of Garuda. *Selamat pagi,* Garuda. Fed the Eagle. Around the feet of the carvings, offerings from about the last ten days lay withering and scattered. The boys were good boys but they didn't get around to everything. And, failed woman, she was not permitted to help them out. Domestic tasks belonged to the *dapur*: to fertile women and to boys. The bold mynah birds, who counted every roof on the West Bank as their property, had eaten most of the rice. She handed the tray back to Petruk. Semar had fastened whistles on the tails of six stay-at-home pigeons, the mere pets. They erupted from the roof and spilled over the water garden, twisted and came whirling back. A sweet, bodiless music sailed through the air.

Derveet untied the sash and tossed it onto Petruk's shoulder. She knelt, hands loose on her lap, staring absently at the relief of Bu Awan. "Why do I do this?" she wondered aloud but as if speaking to herself. "To please you boys? Belief is such a fluid thing. I keep up the rituals because I've done it since I was a child. I feel nostalgia for the supernatural menagerie, because I was brought up by an exile—to whom Bu Awan and Garuda were so very important. What do I believe? Something, nothing. What I believe is hard to put into words. Maybe it wouldn't be worth having if it fitted into words."

The boys pretended not to hear.

Divine Endurance rubbed her head against Cho's arm. "Your human doesn't look well," she crooned solicitously. "It's a bad sign when they talk about religion. You'll have noticed that."

Cho wished to disagree. But Derveet's face, in profile, was too clear a witness: the dark, severe features hollowed with weary tension. She was not sleeping. She coughed and tossed restlessly in the night. It was *very* hard for Derveet to sit still and do nothing.

"What she needs is a distraction," murmured the cat. "Some little thing that won't interfere with your big plans. She needs a distraction to occupy her mind."

Something rattled, down in the gardens. Cho, ignoring the cat, looked out over the balustrade. "Derveet—"

Derveet came to look and sighed in exasperation. "I might have known!" A Samsui bicycle, a type of beast that was rare on the West Bank, lay foreshortened in the red earth alley under the wall of the water palace. It was painted green and purple, Gamarthan colors. It had been painted slate gray and rose, Garuda colors, last time they saw it. It never kept the same pattern on its shiny hide for long. It belonged to Cycler Jhonni.

A few moments later they heard stumbling footsteps on the tower stairs, and Jhonni's rosy face emerged. The Samsui girl clambered out onto the roof, and stood looking guilty.

She should not be here. After they raised the Eagle, it had been agreed that the active campaign should cease. The dancers and their Samsui support team had disbanded. Everyone was lying low. Nobody was supposed to come to Dove House for any reason. The Kops in Ranganar might seem to tolerate a known rebel leader, but that could change in a moment. Derveet was determined not to take chances, now that she had something to lose.

"Is this very important, Jhonni? You know what we agreed."

Derveet smiled, but Jhonni could see she wasn't pleased. She thought of Endang, and that mysterious word scratched in the dust. She knew she was justified.

"It's all right. I'm only on my way to school."

By no stretch of the imagination was Dove House on the way from the Cyclers' compound to anywhere in the Samsui city.

"*Only* school! What an attitude. Don't you realize we'll need well-trained Samsui accountants after the revolution?"

Jhonni winced. At home, she liked her job. At Dove House she was ashamed of it: so unromantic. "I won't miss much. And I've got to talk to you. It's about the camp."

"Oh, the camp." Derveet looked vague, as if what had happened yesterday had slipped her mind. "Come down, we're finished here. We'll give you breakfast, and you can get on to school."

The bathhouse tower was a maze of tiny rooms. Light trickled through broken panels of stone filigree; fragments of wall paintings clung to rotten plaster. Cheeping hives of fur and skin hung in the corners. The air was permeated by the chocolaty stink of bats' shit. Here, the almond-eyed gentlemen of the old Garuda court had relaxed after bathing, waited on by lovely young boys.

Jhonni groped, fending off strings of cobweb, knowing that she'd been wrong to come. But she had to tell what she'd learned! Embarrassment impelled her to chatter like a polite acquaintance.

"How many rooms are there?"

"In the *sudahmandi*? I've no idea. Don't step there—"

Crash.

"Oh. You did. No damage, I hope? To you, I mean—"

Jhonni pulled shards of rotten wood out of her shin. "I'm fine. It's nothing. You could easily find out. You could get some string, and—"

"Ah, the energy of youth," Derveet mocked gently.

"*Ghosts*, Nyonya Jhonni—" A hand closed on her ankle. Semar had come up behind her with a lamp. "The little sister is bleeding buckets, madam. What to do! The Cyclers will kill us for sure."

Jhonni couldn't understand Low Inggris, the Peninsulan language, when people talked quickly. She recoiled from Semar's horse teeth. She was afraid of him. He was ceremonious, calling her "Mrs. Jhonni." But she knew he despised all Samsui, and especially Jhonni. He insisted on helping her after that, gripping her waist with a hard, horny palm, not allowing her to touch the walls of the ruin. She was sure he thought she'd stepped through the floor on purpose.

The ground floor of the *sudahmandi* held, screened by masses of intruding greenery, Derveet's laboratory, where she and a Samsui woman called Kimlan concocted explosives for the dancers—showy stuff, more exciting than destructive. Derveet's terrorism had never cost a single Peninsulan life, not even a Koperasi life. They crossed through to the colonnade, where a staircase of pink marble, miraculously intact, led to a single long room that looked down on the pool.

The walls were thick; the floor was polished stone. A canopied bed stood against one wall, a clothes chest under a mirror. There was little other furniture. Semar bustled, bringing a cushion for Jhonni to sit on and another for her injured leg.

"You'd better fetch an auntie, Semar," suggested his mistress.

But the boys were Jagdanans. They considered the Ranganarese *dapur* hopelessly compromised. "Nah. No good. No healing in Ranganar ladies." He rolled up Jhonni's trouser leg, took off her slipper, made her hold her handkerchief to the blood, and went away, tut-tutting grumpily.

"It's a deep cut," said Cho admiringly. "You might get a real scar."

Jhonni was frightened of getting blood on Semar's cushion. For once Cho's friendly understanding didn't work its spell. Jhonni didn't want to be treated like a child. "About the camp—"

"Ah." A glance passed between Derveet and the doll-who-was-a-person. "I don't think Atoon and I will be going back."

Semar returned with a bowl and a ewer of water, some ointment and a roll of clean rag. He dressed the wound with a long-suffering air while Derveet looked on with folded hands, helpless before the forces of tradition. He knotted the bandage neatly. Derveet nodded approval.

"Could you bring us some breakfast, please?"

He grunted and carried away his first aid.

"But what about that girl?" insisted Jhonni. "Don't we have to find out what made her behave like that? I know . . . I know it was *dapur* magic. But it can't have been good magic. D'you think she was possessed by a demon?" Something held her back from mentioning Endang. Derveet was being strange today: aloof, out of reach, almost unfriendly.

She was looking at Jhonni with reserved amusement.

"Jhonni," she said, as if talking to a little girl who'd been telling her whoppers. "Tell me honestly. Do you *really* believe in demons?"

"I . . ." Jhonni blushed. She felt that Derveet was looking into her soul, and seeing it written there that Jhonni didn't *really* believe in any of it. That to Jhonni everything about the Peninsula was a romance, which she adored. But the gods and demons were not *real*; even *dapur* magic was not real. That was why Jhonni's stupid attempt at exorcism hadn't worked. She had no faith.

She blushed. "Well . . . no."

"Sensible girl."

"Oh?" Jhonni was startled. "But, but *you* believe—"

"Mmm. In gods and demons. Probably *marginally* more than you do, on account of the way I was brought up—"

Petruk came in and laid down a tray with little cakes and fresh *kopi jae*. The energizing richness of strong, sweet ginger coffee filled the room; no one made *kopi jae* like old Semar.

The girl stared in troubled bewilderment.

"I don't understand!"

Derveet felt how hard it was for Cycler Jhonni, as for the other Samsui who'd been involved in her campaign. The Samsui, like the Kops, were familiar with the legendary secret powers of Peninsulan women. And they knew it was all nonsense, superstition, illusion. You might hear some strange things, feats of healing or clairvoyance, but there was always a rational explanation lurking somewhere . . . They were afraid, the way people of sense are "afraid" of ghosts. Not because such a thing seems likely, but because the idea is so unpleasant. The Samsui who had worked with Derveet had passed in a matter of months from magic-as-a-myth to magic-that-works, and the transition was confusing.

"One can see," she said, "how easy it has been for the men and boys of the Peninsula to live alongside the *dapur* without noticing anything strange. The women of your household live apart. You don't have much to do with them, unless you're a boy directly in their service. They talk with those flickering eyes, without words. They examine your dreams. If you are sick, they make you better. If you are in trouble or in danger, they have an uncanny way of knowing it, even at a great distance. If the ladies are angry or upset, then the whole household feels it. Everyone is made miserable without quite knowing why . . . What's so strange about all that? It's just the way things are. The women will not speak to outsiders. What men and boys recount doesn't tell anyone much. What the women *do* is almost too subtle to be seen. That's the way the women of the Peninsula kept their secret for so long."

She had come home from the Black Islands demanding to share the hidden knowledge of the *dapur*. She didn't know what she was asking. Like Cycler Jhonni, she didn't really believe in magic. The women of Jagdana refused to admit anything. Derveet went away to the *aneh* of Bu Awan. She started experimenting with explosives, and blew herself up. By the time the frightened outcasts took her down to Jagdana, the burns were infected. Derveet knew that her sight was destroyed. When the *dapur* treated her, she knew that what they did—without instruments, without drugs—was impossible: and so the secret was out.

She touched the skin beside her right eye delicately. *Without the power of the* dapur, she thought, *I would be blind now.* And how had she repaid the women's generosity? By breaking their precious silence, by bringing *dapur* power into the outside world.

"Not every fertile woman is the same. In many families there is tradition and ritual, nothing more. There are places—coastal Timur, for instance—where Peninsulan women themselves will tell you sincerely that the whole thing was never anything more. And that's our protection."

Petruk fidgeted with the breakfast things and rolled his

eyes at his mistress: scandalized. One did not talk about
these things! Derveet waved him away.

"There are few secrets left," she said seriously. "But this
is one. The Kops know about me, the failed woman Garuda.
They don't mind that. They think I might be useful, when
things really start to crack up. They do not know what it is
that we've been doing. They mustn't find out. Not yet."

The cakes smelled wonderful and Jhonni was starving.
She took one and munched energetically. "But if you can
have good magic, you must be able to have bad magic—"
She sprayed crumbs, realized what she was doing and felt
doomed. It was bad enough trying to argue with Derveet
about *dapur* powers, hopeless with your mouth full. "And
Bu Awan and gods and demons. Isn't it *all* true?"

Derveet took her cigarette case from her sash, opened it,
sighed, shut it again. "I don't think there's much connection."

At least she was answering the question, thought Jhonni.

"You've seen the *aneh*. Oh, not like me." Derveet
stretched out a hand, admired the coppery dark wrist,
turned the petal-colored palm upwards. "Black skin is an
innocent variation, I think, from the human norm. But
you've seen others: the spidery people, buffalo boys,
snake-mouths. I think there's no doubt that once, in ancient times, the women of our Peninsula had truly terrible
supernatural powers. Long ago, they gave up tailoring
human beings as tools or weapons. Maybe of their own ac-
cord; maybe something frightened them into doing so."
She glanced at Cho, who answered with a faint smile of
shared knowledge. "It's my personal belief that what we
call *dapur* powers arose from something . . . *done* in those
ancient days. A slow-burning change that affects only fertile women, and maybe a few exiles like our dancers, who
have slipped through the net, possibly been judged
wrongly; it does happen . . ." Derveet fingered the cigarette case again, tracing the engraving on the lid.

She was wearing a shapely linen jacket fastened with silver, and an unstitched sarong worn the men's way, sashed at the waist with one end loose to trail on the ground. Jhonni thought she looked wonderful.

"But what I saw . . . The dancers have never done anything like that! She . . . she picked me up and *threw* me!"

Strangely, Derveet grinned. "She'll be regretting it now!"

"It wasn't funny!" wailed Jhonni. "It was hideously evil, and terribly dangerous. It's done with something called flowerdust!"

The moment she'd let the word out she regretted it. She felt herself blushing crimson. She saw Derveet's black brows snap together in an awful frown. She knew she'd said something terribly indiscreet, Derveet hated her, their friendship was over—

But suddenly Derveet was laughing. "So much for my powers of evasion," she said to Cho, who was laughing too. Jhonni looked from one to the other, mystified and hurt.

"What is it? Why is it funny?"

Derveet sighed. "Ah, Jhonni, I'm sorry. I'm sorry for what happened to you. I should have realized you would need an explanation, and you deserve one. The young woman you saw was not performing magic. She was drugged." She looked at Jhonni, smiling wryly. "Flowerdust is a special kind of acar."

"She was seeing things on the Rulers' islands!"

"Or thought she was. Flowerdust can make you hallucinate, but its visions aren't to be trusted. Fertile women shouldn't take it. For them it can have unpredictable effects. As you saw—and felt. If it is any consolation, she'll be feeling dreadful today."

"This is terrible! There's someone in the refugee camp peddling a new, dangerous, evil drug—"

Derveet looked shocked. "Oh no, not evil! Abused, the dust can cause hallucinations, madness, maybe even kill you. One could say the same for alcohol. But you drink beer, don't you, Jhonni?"

Jhonni drank beer. She'd been drunk once or twice. She had never smoked. Neither Derveet nor the dancers had ever offered her their green-skinned cigarettes, nor was she in the least tempted. She'd heard her mother, and others, raging about the Koperasis' corrupt relationship with the acar dealers, the ruin it brought to honest trade.

"That's different! Acar's *illegal!*"

"So is dam-busting. And liberating the contents of Koperasi supply convoys is frowned upon in some circles, I do believe . . ." She shook her head firmly. "No, I am not going to interfere. I think it was a mistake to go into the camp. There's nothing I can do, or Atoon. The Timurese won't talk, and the runaway slaves daren't. I agree there's a problem. But if I tried to intervene it would make things much worse."

"But—but aren't you going to tell someone?"

Derveet raised an eyebrow. "Whom should I tell? Physician Mersin? What sort of action do you think she'd take? Weren't you listening, Jhonni? I said: I am not going to interfere."

The prince and the third of Derveet's boys, young Gareng, came into the upper room together. They had been to market. The prince reveled in the petty freedoms of Ranganar. In Jagdana he was a prisoner. On the West Bank, as a modest commoner, he could walk about the street with one watchful servant without exciting any comment.

He didn't live in the main building. It wouldn't have been proper. Derveet was a failed woman; she didn't matter. But the boys had their reputations to consider. What would people think? They had cleared out a small pavilion in the garden, which he shared, resignedly, with the livestock that had become entrenched over the years. Semar referred to this hut as "the prince's apartments." Atoon called it "my studhouse."

He was waving a handful of grubby pieces of paper. Gareng was at his elbow, looking peevish. The prince shook the bills at Derveet. "Garuda, how can these shopkeeper people respect you if you let them rob you?"

"Only a little, my father," tempered Gareng. "Only the decent amount."

Derveet laughed. "Leave me alone, peasant. It's my ill-gotten cash, and I'll waste it as I please."

"Ha. Cash users stick together, I see. What about me? I have no money. My family is utterly destitute of small bits of numbered paper, but where are our handouts from the bandit's bounty? Garuda, as always, makes cause with the landless and treats the rest of us with a stony heart . . ."

The rapid music of the Peninsulan language broke off when he saw the Samsui girl. He greeted her in High Inggris, polite but slightly puzzled. "Ah, good morning, Jhonni."

Jhonni stared. The prince was wearing a hat. A ridiculous conical straw hat, identical to the one she'd lost in the camp.

"Is there something wrong?"

"Your hat—" she blurted, flustered.

"The peasant doesn't want his skin to darken," jeered Derveet. "The beauty is afraid of wrinkles. Gareng, please take the bills away. What will the ladies of Jagdana say if we send their prince back with a mind coarsened by unmanly anxieties?"

Atoon removed the straw cone, touched his hair in the mirror that hung over the clothes chest, and joined them at the breakfast tray. Gareng poured his coffee while Atoon's hands lay as if broken. The boy took the bills away, looking smug. There was no danger that a mere stud was going to interfere with the running of this household. Jhonni was still staring. She could not help herself. There were no male people in her life, only the Koperasi, who had their uses, of course, but who struck Jhonni as barely human. It was the hat, perhaps. It had made him look different. More real? Jhonni was smitten by an inner vision of the pierced and chained naked stud she had glimpsed in the refugee camp.

Her imagination gave that body Atoon's golden face . . . so pretty, just like a girl's.

The prince was smiling politely, unembarrassed by her devouring eyes. "Are you visiting simply for our pleasure, Jhonni?"

"Your ankle looks better," said Derveet. "You should be off to school."

Jhonni blushed red and got up.

"Don't forget your hat."

"My hat?"

Atoon reached for the conical straw from the chest and tossed it to her. "It's yours. You left it behind at the camp. I borrowed it. I was sure you wouldn't mind."

"What brought Jhonni here?" asked Atoon, when they were alone. "I thought the dancers and the renegades were staying away."

Atoon could speak of nationalism as a running sore, but he wasn't free from prejudice.

"The Samsui," she corrected mildly.

"I beg their pardon. The Samsui heretics. Why was she here?"

"The incident at the camp, of course. That, and the word *flowerdust*. I don't know where she heard it. I decided not to ask. The less interest I show the better, I feel. Poor Jhonni is afraid some hideous evil is at work."

"Quite right." Atoon picked up her cigarette case and shook his head over the contents. "The evil part is that I'm not getting any dust. I don't know when there was last a bloom in Jagdana . . . certainly not in my lifetime. I wonder where it could have come from. Do you know?"

"If I'd heard of a bloom, I wouldn't have forgotten."

"What about Endang the clown?"

Derveet looked thoughtful. "Endang," she repeated. "I believe he is the person I knew. My advanced young gentleman seems to have fallen on hard times."

"Will you talk to him?"

She glanced at the doll-who-was-a-person. "Cho tells me that the clown wants me to stay away. I think that is friendly advice."

Derveet stood and walked to the window, the silk of her trailing hem whispering. Poor Ranganarese waited by the pool, which brimmed dark and clear in its basin. It was spring-fed. The water was fresh, untainted by the sea. They'd been lining up since dawn for their day's supply. The West Bank huddled around the wild gardens, shacks oozing into every gap in the walls. The air smelled of brine and flowers. Jhonni did not understand. No Samsui could grasp the outrageous temerity of what Derveet was trying to do. She had dragged the secrets of the *dapur* into the public world. She had turned the subtlety the women used to protect and to preserve their people into a kind of weapon. It was almost unforgivable. Yet Jagdana had forgiven her. Would the others?

Atoon noted the costume that had roused Jhonni's admiration. The fall of the silk was exquisite, the tailoring of the jacket something to make angels weep. Her man's clothes were always perfect. She wore her shame so bravely. It was such intolerable bad luck. The last heir of the Garudas, the only person who could hope to pull the Peninsula together. And she had to be a barren woman: a powerless power, undrinkable water. It was too ironic.

"You're determined to do nothing."

"There's nothing I can do. The people involved are Timurese. I can't tell them how to behave; it would be dangerous indeed for me to try. I've sent word to Handai. She'll be mad. But I think there's little risk of the Kops' taking action out there. They'll put things off, and Physician Mersin will be disappointed."

Atoon nodded. Derveet had ways of knowing what went on in the Administration Compound. "Did you swear Jhonni to secrecy?"

"Not wise. Swearing Jhonni to secrecy would make it an adventure. I hurt her feelings, and I believe I made her ashamed of me. Therefore she won't tell a soul. I think we're safe."

"But dustless." Atoon sighed. He had set up the chess pieces. "Shall we play?"

"Don't you get bored? Where's the fun in winning so easily?"

"It's an addiction."

While the prince and Derveet played, Divine Endurance emerged from inside the filmy curtains of the bed. She and Cho had a quiet conversation. It was remarkable, said the cat, how a little success could change a human's behavior. Derveet's activities against the Koperasi had ceased. Her non-*dapur* friends, the dancers and the Samsui, were no longer welcome at Dove House. Without even noticing it she had put aside those difficult notions of equality and unity. Derveet had believed she must heal even the ancient breach between the sexes. But now look. The stud, Derveet's dearest friend, was kept out in the garden! Very proper and commendable, observed the cat.

Cho was aware of the hidden claws in this approval. She knew Divine Endurance didn't like Derveet.

"She hasn't given up her ideas," she countered firmly. "She's *waiting*. She has to stay in Ranganar, waiting for the emissaries. For people to come, like Atoon, or maybe a sign to be given that we'll recognize and the Kops won't. Don't you understand *anything*?"

Divine Endurance rolled onto her side, caught the end of her own tail, and nibbled it gently. "What she needs is a distraction!"

Cho watched the chess game. Atoon was trapped in the city of renegades: so be it. His *dapur* had sent him to Ranganar, therefore they wanted him to be here. He was doing his duty; that was always enough for Atoon. He was perfectly relaxed. But to Cho's loving eyes, Derveet's restless frustration showed in every line of her body. She looked down at Divine Endurance and suddenly grinned. The cat was like this. She would get hold of an idea and keep on, and on, and on, until finally you were bullied into letting her have her way. This time, the cat was pushing an open door. It was funny; Divine Endurance thought she was so clever about humans. But she never *listened.* Anyone who'd been paying the slightest attention this morning would have known that Derveet was lying: and not just to Cycler Jhonni.

Jhonni biked along the potholed city street that would become the long road to the causeway. The northern quarter of Ranganar was quiet. The causeway was closed to normal traffic, and the camp was bad for business too. The road was practically empty. A few blocks before Cold Storage she wheeled her bike off the paved thoroughfare. A dirt street led through the middle of a Ranganarese kampong, a native village grown up as the Samsui city retreated. She turned into a smaller street that ended at a waterfront. A row of decayed Samsui shophouses stood beside a black creek, facing a mudbank and a leathery tangle of mangroves. The last house in the row was a coffee shop.

The clown was there already. He had cleaned himself up; he wore a faded sarong and a long-sleeved cotton jacket. His matted hair was hidden in a cloth, so it looked like one of those thick head pads coolie boys used for carrying heavy things. He was scrawnier than ever without his layered rags, and taller than she remembered. The only other customers were a couple of Ranganarese in rusty black robes, who sat playing cards out in the front. Jhonni propped her bike where she could watch it, and went inside.

Suddenly, she didn't know what to do next.

She ought to know. She was an experienced secret rebel. She had played her part in raids on Koperasi supply lines;

she had helped to blow up the Garuda dam. But that had been with the dancers. Jhonni had never had to worry about the arrangements. The dancers dreamed that nothing would go wrong, and nothing did. If they dreamed otherwise, everything was canceled . . . When the dancers spoke secrets in public, it was always safe to do so. This time she was alone and she felt horribly conspicuous. She felt terrible about being here at all, without Derveet's knowledge. But Derveet had been so *strange.*

Was this the way it was going to be now that the *dapurs,* the ruling women, had started to acknowledge her? Had it been a fraud, that stirring talk about independence being for everyone? Had Derveet merely been using her Samsui friends? These disloyal thoughts pained Jhonni, but she couldn't dismiss them.

An old Samsui woman came to take her order, her bony feet slip-slopping in outsize yellow slippers. Beaming at the precious new customer, she picked out a cylinder and shoved it into the opera machine that stood by the counter. The puppets on the little stage began to shake and crank into life. Jhonni made out, with difficulty, the opening bars of *The Romance of the Blue Schoolroom,* an old-fashioned tearjerker.

The puppet schoolgirl sweethearts, one rich and one shamefully poor, began to gargle at each other. Jhonni took out her sketchpad and watercolor tablet: her cover. She had to think of an excuse to speak to that boy in the head pad. Maybe she could invent an errand for him. The woman delivered Jhonni's coffee and retreated. She wondered if it really was the clown. How could she be so sure she recognized him?

"Excuse me, Mrs. What is the machine doing?"

Jhonni started. The skinny coolie boy had set his glass of tea on her table.

"Oh," she said. "It's a windup opera. You get sets of metal cylinders, with patterns of little snags. The machinery reads them and moves the puppets, and reproduces the music. This one's a bit worn. For a different act, you change the cylinder. Different opera, you change the stage. It—um, that top part slots out."

Nervousness made her babble. The clown didn't help. He was staring at her dumbly. "This one's called the *Blue Schoolroom*. You see, there's a poor girl and a rich girl and they're in love and they want to get married. You know, marry; it's what we Samsui do. But a good marriage is supposed to be a good business alliance, so they try to keep it a secret. But in fact, the heiress is really a male. I mean a young man. It's something that used to happen, truly. To protect an inheritance, keep a fortune in one piece, a rich woman who kept having male children would dress up one as a girl. He wishes he could tell her. But he's his mother's only child, you see, or that's what he thinks. He must go on pretending or his whole clan will lose their fortune. But really, the poor girl, her, I mean his, girlfriend—"

The clown sat down, slowly, as if his limbs hurt him. He kept his shoulders hunched and his face turned to the ground—as coolies did, hating eye contact with the Samsui.

"—they were changed over at birth, by an enemy who dressed up as a *dapur* midwife and . . . well, there's more: *banyak banyak komplikasi*. It turns out she, the poor one, is the real heiress."

It was done. They were sitting together. Jhonni stopped gabbling and breathed a sigh of relief. At least she had made contact. At least she had not arranged a secret rendezvous and had to give it up because her nerve failed.

"Are you interested in music?"

"I—music? Yes, Mrs. I like music."

"Then I'm sorry for you. I didn't know they tortured the customers like this in here."

Barely, shyly, he smiled. Their eyes met. She was startled again, as at the camp, at finding a human being in there.

"Is it safe to talk?" she breathed.

"Speak Peninsulan."

She supposed that made sense; common coolies didn't speak High Inggris. She hoped she could cope. The coffee shop woman had vanished into her kitchen. The withered hands of the cardplayers slipped in and out of their robes and the broken-down ceiling fan creaked in its slow circuit; the opera jangled on.

Jhonni cleared her throat. "You tell me now what you did not tell. About our friend?"

"Yes. She's in grave danger. You must help me. You must do exactly as I say."

"Is it to do with the flowerdust?"

The clown stared at the tabletop and eventually nodded. "The dust, yes." He looked at the puppets. "What does our friend say about it?"

"She says she'll do nothing. It's not her business."

"Yes. That's what she would say. You must watch her and those around her. You must tell me anything that happens."

"Me tell you?" Jhonni felt she was losing control of this interview. "But how she in danger? You promised you tell me."

"No, not yet. Can't explain yet. We must meet again."

"Not good enough. You tell me now. Do you need money?" She had thought of that. She had a wad of cash in her pocket. It was the Koperasi currency, and therefore polluted. But she'd guessed a refugee wouldn't disdain it.

She'd guessed wrong. He sat up straight. His eyes flashed. "I am, or at least I was, a gentleman. I am that lady's friend. She taught me to believe in the cause of independence. I have suffered for it." His voice shook. "I don't need your money."

"All right!" Jhonni was contrite. "I'm sorry—"

It crossed her mind that the clown was lonely. He could read and write and speak High Inggris. There must be a story behind this: a sad story. Maybe he didn't know Derveet, maybe he didn't know anything. Perhaps he just wanted someone to talk to.

"So, fine, um, Endang. I'm Jhonni, remember. You know, we could find out a bit about each other, talk about ourselves?"

The Peninsulan words came more fluently now. It was easier when she got going. She smiled at him, encouragingly.

"This is Ranganar," he said at last. "It isn't how I imagined. I expected a big city, fancy buildings. Like Sepaa."

"Oh well, you know . . . In the center it's like that. Out here at Cold Storage things are running down. We have a population shortfall. You've seen those big posters saying THREE IS NOT ENOUGH. That means babies. But who wants to have three babies? Go through that business over and over again. Ecch . . . It's a problem we have to solve," she added, suddenly serious, remembering that she was a political activist. "Reproduction is the unsolved problem of the Samsui way of life."

Did he know that Samsui children were fathered by the Koperasi? She was getting confused. He had called himself a gentleman. If he was a male, maybe she shouldn't talk to him about such things. But if he was really a Timurese stud, wouldn't he be shut up? Jhonni remembered Prince Atoon—and the hat, which was no longer to be despised. She thought of a picture once passed around in class. It had been copied from a temple wall, or else from the wall of a brothel in Hungry Tiger Street. It showed a prince, naked astride a prancing horse: the horse's neck curving one way, the man's erect, virile member curving the other. Ignorant, wishing to sound knowledgeable, Jhonni had cried: "It's far too big!" Everyone had collapsed in giggles and she was embarrassed for a month.

Endang leaned across and took the pad and color tablet from under her hand. "Excuse me. May I?" He bent over the paper. She was glad he couldn't read her mind.

"I like music, I like drawing," he said softly. "My favorite subjects at school."

"I'm best with figures. I'm nearly qualified as an accountant." Jhonni had managed to banish the brothel picture. "Accountant" sounded dreadful: no job for a revolutionary. "But the Cause comes first. In dangerous times you have to live dangerously. You have to grasp the blade. Or else you don't exist. Don't you agree?"

"Has our friend a private way to leave the West Bank? To cross the Straits unseen?"

"To cross? I don't know . . . We always crossed the causeway openly and met her on the other side." Jhonni started, horrified. The unfamiliar language had made her say too much.

He didn't raise his head. "Don't worry," he murmured. "You give nothing away. We all know about the dancers, and the bomb-making."

"Fireworks," corrected Jhonni. "Mostly just fireworks. Our friend doesn't believe in violence."

Endang's glance flickered over her and returned to the paper. "Of course. So. She crossed privately by herself?"

But Jhonni balked at this, belatedly realizing she had lost control of the conversation. "Wait a minute. Why should I tell you anything? *You're* the one who wanted to talk to me!"

Endang shut the pad and slid it towards her. His eyes pleaded. "I can't talk. Not now. We must meet again."

She made a decision. She would trust him—not too far, but a little farther. "All right," she said quickly. "Let's plan it. What's the name of this shop?"

"I don't know. I don't think it has one."

The kampong was the nearest place to the refugee camp where you could get anything to eat. Jhonni had told the clown to meet her here because she knew the other volunteers didn't come down this dead-end street. The good food stalls were on the other side of the main road. She'd seen the shabby coffee shop by the water, but had never been inside it before.

She took a stick of charcoal, glanced at the opera machine. "I'll be at the camp often. I'm a volunteer, you know. We'll pretend we don't know each other. When I can meet you, I'll write on the wall by your, er, pitch. Where I met you. I'll write 'Blue Schoolroom.' " "You'll come here the next day, at this same time—"

"At *sore*," he murmured.

Between the heat of the day and the evening: she had forgotten the right word. "*Sore*, yes. If you can come, you'll rub the words out. If you can't, you'll leave them."

The opera machine thumped into silence. The old woman came out and changed the cylinder. Apparently she decided to pass over the ramifications of the plot. Jhonni recognized the start of the final act.

"You didn't tell me the end of the story," said Endang. "The poor girl can turn out to be an heiress. But the young man cannot turn out to be a woman. How can a woman and a man be in love? This does not happen. No happy ending seems possible."

Jhonni chuckled. "You don't know much about Samsui taste. There isn't a happy ending. Opera is supposed to make you cry."

"It's certainly painful," he ventured. "It sounds like cats fighting."

"But you wondered about the changeling." She leapt to understanding. "Do you wish you'd been born a woman?"

"Any sane man wishes that." The clown shrugged. "If he has any desire beyond rutting and decorating himself. It is true, I hate my life."

"That's *good*," said Jhonni earnestly. "That's part of what we're fighting for. When we've cast off the Rulers' oppressive yoke, and reformed land ownership, and made the *dapurs* democratic, the states will live in harmony and so will women and men. There will be no more cruel practices like enclosure and boy-making. Young men like you will go to school to learn a trade; you'll be able to work for a living—" Carried away, she grasped his hand. His fingers, limp and unresponsive, were like dry straw. The skin burned.

"Oh! You're ill. You have a fever."

"No." He pulled away. "We don't get ill."

She had offended him. A moment of genuine fellowship evaporated. She thought of the behavior of people like Physician Mersin, of the fence that was supposed to be going up around the camp. Endang had a right to be hostile. "Of course not, the *dapur* protects you. I know that. I'm sorry." She gathered her things. "I should go. I'll leave first. Watch out for my sign."

"Blue Schoolroom," muttered Endang. He was a coolie again, sunken in his place, avoiding her eyes. "I won't forget."

Jhonni left. On the puppet stage, a pair of stiff and tattered little figures sang a wavering duet. Endang stared at them, the *wayang mesin*, machine puppets. The high-pitched, mechanical words were nearly indistinguishable from the whining Samsui music. He waited until he was sure Jhonni was not going to come bouncing back with another mouthful of childish rhetoric. Then he relaxed his agonizing control. His teeth chattered and his hands shook. He tried to drink from the glass of tea, to ease his parched throat. He couldn't manage it; tea spilled over his fingers. The coffee shop woman came to take out the cylinder: not to waste her valuable resources on mere Peninsulans. She glanced at the coolie and jerked her chin in contempt.

"Heh!"

"*Banyak banyak komplikasi*—" Endang's thin shoulders lifted. "Very, very complicated," he repeated in High Inggris, precisely; as if he were drunk. "No, not complicated. Disgustingly simple."

* * *

When Jhonni looked at her sketchpad, she found her thumbnail scribble had been much improved. It was all there, even more dreary than in life: the wonky tables, battered chairs, the frowsty pair of cardplayers. He'd turned the cardplayers, the Ranganarese women, around. They faced into the picture now, watching Jhonni and Endang, as it were. She peered closer, and murmured in astonishment. Two gray skulls nestled in the dark robes, staring with black pits of eyes.

It was a warning.

"Bad magic," whispered Jhonni.

A thrill went through her.

Until she examined the sketch she'd meant to tell someone about Endang. Perhaps Butcher Handai, since Derveet wouldn't listen. A whole series of secret meetings was more than she had bargained for. But this decided her. She would tell no one. She was alone, against a threat that no one who worked for the Cause would believe possible: evil in the *dapur* power itself.

3

THE COUNTING ROOMS opened off a drab courtyard in the midst of the sprawling Cycler compound. Outside in the dust, flowering shrubs failed to thrive in fat earthenware pots. Inside, superior Ranganarese boys and Cyclers of middling rank tended a forbidding hive of paper and rattling machinery.

Aunt Kwokmei had presided over the Cycler accounts for far longer than Jhonni had been alive. She was a very old woman, whiskery around the chin and parchment-skinned. Her eyes, bright and beady as a rat's, peered from nests of wrinkles. Like a rat she defended her territory fiercely. The Samsui women had a custom of marrying each other, for love and good business, but Kwokmei had never married. She had no child or wife, in the Cycler clan or outside it; no links in the network of personal alliance that bound the trade clans together. But she held her own. When Kwokmei chose to exert herself, even Jhonni's mother deferred to her.

Cycler children hated accounts. Naughty, inattentive little girls were sent to Aunt Kwokmei as a punishment. But Jhonni, who was always naughty, found a refuge in the peaceful dance of the numbers. Aunt Kwokmei, who bullied the bad children unmercifully, soon forgot why this excellent recruit was supposed to be with her. The two became allies and colleagues, while Jhonni was still regarded by the rest of the family as a dreamy, overgrown baby.

Opinionated and eccentric, the formidable old lady regaled her favorite with deviant wisdom. Jhonni learned in school that *Samsui* meant "Three Springs" in an old dialect that nobody used anymore. The Three Springs were: one, physical labor; two, abolish boy-making; three, treat men as equals. Aunt said this was nonsense. If the ladies who came to Ranganar valued physical labor so much, how come they spent their time inventing machines? If they thought the extra sex was so badly treated, how come Ranganarese boys *still* did all the menial work around here?

Boy-making she considered harmless, as long as it was done decently: with the knife, at an early age, no magic! Treating full males as equals was something that happened "in the heart." "If I ever met a man who was my equal, I should immediately treat him as such," said Aunt. "I could not stop myself. But it cannot be forced."

When the Rulers appeared out of the Southern Ocean, the Samsui were already established on Ranganar Island. They were heretics who had rejected the secretive, autocratic powers of the *dapur* and the use of a slave labor force of neutered boys. Ranganar was a small island. The Samsui could not feed themselves and had insufficient sources of fresh water. They were bound to be dominated by someone. Many of them had actively preferred that it should be the newly emerged power. The Rulers were kindred spirits, using machines and distrusting the mysteries of *dapur* government.

So the rift between the orthodox Peninsula and the Samsui grew wider through the years. Since the Great Rebellion, in which the Samsui had tried to stay neutral, the break had been complete. The Koperasi Administration Compound now dominated the Clan Council. The Koperasi had become essential to Samsui life. Most Samsui no longer thought of themselves as Peninsulan. Kwokmei was the only grown-up who ever talked to Jhonni about the past, until she met Miss Butcher and the other radicals.

But according to Aunt Kwokmei, the first Samsui were no mere social reformers. They were a superior race, immune to magic, scattered over the Peninsula ages ago, and gathered again in Ranganar to escape the jealousy of the *dapur*. Aunt K could prove this by the tables of ancestors in the Cycler records room, by the roundness of Jhonni's eyes (a typical Samsui trait), her rosy cheeks, and the flat shape of the back of her head. Peninsulan heads, and the heads of the Rulers too, were universally lumpy.

Despite this racial pride, Aunt Kwokmei had used her considerable power to defend Jhonni's Peninsulan sympathies. She had never met the chief attraction—known criminal, male impersonator—and was never likely to meet her. But she was broad-minded with the tolerance of extreme age. When young Jhonni wanted to join the Previous Heaven Society—a group started by the Butchers to promote cultural ties between Samsui and the Peninsulan exiles in Ranganar—Jhonni's mother had been very doubtful. Kwokmei had persuaded her. *Let the child be; experiments are healthy; it does us no harm to have feet in both pies. What, you want those Butchers hogging all the Peninsulan interest? Big interest, if it comes good and it may yet. Times got changing. This gangster is a good gangster, look at the way she sends the girl home sober. Shows consideration for our feelings . . .*

Hanging fans hissed in the dusty air. It was midafternoon; the working day was nearly over. Big girls darted in to dump piles of bills and receipts and immediately darted out again. Jhonni toiled on without an eye for the clock, soothed by the smell of ink and the unfailing hammering song of the metal keys. The Cycler clan had begun by being in charge of the island's water supply cycle. They had become the accountants for the whole community. There was hardly a transaction in Ranganar—where buying and selling was everything—that didn't pass through this room in some form. Sometimes Jhonni felt that she was sitting at the humming center of the whole world.

She was not a child anymore, in anyone's eyes. After her morning lectures, she came and worked for Kwokmei as of right: soon, her last student days would be over. She was, though nothing had been said, regarded as Kwokmei's heir apparent. The rat-empress passed by Jhonni's stool, casting a sly, sidelong eye over the girl's paperwork. Boys and Samsui minions scurried at their final tasks. "Let me see working-out. Don't tell me you did it in your head. Mark by every figure."

"Aunt, if you think the counting machinery is faulty—"

Kwokmei grinned meanly. "In here, we don't think. We know. Entry in, entry out, figures that add up. Check mark, second check mark, third check mark. That's what we understand. Get a move on. Or you'll be late for your girlfriend the gangster."

The straw hat lay on the counter by the courtyard door, above a pile of rubber-soled slippers. Jhonni glanced at it and smiled. It was Atoon who'd borrowed the hat, investing it with an aura of romance. But that aura now belonged to Endang.

"I'm not going to see Derveet."

"So you say. Be more frank! Always be candid, especially when it will give displeasure. That way, no one gets hurt."

Jhonni had told Derveet that the Samsui were a lost race, and had been downcast to discover that Derveet knew of the theory too. Derveet had pointed out a flaw. The first reformers had planned to raise their sons as equal consorts. That idea had never worked out. The Samsui had depended on Ranganarese studs as well as their own offspring . . . and since the rebellion they had relied, as Derveet tactfully put it, on "other arrangements." If the Samsui had ever been a separate race, it couldn't be so now.

Jhonni had taken this back to Kwokmei, who—to Jhonni's disappointment—accepted the judgment in silence. That was the last Jhonni heard of the wilder margins of Aunt's lore. "You're growing up," she grumbled. "Starting to see through me. Don't be proud. One day you'll need non-senses of your own. Not going to show you mine anymore. You'll spoil them."

Since that day she had been a little sour about "the gang-ster," though she still defended Jhonni's sympathies. She wouldn't admit that she was jealous. Instead she accused Derveet of the mysterious crime of being bilingual. You should never trust someone who could think in two lan-guages. One day, Derveet would become openly crazy and kill lots of people: first among them, most likely, her young Cycler friend . . .

"What, is it someone else you go to see, rushing off in the heat? Nice Samsui girl?"

Jhonni controlled a giggle. "No!"

"I guess I'm behind the times. How old are you? Getting big around the bum, I see. You going down Hungry Tiger Street?"

Hungry Tiger Street was in the brothel quarter, the place where Ranganar Koperasi went to satisfy their base urges with Peninsulan exiles—failed women who hadn't the gall to become gangsters or the talent for the Classical Dance Theater. It was also, coincidentally, the place where respect-able Samsui went to get themselves pregnant. These two facts had been presented to Jhonni, through her childhood, as if there weren't the slightest connection between them. There must be a baby shop somewhere in that haunt of "bad people": a clean and bright place, where the infants were laid out in rows, like fruit. Always girl-infants, for the Samsui. If a male child came home by mistake the parcel was briskly returned, the incident vanished; no one spoke of that baby again.

The topic was so much avoided and Jhonni was so little interested that she might still have believed in the baby shop. Aunt K, robust-minded and tenderhearted, had saved her from the ugly shock that came to many girls when their families decided to send them "down Hungry Tiger Street." Kwokmei's brusque verbal diagrams, with gestures, had ended her innocence. She went on wondering, with deep unease, what happened around the essential act: *What do you do? Do you have to talk to him?*

She would find out. It was a duty, onerous and commonplace. Jhonni had got away with being a Peninsulan sympathizer. She knew she'd never dare to rebel over something that was important to her mother. Kwokmei had chosen not to get a child. She never said why, not really. But Jhonni thought of Endang. His feeling about the relationship between the Kops and the Samsui had begun to color her own ideas.

"I wish I could be like you. I don't want any babies."

"Ha. You say that now. You wait. Baby fever will get you. Ruins everyone's stupid life, one way or other. Now get lost.

"And remember," she yelled as Jhonni tidied her desk (quite unnecessary yelling, since there was barely an arm's length between them), "you pregnant, you stay out of here. No one vomits on my ledgers. No one who can't hold her piss tends my machines." The boys looked around, big-eyed. Aunt cackled loudly. Jhonni hurried out into the sun, scarlet to the ears.

Nobody at home, unless Aunt Kwokmei guessed something, had suspected Jhonni's rebel activities. Her family never took Jhonni seriously. They laughed at her amulets and sarongs. When she joined the Previous Heaven Society and started going off on cultural trips across the causeway, they teased her unkindly. "Promoting cultural ties!" they jeered. Everyone knew why the radicals hung around the dance theater, why they were so keen to recruit those luscious Peninsulan hussies! Everybody knew what really went on at those political picnics! It was a joke. Nobody believed that Jhonni—who didn't even have a girlfriend—had begun a career of riotous lust. They just liked to see her blush and splutter. Jhonni didn't mind, so long as they didn't come near the truth.

They were even less likely to guess what she was up to now.

She had met Endang every day. It was tremendously exciting. She had yet to learn exactly what was happening in the camp, or the precise nature of the danger to Derveet. But she was gaining his confidence slowly.

The frightened hints he let fall had worried her sufficiently that she'd been back to the West Bank on her own account—twice, without Derveet's knowledge. She'd left her bicycle on the Samsui side of the river (that was Endang's suggestion). Remembering Semar's covert anxiety in the *sudahmandi*, she had sneaked into the gardens of Dove House and had a poke around, and actually discovered Derveet's secret exit to the sea.

Last time they met, Endang had given her a magic talisman, from the good *dapur* women in the camp, which he wanted her to place by Derveet's seaway. It was there now. He'd be glad to know that. At this stage, Jhonni didn't know *what* to believe about *dapur* magic among the refugees. But she was certain that Endang was really afraid, and she didn't see how a talisman could do any harm.

Jhonni swung her bike onto the red-rutted kampong street.

For ten days they'd been meeting; it seemed so much longer. He was her own Peninsulan. The dancers had never confided much in Jhonni; and Atoon and Derveet seemed hopelessly out of reach now, compared with Endang. For the first time she had contact with someone her own age from the land of romance. His opinions about Peninsulan politics weren't exactly new to her, but Endang made it concrete. Talking to him, she got a feeling for the human side of Peninsulan politics: how the cultured Jagdanans looked

down on the moneymaking Timurese; how the Gamarthans
were arrogant and brave, but notoriously stupid. The Jagdanans and the Garudas were allies, the Gamarthans and
the Garudas were rivals. The Timurese, with their murderous court intrigues, were mistrusted by everybody. The
Garudas were paramount because they were the tricksters,
always playing one nation off against the others: Garuda
was the puppeteer.

The picture Endang painted of these traditional enmities
was depressing; it didn't leave much room for hope. But she
knew that in spite of his cynicism he loved Derveet. The last
Garuda was his idol. It was something they shared. In Ranganar now, the real identity of the failed woman bandit
who lived in the Garuda water palace was no longer a secret. The Samsui Clan Council would be the last to know.
But Jhonni and Endang had known her and believed in her
for years. They spent much of their time together talking
about Derveet and the vital part she'd played in both their
lives.

Of course, Jhonni had told Endang nothing *important* in
these conversations. Nothing that he didn't know already.
She was careful. She was humoring him, leading him on
until she could break through the barrier of fear and find
out the truth.

The Peninsula side of the city was silent because the
causeway was still closed. The uprising was still going on,
the refugees still trickling into the camp. Garudas and Singhas are old rivals, she thought. Endang said that . . . Suppose Derveet was *wrong* about what was happening in
Gamartha? Suppose Jhonni got to the bottom of the flowerdust affair, and told Derveet, and became Derveet's trusted
adviser, and they all, Endang too, marched off together to
war in the north. Stirred and excited, Jhonni could hardly
wait for this glorious denouement.

"Forever together. Nothing can part us. No difference of
wealth, no cruelty of f-a-a-a-a-ate!"

Belting out the chorus of the first-act duet from *Blue*

Schoolroom, she pulled up outside their coffee shop. The old woman shuffled forward eagerly. In her simple reckoning, Jhonni had become a valued customer. The cardplayers, for once, were absent. Endang wasn't there. But he was always before her. Jhonni stood irresolute, unwilling to go inside. Like a good secret agent, she knew immediately that something was wrong.

Atoon and Cho and Derveet were on the roof of the *sudah-mandi.* It was late afternoon: *sore,* in the Peninsulan style. They were watching Semar as he tended the remaining pigeons. The moon of the third month had been waning when they visited the refugee camp. It was now at the dark and nothing had changed: neither in Gamartha, as far as anyone could tell, nor here in Ranganar.

Derveet had kept to her resolve, though the gossip of the West Bank about the state of affairs in the refugee camp was nasty: things were getting worse. She was right, the Koperasi had not made any serious attempt to impose law and order. But they weren't doing anything to ease the problems, either.

"It's strange," said Atoon, "that no one has mentioned the dust in the tales that come out of the camp. I could almost believe we ourselves were hallucinating that day."

Derveet was sitting with Cho on a bare stretch of coping above Semar's kitchen yard, where the feather balustrade had crumbled. Divine Endurance was curled in a neat brown ball on the sunny courtyard flags below. Derveet hefted a shard of stone thoughtfully. "You and me, and Physician Mersin, and how many others? I suppose the young woman could have been faking."

"And faking the scent of flowerdust, too? I wonder if perhaps you should have interviewed your friend Endang?"

Derveet leaned back against the broken balustrade, rubbing her fingers along the grooves in her fragment of dusty feathers.

"I am sorry about Endang," she said. "When I met him he

was a very confused young man. But he had such anger, and such hopes—"

She had told Atoon the story of Endang, the young stud who had defied tradition by living on after his female relatives died: Gamarthan by birth, Timurese by adoption, educated at the Koperasi college in Sepaa.

She glanced at Atoon and grinned. She knew that Endang's story aroused more pity than sympathy in him. Atoon wasn't surprised that the young man so described had come to a bad end.

"He was a new kind of Peninsulan, Atoon. And he was right to be angry about so much of what goes on. When I met him, he saw nothing good in the Peninsula. He only wanted to escape from our superstitious savagery. He changed his mind . . ." She hesitated. "It wasn't a happy time. I won't say more, it isn't my story to tell, but it wasn't all bad. He lost his faith in our Rulers, and his pride in his fine education. But at least he had found something to replace them: another pride and faith."

"Yet now you believe he's your enemy."

Derveet shook her head. "I don't. We don't even know for sure that it's the same person. Cho met someone called Endang, who seems to be the same as the clown the Samsui identified as a suspicious character. That's all we know."

"And he said 'Keep her away from me!' " murmured Atoon. "Don't you wonder what he meant by that?"

She sighed, her hands slack on her folded knees, the stone held loosely. "I think Endang is in trouble, and he doesn't want to pull me in. I am sorry for it. If I can think of a way to help him and his people, believe me, I will. But I'm afraid there's nothing I can do. The risks are too great."

Petruk came up the stairs, his round pursy face popping up suddenly into view. He asked Semar something. The old boy came over to his mistress, employing the jackknifed, hobbled crawl of a well-trained *dapur* servant, a mode of respect not usually seen in Dove House, where Derveet tried to run things almost as if she were a heretic. The boys adored having Atoon here. His presence gave them license for all sorts of revisionist backsliding.

"Will madam be eating tonight?" he inquired unctuously.

Derveet laughed. "No, madam will be fasting, buffoon."

Since it was the dark of the moon, the official *hari darah* of Ranganar had begun. The boys grinned all over their faces. Devout Peninsulan women fasted through the three rest days of their monthly courses. A failed woman whose blood still flowed—as Derveet's did, at least sometimes—could join the fast and add luster to her household. Their mistress usually claimed she was too busy to starve herself.

Atoon gazed over the West Bank, pretending not to hear this exchange. Petruk went to him (this was a matter of protocol: it was the oldest boy's privilege to address Derveet), murmured to him quietly, and headed for the stairs again.

"Excuse me," said Atoon, rising. "If you will excuse me, madam. I believe I'll go indoors for a while."

He had been summoned, as Derveet perfectly understood, to meet a young person of the West Bank, someone Petruk thought might amuse him. Derveet, who knew how seriously the boys took their pimping duties, took care not to catch the prince's eye.

Semar awarded Derveet's ladylike manners an approving nod. To cover the little awkwardness of the prince's departure, he spoke of the *darah*: a fascinating subject. Nothing could be learned from the blood cycle of a lady who fell in step with her neighbors. But you could read the personalities of the independent kind. The full moon, overbearing and vigorous. The gibbous, envious: a hard mistress. The half-moon, clever and cold. The nail-paring of a young moon, a sweet temper. The waning sickle, melancholy. A woman whose flow skipped from phase to phase was a neurotic, flighty type (he eyed his mistress with wicked meaning) . . . but she might be possessed of genius.

"Nonsense." Derveet grinned. "The *darah* shows that a woman is not pregnant. This meaning is inconvenient for powerful women who have made childbearing a source of power. Therefore it has been arranged that the Peninsula considers the *darah* a highly significant phenomenon. You shouldn't be so easily taken in."

Semar grunted contemptuously. "Madam likes to tease an old boy." He squinted up at the hazy sky. "It's funny that we don't see Nyonya Cycler these days. I wonder why that is, because I know she crosses the river. People remember a Samsui girl on the ferry." No answer. Derveet was absorbed in taking aim, at last, with her piece of stone.

A subtle change had come over the company on the roof, now that Atoon was safely out of the way. There was reproach in the old boy's manner and an air almost of defiance in Derveet and the doll-who-was-a-person. The dark of the moon is a temptation to someone who cannot move freely for fear of watchful eyes.

"The other day, there was an animal in the *sudahmandi*," remarked Semar. "I chased it. That animal wore blue cotton trousers."

He returned to his coops, lifted out a plump she-pigeon with wing coverts of deep greenish-gold: *bunga Gamartha*, flower of the North. She crooned at him, and tried to stab him in the eye with her beak. She had been a little unwell, this one. He was worried about her. He rubbed his seamed cheek against the bird's soft breast and looked back over his shoulder resentfully.

"Madam ought to do something about that animal."

"I mean to, you old misery."

"Hmmph. You will do something stupid. You can never give orders; it is a sign of a weak mind. What are servants for? And you know you need your rest. I heard you coughing again. Late nights are bad for you."

Derveet moved impatiently. "I'm in perfect health. A little cough means nothing." She grinned without turning around. "All I need is a spot of exercise and some fresh sea air."

Semar's anxiety suddenly broke out: he was genuinely angry.

"You want to do everybody's work for them! You want to be a heretic, you want to be a slave, you want to be like the *aneh*. You take *bad* risks because you want to be like a bandit, like a Kop. Why don't you ever want to be a proper, ordinary lady?"

"That would be difficult," said Derveet softly.

She was trying to hit Divine Endurance, who was asleep, or seemed to be. The pebble stopped in midair, made a right-angled turn and bounced over the kitchen doorstep.

"Did you see that? She's cheating."

"Divine Endurance always cheats," agreed Cho.

Semar was mortified by his own lack of tact. But he rallied. "A burglar in the after-bathing house: bad enough. Next, our throats cut. These Samsui girls are of uncertain temper when they pass puberty." The old boy's eyes narrowed with malice. "Maybe she means to creep into the prince's pavilion, sneak a baby off our little father."

Derveet stood up. "I'm tired of this. I don't want to hear any more. And I particularly"—she looked at him sharply—"*particularly* forbid you to mention your imaginary intruder to Prince Atoon. Or to complain to him about my feckless behavior. You hear me? I will not have Atoon worried."

The old boy straightened from beside the coops. He smoothed his sarong primly, with a sour expression. "I knew that."

"Mind you remember it. All of you."

Atoon knew that Derveet was fasting. He would not expect to see her tonight. She passed through her laboratory, picking up a few useful bits and pieces. Cho was waiting in the *sudahmandi*, a dim shadow in her white clothes. Derveet cracked a lightstick, and knelt so they were face-to-face. They had met in the dark, it seemed like a lifetime ago, far away up in the Peninsula, at a river crossing. In her role as Anakmati the bandit, Derveet had been following a strange trail. At the end of it she had discovered this beautiful child. A child who was a machine.

Cho and the cat, Divine Endurance, were angel dolls, *wayang legong*: extraordinary survivals from the ruins of an ancient city. They had come to the Peninsula, Cho said, "looking for the humans," and for another angel doll, Cho's twin. Derveet had learned, soon after she found Cho, that the Rulers had Cho's brother. He was with them; he'd been with them for years. The Rulers had kidnapped Cho when they learned of her existence. But only, apparently, to confirm their suspicions. Derveet had recovered the doll-who-was-a-person without difficulty, as if her enemies accepted as fair this division of the ancient treasure.

They took her from me, thought Derveet. Then they gave her back. Why? It was a question that nagged at her. She told herself it should not. *They're crazy. Inbred, isolated, dying. They don't have sane reasons for anything they do.*

She had found a lost toy and instantly, like a little girl, fallen in love. She had taken the dead past in her arms, and it seemed a right and a good thing to do, a healing and a reunion. But an angel doll, the Rulers had told her, can grant every wish of the human heart. What did that mean?

"Semar's worried," said Cho.

"He's an old baby. I'm not afraid of the Koperasi these days. I have different problems." She laughed suddenly. "The problems of success. It would be politically embarrassing for Garuda to be caught on this trip. Isn't that a joke?"

Before Derveet met Cho, Atoon had found her lost in Jagdana. The Jagdana *dapur* had recognized the doll for what she was, dressed her in white, and let Atoon send her to Derveet. White was the men's color. It meant battle, royalty, and mourning . . . The *dapur* spoke in silence, by potent signs. They meant that because of the angel doll they would support Derveet in her use of the secret powers, in her new kind of warfare. Because of Cho, Derveet's fortunes had changed. Exactly *why* the Jagdana *dapur* had made this decision, Derveet still didn't understand. With an abrupt gesture, she pushed the puzzle aside. The women of the Peninsula had begun to see reason, that was all. It was about time.

"I've been behaving myself. I deserve an outing."

"That's just what I think."

Derveet reached out and touched Cho's face. "You are the comfort everybody needs. You are the perfect something to hug, to keep the nightmares at bay. You soak up terror and loneliness, unhappiness and self-doubt. What do you do with it all?"

Cho didn't know. "I don't do anything, unless you want me to." She frowned. It worried her when Derveet spoke like this. She had been told by the factory, and she knew it was true, that her person would be happiest when he or she forgot what Cho was. It wasn't good for them to be conscious of what you were doing: it might upset them.

"But I belong to you. I'm yours forever and ever."

Derveet put her arms around the doll-who-was-a-person. The slender body moved with her, pliant and open: *growing*. There seemed more of Cho whenever Derveet touched her. She looked like a fifteen-year-old girl, barely old enough to be anyone's lover. Yet if Derveet closed her eyes she was enfolded as if she were a baby on her mother's breast. Safe. "And I belong to you. Never doubt it. Let's go. You and me, back into our private adventure. It's going to be fun."

Cho could have guided them through the secret maze under the *sudahmandi* as if the dank blackness were daylight. But the doll-who-was-a-person had carefully learned how to stumble in the dark. She was so proud of her wrongheaded adoptions of human frailty, it would have been a shame to argue with her. Therefore Derveet, with her cool green-glowing wand, led the way along passages that had once served the amorous intrigues of Garuda courtiers.

They reached a dock, where two boats were moored in the crook of a stone pier. One of them, the catamaran *Visnu*, had carried Derveet across the ocean from her grandfather's island of exile. Semar, Petruk, and Gareng had sailed *Visnu* down from Jagdana, when they were sent by Prince Atoon's family to serve at Dove House.

The *Visnu* shifted uneasily on the loose, bumpy surface of high water. "Sssh, no worries, old-timer. I'm not going to drag you out of retirement." This Garuda would not be taking flight across the sea. Never. She had promised herself that. The other boat was a smuggler's outfit, painted black inside and out, with a wasp-tail engine. Derveet lifted Cho down from the steps: lifted Cho, who could probably lift Derveet on her fingertip. Something rattled onto the bottom boards. Derveet picked up a handful of small stones.

"A little snack?"

When Cho was very young (Derveet had learned that angel dolls were not "built": they grew, like children), she used to think eating was something you could do with whatever came to hand. "I wish I hadn't told you about that. I was only a baby. You wait, they'll be useful."

The black boat slipped away on the tide. A curve of lesser dark appeared ahead; the sound and smell of the sea rushed over them in a gust of warm air. Cho cocked her head.

"Derveet, is that yours?"

"Is what mine?"

"That."

On the rough-hewn wall where the channel emerged from underground there clung a wet, glistening thing about the size of a fist. Derveet brought them in close and examined the object, using an oar to fend them off the stonework.

"No," she said, "it is not mine. I wonder how it got there."

They left the Koperasi-made gadget undisturbed.

Cloud had gathered since sunset, blanking out every star. Under a lightless sky they crept around the west point of the island into the Straits of Ranganar. A patrol boat loomed, growling and flashing lights. Derveet cut the engine and they lay in the bottom of the boat, letting it drift like a sodden log. They passed so close under the side of the Koperasi vessel that they heard a man's voice, humming tunelessly overhead.

Dum didah didodadum . . .

On a calm night like this one there was plenty of time to cross the Straits, complete a simple errand, and return before dawn. They skimmed along, cooled by their own speed, without event. Soon a mass of lights appeared on the horizon. It was the big Koperasi barracks and supply complex west of the causeway's end. Its blazing lights had been used as a seamark by generations of grateful smugglers. The coast of the Peninsula loomed, black against charcoal. Before long they met the mangroves and entered a maze of creeks. Derveet cut the engine again and sculled, stopping often to think and review her passage.

"Knowing that I was nearly dead of inactivity, some angel sent the flowerdust . . . Nothing personal, Cho. This angel is the human kind. But who? A cartel of Timurese peasants? I wonder. Fertile women should not take dust. Everyone knows that. Did the woman who caught my attention know what she was risking? I wonder. And Endang was supposed to entrap me. He couldn't bring himself to do it . . . Yet someone knew I would make this trip and had a Kop device planted to signal my exit. This could be a trap, Cho."

The Occupying Army on the Peninsula were a different breed from Ranganar's Kops: much less tame and far from harmless.

The channel was too narrow for sculling. She stood and poled them along with one oar.

"But I don't think so. I don't think there's an Occupying

Army reception committee waiting for me here in the bushes. There's something *personal* behind this scheme. How much depth have I ahead?"

"Not a lot," answered Cho. She leaned over and slipped her arm into the water. "I'm touching bottom . . . None."

The black boat—it didn't have a name—slithered and crunched. They stepped out. Ahead of them the Koperasi complex blazed, illuminating a wilderness of knotted stems, strangling air roots, and crowding leather leaves. Harmless insects chanted: *zoing zoing zoing.* The Kops were terrified of Peninsulan swamp and forest, even at the gates of their own installations, which was convenient. In reality the mangrove forest was a gentle place. Aeons of human interference, both brutal and exquisitely subtle, had banished or disarmed almost every noxious species, except one.

"Now for the treasure hunt. When I was the bandit Anakmati—before I met you and became a reformed character—I was like a pirate of the acar hills. Pirates always have some buried treasure stowed away. We lack the secret map. But I can remember." She chewed a knuckle. "I *think* I can remember. But don't you help me, angel. No fair."

They tied the boat up, and paddled and clambered through the chaos of branches until they reached solid ground, a cleared and brightly lit band of earth in front of the Kops' perimeter fence. Cho looked up at Derveet dubiously.

"They never come out," murmured Derveet, in answer to her unspoken question. "Except by the hard road, in full array. This is very safe. Really."

"This treasure," she whispered, "came to me while I was in partnership with a Koperasi officer. It seemed appropriate to hide it where the Kops could watch over it for me. I was trying to be clever; I thought my partner would never guess. I'll be honest with you—the complex was smaller then. I didn't expect them to develop the site the way they have. What *do* they plan to keep in all those sheds?"

They waited. A pair of Kops tramped by, shouldering weapons. Then Derveet led the way, bent double, racing toward the corner of the compound. Halfway along she tripped, fell. The men heard the thump and stood debating. They began to come back. Flat on her face, and smothering laughter at her own idiocy, Derveet pulled a handful of small discs out of the bag slung at her waist. She twisted fuses together. But Cho was quicker. The Koperasi heard a rattle of stones behind them, instantly swiveled and thundered off towards the new noise. Derveet and Cho scooted on.

Beyond the fenced compound there was waste ground, dotted with heaps of gravel and stacks of planking. Derveet flopped behind a pile of heavy sacks to catch her breath. She was still choking back laughter. She felt invulnerable, exhilarated by the game. She felt as if nothing could go wrong for her, nothing ever again. Something rustled: a dry flow from a tear in one of the sacks. She touched the stuff curiously. It was rice.

"Idiots!" she breathed. Rice rotting on a building site: cement dust no doubt delivered as food to some unfortunate plantation slaves. "You'd think they'd do something useful occasionally, just by accident . . ."

The floodlights leached darkness from ground level but left the cloudy, moonless sky untouched: an odd effect. They followed a gray path under the black sky, until there was swampy brush on either side of them. Soon, a dark, tall shadow showed through the undergrowth. The ancient stump might have been a relic of the forest that grew here before the Koperasi came, before the salt water moved in. It was higher than a tall man. Ferns and orchids, alien to this sea-infected terrain, perched like roosting birds in hollows where fresh water gathered. They climbed up. The center had rotted, or maybe had been burned away. Derveet leaned down, reaching at arm's length.

"There's a ring here. Should be . . . Got it."

Her hand came up easily, pulling a line. It was Koperasi twine, slick, tough, and impervious to rot. She pulled until she held the loose end.

"No treasure?" wondered Cho.

Derveet thumbed the severed strands. Her other hand beat out a complicated rhythm on the rim of the stump.

"No treasure."

She did not seem surprised.

How still the night was. Derveet reached into her sash—an uncompleted gesture. She knew that her smoking depressed Cho. She put her arm instead around the doll-who-was-a-person, and inhaled the bliss of freedom. The damp air was cool and sweet after stifling Ranganar.

She considered the irony of this escapade—dodging the Kops and playing with fireworks, when she had at her command the magic of the angel doll. Ask, she had been told. Ask for anything and it will happen. She had never tried to find out if this was true. She had made a decision, and she would stick to it. She would not be beholden to the weird powers tapped by a lost world in its death throes. She would never ask Cho for any more than her love and companionship.

"I like outings," murmured the doll. "I wish we could live outdoors forever."

"I need to do the Timurese a favor. That's the real bait in this curiously transparent trap. The Timurese are so cynical, and they have no friends among my friends. I thought everything would fall into place after Jagdana declared for me. It seems I have to make a separate peace with each of the princedoms, even Gamartha eventually. Don't know how I'm going to manage that."

Cho sighed.

Derveet pondered. "Everyone pities me; I pity myself, because I am a failed woman. But it occurs to me . . . if my grandfather planned things this way, he never told me. But if he did decide the Young Pretender would be better off barren, he was wise. Supposing I had returned a proved woman. To take up residence, say—not to show favoritism—in the ladies' palace of Timur? Or Gamartha? I suspect my child and I would be long dead . . . Unfortunately, emergent divine powers don't seem to improve the character, not necessarily. *Dapur* women can be good, or bad, or *nasty,* same as the rest of us . . . This way, however outrageous I am, I'm less likely to offend the dangerous ones. I command a kind of respect but I threaten no one."

She laughed bitterly. "What a joke if I'm no relation after all. If I'm some island orphan the old man picked out and trained up for fun." She pushed back a lock of heavy hair with her free hand. "Atoon's family acknowledged me, and I suppose they would know. But it proves nothing. The Hanoman *dapur* wouldn't let the facts get in the way if they'd decided the world needed a semilegitimate Garuda on the loose."

Derveet paused, half hopefully, her chin on the doll's hair. Cho could feel her pain: a humiliating sore place that only Cho was allowed to touch. She wished that she could say *You are real, it is true.* But Derveet's hunger for legitimacy was one of these strange human appetites: the things that they wanted and hated themselves for wanting, so that giving them their desire would be the worst way of making them happy.

"It's so complicated—" she whispered sadly.

Derveet drew back, smiling in the gloom. "I'll never know," she said, "if I have the right to do what I'm doing. It's not something you can help, Cho. No one can tell me, not so that I could believe them. But like Atoon at the chessboard, it's an addiction. I can't stop now."

Somewhere back along the fence, the cracker-disk that Derveet had dropped suddenly went off, with a flare and a bang. There were sounds of Koperasi agitation. Laughing, Derveet and Cho jumped down and plunged into the brush.

* * *

Hari darah infuriated the Samsui. They didn't mind not being pregnant, and saw no significance in their own blood flow. The regional variations and local shifts of the *darah* tables were the bane of business travelers. It was impossible to keep track of the Peninsulan rest days. In Ranganar it was as bad. Devout Ranganarese kept their coolie boys at home. The Kops went on half-duty, taking any excuse for a holiday.

At the camp Jhonni found the Cold Storage building deserted. Heaps of sharpened stakes and bales of wire lay about. The fence the Kops were supposed to be building proceeded slowly. There was just enough of it to form a potent symbol of fear and distrust and poison the poisonous atmosphere even further. Things were so bad now that the volunteers didn't stay here past *sore* unless the men in red uniform were here. And the evil atmosphere was spreading. Around Cold Storage, Samsui kept off the streets.

Her charcoal scrawl had been smeared off the wall. There was no sign of Endang at his watching place. She waited. The sky was overcast; the camp smelled worse than ever. Robed women passed the end of the alley. Invisible faces turned to her: she imagined skulls looking out of darkness.

Endang had told her his life story. Jhonni had been enthralled. At home she had lain awake at night, wondering how it felt to be ordered to commit suicide by your neighbors, by ordinary people who'd known you all your life! Just because the fertile women, your mother and aunts and sisters, had died, and therefore your life was supposed to be over. How did it feel to be chained up naked like an animal, if you were . . . not like that stud in the peasants' shack, but *Endang*, a person? To be forbidden books, forbidden to write, to be beaten? She had sat with him in the coffee shop, drunk with admiration, thinking how good-looking he'd be if he weren't so thin, and if he were a girl. Thinking, If only he were a girl.

Because he'd refused to commit suicide, and later taken

up the cause of independence, he'd been sent to live with some cruel, brutal people who were distant relations. They had turned out to be criminals. They were the ones who were peddling the terrible drug flowerdust . . . They forced him to work for them, running errands and keeping watch. But Endang had bravely made contact with Jhonni and told her everything.

She walked about in aimless, horrible restlessness, and understood that Endang had told her nothing. She was the one who had done the talking. She had told him things that she should not have told, and done things that she should not have done. She had no idea why. She could not recover the chain of reasoning that had led her to trust the clown. He was her *own Peninsulan.* Though he was a man she had treated him like an equal, from the heart, just the way Kwokmei described it. Shame and fury swelled in her.

"I must have been mad!" she muttered. "Must have been mad!"

Darkness fell. *It can't be true,* she told herself. *He's in trouble, something's happened to him.* Cold chills went through her. She sat with her back against the tin wall of a shack on Endang's patch. She didn't know what she was waiting for.

The wall was built up with earth at its foot. She remembered how Endang had written on the ground. She scratched at the caked dirt, not meaning anything by it. A crust came away in her hand. She felt something like a hard, whippy piece of string. She went back to her bicycle which she'd left at the gates, lit her lamp and brought it to the alley, hiding the light inside her jacket as she crept across the open ground. She dug a bit more, and pulled out Endang's secret.

At last he came back. She didn't know, though they'd met so often, which of the refugee huts was his "home." He emerged from the shadows, settling the rags of his fancy dress and shaking out his matted locks. He saw Jhonni, sitting with the bicycle lamp in her hands, the Koperasi-made wave-communication box smashed between her feet. As soon as she could see his face, Jhonni gave up hope. There was not going to be an innocent explanation.

"You shouldn't be here," he said. "It's dangerous."

"I was waiting for you." Jhonni could have cried with fury. "How stupid do you think I am?" She grabbed the box and shook it at him. "This isn't magic. It's a *wave* receiver. I know about these things. I'm not ignorant! Who have you been talking to with this? The Admin Compound?"

"It's for picking up signals," he explained. "From the detector I got you to leave on the wall of the sea tunnel. My ladies wanted to know when she left to cross the Straits. I hid it here because it would be dangerous to keep a thing like that in our shack."

Jhonni had expected him to deny everything, or to break down and beg for mercy. She gaped, stupidly dazed. "You're crazy. We're lying low. The Straits are full of patrol boats. Why would Derveet do anything like that?"

"She's done it," said Endang. "That's why I wasn't at our rendezvous, Samsui. It's the first night of the dark of the moon. I knew I didn't need you anymore."

Jhonni stood up. "You never told me"—the words came hard—"exactly what happened when you first met Derveet. What did you do for her up there in the Timur hills?"

The clown laughed. "I betrayed her to the Gamarthans."

Endang was taller than Jhonni, but he never stood straight. She looked into that so human face, so like a girl's. Endang looked back. For a moment, unthinkable things were admitted. Then she hit him, first with her fist and then with her open palm.

"I trusted you!"

"That was your own idea." He licked blood from his upper lip. "It's not my fault that you're so easy to fool."

"What have you done?"

"Stupid Samsui."

She hit him again. This time Endang hit back, with an unleashed, luxurious savagery that smashed through their false friendship, telling Jhonni that he hadn't only deceived her, he'd hated her from the start. They punched at each other, both sobbing and gasping insults, until she gave up in disgust.

Endang was on his knees. He dropped onto his side. "You can't do anything. She's gone. When she comes back, my ladies' bully boys will be waiting." He rolled over and lay looking at the sky.

"*Why?*"

"Because nothing can be done," said Endang distinctly. "We're all doomed. Garuda irritated me. She's dead but she won't lie down. But I wouldn't betray her for that. I betrayed her to save myself a beating. It's a good reason."

"You're coming with me to Dove House. Get up."

"It's too late for the ferry. It's too late anyway."

She hauled on his limp, hot hand. Endang laughed, a weak, infuriating sound. His head rolled back. He was sick, sick in his mind: she knew that now. His eyes had closed. Had she killed him? Evil compunction filled her. She had been attacking a helpless maniac and she wanted to hit him again, beat him to jelly. If she hurt him enough she might wipe her shame out of existence. She hauled him upright and locked her arm around his skinny waist.

"Come on, you're coming with me."

As Cho and Derveet made their way back through the patrols, the benign cloud cover finally broke up. Dawn was not far off. Derveet cut the engine for the last time, relying on her sure knowledge of the currents. They rode the water snake, lying on the bottom boards in each other's arms. Stars floated over them.

The black boat drifted into a gray cove where stonework jutted through dark masses of shrubbery. The seedlings of long-dead ornamental trees had become twisted giants, frozen in the act of tearing apart a shallow flight of steps.

The boat slipped towards the hidden entrance. A long rattle of sound burst out of the trees. The boat jumped and jerked, as if trying to bend double on the surface. Koperasi rubber bullets, hard as iron nails, whanged and rattled. Blurred figures scrambled out from the shrubbery. They threw down their *senjata* and waded into the water. They grabbed the hull of the smugglers' boat and groped inside, searching for the precious cargo. Some of them peered around for the body of the person they'd been shooting at. They hissed at each other, getting anxious. Who had seen someone in the boat? Had there been anyone in the boat? Which of them was it who had started shooting?

"Are you looking for someone?"

A tall figure stood on the gray sand, enclosed in a sheen of glimmering phosphorescence. Silver droplets shimmered from its raised arms. It made a flowing gesture which persisted in the air, so that a green-and-silver snake seemed to twist between its hands.

"Is this yours?"

On the other side of the little cove, a small person in white clothes was helpfully holding out the Koperasi gadget.

There were six of the boys. They were big, husky creatures, but they didn't like what they saw. They looked around wildly: the only means of escape was to swim out to sea or dive into the tunnel. "Don't go inside," the dark figure on the sand advised them kindly. "You'll get lost. And there are ghosts." The boys stood waist- and thigh-deep, staring.

"Go back to your ladies," said the dark woman who held the twisting serpent, harmless in her grip. "And tell them Garuda is merciful. Your family won't be punished for this."

Then one of the boys took courage and ran at the shore where the doll had been standing. The sand was empty. In a moment, the other five had followed, and were crashing away through the trees.

Derveet and Cho collected the firearms.

"So much for the Timurese," said Derveet. She grimaced at the weapons: homemade things, equally dangerous at either end. "I wonder how many of *these* there are in the camp. Poor idiots. The ladies back at Cold Storage are not going to be pleased!"

They returned through the passages to Dove House.

Atoon was waiting for them in the upper room. White early light streamed through the long windows. He was setting out chess pieces with exaggerated care. "I was wakened very early," he said, without looking up, "by the sound of *senjata* fire. It seemed to come from the shore, too close for comfort. I went to find you, but you were not at home. I know that there is a passage under the *sudahmandi* to the sea, so I went there. Semar intercepted me and sent me back."

"I'm sorry—" said Derveet.

"I'm sorry you felt you could not trust me, madam."

He set the white prince on its square, with precision.

"I see your point of view. I am a valuable piece of livestock, I must be protected. On the other hand, I have an heir. I am nearly thirty years old, quite past my prime. It had seemed to me that my family in sending me here made a clear decision. I do not believe they intended me to act as a garden ornament. But naturally Garuda will know the mind of the Hanoman *dapur* better than a mere male—"

He placed his pawns. Each exact movement of his fingers was taut with governed emotion. From Atoon the imperturbable, this was an unthinkably violent outburst. Derveet was astonished, and ashamed. She came into the room, dropped her sodden jacket on the clothes chest, pushed back dripping hanks of hair. "I've been across the Straits," she said. "There was something I had to find out. I meant to tell you—"

Suddenly there was a commotion on the stairs. Cycler

Jhonni burst in, the boys behind her. She was dragging a bizarre figure in colored rags. She threw down a shattered box that vomited a knot of wires.

She gasped for breath. "We couldn't get across the river. We've been out all night. I wouldn't let him go—"

The boys, at a glance from their mistress, melted away. Jhonni relaxed her grip on the clown and stared at Derveet.

"You're safe," she said. "You didn't go?"

"I'm safe," agreed Derveet. She was looking at Endang.

She raised a hand: a film of silver-and-green light slithered across her fingers. She passed her thumb across the firefly light and smoothed it out of existence. "Magic," she remarked. "Why shouldn't I be safe, Endang?"

Atoon was on his feet. He had moved, swift and silent, across the floor. "The clown!" he exclaimed.

It was Jhonni who answered Derveet. "He fooled me! He told me you were in danger, and he had to meet me outside the camp, and he said there was bad magic. We met and we kept meeting, he got me to find your seaway, he gave me a magic charm to put there, to protect you . . . Oh, I don't know what I was doing. I've been such a dreadful fool."

No one denied it. Jhonni saw Endang's talisman lying on the clothes chest by Derveet's wet jacket. The palm-leaf decorations and little twiddles of gold foil had come off. It was obviously a Koperasi sending device. She hated herself.

But Derveet didn't look at Jhonni. "Well, Endang. It's been a long time. I got your warning, by the way: thank you. Speak up. Who *are* your people working for?"

The clown suddenly made a staggering dive for the doorway. Jhonni yelled and lunged after him. But the prince, who had been watching Derveet carefully, held her back.

"No," he said. "Let Garuda deal with this."

She caught up with him under the *sudahmandi*. He was trying to climb into the ruined stairwell, but his limbs wouldn't obey him. He backed against an invasive tree trunk. Blood ran from his split upper lip. Derveet remembered an intelligent and beautiful young man, righteously defiant towards outworn tradition. The wreck of the human being she had known, when they were both young and untarnished, faced her. She had seen too much human wreckage.

"What happened to you, Endang?"

"Since we last met? A lot. You too, Garuda." He sneered. "You were a decent lady outcast when I knew you, and I was the renegade. We've changed places, haven't we? Koperasi whore."

"I'm not a whore. But I don't judge anyone who is. We all get by as best we can. I have no enemies. I can't afford them."

He looked hatred.

"And the doll." He pronounced the term with evil relish. "Garuda, with a doll in the shape of a child. *Do* you fuck her? It's something people wonder about, in the camp."

"Yes, I do," she said evenly, taking no offense at the gross Koperasi term.

"Fucking a doll, a *machine*. Don't you worry about that?"

"I worry. And I worry about how the doll feels, when she knows how I worry. I can't protect her from that. I can't protect her from anything."

"I did not betray you to the Kops."

"I didn't think you did." She shook her head. "I don't underestimate Cycler Jhonni. She is my good friend. But in *our* world she's a helpless child. If there are machines, it must be Koperasi business. If there's 'magic,' it must be the Peninsula. She does not see things blurred, the way they are. And she's very romantic about the *dapur*. She'll believe anything you tell her on that subject. Unless you talk about common, human villainy."

"Derveet." His face twisted. "I told the doll to keep you away from me. But there was Jhonni, it was so easy to play her. I couldn't fight my *dapur* when they said to use the

Samsui to get at you. I couldn't fight them. I'm in such pain."

Derveet frowned. "Pain?"

He crumpled. He could no longer sustain the will to hurt her. "I know," he sobbed. *"I know how hopeless everything is. Can't stop knowing. And they won't give me the dust. It hurts."*

Derveet stood looking at him, a new expression dawning in her eyes. It was not entirely sympathy. "Ah. Interesting. You are suffering because the Timurese withhold the flower-dust?"

"Can't sleep, bad dreams, can't eat . . . Sometimes my hands and feet tingle, numb, won't obey me. Pain in my mind, can't describe it. Things get worse and worse at the camp, they get angrier, they beat me, I see horrible things, horrible things."

"I think your ladies don't control the supply."

"They never did."

Derveet sighed. *"Baik,* good. Enough. We'll sort out this tangled coil. The Timurese, I must say, have a strange way of asking for help. But since they *do* ask . . ."

Semar was waiting. Atoon had spoken to him. His expression was that of a Jagdanan servant confronting a young gentleman who has sneaked out and come home bedraggled from some disreputable bathhouse. This demeanor drew reserves of courage from Endang, who straightened his back and brought his head up.

"Go with Semar. Get yourself tidied, and then we'll talk." She smiled faintly. "I'll send Jhonni home."

Endang flashed a look of fervent gratitude. He had been dreading, above all, the moment of facing Cycler Jhonni again.

"What about my family?"

Derveet grinned. "I met some of your relations on the beach. They'll be getting back to the camp. If your ladies are anxious by this time, it will not be for *your* safety."

4

THE BOYS STRIPPED and scrubbed him. They laid him out on a hard wooden bed and gave him a good rubdown, using a very pungent sweet oil. It was like a dream of childhood. He lay passive, feeling the ghostly contours of the old *sudahmandi* at home gather around him: the little wooden bathhouse beside the main courtyard, where roses grew. The whisper of wind music from the eaves of the big house that were hung with bamboo chimes. Mountains all around, the forested valleys filled with mist in the early morning. He had not remembered the wind chimes for years.

Garuda's boys talked to each other and to him while they handled him as if he were a baby. It was a long time since he had had boys serving him like this. Their soft hands petted him as if he were the favored son that he had been. It was instinctual, nothing to do with the facts. They lifted the matted coconut-fiber mass of his hair, and stroked it as if they were admiring a prince's sheeny flowing locks.

At home things had been modest but good: the oil, the towels, the toiletries, the boys. They weren't servants; home was too small a place for that. They were his uncles, cousins, his brothers, half-brothers. He had accepted their intimate subservience as of right. He remembered the faces, their light voices: not a single name.

"It has to come off, sir. There's nothing else to be done."

He thought they were saying that they would make him a boy. The Timurese peasants had not considered that solution. To castrate a grown man was an offense against their religion. Maybe the cut would make him feel better, at last, about those nameless brothers and uncles. He was startled when the youngest boy patted his knee and reassured: "Don't worry. It will grow again."

They sat him in front of a mirror, a dim, long glass in a heavy frame. Some of the carving had come away. There were wormholes in the wood. The room was bare and damp, a musty undercroft. Endang's eyes slipped from side to side, noting the ill-fitting wooden door, the tumbledown walls, an unglazed window. He was thinking of escape because he always thought about escape. But he didn't know where he could go.

They cut his hair. They helped him to dress. He stood up clean and smooth: an emaciated young gentleman clothed in bright and elegant taste. His cropped head was light to carry. The face in the glass seemed no more to belong to him than the clothes.

"Your looks have improved, anyway."

The Peninsulan who had come to the camp with Derveet stood in the doorway. This person had caused excited speculation among the refugees. Endang considered the lovely face, the small, strong figure arrogantly held. He wondered if the camp had identified the black Garuda's friend correctly. Was this indeed the Hanoman prince of Jagdana? Now I know too much, he thought. They can't let me go. The man smiled, waiting for some response. But Endang was falling, willing himself to fall, back into the hell that kept the real world at bay. In a sense it was easier to bear. Frightful things stood in the air. *No one can help me.*

"Come out to the pool."

So he followed to the pool, groping his way through ghosts and floating skulls. This was the way it had been since they took the flowerdust away. And before that . . . ? Derveet was beside the water, with the doll machine. There was a tray laid with a platter of grubby-looking unhusked rice and two small dishes of vegetables. He was surprised that the food was so poor.

"Will you eat with us?"

He remembered talking to Jhonni, in the *Blue Schoolroom* coffee shop. How had he managed that? It had been possible somehow. But now the puppeteer had dropped the strings. He did not want to eat. He wanted to tear open his chest with his nails and squeeze his heart until it stopped beating. He imagined pulling the flesh apart: peeling skin and muscle, reaching inside the raw chicken cage of bones. The faces wavered. His fingers scrabbled at the fastening of his borrowed jacket.

"Stop that," said Garuda.

Endang moved a mouth that seemed thick with unuse, as if he hadn't spoken for a thousand years.

"I won't eat. The food is dirty."

The doll-who-was-a-person laughed, a sweet sound. "I expect he's used to better meals at Cold Storage. You can get anything in there, for cash. It's hard on the people round about. The price of a box of matches in the kampongs has gone through the roof!"

"Endang—" Derveet caressed him with false politeness, a charade of welcome. "You and Cho met each other, I think. Let me introduce my friend Atoon."

Now I know too much, he thought again. He couldn't understand why they weren't afraid that he would betray them. He wanted to scream and cry. He wanted to make these two (a doll could feel nothing) feel the same pain he did: to reach in and tear out their hearts. He became the clown. He dropped to his heels, elbowed past Garuda to the platter, grabbed a handful of rice and stuffed it into his mouth. He pretended to gag, sprayed masticated rice over all three.

"If the food is poor," said Atoon, "appetite might help. We'll swim. You can swim?"

He could have fought them if they touched him, but no

one touched him. Confused, he followed Atoon's example and stripped off his borrowed clothes. Atoon dived neatly, Endang stumbled into the water. His body took over. Apparently it craved passionately the refuge of physical effort. The pool was wide. He measured it twice, and then Atoon had to haul him out of the water. Derveet and the doll had gone.

There was a cloth laid down on the stone rim in the shade of a mango tree. More pummeling. Atoon's hands, which looked so delicate, were hard and strong. In Jagdana they believe that vigorous *pijat, mass'azh,* as it's called in High Inggris, soothes any kind of suffering of mind or body. He was home again, drowsing in his own room. In a moment, his mother's speaking boy would kneel beside him and whisper: *Wake up, little father. What did you dream?*

When he woke he remembered no dreams. He lay in a cloud of miraculous physical ease, feeling the stone beneath him as a comfortable bed. He opened his eyes. Garuda was sitting there, alone. It was almost dark.

"Could you eat now?"

He sat up, wrapping the cloth beneath him around his naked body. He saw the remains of the meal he had refused. At the camp, the boys would have taken those scraps and thrown them to the chickens. Not to the poor. His ladies didn't encourage the poor sort of refugees to hang around. He put rice into his mouth and was astonished to find it tasted of food, not shit and ashes. He ate about half a cup of unhusked rice, and had to give up: exhausted. He drank some water. The boys came and took things away. Endang tried to recover his shattered thoughts. He would escape. Soon, probably, the boys would take him and lock him in that undercroft. He would find a way to break free. Then, into the pool. He would drown himself.

They sat in silence for a long time. He watched the dark reflected sky. A long, tiered glimmer of light rocked on the water, falling from a lamp lit somewhere above them. When at last she suggested they go indoors, he followed her like a house cat.

There was a bed made up on the floor of Garuda's room. He lay down. The oldest boy was putting red-tipped tapers into an incense holder on the floor by his head. The boy and his mistress murmured together. The doll must be near. Endang could feel how Garuda's mind rested on her presence, somewhere close in the lamp-lit shadows. The love between those two made him feel so lonely.

"I was the puppeteer," he said. "I was the cruel overseer, and this helpless creature Endang was my slave. I made him betray Jhonni. I passed on what the women did to me, to myself. Do you understand?"

He did not say *betray you*. Once Derveet had given him the painful gift of hope. He had lost the hope. But there was still the pain, which she had shared then and shared still. She knew that whatever he had done, he couldn't help himself. There is so much injustice in the world. One can do nothing against it. Derveet could not be betrayed, because she had never asked him to be faithful.

"It was for the flowerdust," he whispered.

"Was it? How do you feel now?"

"Haunted. Everything hurts. They stopped giving me the dust."

She laid her hand on his forehead. "No fever. You're cooler than I am. Endang, you don't know much about flowerdust, do you?"

He opened his eyes wide, surprised.

"What is there to know?"

Garuda looked down at him, with a cool curiosity that made him frightened. The lines of her face were drawn sharply by the lamplight. "How often did you take the dust? Tell?"

He felt obscurely insulted. "Three, four times, a full glass."

"And then no more."

"Everything hurts," he whispered.

"You are not addicted to flowerdust. If your ladies let you believe that was possible, it was a lie to scare you. The way you scared Jhonni with your bad magic invention. I don't know quite what is wrong with you, but the dust cannot be to blame. For fertile women, flowerdust is unpredictable: but even for them, there's no danger. The dust is not poisonous even to them, unless they become addicts, and that is difficult to achieve. You'd have to live on the stuff for months—a very expensive hobby."

"Can't sleep. Fear everywhere. Can't stop seeing horrors, feeling pain. All the pain in the world."

She laughed shortly, without humor. "I have the same problem, sometimes. And I, young man, haven't had a *sniff* of the dust in years."

Stung by her disbelief, he turned his face away. At once he fell helplessly into the dark.

"Well?" said Atoon to Derveet, by the poolside. She and Cho had left Endang in possession of their room. Semar would stay beside the young man's bed and watch through the first part of the night. Fireflies winked green over the dark water. The white stars bobbed within it.

"He's asleep again. Dropped into it like a stone falling into water. I don't know where he got the idea he's a dust addict. Yet he doesn't seem to be faking, whatever it is that's wrong."

"Maybe not. Those eyes! But he's a Timurese. They're good liars."

"A very rational deduction," agreed Derveet gravely. "Except that he's a Gamarthan, remember." She laughed. "Gamarthan, and clever, and a good liar. So much for one's prejudices. You'd better keep a close eye on this strange creature if you've become my bodyguard." She had seen the way he moved when the two intruders burst in. She was touched. "Not that you'd need my orders," she teased, "to keep a close eye on looks like that."

She sobered. "Atoon, I am sorry I deceived you: about the dust, and about my plans. It was wrong of me. Give me a few more days, which will give Endang a chance to recover, I hope. And I'll be ready to explain."

He inclined his head, and lifted a hand, in a faint and graceful denial. "Not at all, madam," he said, leaving Derveet unsure whether he accepted her apology or whether she was not at all forgiven. If it was the latter, she decided that she deserved it. It is strange to come face-to-face with prejudices you didn't know you possessed.

"I hope there's nothing seriously wrong with him. Poor Endang, he has had a hard time." When he was naked they had seen ridged scars layered along his back and ribs, and the chain galls on his wrists and ankles.

But Atoon wondered, "Whose side is he on now?"

"His own, I would assume. Do you blame him?"

Atoon could guess how Timurese peasants would treat an extra stud with the distinction of a Koperasi education. But his own life had been, in principle, the same. The *adat*, the law, is neutral. It is people who make it good or evil. "Tradition has never hurt me."

She glanced at him quizzically. "No?"

The prince retired to his studhouse. Derveet and Cho spent the night awake, sitting by the pool, watching the stars. In the upper room Semar watched Endang's sleep, wiped the sweat from his thin body, and kept the sweet incense burning.

There were fish in Derveet's pool, long as a man's arm. Their scales were mottled rose and cloudy blue. They gave way in front of him under the water, keeping their distance without fear. They were above and below, cool shapes of calm. The pool was floored with large, rounded pebbles. He drifted over the dim landscape, then rose like a bubble from the hidden springs until his face broke the surface. Breathed, and dived again. Down into the rose-blue world, up into the yellow-blue of the sunlight. Tracery of silver, tracery of gold: down and up, down and up. The rhythm was his breathing. The air and the water held him alternately, more tenderly than the earth had ever carried him. He breathed, and slept.

The next morning he was better. His joints ached; his memory of the recent past was hazy and full of holes. He didn't know if he was a prisoner, a patient, or a hostage. But he was better, he was in control. Derveet—Garuda—watched him while he ate breakfast in the upper room. Unsmiling, she leaned forward and snapped her fingers in front of his eyes: crack, crack. He flinched away.

"You're seeing what's in front of you today. Good."

She questioned him a little, but not about the flowerdust. What was happening in inland Timur? What had made his adoptive family pack up and head for Ranganar? What was the journey like?

Endang refused to meet her eyes. "I can't help you. I'm an unwanted male. No one told me anything. I was baggage."

"*Baik*," she said, nodding. "All right." Meaning *I'll accept that for now*. Of course she wasn't satisfied.

The doll smiled at him kindly. He remembered that it had promised, a long time ago at the camp, to give him his heart's desire. It was a thought that chilled him for a moment (the clown had been desperate . . .). But he was strong enough this morning to feel insulted by kindness from a machine. He would not look at it.

Derveet had said he was not an addict, and the flowerdust did not give him his bad dreams. *What does she know?* he thought scornfully. But the question frightened him: he fled from it, clinging to his fragile sanity. After breakfast, Atoon asked him if he knew *pencak silat*. The practice of native unarmed combat had been illegal since the Great Rebellion, and Endang despised the mindless, masculine cult of the physical. But he remembered how it had felt to swim, in the pool and in his dream. His body longed for that release.

"Not since I was a child," he said.

The two young men sparred for an hour in the water garden, Endang surrounded by the faint ghosts, good ghosts this time, of the mountains that had looked down on the practice yard at home.

Two days passed in this way. *Pencak silat,* swimming, *pijat;* meager meals, sleep like death. Atoon sparred and swam with him; Derveet came to sit by the pool and talk, at firefly time. He told himself that this separation between them was a trick to weaken his defenses. He knew that when he faced them both it would be an interrogation. He prepared himself for that moment. He and Derveet talked about Cycler Jhonni. No one said a word, after the first day, about flowerdust.

Cho did not come near him.

In the heat of noon on the third day, he and Atoon were under the mango tree. Endang lay on his belly and the prince massaged him. "You're better," remarked Atoon. "I can feel it. You are inhabiting your body. When I first pummeled this thing I was kneading dead meat."

"You've both been very good to me," Endang muttered dutifully.

"Don't be too sure. She wants you for something. All will be revealed quite soon." The prince's hand rested lightly on Endang's naked side. "Meanwhile, since you are well, would you like to practice a different sport?"

Atoon was a Jagdanan, and completely shameless about his well-developed male appetite. He was very funny about the privations of life in Ranganar, away from his household: about his social gaffes with the West Bank youths Derveet's boys procured for him. Endang lay still, feeling the touch which had magically, expertly changed its meaning—from impersonal skill to caressing lust.

"No, thank you."

"As you wish."

Endang should have left it at that. But his resentment of this privileged, contented animal boiled up. If Atoon had been faced with Endang's duty when he was fourteen years old, he'd have picked up the knife cheerfully. Nothing could disturb Atoon. Nothing could reach him through the swaddling of the *dapur*, through the blinkers of tradition.

"The Kops banned the practice of honorable suicide. Unwanted studs were to live. Did you know that? It was our people who started it up again. Our sadistic ladies and their boys."

He heard the prince's voice, placid and unjudging. "I know that. Horrible things are done in the name of orthodoxy these days, even in Jagdana. But who is to blame? When life seems worthless, then one clings to tradition."

Endang kept his face buried in his arms. "I got away from the peasants twice. I sold myself to the Kops on the coast. I didn't do it just to eat, either. I enjoyed going with them."

"I would hope so," said the imperturbable voice. "If one accepts the necessity of staying alive, what else is there to ease the pain if not pleasure?"

Endang sneered. "Fucking isn't about pleasure. It's a matter of power and who is in control. Being fucked by the Red Men was no different from being fucked by my fellow Peninsulans. Merely a little more honest." He had a sudden longing for Jhonni, imagining the same question from her: stupid, clumsy Samsui blockhead. *Did you, uh, you know, "do it" with the Koperasi? What I mean is, are you in their pay after all?*

"The third time I got away, I took day-laboring work." He bared his teeth, but couldn't make himself look up. "I made sure they knew it. I wanted to be polluted, so they could never use me as a stud. That's when the family really let themselves go, when they got me back home. But I was safe from the foul privilege of rutting . . ."

"Don't think about it," said Atoon. "Put the hurt away. Tell yourself you will think about it sometime, but not now." He touched Endang's arm. "Move into the sun. The heat is good sometimes. It sweats the devils out."

Endang rolled over and found he was alone. He stared up into the leaves of the mango tree. To have refused a prince: what a memory to treasure! It would have been wiser to accept. But that might have been embarrassing. At least the Red Men didn't expect any response from you.

He closed his eyes. They seemed so confident, the Hanoman prince and the spoiled Garuda! The refugees in the camp were excited about it: Garuda had raised the Eagle and the Jagdana prince had come to her call. It was like an old story; it was as if the Koperasi didn't matter anymore. Maybe they didn't; everyone said they were falling apart . . . Endang smiled to himself, bitterly. Garuda and Jagdana allied, and Gamartha up in arms in the north. A return to the good old days. Could Derveet really hold the Peninsula back from that inveterate pattern? He began to shiver. He must not start calculating the chances of Derveet's success. That was madness. He would not think about it. They could question him as much as they liked, try every means to worm their way into his trust. He would keep his secret. He didn't have the information they wanted, but he had a secret. And nothing, no power on earth, would tear it out of him.

She wants you for something. He wished Derveet would pick up the puppet strings. He didn't care who took charge; only he must be used. That was his refuge: to be an empty tool, to be a vessel, a vehicle, a beast of burden. That was the escape.

Endang woke early and sneaked out of the upper room. He groped through the wet, shadowy confusion of the water garden. He'd just found a gap in the wall when he heard Derveet's voice on the other side. She was talking to the boys with the *pagi-pagi,* the morning-business cart that carried away each day's supply of shit and piss from Dove House. The boys sold their redolent freight to the Samsui.

He froze. She came through the break in the stonework and caught him there. It was hardly light. He couldn't pretend to be doing anything but trying to get away.

"Good morning," she said, with good humor. She'd been out since the afternoon before. "Bad news, apparently. The Samsui factories are making production cutbacks, gas demand is falling. The bottom's dropped out of the *pagi-pagi* market." She grinned. "Sorry. Were you going somewhere?"

"I couldn't sleep." Helplessly, he walked back to the pool beside her. Why had he been running away? He didn't know.

"What will you do, Endang?"

He didn't understand the question.

"I wouldn't advise you to return to the camp. That is, not unless you're playing a sneakier game than I know."

He was too shocked to speak.

"But you can't stay here. The Kops—to humor the Samsui, of course—have made it a serious crime for us native inhabitants of the island to harbor refugees. And my relationship with the Administration Compound is delicate . . . Well, you see my problem."

Perhaps she'd been up all night reviewing his fate with her cronies in the Admin Compound. Nothing would surprise him. She sat cross-legged on the pool rim in her best bandit's suit, chewing a toothpick, her chin propped on one hand. A wing of heavy black hair shadowed her face. His pride deserted him.

"I'm still sick. If you and the prince stop treating me, the craving will return, the visions—"

Derveet trailed a hand in the water. "I told you, you were never an addict. Nobody's been treating you. If you needed to be cured, you've cured yourself. I don't think you were sick with anything more than misery and hardship. But

Semar says perhaps you have been getting too close to the hearth . . ."

Endang started. Derveet saw his whole body stiffen. "I don't know what you mean!" he protested hoarsely.

Different states had different customs. A stud's needs, over and above his duty, were recognized and satisfied one way or another. In the silence of the hearth quarters, women did as they pleased. There is no shame in physical appetite, so long as decorum is preserved. But between women and men, there was only the act of procreation. Anything more personal, in the way of a physical relationship, was repellent, inconceivable throughout the Peninsula. The failed women who whored with the Koperasi were committing blasphemy, but even they did not lie with men for pleasure.

"Getting too close to the hearth" could have two meanings. One was that you, man or boy, had offended some malign lady who wasn't ashamed to use her secret power for harm. The other was insulting.

Derveet continued blandly. "Only that your ladies may have been abusing you in more ways than one. What else would I mean? I don't like to admit it, particularly not to a Samsui, but Jhonni is right. There can be such a thing as bad magic."

Endang relaxed, laughed, incredulous. *"Them? No!"*

"Well, we won't talk about it anymore . . ." She pursued her own line of thought. "I think you should try to register with one of the clans, as a second-class citizen. I believe the Cyclers would take you on. They have plenty of office work."

Clerical work was permissible, better than physical labor, anyway. Of course she would think of that. Derveet the rebel had always been steeped in tradition—she used to laugh about it. A Samsui clerk. Ridiculously, he felt insulted. He couldn't believe that she would let him walk away. "And the dust?"

"Never mind about that. That's over, for you."

"You know how it will be. My family controlled the camp because they had the flowerdust. Soon I guess it will reappear in the hands of some rival women. It's being done deliberately. Whoever's behind this can go on playing that game: stopping and starting the supply. There will be more killings, more fighting. The Samsui already hate us, the local Ranganarese are suffering. The Koperasi will have license to do what they like—"

"Don't get upset. I have taken on the problem. Relax."

"Oh, thank you so much. You have taken on the problem, I mustn't worry my pretty head. Typical *dapur* thinking. Helpless, spoiled babies are so much easier to handle. Derveet, I knew a different woman. You convinced me once that there was another way for Peninsulans to live. That the *dapur* power could be used openly, for the good of all. You've changed!"

She stared, in what seemed genuine astonishment, and laughed, getting to her feet in one limber movement.

"You *have* recovered . . . both of you! Is this a conspiracy?" She looked down, sardonically amused. "It's not so easy to abandon responsibility, is it? As pleasant as the prospect sounds." She went indoors, leaving him to contemplate the blank abyss of his untrammeled future: a life of his own.

Jhonni came to Dove House with trepidation. Petruk, the middle boy, had brought a summons to the Cycler compound. He was gone before she could get away from the counting rooms. They were awash, as always these days, with state-of-emergency paperwork. Jhonni was surprised that Aunt let her go at all.

The message was that she should come alone, but she was tempted (she had made such a mess of trying to help Derveet) to run around to the Butchers' and ask what was going on. She didn't. She had a strong feeling that this summons concerned the flowerdust, and therefore it was common sense to keep Handai out of it. Handai was a radical and a Peninsulan sympathizer for upright, moral reasons. She would hate the way Jhonni had heard Derveet speak of the drug: amused, almost approving. It would make trouble between them. Feeling responsible and wise, she set off alone.

The first person she saw when she walked into the upper room was Endang: her own Peninsulan, with cropped clean hair and wearing new clothes. Derveet had told Jhonni, before sending her away that horrible morning, that Endang was not working for the Kops. Things were complicated, but he was not a traitor. Jhonni had been glad to know it. But she had been hoping she would never have to meet him again, ever. Her mood crushed, she crossed the room with her eyes averted, begging her cheeks to stay cool.

"Jhonni, Endang, Atoon." Derveet sat in a window embrasure, the doll-who-was-a-person beside her. The brilliant light of *siang*, the heat of the day, framed them, making a shimmering aureole around Cho's cap of pale hair.

"Now that you're here, Jhonni, we can begin. This is a meeting to plan our solution to the problems that flowerdust is causing in the refugee camp."

"I knew it," cried Jhonni. "I knew you'd change your mind!"

Atoon and Endang had been playing chess. Atoon tipped over his prince. "I resign, sir. Garuda's rare confidence in two mere studs requires our full attention. Unless, perhaps, madam would prefer us to retire to the garden?"

Jhonni wondered what had been happening. It was hard to imagine Atoon quarreling with anyone, much less Derveet. But there was a definite edge in his tone. Derveet gave the prince a look of rueful amusement. "Stay where you are, gentlemen. Jhonni, don't stand there gaping. Please, sit down. I have a confession to make. I believe the flowerdust in the camp used to belong to me."

Jhonni's expression fell comically, from eagerness to shocked mistrust. "It belongs to you? This horrible drug?"

Derveet sighed. "You Samsui . . . flowerdust is not horrible."

She dropped from the window seat, and settled on the floor, spread her hands like a storyteller.

"For your benefit, Jhonni: a short history of the dust. They say that the *dapur*, in ancient times, set itself to eradicate all harmful things from the Peninsula, including harmful pleasures. I have no idea whether this is true. But there is a white poppy that grows in Gamartha which, legend has it, was once the source of a pleasure so compelling that people died for it by the millions. The poppy plant no longer has any interesting properties; and don't think people haven't tried. What other delights were lost we'll never know. We were left with alcohol, a poison that appeals to few Peninsulans, and acar, because it is harmless. But life is cruel and the weed is weak. So the ruling women relented and invented flowerdust. It is a variant of acar: a bloom which does not set seed, which cannot be grown commercially or produced artificially. Which appears as a gift from heaven, and then vanishes for generations. One takes the finely powdered flowers in water: our golden wine."

Atoon was looking—as near as his lovely and perfectly trained features could come to it—disgusted. " 'If I'd heard of a bloom, I wouldn't have forgotten . . .' " Your exact words, Garuda."

"Would I lie to you? There was a bloom. In the days when I was Anakmati the bandit, on a farm of mine. I didn't want it to reach the market—not at that time—and I didn't want to have to waste my time guarding such a covetable treasure. So I arranged a hideous accident. The whole farm was burned out, just at harvesttime. Accepting heartfelt commiserations, I packed the bales myself and hid them. The dust keeps well. I knew I could leave it for ten or fifteen years if necessary, without losing anything. It's not something one would forget, but I had not thought of it for years. When we went into the camp and saw the evidence of dust, I remembered my vintage at once. Blooms are *rare*, Jhonni; once in a hundred years is no exaggeration. So I waited until the dark of the moon, crossed over, and found my hiding place empty.

"But let's forget where the dust came from originally. How did it reach the camp?" She looked at Endang, calmly expectant.

At dawn she had caught him trying to escape, and told him that he was free to go. When he had come in from the pool, she had warned him that Cycler Jhonni was on her way. She told him it was time to talk about the flowerdust, but had given him the choice of staying out of sight . . . She had known he wouldn't take that choice, the same as she had offered him his freedom knowing that he wouldn't take it.

And now he was trapped, manipulated into her plans. He had been bracing himself for the interrogation, and here it was. Jhonni sat across the room, her round eyes lowered, clearly still hating him. He looked up at Derveet, who smiled back innocently. *Dalang,* he thought. Oh, you puppeteer!

But he answered. It was like the pull of physical exercise. The temptation to be part of something was too great.

"We left Timur because our neighbors were leaving. There were rumors of an army coming down from the north. Everything was quiet in our countryside, but fear is a fever: everybody had to be moving. The women of my Timurese family, the peasants, went with the rest. They are moneylenders. They had a hoard of cash before they left for Ranganar. I know that, and I know it was gone soon after we reached the camp because the speaking boy Parangtriti let me see the empty chest. Parangtriti doesn't—didn't—like me any better than the rest, but he sometimes talked to me because I can read and write, I was a student, it flattered his self-esteem. He was boasting; he said he'd helped the women to make a tremendously good deal.

"I don't know any more about how they got the dust. It must have been on the road or very soon after we arrived. I think someone picked us out just *because* the ladies were moneylenders, not acar dealers, and had no contacts in the trade. I don't think they knew much about flowerdust, any of this lore about the once-in-a-hundred-years bloom. It was a specially strong and profitable kind of acar, nothing more.

"I saw a packet. Small." Sitting back from the chessboard Endang cupped his hand. "No bigger than a woman's palm, almost flat. I saw that. Parangtriti never got to handle it: I saw it through the women's curtains, being passed from hand to hand. They gave me the golden wine from their own hands." Endang smiled wryly. "To test it, I think: to see if I would die. Then I started to work for them. They'd never had a use for me before. But though we'd just arrived, there were neighbors from Timur around us. It was useful for them to have someone whose face wasn't known. I dressed up as the clown and ran errands for them, and kept watch. In the course of about ten days, because we had flowerdust for sale, my moneylenders became the rulers of the camp. I had, I think, two more drinks in that time. Or three."

"Then?" prompted Derveet.

He shook his head. "No more dust. There was supposed to be more; they'd handed over the cash. But there was none. Trouble. And then Parangtriti had a new job for me. *You* were to be allowed to find out that there was flowerdust in Ranganar. If you hadn't come to the camp I would have been sent to the West Bank. Your visit was useful. When you knew, we were to keep watch on you. That was my job, to trace your movements with Kop gadgets. You would leave the island secretly, and return almost at once. When that had happened we were to report back. The rest—" He grimaced. "The ambush was the women's idea.

To them it was obvious that if you left the island, you were going to fetch the dust.

"Believe it or not, I don't know any more. I tried to tell them they were being used by the enemies of the Peninsula. What did they care? If you want to know what I think, I think the Kops are involved. My ladies have dealt with Kops before. I think there was only one dust transaction. I don't know how they got their instructions about you." He looked up angrily. "And I don't know how you're going to find out. You could try to haul Parangtriti out of the camp, question him. But you've left it late! You've given them four clear days. Do you know what it's like in there?"

He caught Derveet's brief smile. He realized that he had no idea how she'd spent those four days; certainly she hadn't been at Dove House for much of the time.

"What are you going to do?" he asked.

"About the dust in the camp?" Derveet frowned. "Nothing—directly. I meant what I said, that part at least. You're right, Endang, it would be madness to try to tackle the problem at this end. I won't go back to the camp. But I have another approach. I believe I know who has the dust, and where."

"Another bandit?" blurted Jhonni, and blushed red.

"Worse than that. A Koperasi officer." She looked amused, and a little guilty, thought Endang. "A few years ago I was dealing acar, as Anakmati, in partnership with a young Koperasi officer in the Occupation Army called Gordon Bennett Hamzah—Jeeby to his friends. We had more in common than you might think. We were both using the acar trade as a means to our separate ends. Jeeby was ambitious on his own account, and the OA runs on weed; I had my political schemes. Jeeby could have found out about my bloom. And I think he is the only one of the few who *could* have known who is actually still alive."

She paused for a moment, thinking maybe of brief lives, of all the lost souls of the outcast world.

"Not only alive, but thriving. He's a Provincial Commander now. I've been catching up on his career. He's recently been sent to take command of a new kind of Kop institution in the wilds of central Timur—a wise move, apparently. The Kops here say Jeeby's on to a very good thing."

"We congratulate him," said Atoon dryly. "But the dust?"

"You see, I have a piece of information about my former partner. I've never felt like using it before; obviously fate was saving it for this occasion. If Jeeby has my dust, I can get him to give it back. The problem is, my pressure won't work from a distance. We'll have to go to him."

"We?" repeated Jhonni, bewildered.

"The five of us here, yes. Up to Timur and back. It can be done quickly, a matter of days. I've already made most of the arrangements. We're ready to go—that is, if you three will agree to play your parts." She turned to the prince. "Atoon—"

"Madam."

"Are you still as good a dancer as I remember?"

Atoon made a self-deprecating gesture.

"The *dapur* roles?"

"Anyone who dances seriously must practice Sita."

"*Bagus* . . . Now, Jhonni, I have a job lined up for you in the camp itself, Jeeby's institution. You'll be taken on as a temporary civilian accountant. You'll have freedom of movement, and Koperasi safe conduct. They won't suspect a Samsui. When I've recovered the dust, your part will be to take it out of the camp. You won't be alone. You'll need a clerk; that's Endang. His second-class-citizen papers are ready, waiting to be picked up. I hope your family won't object to your working for the Kops temporarily?"

Derveet's eyes evaded the astonished questioning in their faces, rested tenderly on the doll-who-was-a-person, who was smiling in delight. Cho loved games.

"Jeeby's new camp is a reform school for recalcitrant

slaves. We will need a recalcitrant slave. That will be me. Cho . . . will be everything else."

"But, Derveet—"

"Garuda, is this—"

"I know, I know." The puppeteer's hands soothed the air. "I said we must lie low, until Gamartha is quiet again. But I'm not undertaking this lightly. The state of affairs in the camp is a real problem. The refugees are also Peninsulans. They deserve protection. The boys will keep house here, repel boarders, give out that I am seeing no one."

"What about Handai?" cried Jhonni. "And the others? What'll they think if I disappear off to Timur? And the dancers?"

"Leave Miss Butcher to me."

Jhonni's head was spinning. Cross the Straits, travel into Timur, blackmail a high-ranking Koperasi. She was astonished, and beginning to be very frightened.

"When do you want me to leave?" she demanded, as eagerly as pride decreed.

"Very soon," said Derveet. "You and Endang will be traveling together. I want you to take him home with you now." She did not see, or pretended not to see, the expressions of sheer horror on the faces of the accountant and her new clerk.

She smiled around. "Do you all agree? Then let's get down to the details. Any questions?"

Jhonni and Endang left together, bristling like two strange cats forced into confrontation. Jhonni wheeled her bicycle between them. "I'm sorry," she said at last, when they were almost at the ferry. "I'm sorry I misjudged you."

"You didn't. I cheated you."

He had changed his clothes again for the new role. His loose black pants and shabby blue jacket looked like what they were, Samsui castoffs, provided by Derveet's boys. Nyonya Cycler and her native clerk bumped the bicycle down the wooden steps between them. *Start playing your parts at once,* Derveet had said, and how could either of them protest that this was impossible, that they couldn't do anything together? Jhonni was thinking how different he'd been when he was talking in the upper room: so clear and sharp, like someone she'd never met.

Petals from the flower market above made slow whorls on the black and sluggish water. Ranganar's river barely deserved the name. It was merely the widest of the hundreds of brackish creeks that threaded the island. They clambered into the ferry and stowed Jhonni's bike among the live chickens, fruit baskets, oil tins and lumpy secretive bundles. Jhonni paid their fares. Endang kept his eyes down and would not speak. The coffee shop on the little street with no name might never have existed.

Derveet studied the chess pieces. "You were losing anyway."

Atoon had the grace to admit it. "I was. Endang is a very good player."

"Good-looking, too. But not as friendly as he might be?"

The doll-who-was-a-person chuckled.

"Do you good, for once," remarked Derveet obliquely, with a sly grin. The prince gave them both a repressive glance. They were impossible. He did not object to their knowing he had been turned down, but there are rules of behavior. When the boys were out of the room, decorum ceased to exist in this house.

Outside, the afternoon water queue was being served. The chatter and laughter of the Ranganarese boys rose like birdsong into the upper room. They could be cheerful over so little. They were probably laughing at the latest Kop rationing scheme: starving people by numbers.

"There is more to this," said Atoon at last, taking a resin-and-tobacco cigarette from Derveet's case. "It's not just the flowerdust."

"You could be right." She took a cigarette herself, lit both of them and went to the window. Semar was concerned about everybody's teeth. The Ranganar *dapur* was a feeble affair, and the Samsui heretics were worse than useless. Without fresh produce from over the causeway, living on practically nothing but rice and dried beans, people would get gum disease and lose their smiles.

"You aren't actually going to let those two children courier the drug back to Ranganar?"

"Probably not. But we may well need somebody on our side in the Kops' office. More to the point, I don't think the boys will be able to keep my absence a complete secret. And if I leave Ranganar, I won't leave Endang and Jhonni behind."

Atoon raised an eyebrow. "As bad as that?"

She had spent the last four days finding out the state that the city was in: talking to the dancers, talking to Miss Butcher, prowling the underworld.

She nodded grimly. "As bad as that. Endang's ladies have recovered from the failure of their ambush. They're very angry and looking to punish me. And they aren't the only ones who are making the city dangerous. The way things are, I don't believe Jhonni or Endang would be safe, not even in the Cycler compound. A trip to the Peninsula could well be safer."

She thought of the senior officer from the Admin Compound, the Red Man she had talked to in a Hungry Tiger Street bar three nights ago. *It's a madhouse up there,* he'd told her. That was the line the Ranganar Kops always gave you. *It's the OA, they're monsters, it's not us, we're nice, we're good to you people.* He was happy to fix her up with a job for a Samsui girl in Jeeby's institution. It would be easy. The Occupying Army staff at Sepaa were looking for a way to get some dirt on Jeeby Hamzah, and it wasn't a job you could give a Kop clerk—divided loyalties and all that. Provincial Commander Hamzah wasn't liked at Sepaa. He'd traveled too far, too fast: too clever by half.

The Red Man was grateful for a chance to do the warlords

in uniform a favor. You had to keep in with the OA now, and it was tricky, trying to guess who'd come out on top when the final collapse came. His sad, rheumy eyes—those water-colored eyes that hated the sun—pleaded for reassurance. Derveet, Anakmati, Garuda: he didn't care what she called herself, if only she could bring back the good old days. When you could rely on things. When the behind-the-scenes deals could go on in peace, and you didn't have to worry about the scenery falling on top of you.

The failed-woman whores passed by their booth, but the Red Man ignored them. He only wanted someone who would listen. *This fucking senseless thing with Gamartha, you know: it's the end.*

No, there was no question, she must go. She had been waiting for emissaries. Well, in a roundabout way, Timur had called on her for help: and she would not refuse. She wondered what was going on in G. B. Hamzah's mind. What was behind his strange behavior? But there was no need to wonder. She would find out.

The Ranganarese boys chattered and laughed by the pool: the sound that meant the causeway was still closed, and too many days had passed. She and Atoon were still alone, and the rising in Gamartha continued, a rebellion in the old, hopeless style. There was no sign that the women of the Peninsula were taking the kind of action she'd hoped for. It was getting hard to believe that they would. All to do again . . . all the work to do again. No matter what she found in Timur, it would be a relief to escape for a while from this knowledge.

She leaned forward to flick ash from her cigarette into the garden, and became aware that Divine Endurance had jumped up into the embrasure. The cat was sitting precisely upright, and purring, her blue eyes slitted in approval.

"What are you so pleased about?"

Divine Endurance took a dainty step and pushed her sleek, throbbing head against Derveet's arm.

Derveet moved warily out of reach. "You like the sound of my picnic? You are not invited."

"She'll come anyway," said Cho, from the floor, resignedly.

"Not with my blessing."

The cat's eyes opened wide in a defiant glare; and between one moment and the next, she had vanished. Derveet looked to Cho. It happened so rarely that you thought you'd imagined it, when the marvelous toys forgot their adopted limitations.

"Cats can do that," said the doll, worried by Derveet's expression. "Disappear quickly? It's allowed, isn't it?"

For peace Derveet agreed: real cats could pretty well do that. She felt a shiver of disquiet. She did not consider Divine Endurance's approval a fortunate omen. But she refused to be made nervous by the ill will of a toy cat.

Atoon, having smoked in silence for a while, began to rearrange the chess pieces. "Have you considered we may be taking a traitor with us?"

"Of course. But I'd rather take him than leave him behind."

"I see that." Atoon thought of Endang's confessions: the young man who had never experienced pleasure, who despised and punished his own body. Day labor, to the orthodox, was even worse than whoring for the Kops. A stud's body is sacred, the way no woman's body is sacred. Women live in the mind, and in their children. What does a man have if not his physical being? A male who sells his physical labor is polluted forever. Atoon was less shocked than the young man had doubtless hoped: Endang *wanted* to be despised. But still!

"I'm relieved to know you don't trust him."

"I *trust* him," temporized Derveet, "as much as I trust anyone, I suppose. But there's something I don't understand . . ."

"He doesn't like me," remarked Cho, without rancor.

Atoon waited, but Derveet shook her head, declining to discuss the mysterious young man any further. "It could be nothing. He's not a willing traitor, I'm sure of that."

"You're giving Jhonni a heavy responsibility."

"Not more than she can bear. This isn't the first time she's worked with me, remember. She won't let us down."

"But will I?" wondered the prince. "Derveet, are you sure?"

She knew that he'd been working up to this question since Jhonni and Endang left them, steeling himself to ask and hardly daring, in case she said: *You could be right, you'd better stay behind.* Was she really planning to take two studs with her on this adventure? In Peninsulan received wisdom, it was suicide to involve full males in any affair requiring self-control. Semar would tell her she was crazy . . . She almost laughed at Atoon's secret eagerness, but conscience struck her. In Jagdana men are not chained. But there can be chains in the mind, and a friend can refuse to see.

"You told me. You're here to make yourself useful. And what can go wrong? You said yourself, you have an heir."

It was the brutal truth. The Hanoman *dapur* had sent their prince to Derveet: a wonderful gesture. But if it happened that they wished to withdraw their support . . . If for instance Garuda failed to win over the other two great princedoms, Jagdana would not be exposed in Derveet's failure. The practice of enclosure can be useful. *No, that was not our prince,* they would have their speaking boys declare. *Someone who looks a little like him maybe.* Later it would be announced that Prince Atoon—who had of course never left the palace—had abdicated in favor of the heir chosen by the ladies from among their male children. It was the way things were done. Risks could be taken, but never so as to endanger the hearth.

The prince and Garuda smiled at each other, comfortless

knowledge in their eyes. Atoon turned the board around. He held out his fists across the game of soldiers, still smiling.

"What, *again?*"

"There's one thing that puzzles me," he remarked placidly, as the game went on. "Your leverage with the Provincial Commander. I don't doubt you, but I don't see it. What kind of revelation could be so powerful?"

"What kind . . . ? Atoon, are you joking?"

He stared, until enlightenment dawned. "Ooh." He shook his head. "No, not joking. A little stupid. You know how it is with us studs. Not enough blood gets to the brain."

5

ABOUT HALF A *batu* from Straits Control on the Peninsulan shore, heavy machinery was at work. The Kops were digging up the road. The long-journey treader, a dun caterpillar with deep-set window-eyes along its flanks, swooped wildly towards the seawall. Red mud spattered already filthy glass. Jhonni ducked instinctively. Another earthmover stood dead ahead. The treader pulled up. She watched an antlike line of refugees climbing over the gouged road surface in the other lane, and contemplated the hideous prospect of being stranded in neither country, between Ranganar's Koperasi and the Peninsulan Occupying Army.

"What are they doing it for?"

"Essential maintenance," suggested Endang, without warmth, without glancing her way. "It's essential for them to find and smash the water mains before peace breaks out in the north. Otherwise life in Ranganar might return to normal, and the Samsui might forget how much they need their Red Men."

Jhonni slipped a hand inside her jacket. Her wallet was still there, with the painfully new certificate of her professional qualification, the special *permisi travel* documents for herself and her clerk, the letter confirming her appointment at the base in central Timur. A wad of paper money; adult clan papers also painfully new.

She checked Endang too, trying to do it covertly. He seemed to feel her attention. His profile became even more rigid, more reserved. *I've apologized,* she thought. *What else can I do?* But they had wronged each other; it couldn't be fixed. That false friendship stood between them forever.

Maybe she should have told Derveet that the partnership was a bad idea. But when Derveet had given them their roles to play, they had both known they must accept. Jhonni was sure of that. The flowerdust was the first priority: to get hold of the flowerdust, and make sure that no more of it reached Ranganar, bringing madness, violence, and fear. If the drug was in the camp, it wouldn't be long before it was on the streets of the whole city. She shuddered at the thought.

The driver decided that he could, after all, edge through the space between the earthmover and the sea. Her whole body sighed in relief. As long as they were moving, nothing terrible could go wrong.

The last time Jhonni had seen Straits Control was the day the Previous Heaven Society blew up the Garuda dam. She was shocked at the change. The customs buildings looked as if they'd been deserted years ago. The garbage in the puddles was old and faded. There were no trishaws jostling for custom, no food vendors, no hawkers; no ice-boys wheeling chunks of dirty ice wrapped in sacking and screaming frantically "Es! Es! Gangway!" In the parking lot stood two massive armored treaders. Even they looked as if they'd been abandoned. Beyond the farther gates a listless frieze of Peninsulans hung on the wire, like a tattered creeper with faces and hands for flowers: more refugees waiting to be processed.

The causeway was officially closed to northbound traffic, but trade must go on. If you were hardy enough, if you had the contacts, and if your business was somehow going to benefit the Koperasi, *permisi travel* could be arranged. About half the people traveling this morning were

Peninsulan Kops returning from leave. The others were Samsui. There was an assortment of boy servants. Jhonni eyed the camouflaged treaders, wondering where on earth you would find vegetation that resembled those muddy splotches. She was reminded that on this side of the Straits the Kops were an army, the OA: they were *serious*. She recognized none of the Samsui, which was a relief. The only thing she knew about these women was not reassuring. They all must have important contacts in the Admin Compound. She muttered this bad news to Endang, as they shuffled in line to have their papers checked.

"One thing we have in common," he murmured. Jhonni giggled, caught his eye, and earned a grudging smile. She reached the counter, Endang half a pace behind with his eyes on the ground. The Kop leafed through her *permisi*. Jhonni kept anxious count: *must get every single one of them back*.

"You're an accountant, Cycler. Plenty cash, eh?"

He riffled imaginary paper money, his eyes speculative and hard.

"Not at the moment," grumbled Jhonni. "The troubles are bad for business. That's why I've been sent to this job in Timur. Where I'll probably get shot."

"Hmmph. There's no shooting in Timur. Not yet. Next."

They were through. They found space on one of the benches. The same treader that had brought them from the city would carry them north, but it wasn't leaving for another hour. Or so.

Jhonni made an inventory of their companions. There were thirteen Koperasi and six Samsui besides herself. The Koperasi had three boys among them. The Samsui had another five; and there was Endang. Twenty-nine people. She wondered how far the rest of them were going, and how many of them were spies. Two of the Kops weren't in uniform. They were slumming it in Samsui clothes, custom-made outsize versions of office workers' dark cotton suits.

One of them wore a brightly colored length of painted silk slung around his neck. Jhonni couldn't decide whether the effect was friendly-looking or sinister. None of the other travelers looked either interesting or trustworthy.

"I wish we could get some coffee," she muttered.

"Or tea."

The ghost of the *Blue Schoolroom* coffee shop rose in the dank, hot transit hall. It was bare of any kind of facilities, except for a washroom door under which was seeping an ominous muddy trickle of liquid.

"I hope I can do the job the Kops have hired me for. What if I can't? That would ruin everything."

"You're qualified."

"Friends in high places," Jhonni pointed out gloomily. Gathering confidence, and clinging to the tail of the ghost, she asked him: "Endang, are you frightened?" She chose her words; they could easily be overheard. "Anything could happen up there. Is the trip worth it?"

"Banyak banyak cash involved. You didn't think of that?" He made a secretive, cynical grimace. "Maybe we'll get our cut."

She was shocked. "Derveet doesn't want the flowerdust for profit!"

He could still be a traitor. Derveet had not said so; it didn't need to be stated. Jhonni had realized almost at once that Endang had to come to Timur. It was safer than leaving him behind, perhaps to reveal their plans to the people he was really working for. This was one good reason why she couldn't refuse his company. Belatedly, it struck her that Endang was smart enough to see this for himself. No wonder he wouldn't talk to Jhonni. She was his jailer. She wanted to reassure him, but she couldn't find the words. Supposing he *was* a traitor?

"You did that before," she hissed, discomfort making her angry. "You say something you know will frighten me, to put me off balance, and then take advantage. It won't work again."

Silence.

"Couldn't you *try* to level with me, trust me?"

He shrugged. "I've been passed from hand to hand like a piece of dirty paper money. My trust means nothing."

Jhonni was heartily sick of those coolie-boy shrugs, the lowered eyes. "You're overdoing it," she snapped. "You're my confidential clerk. We can converse. You can *look* at me."

Endang laughed without making a sound, a trick she remembered from the *Blue Schoolroom* times. "You too are being used, played by the puppeteer. Are you certain that you know what she's doing? Are you certain that *she* knows?"

He turned his face to her as he spoke, mechanically, the prisoner obeying an order from his guard. She studied his features: wide brow and cheekbones, pointed chin, long almond eyes, full lips. The high-bridged nose that snub-nosed Jhonni had seriously envied. His complexion was clear copper, the color that golden Peninsulans turn when they can't hide from the sun. She tried to find the person who had seemed such a kindred spirit. There was nothing but a mask. How could someone behave like that? *I truly liked you*, she wanted to say.

"Is there something wrong, ma'am?"

"No. I was trying to work something out. But I give up."

Before Derveet blotted out every other passion—the sun blotting out the stars—Jhonni had been prone to secret crushes. She recognized the symptoms. She had to admit, she had been suffering a kind of crush on her own Peninsulan. The moment of walking into the upper room at Dove House returned to her: Endang in those lovely Peninsulan clothes, with his hair short as her own. He'd looked like a girl dressed up. It had given her a shock. She was starting to blush at the thought. If he guessed! But how could he? She dived her hot face into her hands.

"I'm so thirsty, I feel quite ill."

"I could look outside," offered her clerk in a neutral tone. "There may be a drinks vendor."

"No!" said Jhonni sharply. "Stick together."

She was responsible for this possible traitor. She mustn't let him out of her sight.

This was going to be awful.

Aunt Kwokmei's reaction to everything had been astonishing. Her favorite needed to qualify at once, needed to leave at once for Timur, where she would take up a temporary job attached to a Koperasi base. And at the Admin Compound there were papers waiting for a strange Peninsulan . . .

Jhonni had brought her story straight to Kwokmei's counting rooms from the ferry, from Dove House. It didn't occur to her to do otherwise. The old lady heard her out, while the messenger girls flew to and fro and piles of state-of-emergency paper grew on the desks of the sweating boys.

"You told your mother?" she asked at the end.

"I—I hoped you'd talk to her. It's very important, Aunt."

Kwokmei, the childless, looked at Jhonni for a long time. "To Timur, eh? To the fighting."

"The fighting's in Gamartha. Hundreds of *batu* farther north."

Kwokmei lifted a skinny parchment hand, and moved a strand of damp hair from her cheek. Her eyes wandered from the row of machines to the boys and women feverishly at work to the door through which sunlight fell from the dusty courtyard where the oleanders were dying—as always—in their tubs.

"Stupid girl. Nobody knows where the fighting is. Not even the people being killed. Your gangster, she's fixed you up with this job? Fixed papers? Nice. Bit sudden, but it's nice you know someone who can get you outside work. Good experience."

Jhonni's expression must have melted into abject gratitude, because Aunt Kwokmei cackled loudly, reached out, and gave her a stinging slap around the ear. This was her usual response to sentiment.

"What about the boy? Let's see him."

Jhonni, head ringing, beckoned to Endang. He came into the room briskly. They were so awkward with each other that she hadn't been able to discuss tactics. Fortunately he seemed to understand that the shifty-eyed-coolie act wouldn't do here.

"Stand at desk, boy. Write name . . . good. Add this column . . . Ah, not good. Maybe you can wash clothes? Make tea?" She studied the crop-headed Peninsulan in his ill-fitting trousers and jacket. Her rat-bright eyes narrowed.

"Let me have a word with you, girl."

She drew Jhonni into the noise of the machines. Experts of the counting rooms could hear each other clearly within the clatter. Their ears grew filters.

"This is not a boy."

"I know," said Jhonni.

Kwokmei looked very interested, so interested that Jhonni couldn't keep the picture of that temple painting, the naked prince, the springing curve of his member, from filling her mind. She felt ridiculously uncomfortable.

"My, my. This gangster of yours, she is one serious revolutionary. But you better take care. They see he's a full male, Kops can pull him in. Studs are not allowed to roam."

Then the rat-empress, who never touched except to pinch or slap or drag you around, laid her hand firmly and gently on Jhonni's shoulder.

"This is a bad time. You don't understand because you're a child. You've never known the streets without armed Kops every which where. You've never known a year when the Council wasn't yelling at the Butchers for talking Peninsulan sympathy, and the Butchers weren't yelling back: 'Cowards! Fools! Don't You See, We'll Be Next!' " (This was the text, more or less, of one of Handai's infamous big-letter posters.) "You think the way we live is normal, can go on the same. No, you should listen to your gangster. She sees what's coming. We should all listen."

Aunt Kwokmei, to Jhonni's bewilderment, let go of her shoulder and made a sign with her two hands, thumbs hooked and fingers spread, like a pair of pinioned wings. Jhonni didn't know what it meant. She saw, over Kwokmei's shoulder, that Endang was impressed.

"*Baik-lah.* You go and pack. I'll talk to your mother. Wait." She jerked her head with an amused look—a very odd, complicated look—at the stranger. "You need a chitty for *him.* Clerk clothes, toothbrush, what-all. Bet he didn't bring much over the water."

Jhonni had asked Endang about the sign when they were in the clothes cupboard, she picking things from the shelves and laying them on his outstretched arms.

"It is the Eagle's wings. Some of your people used that sign in Ranganar a hundred years ago, when the last Garudas brought the princedoms out. It showed a little low-risk sympathy for us. It was as far as a Samsui would dare to go."

The cupboard, which was large as a room, was musty and dark—inevitably musty, in spite of the hanging bundles of water-sucking plant. Jhonni inhaled the scent of childhood: the everlasting warm damp of Ranganar, the sharp herb scent that somehow meant Aunt Kwokmei. She was suddenly miserable. Kwokmei was very old. *Aunt might die while I'm away.* Endang's explanation seemed to contain a sneer directed at the rat-empress. She told him—speaking in character, as to a coolie boy—to bring the clothes and follow her: don't dawdle!

The accountant papers were no problem. Aunt Kwokmei could have processed them months ago, if she was ever quick to surrender any kind of power. Mama was difficult. She was uneasy about the Timur job. It was necessary to co-operate with the Admin Compound. But the balance of opinion in Ranganar was shifting daily. Actually to *work* for the Koperasi was low standard, not high class. It would give their enemies in Council a handle, it might cost the clan business . . . But whatever Kwokmei said to her, it must have been convincing.

Doing favor for the Kops: got privilege! Don't worry if it dirty. Going to need all sort small-percent advantage soon. Never mind profit, if we mean to keep fed!

The transit hall was deadly quiet. Jhonni thought about the Eagle's wings. A hundred years ago: that meant the Great Rebellion. Even Aunt wasn't old enough to remember the Rebellion herself. Someone must have taught her the sign. Jhonni imagined how it must have been. Respectable tradeswomen handing things over a counter, casually making that gesture with the hooked thumbs. On a street corner; or someone sitting on a park bench watching children at play. Samsui of Aunt's mother's generation, exchanging the sign that meant *Are you a person I can talk to?* She was amazed. The Butchers had always been radicals, but she'd never thought of Peninsulan sympathy having a history in her own clan. She'd assumed she was the first Cycler in hundreds of years to be a "Peninsulan."

The Kops in Samsui clothes were chattering with their heads close together, their noise in this silence sounding like the bravado of naughty girls at the back of the classroom. Most of the passengers seemed to be doing the same as Endang, falling asleep with their eyes open. There were two armed Kops standing at each of the doors to the outside world. Jhonni hadn't noticed them before. She wondered if they would have stopped Endang if he'd tried to leave. She'd been right to prevent him. Neither of them should do anything to attract attention.

Idly, she experimented with her hands on her lap, hooking her thumbs with her palms turned inward, backs of her hands out. She flapped with her fingers. Eagle's wings. Endang stirred beside her. She quickly tucked her hands in her pockets. She decided she'd better go over the plan in her mind.

When they reached central Timur, Jhonni would take up her post at the base, at G. B. Hamzah's Reform Project. Derveet and Atoon and Cho would have made the same journey without benefit of Koperasi documents. Derveet would be inside the base, but she and Jhonni would not know each other. Derveet would let Cho and Atoon in. They would help her to work on the Koperasi officer (whatever that meant: Jhonni only knew the details of her own and Endang's part) until he handed over the dust. Endang and Jhonni would have rooms in the Peninsulan town outside. The bales of dust would be delivered to Jhonni, who would smuggle it off the base. Then one or the other party would carry the drug back to Ranganar, and the other would be the decoy—just in case G. B. Hamzah changed his mind. *One or the other . . .* Jhonni slid a glance at Endang. Derveet had left that undecided, and Jhonni guessed she knew why. She wondered if Endang had noticed. It must be hateful not to be trusted.

What if she was the courier? What then?

"Bales" sounded alarming. But Derveet said a full bale of flowerdust was no larger than your hand, and weighed no more than about a *kati*, a Peninsulan measure of weight near to half the Kops' kilo. There had been twelve of these originally. If what Endang said was true, only a half-bale had been sold in the camp. There might be eleven packets left. Eleven or eleven and a half lightish objects about the size of hands, to be concealed in two people's baggage. It wouldn't be difficult. A Samsui up-country outfit was voluminous; it had plenty of hiding places. But Jhonni fretted over the vagueness of the Peninsulan mind. "Lightish," "hand-sized." She wished Derveet had given precise measurements.

She knew they'd be lucky if hiding the stuff on the way home was their worst problem. But she had to fix on something limited to worry about or she would start to panic.

At last the hour (or so) was over. Their driver was a civilian, a middle-aged Ranganarese. He and two tiny, skinny assistants shoved bags into compartments in the treader's segmented flanks, between the four pairs of long, massive caterpillar rollers. Jhonni stood watching, making sure their bedding, the three big bags, and her traveling desk were stowed well, and not "accidentally" left behind to be collected by the team's confederates. Her mother had made her promise solemnly to take *nothing* for granted.

She looked around for Endang, who should, strictly speaking, have been taking care of his mistress's baggage. He was standing on the edge of the group of travelers, staring at nothing. No. He was staring at the refugees. Jhonni saw that her own Peninsulan was ashamed to be where he was, ashamed to be on the right side of the fence, to have clean clothes, to have food in his belly. She felt as if someone had taken hold of her heart and squeezed it. Tears stung her eyes. She abandoned the bags to their fate.

"Endang."

"Ma'am?" He'd whipped the mask back into place, but she wasn't fooled anymore. She didn't know what to say.

"Endang . . . we're going to get the buggers. I s'pose we can't go and fight in Gamartha. But we're going to *do something*."

"If you say so, ma'am." Jhonni's face fell: rebuffed again. Endang grinned, fractionally, and added in a rapid undertone, "But not if we chatter and *fidget* in public, ma'am. The Peninsula is *not like Ranganar*."

"Oh." Jhonni blushed like a tomato.

The Kop with the sarong around his neck leaned out of his seat as they clambered past him down the aisle.

"Nice-looking boy. D'you always chat to them like that?"

"He's not a—" for a moment, she experienced death "—an ordinary boy," she recovered, heart thumping. "He's a Timurese. A refugee. Educated in Sepaa. We took him on, on spec: doing our bit, you know. We're very pleased, so far."

"Took on a ref? Good on yer. Wish we could empty the whole bloody camp. It's a shit, poor bloody bastards living in their shit, and shit like that—"

Something jabbed her in the spine. Endang, who had charge of their hand luggage, was poking her with a roll of palm-leaf mats.

"Move along the bus!" the friendly Kop said, grinning.

They took their numbered seats. "I'm sorry," muttered Jhonni. She'd thought she was in charge. She was obviously mistaken! "I couldn't help it. In future I won't talk to *anyone*."

The opera cutout book was not in Jhonni's baggage. But she had brought along a dog-eared notebook that held her first Peninsulan vocabulary. The list was decorated with drawings (very poor) of Jhonni on horseback (something she'd never tried) and the girl she'd been in love with when she was eleven. It was made up of borrowed words that everyone, Samsui and Kops, used constantly. To eleven-year-old Jhonni they had glowed with romance.

baik-lah	good, fine, terrific
bagus	same only more
enak	tasty, fresh (same only more slangy)
makan	a meal, eat
masuk	enter, let's go, let's do it. Also, <u>the act of procreation</u>.

These last words, solemnly underlined, had been a source of enormous fascination. When she was eleven, Jhonni was not at all sure what humans did to "procreate."

diluar	outside
sudah	already (done it, had it, seen it, thank you)
masih	still available
belum	not yet

terima kasi	thank you
tak bisa	can't
boleh	you can, you may
habis	finished, sold out, go home, show's over
cukup	enough

"*Masuk!*" shouted the driver's boy, swinging perilously in the rear doorway. The treader started to move. It lumbered through the gates of Straits Control, past the refugees, onto a red dirt road. That was it. She was committed. She was a drug smuggler. It sounded much worse than blowing up the Garuda dam. If she was caught, Mama would never, ever understand.

The windows had been washed at Straits Control. The one beside her was ill-fitting and rattled violently. For the first time, excitement gripped her. She was going up-country, farther into the enchanted land than she had ever dreamed possible. There would be mountains, forests, temples, waterfalls.

Jhonni dozed. Koperasi plantations rolled by: oil palm and rubber. This was Occupied Territory, land that had once been the Garuda princedom, now known simply as the Territory—or the *sawah,* the rice field. Endang watched them. On the edge of sight, the trees flickered and began to distort. A hollow-eyed face, a bundle of naked limbs . . . The nightmare illusion ate across his field of vision, steadily. He saw rows of dead bodies, upright. The trees were bodies of starved and naked slaves, waiting to be shoveled up and packed down into fuel for the Rulers' engines.

Why did he have to say that to her, about Derveet making money from the dust? It was nonsense. Why did he have to hurt poor Jhonni? He couldn't stop himself. He needed to hurt someone. The knives came out and twisted, because he was himself in pain.

Poor Garuda, he thought. Still playing out her stubborn game of diplomacy, of everybody wins. Help the Timurese if they're on your doorstep and they need help—even if the Timurese concerned are heartless criminals who've just tried to kill you. He pitied her sincerely. He pitied them all—almost as much, he conceded with sour honesty, as he pitied himself.

Derveet suspected that the women of Endang's family had been working on his mind, abusing their powers to keep him helpless. She was wrong. *The* dapur *is helpless,* he thought. He stared through the window while horror ate at his field of view until there was nothing else left. He was not cured. He never would be cured. *No one will listen to me,* he thought. *I will become a puppet again, with new hands on my strings. I will tell no one, never. I will keep my secret.*

On the southeast coast of the old Garuda territory, down below Sepaa, a flat-bottomed river valley opened towards the sea. The slopes on either side were rice-terraced to the sky, in the immemorial pattern of the Peninsulan land-scape—where human use is the most natural and pervasive of all natural features.

The tiers of the amphitheater, green stages for ten thou-sand thousand dancing goddesses, were deserted. The net-work of earth walls and channels had dried and crumbled. The terraces were thick with spear grass and thorny scrub. But there were people planting rice in the flooded fields below. From a distance it was a lovely scene. The drab clothes and dark skins of the workers set off the tender em-erald of the young rice. The sway and fall, sway and fall of the ranks had a silent music; the ocher water of the fields glittered in the sun.

Three people sat together on one of the terraces, hidden by a thicket of spear grass and tall purple ground orchids. Two of them, a young girl and a man, wore lumpy head-cloths wound low over their brows, and waistcloths of diamond-patterned bark cloth that looked like snakeskin. They were evidently forest tribals. Small communities of these people—truly, unreachably decadent savages—lived in the forests that covered the spine of the Peninsula. The Koperasi didn't bother them. They would sometimes emerge by the road and beg a ride from a passing treader, seeming to regard the lumbering vehicles as a natural phenomenon.

The third Peninsulan wore a tattered jacket and breeches that bore signs of vanished dandyism, and could have been male or female. In the wilds, a bandit and a failed woman could be hard to tell apart. They watched the rice planters.

"It looks so pretty," murmured Atoon viciously.

"It *is* pretty," Derveet corrected him. "You object to the overseers and the whips, and the fact that the laborers are skin and bone in the richest land in the princedoms. I am grateful that they are planting food. There is a limit to the amount of rubber that people can eat."

"She's such a know-it-all," remarked Atoon to Cho. "She has Kop land use at her fingertips; she has studied everything and then everything else." He was unhappy about Derveet's plan, now it came to the point. He did not like to think of Garuda humiliated among the slaves.

"You're hard to please. Would you rather I'd left you in Ranganar?" Derveet took his hand, closed the fingers over a large and flashy ruby ring. "Poor taste, I know. But the stone has been judged good, if gaudy. You don't have to wear it. Wait and see what happens to me below. If all goes well, you two get down to the road. Watch the gates to the base. If I can, I'll let you know what's happening. But whether or not, as long as I get inside you hitch a lift on the next treadie that passes. In Sepaa, show the ring to the boys at the Northern Transport Depot. Tell them where you want to go. Say: *Express.* And I will see you in Timur."

To deal with the Koperasi you must step into their world, where time moves at a different rate, where the treaders churned incessantly up and down the wide graded roads. Atoon and Cho might be in Timur in less than a day. Derveet hoped to be close behind.

"*Baik.*" Atoon looked as unhappy as he could ever permit

himself to be. Isn't that the way? Derveet thought. A little freedom always makes people discontented.

"Atoon, slaves are fighting for places in Commander Hamzah's rest home. No one is going to harm me. Even if that weren't so, one of us has to be inside the system. And they don't keep studs."

She turned to the doll-who-was-a-person. Cho's sweet face peeped out from under the absurd headcloth, alight with pleasure. To her this was sheer joy: an adventure, a game, and a chance to make herself useful. "Dear child. Take care of the little father. If you come to sell the ring, don't let him get into any dice games. A prince who takes to gambling can get into bad, or at any rate extremely long-winded, trouble."

She referred to an episode in the Peninsula's Scripture, in which a prince carelessly dices away his family's inheritance. It was a mishap that triggered a devastating war and a million or so interminable lines of sacred poetry. She stood on the verge of the drop to the stage below, bent to touch the pure curve of the doll's cheek. She was gone.

"One of these days," said Atoon gloomily, "she will go off and leave us that way, and she won't ever come back."

The doll nodded. "I know."

Scripture: at the heart of that endless story of the great family, of humanity, five brothers served their single wife. This arrangement, very odd by Peninsulan standards within historical memory, was explained as a symbol of the relationship between the Garuda family and the princedoms . . . She slouched down the dry terraces, adopting the slack, foot-sore gait of the Peninsulan vagrant. To woo my husband Timur, she thought, I humble myself.

Insofar as Timur could be wooed, by Garuda's care for the inland peasants who'd fled to Ranganar. But it might make a difference . . .

I hope this works.

She spared a thought for the new Peninsulan, and his fall into every kind of chaos. What would become of Endang? She pitied him . . . and almost envied him the experience of a world of pains and pleasures that she could not imagine.

She walked down the terraces. White-and-purple orchids bobbed thigh-high. Tiny lizards dived for pebble cover; something larger caused a submerged kerfuffle in a stand of orange-flowered shrub. She did not try to conceal her approach. There was nothing to conceal. She was no one, a scrap of human detritus cast adrift by these hard times. Identity fell from her as she walked. The prince of Jagdana's friend, possessor of the marvelous angel doll; Anakmati, the wily paragon of bandits; Garuda, the doubtful pretender to an ancient throne. None of those. Not for a while.

The rice-planters were closer. She could see the sores on their legs and the marks of hunger on their faces. What a relief it was, a secret joy, to join them. Her inner eye lingered on the child's face. But Cho grew indistinct. Now she was only Derveet.

Not even that.

Sway up, sway down. Long ago, before the *dapur* retired into itself and women gave up outdoor work, the young girls used to sing when they were planting out the rice. Then the boys used to sing: sing and plant all day, stay up singing and dancing all night. This vast field was silent. Derveet went to the nursery trailer. She looked at the rice and sighed. She made a sling out of her ragged scarf and loaded it with seedling bundles. In the distance a man with a hat (the only hat in sight) sat in the cab of a mud-covered agricultural treadie. A group of figures, huskier-looking than the planters, were hunkered down on the track in its shadow, their backs against the tall slatted rollers.

No one paid any attention to her. She took her place at the end of a ragged line. Sway up, sway down. The opaque water reached her knees. The mud under it was ankle-deep and contained things that wriggled and bit. Fish, perhaps;

the leeches were more discreet. Thrust a hand and a green seedling into the mud, sway up, move on. The pace was slow for her energy; she had been eating too well. It took her a while to catch the rhythm and leave her plants upright. After that it was easy. Others didn't find it so. Many of the slaves were hardly trying. They moved up and down to satisfy the eye of the overseer—but like broken gears, catching on nothing. Emerald tatters floated on the surface of the water.

What stupid stuff rice is, she thought. Stupid domesticated brute, helpless without human nursing. Whereas acar was a plant that knew how to look after itself. Its careless hardiness, the speed of its responses to water, to light, to shade, had delighted her when she was a grower. And when the bloom came . . . ah, that had been a wonderful day, though the gift was useless to her. It was love returned.

She thought about getting close to her ex-partner. It was an advantage that Jeeby was Commanding Officer. That meant a private life, private quarters. And—unless his habits had altered dramatically—no intimate servants, no personal friends among his fellow officers, no confidants. Provincial Commander was an impressive rank. But she didn't believe success would have changed her old ally. Jeeby would still be an outsider.

She managed to ease herself farther into the line. On her left, a young girl. On her right a wizened boy who might be any age from fifteen to fifty. The girl was pigment-deficient. Her hair was an extraordinary color, orange as a flower. She wore a sarong knotted under her arms, nothing else. All her bare skin was blistered, raw and seeping. The sun—it was soon after midday—burned down. Derveet watched her neighbor's misery, and decided the brutalizing effect of slavery was not part of her act. She shrugged off her jacket: "Here."

The girl didn't notice what had happened any more than a piece of earth might. The boy, however, was intrigued.

Derveet saw his eyes flicker over her. She would have to remove herself from that dangerous spark of interest.

She moved into the next row. The boy moved with her. Derveet went on planting, a frown briefly creasing her brow. He might be a problem; there would be problems. She felt herself slip into the state of fluid open-mindedness that went with these adventures. An object in view, but no fixed plan. She was ready, like water, to fall in whatever direction offered least resistance.

A short time ago Derveet had been Anakmati the bandit. There were wanted posters of the black-skinned ruffian with the eyepatch, the braids, the nose like a dagger. Anakmati was famous. But every Koperasi wanted poster Derveet had ever seen showed a black-skinned ruffian with a nose like a dagger. The people who made up those posters were locals, with ambivalent feelings about bandits. In traditional iconography, black was the color of courage.

Ranganar was small, the Peninsula was large. The Occupying Army was no longer a coherent force; an obscure base in the Occupied Territory was beyond the end of the world. The Kops here would have heard that some terrorists blew up the Garuda dam. There was no reason to fear they knew more. She did not know what would happen if she was recognized up here. For a moment she woke up, like a sleepwalker on the edge of a cliff. *This could go horribly wrong.* But that vertiginous thrill was a familiar sensation. Derveet was always waking on the cliff's edge. Oh well. Better get on with it.

She straightened.

"Stop what you're doing, people!"

The boy who was too interested slid her a beady glance. Derveet emptied the bundles out of her sling. She splashed along the row, grabbing seedlings out of hands. A few of the slaves started yelling at her, others speeded up their rhythm. In distant parts of the field, figures came to rest, glad of any respite.

The man in the hat splashed over.

"What's this? What's going on here?"

He wore an ancient uniform jacket with the sleeves torn out, a grimy pair of brocade breeches he must have stolen from a bandit, high rubber-and-canvas boots with laces. He carried a buffalo goad, which prodded and slapped bodies aside until he reached the offender. He had never seen Derveet before. If he noticed this, it meant nothing to him. His face was yellow as a pumpkin, and almost as round.

"Plant rice! Go on, plant rice! What do we feed you for?"

"I'd be happy to plant your rice. I'd be *delighted*, if it would do any good. But you see, this is not delta paddy." Derveet, leering affably, held out a handful of seedlings for his inspection. "You know how it is. Muddles happen. This water here is salt. Taste it, you'll find I'm right. This kind of rice won't grow." She tore up another handful of young plants, and tossed them aside. "Might as well junk the lot . . ."

Pumpkin-face could have started hitting her. He did not. This man was not automatically violent. He stood, scowling, looking bored and irritated. "Crazy man-woman." He wheedled. "I don't want trouble. You don't want trouble."

"STOP WHAT YOU'RE DOING, EVERYONE. THIS IS ORDERS!!"

The shout came from the wizened boy with the bright eyes. He danced from foot to foot, dipped and splashed a creamy wave of muddy water into the face of the man with the hat. He was grinning wildly. "Taste! It's salt!" He hopped around, waving his arms. "STOP! STOP! DON'T MAKE YOURSELF TIRED!" He had a voice like a bull-frog's, an extraordinary volume from that narrow, concave rib cage. Derveet and the overseer stared at him, united in disgust. Slowly, the overseer's face changed. He gave in resentfully.

"*Bagus!* You both want trouble. Come out of here!"

The man with the hat cut the two of them out of the row.

He drove them ahead of him, back to the track. The trusties who acted as his guards took over. They ushered the recalcitrants into the back of the treadie, without any violence at all, and shut the doors. The senseless planting of rice that couldn't grow went on.

There were no Peninsulan towns in the ex-Garuda territory. There was no significant population outside Sepaa except for the slaves and the Koperasi—and the acar growers in the hills. The bases strung along the coast each had a slave farm next door for fresh food, for servants, and for sanctioned "comfort boys."

There were no comfort girls. The women whores in the big Kop towns and in Ranganar were treated with a kind of respect by their customers. Any girl children who were abused up here—in desperate acts of daring, because a girl slave might be fertile, might possess the terrifying powers and no one would know—had nothing to do with comfort. And they received none: no extra food, no little privileges. They were pits of terror.

It was stinking hot in the treadie and pitch dark. The air smelled of piss and sweaty bodies. The wizened boy tried to make conversation but she ignored him. She was thinking about Merpati, the heroine. Who had been brought, perhaps, to a base like this, in a dark metal box like this one. Derveet didn't know. She had never asked her grandfather, *What happened to my mother? Exactly what? Where? Did she tell you? Could she?* He wouldn't have answered. He repelled direct questions about that time. She felt herself that curiosity was an affront to the other woman's experience. There was only one decent way to find out.

They were delivered to a large concreted yard. There were glimpses of the docks between gray walled buildings, chopped rectangles of dark blue water. On the land side, beyond a tall fence, you could see the farm barracks: long, moldering, sagging shacks of palm-leaf matting. The boy pointed. "That's my house. That's where I live!"

The overseer was talking to a pair of Kops who wore the brick-red uniform of the Occupying Army. "I've brought something for The Office," she heard him say, in a tone of reverence. She felt how The Office was the source of all his joy and grief, his *dapur*. Derveet scowled at the boy from the field.

"Why did you tag along? Who asked you?"

He pursed his lips, posed his hands coquettishly. "To be noticed! A handsome officer will see me, and make me his own."

"Liar. You want to be sent to the Reform Camp."

He bridled. "What if I do? Why should I not?" He looked down his nose—quite a feat; his head barely reached her elbow. "They won't have *you*. You are black, you are deformed. The Reform Camp is not for *aneh!*"

She was taken inside first. She was marched to a small gray cell with a drain in the floor and a shower nozzle in the wall, and told to strip. The water was blindingly hot and stank of disinfectant. It almost knocked her out, after the heat of the field. A young officer, a fresh and innocent-looking specimen, came in. He looked at her teeth, tapped her ribs, lifted her arms, felt her buttocks, inserted neutral fingers into her mouth, rectum, vagina. The examination was perfunctory, his hands were eerily gentle. He gave her a pair of clean cotton drawers to wear.

She was taken along the corridors, into a room where there were fans in the ceiling, red rubber matting on the floor, notice boards on the walls layered thick with printed and handwritten papers. There were young men, old men, fat men, thin men, all in the brick-red uniform. Startling numbers of men, to a Peninsulan eye. They ambled from desk to desk, or sat staring like cattle at the mounds of paper in front of them. The place looked like a Samsui office in Ranganar, but totally devoid of the women's manic bustle. Derveet's unregenerate instinct wondered, as always, how studs could run a business. Let alone a country. She knew the answer: they couldn't. In a smaller room beyond, a large middle-aged man sat behind a desk. There was a hard chair in front of it. The young Koperasi told her kindly to sit down. Derveet folded her legs awkwardly onto the alien furniture.

"A woman." The older officer sounded dubious.

"Male impersonator, sir. Quite harmless."

"Can she understand Inggris?"

"I think so. The underworld usually can."

"You think so." The old bull's eyes were heavy with distrust for the younger generation. "You examined her."

"I find it hard to converse with a woman when I'm treating her like an animal."

The young officers were often soft to start with. In the Peninsula's experience, it didn't last. Their hearts broke soon, and a broken heart is more cruel than a heart of stone. Poor kid. Let him stay human, she prayed. Let him have a chance.

"No records, of course. Does that farm keep *any* records?" It was a rhetorical question. He heaved a sigh, drew a sheet of paper from one of the heaps, apparently at random: addressed the slave.

"Name?"

"Diponegoro."

It was the name of a mythical hero. The Kop grunted and filled in the four letters that fitted on his form. She was Dipo. That was all right. It had a ring to it.

"Mother's name."

Silence.

"Mother's name."

"She can't tell you that," protested the young one. "They never answer that one. The names of their women are sacred."

This was not exactly true. Between one respectable Peninsulan and another, "Mother's name" was a greeting, the most commonplace of questions. But respectable Peninsulans did not talk to the Koperasi. Ironically, the most eagerly Peninsulan Kops knew only the etiquette of the outcasts, of the dispossessed. The bull gave the bull calf a weary glare. "Don't try to teach me Peninsulan culture, Doctor. I've been in this country a long time. Father's name."

Derveet leaned over for a look at the nameplate on the desk.

"William Green Noto."

He looked old enough.

The young Kop choked. The older man reached over and slapped her hard across the face, a routine blow, without malice. She thought it was directed at the doctor. He tossed his sheet of paper aside. "Oh, what's the point? Make something up. Isn't that what we usually do?"

There was a moment's pause.

"She's underweight, sir. And I didn't like the sound of her left lung. We were asked for healthy subjects."

Derveet was outraged. So was the senior officer.

"Underweight?" he repeated, with withering emphasis. "Are we in the fat stock business? Apparent good health, normal intelligence, resistance to discipline. That's all I need. Send in the boy."

"Come on, Mrs. er, Mr. Diponegoro."

The lieutenant opened the door to usher her out. Derveet looked up. She was tall, awkwardly tall, even among the chunky Samsui. In this world, she became small. She grinned in triumph, because she tried never to miss a chance for a human gesture. But he had difficulty returning the smile.

She and the irritating boy were shut up together in the back of another treadie. It was an improvement on the last one. It was windowless, but there was a hatch in the roof which seemed to have lost its cover, and the bare interior was quite clean. There was even a clean, covered nightsoil bucket clamped to the wall.

"Were you insolent?" he asked. "I was insolent. It makes

them think you are strong, that you will survive the journey. I got by on that, though my buttocks let me down." He smirked vindictively. "The see-over hated me. I have been naughty as naughty, but he would not send me to The Office before. Even though he *knew* our Office Red Men were in trouble for not sending in any re-cal-ci-trants. He's a bad man."

Derveet, chin on her knees, wondered what the soft Kop knew. From every other source, she had heard that Jeeby's Reform Project was slave heaven. If only you could be bold enough to be recruited . . . and not too bold. If you were unlucky, chose the wrong overseer or wrong officer, you might get beaten to death trying to prove yourself both re-calcitrant and healthy. She was not unduly dismayed. There would always be unexpected dangers. So far, things were going remarkably well.

"So, I don't find out," she said. "I suppose I never will."

The boy was puzzled. They sat facing each other, backs against the stripped metal sides. The square of light and air beamed down on them.

"What is it you didn't find out? Something for your plan?"

"What plan?" He was still grinning, with more gaps than teeth. His ribs were laced with whip scars. "What's your name?"

"Gani." He cracked his knuckles. "I know who *you* are."

Derveet thought of the nameplate on Officer Noto's desk. "No, you don't. Do you know where they're taking us next?"

"Straight to the Timur hospital, of course!"

"Ah. The hospital." She considered this title, which was new to her, and put it together with the young Kop's unhappy eyes. Gani delved into his clean drawers. He brought out a handful of slippery, shiny gray fish, about a finger long. "Lucky you," said Derveet. "Nobody told me we had to provide our own rations."

"We can share!"

He delved again, and to her amazement produced a small paper notebook. "They have too much," he explained. "I call them the paper people. If they stay out of the sun their skin is white like paper. You see. I can help you in many ways."

"Is that so? Let me have that notebook, for a start."

She began to tear sheets out, ignoring his wails of protest. Soon he got the idea and started copying her. By the time the treadie moved, its floor was littered. Gani looked at her with bright, avid curiosity. "What are they for?"

"None of your business."

She stood, grasped the edge of the hatch overhead and swayed, listening for their passage through the gates, out onto the graded surface of the highway. The treadie snarled up to a jolting, inhuman speed. Gani hid his face and moaned. "Why drive too fast, Mr. Kop!" Behind it, a flurry of white paper wings tumbled down the air, and fluttered into the gray spattered verges.

6

"THE *DAPUR* DON'T achieve a thing. They don't call up demons, they don't make rain, they don't cure fever, they don't tell the future, they don't find lost property. Anything like that, no matter who says otherwise, I guarantee it's a fake. Yet you show me a genuine, native Peninsulan and I'll show you a fucker that believes, no matter how many fakes you unmask in front of him.

"You see, to *them*, *dapur* power is something different. Your native Peninsulan obeys his mother-sisters because he's used to doing that. And you'd better be sure, if you make a contract with a Peninsulan, that you get it thumbprinted from the women of the family, because nothing else works! But the *dapur* is bigger shit. The *dapur* is the ruling cabal of the native state, and your mother-sisters are part of it in a kind of a mystical way; and if the *dapur*'s on your side it's like having your CO by the short and curlies. More so. It's *enak sekali*. You can walk on fire. Bugger it, you can walk on *water*.

"Your servant will take the cash out of your jacket while you're sitting there looking at him. Why? He's feeling lucky. He's convinced some noble lady behind closed doors is saying her prayers for him. If he gets caught . . . then, fuck it, he made a mistake, she was praying for some other bugger. D'you see what I mean? The *dapur*'s infallible. You can't argue with the magical worldview."

Jhonni listened to the voice of the friendly Kop. She was half-asleep, her head rocking on the back of the seat to the treader's slow, hideous jolting. She kept hearing *dust* when he said *dapur*. She would start up, convinced that all was discovered. The bale of *bungadebu* was about to be dragged from under her seat. She was going to be shot. She was going to be thrown into a slave camp. Then she would realize she had been asleep. There was no bale of drugs. Not yet.

It was the second day of the bus journey. Jhonni had no idea where they were. Her mother had given her a map of the Peninsula and another of Timur. They were no use, because she was afraid to get them out in case the Kops confiscated them. Mama had said that was bound to happen sooner or later. The treader heaved itself along like a crippled beetle, with such agonizing slowness you prayed for death to end its misery. Every hour there was at least one halt to tinker with the rollers. And at least one roadblock. The Koperasi were different up here. They carried different weapons. The troopers were thinner and smaller and shabbier, the officers more alien. While the shabby, nervous little men in uniform were walking up and down the aisle, everybody would go completely quiet. Everybody—even the off-duty Kops—seemed to be trying to surround themselves with a shell of invisibility: *don't notice me.*

At the first block Jhonni was convinced they'd reached the fighting: things were far worse than anyone had guessed, the whole Peninsula was up in flames. At the next block she was sure that there'd been a tip-off. The Red Men were looking for the *bungadebu*. Gradually it dawned on her that this level of intimidation didn't mean anything special. This was normal life.

She was dismally disappointed in the scenery. For the stretch of road where you were able to see Bu Awan, the great Mother Mountain of the south, it had been dark. Now it was daylight again and they were back in the plantations.

Sometimes the treader would crawl past groups of people trudging by the side of the road, heads down. But there were no towns, no villages, no proper houses: only, occasionally, a row of swaybacked shacks in a bare, wired yard.

The journey had shaken people down. The treader was a network of the temporary alliances decreed by proximity, and Jhonni had been unable to keep her rash promise to talk to no one. Across the aisle there was Commercer Lian traveling with her wife, an Assistant Physician called Pao, selling medical supplies: they talked a lot, in contracted, very Samsui jargon. Behind them sat a Builder called Yen, and the Commercer-Physician's boy, who didn't talk and remained nameless. In front were two youngish Pabrikers, who were heading for the Timur coast and kept offering Jhonni sweets and cakes. They were going to supervise the installation of an improved production line, which their clan had sold to the Kops. The Pabrikers were a clan without class, known for their coarse manners and poverty-stricken greed. They preferred not to discuss the nature of the goods involved in their deal with the Peninsulan Army. But they were unpleasantly sympathetic about Miss Cycler's demeaning Koperasi appointment.

The two friendly Kops talked to everybody. The little dark one with the sarong was called Ken. His companion, Daoud, was the archetypal Kop: huge, red, and bristly as a pig, with whitish hair and eyes the color of water. It was Ken who did the talking. He kept up the running joke about Commercer Lian's sample case, and how useful it would be if the treader was waylaid by brigands. And the other running joke about Pabriker Feng's samples. The uniformed Kops didn't talk much, and addressed none of the women.

Ken brayed on and on. His voice had a maddening, toneless, grating timbre, but at least it sometimes drowned the vile rattle of that ill-fitting window. A feverish doze swallowed Jhonni up again. She started, opening her eyes. The treader had stopped. There were buildings outside.

"Where are we? Why've we stopped?"

"Anganangrek. We've got to collect our bags."

"Is it a meal break? We don't have to get our bags. We're through-passengers."

Endang gave his soundless laugh.

The only long halt they'd made had been at night, at a big river crossing somewhere near Bu Awan. Jhonni had been too sleepy and resentful to find any romance in the situation. She climbed down, spirits lifting. She was a daring secret agent, arriving in a mysterious Peninsulan town called Orchid-dream (or something like that). Orchid-dream was not prepossessing. She could see no temples, nothing old, not a scrap of decoration. Nothing was pretty. The buildings were made of cement and sheets of tin and had no glass in the windows. A few of them were shops, displaying the same kind of cheap shoddy goods that you could see in any Ranganarese kampong. Some produce stalls stood in the middle of the square, surrounded by debris: rotten vegetables, limp corn husks, tatters of rag and bone.

"I wanted to buy some souvenirs," she joked. "Aren't there any handicrafts?"

"It's a base town," said Endang. "Most towns on the treader roads are. Occupying armies don't encourage fine architecture. You won't find any handicrafts. Anything anyone who lives here grows to eat or makes to use has to be produced *after* they've worked for the Kops. People don't have the time or energy to make their lives beautiful."

Jhonni was glad he was talking to her. "That sounds like Derveet."

Endang nodded. "It was. I used to be ashamed of being a Peninsulan. I saw mean little places like this, and I didn't want to be part of them. I didn't feel guilty; I thought the choice was a matter of my superior taste. Derveet makes you see things differently. She makes you see *more*."

Jhonni wrapped her arms around herself and shivered. "So this is the Peninsula. And we're still quite close to civilization. What will it be like when we get over the border?"

"We've crossed it. We're in Timur."

At the sound of that word, something strange happened to Jhonni. Something touched her, like a hand on her shoulder. The touch brought a shaking wash of dread, as if she were a very little child and Mama had caught her doing something childishly but horrendously wicked. Was that touch her mother's hand? She was afraid to look around.

Endang was smiling thinly. "I apologize for Timur."

"Uh, sorry. I didn't mean that the way it sounded." *Still close to civilization*, she had said. That was the way you discovered your own prejudices. The Peninsula meant romance, but civilization meant Ranganar, Sepaa, the coastal towns, the Koperasi. Endang was watching her with an odd expression. "Did I look strange? I felt strange for a moment. It's just . . . not a good first impression."

The Ranganarese driver had hauled everybody's bags out and dumped them on the ground. The Kops seemed unsurprised. Some of the Samsui were arguing with the driver and his boys. The others stood around, gazing at the hateful treader with lost and bewildered expressions. Now they were about to lose it, it seemed their one friend in a strange and hostile world.

Jhonni knew that Mama would have been tackling the driver. But she was unable to concentrate. The flurry of Samsui indignation looked so pointless. It was late afternoon, *sore*, the time when she and Endang used to meet. The sky overhead was blocked in with purple masses of cloud. There was a storm coming; maybe that was why she felt chilled. She heard herself humming "And I will hear your step" from the *Blue Schoolroom*. She panicked because *the tune was a sign.* She must not make secret signs!

Commercer Lian came up, yelling the bad news in Jhonni's face.

"He's not taking us any farther. He says we stopover here, find our own night-stay bills. Can you believe it? He says that's what his *dapur* agreed with the Admin Compound. Tomorrow morning, a Timurese treader will pick us up. That wasn't the arrangement! We bought straight-through tickets, inclusive! You did too! Tomorrow morning! We'll be *two days* behind schedule! My mother, someone's going to hear from me! Chiseling Kops! Chiseling Ranganarese! Bunch of red-backed kites!"

She was a big woman, square cut in the face and body, with a bob of thick iron-gray hair: a woman who thought well of herself and was used to respect.

"D-don't worry." Jhonni's teeth were chattering. "I expect the fighting will still be g-going on. Still be a good m-market for cheap painkillers and secondhand bandages . . ."

The Commercer, as Jhonni had already discovered, was armor-plated against sarcasm. She groaned. "Suppose you're right, Miss Cycler. Travel on the Peninsula in the troubles, bound to be like this. Always we Samsui got to work hard, want make profit."

Two days . . . Jhonni had fallen out of time. She had lost all sense of urgency. She stared at a mound of green melons on one of the bedraggled stalls. Some of them were split to the red flesh, others sunken and puckered like deflated footballs. She thought how much they resembled a pile of battered heads. If she stared hard she could see eyes, mouths, bruises and missing teeth. The Commercer peered into the girl's face, muttered something, and stamped off. Jhonni screwed up her eyes, and opened them again. The heads had turned back into melons.

They took refuge in the hotel, the only two-story building in sight. Commercer Lian negotiated rooms for the Samsui, while the travelers spread themselves over tables in the ground-floor dining room. The table arrangements went more or less faithful to the seating plan of the treader. The uniformed Kops took a long table together and ordered beer. Ken and Daoud took a table among the Samsui; the boys sat with the boys. Jhonni, by hanging back cunningly, managed to avoid Lian, Pao, and the Pabrikers. She took the last table, alone, spread her traveling desk over it and pretended to be working.

There were no local customers. Maybe the townspeople were not allowed to mix with foreigners. Timur was supposed to be a traditional princedom. But the royal family had had to step down because they had no male heir. There had been a bloody interregnum, with murders and mysterious deaths; then the Koperasi took over. They'd put an infant nobleman on the throne, and in theory, they'd hand the government back to *his* family when he came of age. No one expected that to happen. No one seriously expected the prince would stay alive that long. Jhonni watched the aged waiter who hovered beside the Kops. He was smiling as if there'd been a death in the family, a tragedy which had to be kept from these crass strangers.

She noticed that Ken was doing something furtive. Sheltered by Daoud's bulk he was delving in his kitbag under the table. Strange weeping and wailing noises emerged faintly. He must have a communication set in there. That was contraband. In coastal Timur you could buy things like wave sets and music bands almost openly, but possession was still a serious offense. Jhonni had been the set operator with Derveet's gentle terrorists. She tried hard to listen, longed to get her hands on the controls. But she heard nothing intelligible. One of the uniformed Kops got up and passed by Ken, as if by accident. Jhonni saw him bend and murmur something: a warning? The weeping noises stopped. Ken's hands were on the tabletop.

She realized that everyone in the room had been riveted by the hidden machine. The women and boys, frozen in their seats, tried not to look at each other; gradually, anxious and desultory conversation began again. What was everybody expecting so intently? News from Gamartha? The death of a prince? Things were different up-country. The rules were slackened; you were allowed to see things that were invisible at home. But that wasn't because . . . it wasn't a *good* sign.

Jhonni couldn't eat her food when it appeared. There seemed to be something stuck in her throat. She heard Ken braying at the Timurese waiter in garbled Peninsulan. *"Apakabah,* old dickless. What's up with you? *Satu lagi rajah mati?"* Is the prince dead? He was making a poor joke. But Jhonni guessed she was not the only one to be feeling the strain. They were stranded; it was natural. The pressure of unknown bad news surrounded her. Her guilty conscience writhed. Perhaps everybody on this journey had a guilty conscience.

Ken was getting drunk, talking loudly and waving his arms. "They say there's no disease in the traditional Peninsula," he shouted. "If it's true, it's because they chuck the weaklings out. Most of our troops are *dapur* rejects, dirty little things. Not me! I'm a proper son of a whore." He grew solemn. "No, seriously, I trace my male line back right to the Rulers."

The boast struck Jhonni as funny. It sounded like Aunt Kwokmei: "Samsui are different, a pure, untainted race." *But the truth is, we're all Peninsulans,* she thought. *Everyone in this room.* She pushed her hair back from her throbbing temples, half meant to stand up and make this announcement. But a fight had broken out between Ken and Daoud. Some of the uniformed Kops waded in and dragged Ken away, yelling, his face suffused and distorted. The giant Daoud came up to Jhonni and made an apology.

"He's been drinking, miss. The bad news from Timur, it's getting him down."

"You mean Gamartha."

The giant's blind-looking eyes couldn't focus on anything.

"As you say, miss."

Jhonni looked around and discovered that the dining room had emptied. A broken stool lay on the floor; a brown bottle was rolling in a pool of liquid. "Where did everyone go?" she said, finding a gap in her memory. Guilt flooded her. "Where is everyone?" Someone took her arm and led her upstairs.

The room had yellow-washed walls and two dirty beds. The lamp showed thin trails of cobweb hanging from the ceiling. The floor looked as if it had been freshly laid and there was a smell of wet cement. Jhonni thought of a hastily buried corpse. She blessed the convention that made it natural for her clerk boy to share her room. She had hardly thought of Endang all evening, but she would have hated to sleep alone in here.

"Was I drunk? Was I shouting?"

"Not at all. You fell asleep." He hung the lamp on a hook between the beds, and laid their palm-leaf mats over the mattresses. Jhonni sat down heavily, trying to get the measure of the weight that had descended on her. When? In the town square? She didn't have the nerve for an adventure like this.

"Oh, you're doing women's work. I'm sorry."

He gave her a glance, unreadable in the lamplight.

"It doesn't matter."

"The plan" rattled through her head, the words and no more. She could not imagine carrying out all that activity: fooling the Kops, couriering drugs. She wondered if her *darah* was coming. But it shouldn't be, and the psychic thump of *darah* on its way had never been like this. If *dapur* women felt like this every month, unless they were pregnant or had just given birth, no wonder they never managed to throw the Rulers out.

"Endang, do you think we're under the protection of the *dapur*? Is Atoon's family looking after us by magic because they've declared support for Garuda? Does Derveet believe that?"

Endang sat on the other bed. There was something human between them again, some fellow feeling. But Jhonni didn't know quite what it meant. He was watching her intently.

"The royal Hanomans have acknowledged Garuda. They

will serve her cause if they can, as women can. I don't know if drug running was included in the contract." His tone was light, his eyes were bleak. "The *dapur* has never protected me."

"You don't believe—"

"Oh, I believe."

She found that thinking about the *dapur* was a mistake. It made her feel worse. "I'm sick. I'll go to bed."

There was a slow, creaking fan. Shadows crept on the walls. She was afraid she was going to start seeing things in them, but she knew the darkness would be no protection. There were certainly bugs in the mattress. Everything in this country was crawling, unhygienic, dirty. No wonder she was ill.

"What's wrong with me, Endang?"

No answer. He was sitting beside her. He'd lit the lamp again and got hold of a pitcher of water and a glass from somewhere.

"How long have we been traveling?"

"Two days."

"It seems like forever. I thought people on the Peninsula didn't get sick."

"You're not sick. You're imagining things."

She couldn't believe it was malice she saw in his eyes. "Is Ken sick too? Or was he drunk? I think we're all coming down with something . . . dirty food, bad magic . . ."

"Drink some water."

She held on to his hand around the beaker. His skin was cool. She would not have been outraged by his treachery if she hadn't liked him so much. He was a stud. He mustn't know how uneasy it made her to have him so close.

"I feel disgusting. Head, belly, aching all over. I wish I could sleep. I hate the Peninsula. It's vile, those marching trees and things, exactly the same. They're like dead people."

Endang was looking at her with such a strange expression that she was frightened. He dipped the end of his scarf in the pitcher of water, wrung it out and wiped her face.

"It doesn't make sense. It's as if . . . If your house is broken into and your valuables are gone, at least you know someone's better off. But the Rulers have *trashed* everything."

"Not many Samsui see that. Not even those who come up-country."

"Not people like Commercer Lian. Maybe I'm not a Samsui." She giggled weakly. "I come of ancient Peninsulan lineage. I was swapped at birth, like the girl in the *Blue Schoolroom* . . ."

He agreed soothingly. "You come of ancient Peninsulan lineage."

Then Jhonni was frightened again. She did not want to suffer. "I'm not. I'm a Samsui, a Samsui. The Three Springs are: One . . ." She couldn't remember another word.

"Try to sleep."

"I can't. The bad *dapur* is using evil magic on me."

"Then use your own magic, fight back. Think of somewhere you'd be happy and feel safe. Imagine yourself there."

The oil lamp flickered. Jhonni dozed and woke and dozed again. At last she woke and found the lamp had gone out. A faint, chilly light seeped through the unglazed window. Endang was asleep on his mat on the floor, his shoulder hunched away from her. The other cot, mysteriously, was up against the door. She blinked at it, vaguely remembering noises: a loud sobbing that had been startlingly like Commercer Lian's voice. Had she heard gunfire? There wasn't a sound now. True morning must still be far off. She closed her eyes, imagining herself in a safe haven: this dirty room, with Endang asleep beside her.

Breakfast was hot chili noodle soup with an egg broken into it, Jhonni's favorite. Yen the Builder came and joined her. She was traveling alone to join a contract team on a

Koperasi bridge. She was a poor woman. Her hands were gray and gnarled with ingrained dirt. She didn't make snide remarks like the Pabrikers, but made it clear that she was heartened and comforted to know that Miss Cycler was also going to work for the Kops. Jhonni, to her own shame (because Yen was a likable person), had been insulted. She had longed to explain that her position was different. The Builder said she was going to leave the group. There was a bigger town off towards the mountains where she could pick up another treader going north.

"How will you get there?"

"Walk." Yen looked around at the subdued travelers. No one was talking much this morning. Eyes were heavy, faces glum. "You won't reach your base if you stay with this lot," she said seriously. "There's been some kind of bad influence with us from Ranganar. Maybe a demon."

"You mean, one of us is a demon?"

"If you'd been up here much, you wouldn't laugh. You should come with me, Miss Cycler. I know I'm not your sort. But if you're late, you'll lose the job. The Kops are like that." She looked into Jhonni's bowl. "These Timurese are filthy. That's a bad egg, can't you smell it?"

There was nothing wrong with the soup. Jhonni sipped at the fiery chili broth, but shoved the rest aside. Everybody was going mad. Was it something they'd eaten?

The Timurese treader was ancient and peculiar. It had no baggage compartments. Everything had to be bundled up and tied onto the roof. Instead of rollers it had eight wooden spoked wheels with rubber tires, like an oxcart. Jhonni gave up hope when she saw that. She couldn't imagine wheels lasting any distance, hauled by an engine on an Occupying Army highway. Twenty-eight of them climbed on board, and arranged themselves much as before. Shortly, the treader stopped again at an outlying huddle of dwellings. A pile of local people crowded on. Of course, the Samsui protested. One of the uniformed Kops gave a bark of laughter, and the protests ceased.

Instead of glass in the windows there were slatted bamboo blinds, raised or lowered by means of a cord with a knotted end. The blind at Jhonni and Endang's seat was stuck halfway. She tugged and fiddled with it for a while, longing for more air.

Jhonni started. Endang had leaned over and taken her hand.

"Was I shouting?" It was ironic that she should get seriously ill now, for the first time in her life. "I've always wanted to be delirious. I thought it sounded exciting."

He put her hand down carefully.

"Please, Miss Cycler. Leave it alone."

Timur Kering means "The Dry East." There were no more plantations. There were stretches of small irrigated fields, divided by stretches of stony semidesert. The granite peaks north of Bu Awan, far off in the west, wrote a message on the sky. Jhonni read the black letters. Strangely enough, the words were in Inggris: BLOODY FLOWERS BRING DESPAIR. Jhonni felt her forehead with a sweaty hand. It was as cool as could be expected in this furnace-hot moving torture chamber. She heard Commercer Lian saying loudly, "I expect Yen *was* the demon!"

When they stopped for a meal break it was at another river crossing. There was a big shed with benches and tables and a dirt floor. It was gloomy inside but no cooler than the treader. On the counter stood an earthenware urn of water with a communal scoop, and a large metal dish piled with grayish fritters that seemed to be made from crushed beetles. They had left the realm of plates and glasses and decent food behind them. The local people wisely stayed outside in the sun and ate their own provisions.

The Pabrikers sat staring ahead, dead silent, with identical blank faces, like twins joined at the hip by mutual disgust. Ken, whose voice hadn't been heard today, had laid his head down on a tabletop, with his grubby sarong wrapped around it.

Jhonni was struggling with a fit of diarrhea. She found

the squalid latrine and squatted there, to void herself of a rush of stinging yellow liquid. There was no water. She wiped her bottom with a piece of cotton torn out of the lining of her jacket, and crouched over the pit ready to cry in abject misery.

Outside, the driver lay like a log of wood in the shadow of his machine. The sky was the color of mud. There was nothing green in sight. Fuel barrels stood in a stinking black puddle. Commercer Lian was looking down into the broad, dry gully where the river had been. She was eating a dirt-and-beetle fritter.

"What happened to the water?" asked Jhonni.

"Diverted to the south. Big project, good profit. You should ask your mama about it, Miss Cycler." She threw away the remains of the fritter. It joined a lava flow of garbage that must have been dumped in this desolate spot over years. "What kind of world are we leaving for our children?"

"D'you have children, Commercer Lian?"

"I have three daughters." Suddenly the woman yelled, "Shut up! Shut up!" and slapped Jhonni across the face.

When they moved on again, half the Kops had stayed behind.

During the afternoon there was a rainless electric storm. Grit and dust blew through the blinds. The passengers huddled with covered faces in an ocher gloom. Perversely, the driver started to pick up speed until they were racketing as fast as a galloping horse. Jhonni was frightened. She pulled Endang's scarf from his face.

"I think the driver's lost control!"

He couldn't hear her. He was absorbed in a sheer effort of endurance: his mouth contorted, fists screwed into his eye sockets. She staggered up the aisle, counting passengers. The treader had emptied again; there were vacant seats. She counted sixteen of the original twenty-nine among the Timurese, identified by patches of uniform or dark Samsui cotton that showed through the dust. There should be more, surely? She didn't remember the others leaving.

"Stop! Stop! Pull up until it's over!"

He was driving with his head swathed in cloth, a dark sliver left open for his eyes. He didn't acknowledge her, but he braked suddenly and stopped. Thunder boomed. The wind reached the climax of a spasm of noise. Jhonni dropped to her knees and hid her face in her arms. When she looked up the driver's seat was empty and the front door was flapping open. She climbed down and found the driver. He was squatting on his heels in the shelter of a leaf-less thornbush that was dotted with twisted little yellow gourds. The dust storm buffeted around them.

"Is it us?" she yelled, in the driver's language. "Are we doing this? Is someone on the treadie a demon?"

"You all are demons."

A cloud was coming down the road from the north. It was the color of dried blood, crossed by shivers of fiery light. As it came closer the blood color resolved into a mass of limbs: the dancing limbs, the muscle-barred bellies, the gleaming teeth and fiery eyes of an inhuman crowd. The cloud of dancers was going to engulf the treader. Jhonni meant to keep her eyes open. She couldn't; she hid her face. Insubstantial boulders rolled over her, a torrent of emotion: fear and horror and dread.

When it had passed Jhonni looked up and saw, as she had suspected, that the path of this dust storm lay along the road. It had come to meet the travelers from Ranganar, and having greeted them it had faded away. Thorny scrub and acacia trees stood calmly in the limpid heat of the declining sun.

"What was it?" she asked.

The driver uncovered his face, shook a bushel of grit out of his scarf, hawked and spat yellow. "It's not your fault, *nyonya*. They are leaving us. These events happen more and more. *Dapur* things outside the *dapur*. Bad news for everyone." He shrugged. "Maybe someone murdered the prince today."

At sunset on the third day of the journey they were traveling through the smoking remains of a burned-out forest. It was a gas field, laid down by the *dapur* in the old days. Between the shriveled hulks of great trees, standpipes stood beside the road, topped with crowns of purple flame. They should have reached the town beside Hamzah's base about fifteen hours ago, according to the schedule. But Peninsulan bus schedules were a fiction at the best of times. They weren't doing badly: that was strange, when everything was strange. Jhonni stared out of the window, smoke in her face and stinging her eyes, listening to the mutter of other people's dreams. She didn't know if she was delirious and imagining the whole thing. Or if everybody on the treader was delirious and sharing the same nightmare.

She wouldn't have minded the hallucinations. They were eerie, scary, nasty, but it was interesting to have a nightmare while you were awake. It was the awful feeling that went with them. She had never been so miserable in her life. Her soul was lying under a pile of lead weights.

BLOODY FLOWERS BRING DESPAIR.

Between twilight and full dark she opened her eyes to find the treader filled with a bluish light. She was sitting beside a rotting corpse. Across the aisle there was a Peninsulan woman, half-naked as if she were in her own house, dead and propped slackly in the seat, with a dead male child at her breast. Jhonni saw the remains of the Samsui cotton suit and knew she was looking at Commercer Lian. She got up, shoving her way past the dead thing beside her. Packed tight, stifling tight. Everyone was trying to get out. There was no light now, but a glimmer on teeth and the whites of eyes. Jhonni used her elbows, shoved and pushed. She heard voices crying. She couldn't understand a word, but she didn't need to be told that the doors were locked from the outside. The treader, with its bursting freight of bodies, was racing through the dark to some terrible destination. She knew she couldn't escape but she could not stop herself from fighting, kicking aside the weaker prisoners, the screaming children . . .

She fell down the steps at the front of the treader. Someone's foot crunched on her hand: a Koperasi boot. Jhonni yelped and rolled away. She scrabbled to her feet and ran, as bodies were running all around her, blindly into the night.

She found that she'd stopped running. She was alone and sitting on the ground. The air was moist and cool. She felt large things around her, and her head was ringing as if she'd just run it into a brick wall. She groped in her jacket for her pocket light. Her hand came out wet, smelling of lighter fuel. The cap had come off the reservoir. She put her other hand carefully in her other pocket and found her matches. She managed to strike one without setting fire to herself. She was in a living forest. The black trunks of trees stood on every side; foliage closed off the glimmer of the night sky. She saw someone moving—a long-boned, intensely familiar shadow that she could never have mistaken for anyone else's.

"Is that you, Endang?"

He stumbled. When she reached him he was doubled over, retching.

"Endang?"

He stood, wiping his mouth. Jhonni was on her fifth match by this time. "What's happening? Is this real? Builder Yen said we'd brought a demon with us from Ranganar."

"It's real," he said hoarsely. "It's me. I am the demon."

The match went out. Jhonni shook her burned fingers and dropped the box, scattering matches into the invisible wet leaf mold. She and her own Peninsulan stood in the dark. But she could see a little. There was light coming from somewhere.

"There's some kind of light over there. Let's go to it."

They groped their way onto the shore of a wide lake that lay black and white in starlight. There was a steady, quiet roaring sound. About a stone's throw off to their left a tower of moving silver fell as if out of the sky: a waterfall. Endang sat down on a length of tree trunk, Jhonni beside him.

"In Ranganar," she said, "you were keeping something back. There was something you weren't telling. Is this it? Is this what's happened? Is this really why the refugees ran away? Is everybody up-country having visions . . . going crazy?"

"No." He rubbed his hands over his face. "You didn't listen. *I am the demon.* The visions are mine."

"I don't understand."

Endang heaved a sigh. "I didn't tell you much about the first time I met Derveet. Did she?"

"No. She—she doesn't gossip."

"No. I can believe that . . . It was the year when the succession failed. I had graduated from the Peninsulan College in Sepaa. Major issues that affect the whole federation—like a change of dynasty in one of the princedoms—are decided, traditionally, in a town called Canditinggi, in the Timur hills. *Dapur* delegations come from all over the princedoms and debate behind closed doors. I was very young. I didn't see why I should be shut out because I was a man. I went to Canditinggi, calling myself an independent observer."

The waterfall made Jhonni's mind completely quiet. She didn't know what this had to do with demons, but she was happy to listen to Endang. They had talked so much, but he had told her so little.

He laughed, a smothered chuckle of pity and scorn for his pushy, ignorant young self. She knew the feeling exactly.

"It was ridiculous. I ended up staying in a terrible dive, a den of thieves. I had no idea how to look after myself, you see. I met Derveet, who was with the *aneh* delegation. But she was staying in my dive, with the bandits. She was very kind to me, she didn't laugh at the idea of a man coming to the debate, though it was *stupid*. I had no idea who she was. When I arrived up there it wouldn't have meant anything if I had known, because to me independence was dead, a day-dream. I wouldn't have given her away; I'd have felt sorry for her and curious, like a tourist, I suppose. I'd have been interested, no more.

"Well, the bandits were indiscreet; and Derveet and I meanwhile had long talks. I mean it in the best way possible when I say she is a very slick operator. She changed my mind, against my will. I found out that I had been converted to the cause, and that the patient, funny, clever outcast woman who had done me this favor was Garuda herself. Do you know what happened at that debate?"

"I should, I know . . ."

"It doesn't matter. It doesn't matter anymore. At the time, it seemed terribly important. The Assembly decided to choose the family that the Koperasi wanted them to choose . . . a cynical tribe of collaborators. In fact they'd made the right choice, the yielding choice: to save lives. But I decided to try to change the result. I went to the Gamarthan delegation, using my original family name, and told them Garuda was in town and what her choice would be. The Singhas don't like the Garudas, but Gamarthans are sticklers for precedent and for loyalty. So I thought I'd solved everything. Well, apparently someone followed me, a spy overheard me . . . The Kops had a tip-off and Derveet was nearly in bad trouble. That's why I said I betrayed her."

"I didn't take any notice," said Jhonni quickly. "I knew you were saying it to make me feel bad."

"Ah, Jhonni." She felt the soundless laugh in the dark.

"But Derveet got away and my plan seemed to work. When the public announcement was made, the family Derveet favored were Timur's new royalty. A young man called Ida Bagus Sadia was our new prince." He drew a breath. "You probably remember that name."

"Was he the one who got murdered? Was that the year of the three princes?"

"He was raped and mutilated shortly after the election, certainly on the orders of one of the other candidate families. He killed himself, and that began a round of palace murders. That's the way we Peninsulans are. We destroy ourselves . . . Sometimes still, I think it was all my fault. I was the one who interfered."

"Don't be *stupid!*"

"You're wondering when I'm going to get to the demons. You don't know what it was like in Canditinggi when the debate was ending. The world closed in on us. I think the mind needs *possibility* the way the body needs air. There were no possible moves left; we were suffocated. I didn't believe in *dapur* magic. But when the women could not see any way of saving Timur, and chose among equal evils, everyone in the town felt it. That is the *dapur* power. It isn't protection: it is knowing too much. If you had been there you would understand why, with all that they can do—seeing the future, having the power to change the world—the women *don't do anything.*"

Jhonni saw a vividly colored pageant painted on the darkness—almond-eyed princes, royal ladies in cloudy robes, the flash of a hidden dagger in a pavilion of fretted marble—the glamour that had stolen her heart. It was a dance of death.

"I can understand why you hate them."

She felt him stir, laughing without a sound. "I can't fool you, can I? Yes, I hate them. I hate myself. I am a monster. I have *dapur* powers."

The water roared and roared, softly in the dark.

"I didn't know, at Canditinggi. I started to understand what I am soon afterwards, when I was far away from the *dapur* Assembly, and the bad dreams went on. I'm a male,

I'm a stud. I have this fragment of the power by some freak, but it doesn't do me any good, it only does harm. I don't know, but I think Derveet guesses. She pities me. And the Timurese, they knew something wasn't right. I dream true, I dream while I'm awake. My dreams are nightmares, and now apparently I can share them. Can't stop."

He buried his face in his hands. "I've been glad. I've *enjoyed* watching you all suffer, all the way from Ranganar. Especially you. You didn't know what was happening to you—poor Jhonni, I enjoyed that too."

He looked up. Jhonni was frowning in concentration.

"So, what is wrong now?" she said.

"What is—?"

"You have *dapur* powers of some kind. All right. The dancers aren't supposed to have these powers, because they're failed women, but they do. So, I suppose the same can happen to a stud. You get the horrors when something bad is going to happen. Last time, it was the succession debate that was going to end in awful murders. What is it now?"

"The horrors," repeated Endang. He peered at her, trying to fathom this calm reaction. "Take your choice. The Peninsula is dying in agony, there are endless horrors. It was the dust, this time. *Dapur* powers and flowerdust don't agree, Derveet said so. The dust opened doors in me that I don't know how to shut."

"But, Endang—" Jhonni was incredulous. "Can't you tell yourself there's hope? The Rulers don't care anymore, the Koperasi are falling apart. Derveet's ideas are winning. And there's Cho—"

"No," he said. Softly, immovably. "The Peninsula was a *good* place, Jhonni. Not altogether, no more than humanly good. We had a government that had turned away, of its own free will, from most of the abuses of power. We had devoted ourselves to the perfection of human life. Health, comfort, pleasure, beauty: a minimum of suffering, real happiness for most of the people a lot of the time. No one worked too hard, no one was very rich or very poor. You're a Samsui, you can tell me everything that was wrong with our paradise. I'm a stud—do you think I don't know? But now? It's too late. Nothing can save us. Even Derveet is not as hopeful as she makes out.

"Dear God and Mother Sky," he wailed. "Everybody knows we're dying. But the *dapur* women, those who aren't as self-serving and oblivious as the rest of us, have their resignation. You others can pretend, live for the moment, shut your eyes to the reality. I can't do that. I can see clearly. And I'm a stud. I'm not strong, not wise, not resigned—"

Jhonni sniffed and wiped her eyes on her sleeve. She felt terribly clumsy, too stupid for words. She hoped she was right not to argue with his mad despair. She took his hand and squeezed it hard. "What do you want to do? Is there anything that would help? Would it help to go to Gamartha and fight? I'll come with you."

She felt him start. "You're forgetting. We're supposed to be going to central Timur to help Derveet recover that cursed flowerdust."

"I think," said Jhonni deliberately, after a pause for thought, "that Derveet doesn't rely on people. Except maybe on Cho. She knows fixed plans don't make sense in our situation. If we don't turn up she'll think of something else. She won't blame us, either. She loves people without having expectations."

Endang turned and looked intently into her face, trying to make out her expression by the bare glimmer of starlight.

"You are serious, aren't you? You would come to Gamartha with me, get up and come with me now?"

"Well, yes. If it would do any good."

"Dear Jhonni. You are a true friend."

He put his arms around her. Jhonni returned the embrace as if it were the most natural thing in the world, and she felt that the resentment between them had vanished. They would be able to look back on the *Blue Schoolroom* coffee shop with affection. There had never been a sham friendship; it had always been real.

"You are an astonishing person. I don't deserve you. Going to Gamartha is a stupid idea. But the heart that thought of it—"

"I know I'm an idiot."

"Only sometimes."

Jhonni meant to say that friendship was the most important thing in the world. It didn't matter that they were a stud and a Samsui. In the new world, when all error was swept away, there would be hundreds, thousands of pure and true friendships like this. The speech never began. Instead she took her arms from around his back, cupped his face between her palms and kissed his mouth. She knew it would be all right and it was. He kissed her back, and still everything was natural and good, tender and friendly.

Then, by a shift she could not afterwards remember, she was gripping her own Peninsulan hard by the shoulders and kissing him by no means in friendship. They were kissing openmouthed. It happened so easily, impossible to follow how. The kissing went with moving hands, hands sliding under clothes, finding the wonderful smooth warm-and-cool skin. They slipped from the log and were down on their knees in the soft earth, pressed together breast to breast, crotch to crotch.

It stopped. Somebody, both of them, pulled away.

Jhonni's blood thumped in her ears. She tugged her clothes into order. Endang dragged his hands through his cropped hair, down his cheeks. There was nothing to be heard but each other's breathing, a loud, shocked panting that drowned the waterfall.

At last he said, "Let's not talk about it."

"No," agreed Jhonni fervently. "Not ever."

The treader was standing by the side of the road. The folding rubber door at the front stood open, trailing like a broken wing. The driver's lights were burning. They were jam jars filled with oil and tied to the engine housing, with cloth wicks and reflectors beaten out of the lids of old tin cans.

Beside the treader stood a dark bulk of building. Jhonni blew out one headlight and unfastened the other, held it up to examine the place. There were Koperasi notices, something to do with waterworks. A door was standing open. Since there was no one about outside, they went to look inside. There was an office, with a treader company's sign up on the wall. Still nobody about. They climbed a rickety flight of stairs and found, in a loft above the waterworks, a huddle of silent bodies.

"In the morning," said Endang very quietly, "they won't remember. That's the way it is. When the *dapur* knowledge spills out it fills all the minds nearby: and then it evaporates. You'd forget too, except that you will still be with me." Someone stirred; Endang asked a question and got a sleepy answer. This was their stopover for the night. They looked at each other.

She hoped she'd done right. When your—male!—friend tells you, *I have* dapur *powers,* and he's obviously terribly upset, and strange things have certainly been happening . . . It had seemed like the best idea to keep calm and accept what he said.

"Still friends?" she asked humbly.

"Most certainly."

The sleepy voice said, in Peninsulan, *Put the light out, please.* They separated, to settle as best they could: Jhonni among the Samsui, Endang with the boys.

7

DERVEET WAS IMPRESSED by the scale and the sheer class of Jeeby's enterprise. Everything was new, everything was clean—from the Reception Block where the clerical Kops shuffled their paper to the recalcitrants' latrines. The white-painted dormitories stood in green lawns; the officers' quarters had a rose garden.

Discipline was lax. New arrivals soon learned how to behave. Rule one: *Don't bother us, and we won't bother you.* But Dipo was one of the nervous kind, the ones who could not believe their luck. He was always looking for little ways to ingratiate himself. When he dropped out of line on the way back from work in the vegetable garden, the guards were not disturbed.

"Hey, Dipo. Where you off to?"

"Only trying to help, sir. Want to fix up the Commander's beautiful flower trees, give them a haircut."

"Let him go," suggested the first of the two Kops. "Her. Shit, I never know what to call them, the men-women. It's his little fancy, pruning the shrubs. He's harmless."

Derveet ambled away across the slick blue-green herbage. To her right, the officers' quarters and the Command Block, standing by itself, where Jeeby Hamzah had his private office. On her left, the distant perimeter fence—which looked impressive but was as porous as a sponge. The ground between had been flattened and marked out as an airstrip. There probably wasn't an operational flying bubble left in Timur: Koperasi aircraft maintenance was a disaster. But one had to admire Jeeby's style. Derveet considered the daunting task of clawing together the resources for this place out of the fragmenting chaos of the Peninsulan Administration. No wonder the staff officers at Sepaa resented Commander Hamzah. They were plain jealous of his initiative. But then, Jeeby was no ordinary Kop.

Around the dormitories there were stands of flowering shrubs, a few months old but already riotous: scarlet hibiscus, purple bougainvillea, yellow allemanda, thrown together with a profligate and hungry eye for beauty. Most of the Koperasi officer class were Samsui male children, raised in Sepaa and educated with care, along with a few extra sons from Kop-influenced families of coastal Timur. Jeeby Hamzah was not a graduate of this system. He had come up through the ranks, seen some very hard times. Jeeby had never talked much about his childhood. Derveet applied her pruning hook gently. She was glad about the flowers. Good for you, old friend. There was no one in sight, not a Kop and not a single recalcitrant. She stepped behind a veil of bougainvillea and joined Atoon and Cho in the hollow in the middle of the bushes.

They had used Anakmati's ring to good effect and traveled to central Timur as smoothly as Derveet. Whereupon it had turned out there was no difficulty in getting in or out of the Reform Camp—along with the vegetables that sneaked off to market in the Peninsulan town next door, the highly illicit trade in smokes, the Koperasi tools and materials that walked out of the trade workshops, and the lively traffic between recalcitrant boy whores and their patrons. The only difficulty the conspirators had found was in avoiding the other users of the hollow bushes, the empty storerooms, the unguarded bolt-holes under the fence.

Atoon and Cho wore the same blue cotton shirt and pants

as Derveet, the recalcitrants' uniform. They couldn't rely on always keeping out of sight. Atoon's river of hair was a problem (one wouldn't *dare* to suggest the simple solution). He wore it bound up in a tight cap of braids under an oversized Peninsulan Army cap, which made him look very odd, conjuring an impish, bold personality nothing like the Atoon Derveet knew. He was in the process of folding a sheaf of fine dark tissue into a scarf, which he would wind around his waist under the blue shirt.

"Does the ghost walk?" whispered Derveet, grinning.

"The ghost walks. And your friend likes it less and less."

Derveet took no part in the plaguing of G. B. Hamzah. She stayed away from the officers' quarters. She was saving herself. "Well, serves him right for making off with my property. It'll be tomorrow night, I hope."

"About time," declared Atoon. "I want to see you out of here before something terrible happens."

Derveet chuckled. "I told you: we're supposed to be *healthy*. At the first sign of trouble, I tell the Kops about my bad chest and they'll have to throw me out."

"I don't think that's very funny."

"Your concern is touching. Would it extend to letting me have a smoke?"

"No. You'd go away smelling of it, find yourself locked up in the punishment cells, and ruin everything."

G. B. Hamzah had a twisted sense of humor. In the reformed acar dealer's Reform Camp, the one serious crime an inmate could commit was to be caught smoking.

"I don't think there are any punishment cells. Cho?" Derveet wheedled. "Please?"

The doll shook her head, mouth prim and eyes gleaming. "No. This is doing you good."

"Heartless despots. How quickly power corrupts. I am shocked. Well, your reign will soon be over if Gani produces the goods."

"Gani." Atoon frowned. The camp slave who had at-

tached himself to Dipo down in the south wouldn't be
shaken off. The prince could see it was necessary to humor
him, but he thought Derveet had gone too far. "Is it fair to
involve a boy in such a risky adventure, madam? Or wise?"

How quickly freedom corrupts. Is it fair to involve a
stud? she wondered. She didn't say it.

"It's a waste of time your softening Jeeby up if I can't get
near him. It's better to use Gani and move quickly, rather
than linger and risk complications. The essence of this adventure is speed. I want to be back in Ranganar."

She left the hollow and strolled on across the lawns,
going virtuously to return her billhook to the tool depository. She was arguing with herself about the extra sex:
about Endang, Atoon. It's the natural way, she thought. Society is made of mothers and children. You have one male
to be your stud and drive off the rest. That's how things go
in the animal world, generally. The majority of full adult
males are not "people" to the rest of their kind. They are
merely one danger among others for the females and their
young ones, the ones who make up the social group: normal
life. Isn't it an improvement, isn't it civilization, to make the
extra males into boys, instead of driving them off? They
couldn't *all* be studs.

She reached the complex of buildings that extended out
of the back of the Reception Block. Koperasi clerks were
hanging about in the corridors, gossiping and drinking
tea. They greeted Dipo with genuine friendliness: good
old Dipo, eager to please, always ready to giggle at your
jokes. One young man pretended to offer him-her a fag.
"Oh no, sir, no, thank you. I wouldn't want to upset the
Commander . . ." Dipo's face was a picture of helpless longing as he backed away. The youth and his friends laughed.

Inside the depository she took an empty sack from a pile
of miscellaneous rubbish. She wandered through the of-
fices, diffidently opening doors and peeping in, dragging
her sack after her and stuffing it with crumpled paper from

the clerks' wastebins (there were, alas, no fag ends). The
Red Men ignored her, until she met Sergeant Tomo.

"Hey, you, what are you doing?"

In a corrupt institution there is always somebody, buried
deep in the swamp of lies and idleness, who knows what is
going on. In Hamzah's Reform Camp the somebody was
this Sergeant Tomo: with the paunch, the receding yellow
hair, the solemn, brooding, cynical smile. His official post
was not impressive. He was a plain sergeant, in charge of
Building Maintenance. His appearance was deceptive. He
was as sloppy as the sloppiest—uniform tunic open over his
soiled and bulging undervest, ancient Peninsulan slippers
instead of the regulation laced canvas boots (he suffered
with his feet). But Tomo was the one who knew.

Dipo raised an idiot dark face, hurt and frightened at the
churlish tone. "Collect paper, sir." She straightened, explaining in Peninsulan with a few proud words of the more
impressive language.

"Our Rulers say, paper is *rsuble, rsource!* Must not waste.
Collecting for mash and roll-out again, sir!"

"Hmmph . . ." The brooding eyes looked her up and
down—a long, suspicious, sourly weighted stare that had
Dipo squirming abjectly. Most of Jeeby's staff were young
and as grateful as the inmates themselves for this haven out
of the storm. They were so innocent they took Dipo's fawn-
ing for genuine goodwill. Sergeant Tomo was not impressed. The stony eyes didn't waver. But he shrugged.

"*Bagus.* Carry on. Good lad, uh, girl."

The temporary accountant was alone in her office, standing at a high desk with her back to the door. A small abacus
with worn black wooden beads chattered under her fingers.
A Koperasi counting machine lay rejected on another table.
Dipo shuffled up behind her, dragging the sack.

"Is that you, 'Veet?"

Derveet leaned over the Samsui's shoulder.

"Lucky it was. Don't work with your back to the door."

Jhonni was too absorbed to be abashed. She lifted her face, frowning distractedly. Her coarse curly hair stood up in corkscrew spikes; her cheeks were flushed with concentration. "I can't move the furniture. It's fixed down."

"Found anything interesting?"

"Well, yes, I have. There's something funny going on. But it's not what you'd expect." Jhonni's voice expressed fascinated puzzlement: she was in her element. "There's plenty of the sort of thing you *would* expect, petty fiddling, and not well concealed. But the amount of filching, it's trivial compared with . . . there's a *lot* of work hours unaccounted for. I mean, cash. A real lot."

In Ranganar, the Samsui used Koperasi paper money freely these days. But Cyclers still made up their accounts in the old style, where the shifting value of an hour's work, of *time*, was the unit of exchange.

"It doesn't surprise me if there's a big drain on the camp's finances. I should imagine there are several tiers of payoffs involved. That's the way things are in Koperasi-land."

"No, you don't understand. There's *more* money here than there should be . . . much more."

Derveet was rooting in the wastebin. "Aha!"

"What?"

"Nothing, nothing," murmured Derveet, stowing a small object into the rolled cuff of her sleeve (the inmates' suits had no pockets).

"I'll have to do some more digging. I still can't work out exactly what's happening . . ." Jhonni pondered, her eyes dazed with calculations. A Samsui works like a machine, thought Derveet. They don't know how to stop. Jhonni had clearly forgotten that she was not *really* here to audit Jeeby's accounts.

"Don't dig too hard. Stay with the trivia. We're here for the flowerdust. Keep that in mind."

The door of the office stood open, an elementary precaution. Thumping Kop footsteps approached. Jhonni returned to her ledger. Derveet became Dipo, a subtle and curiously effective transformation. She stowed her wastepaper— eyeing the Samsui girl with some kind of secret curiosity.

"Still no clerk with you, Miss?"

"Oh." Jhonni's head bent lower; her hand shaded her cheek. "He's still not well. He's getting better."

"*Baik-lah.* Give him my regards."

Alone again, Jhonni sighed, pulled her curls, returned to the fray. Absorbed, she trod the maze of numbers, following the hidden footsteps. There was the superficial corruption. But on a larger scale, no one was siphoning money out of this project. Funds were pouring into it. Tomo's private enterprise, and the unheard-of luxuries provided for the slaves, scarcely made a dent in Hamzah's resources. So where was it going to? And where—in the Koperasi financial system that was so perilously near total collapse—was it all coming from?

Derveet fell in with a gaggle of inmates who'd finished a literacy class. Nothing much happened in these classes—to Derveet's obscure relief. If the Kops had actually been teaching slaves to read and write, that would have been a little *too* bizarre. There were plenty of *aneh* among the healthy recalcitrants, a few as dark-skinned and as gangling tall as Dipo. For once Derveet blended into the crowd.

Gani was making up to the class teacher, a Koperasi lieutenant with a pink face and a shock of pale brown curls. The boy's plucked-chicken physique had filled out already. No longer ageless, he had become young and almost pretty, with a vivacious pair of black eyes. He winked lewdly at Dipo while the teacher's attention was briefly with another student. "Tonight!" he hissed. "You see! At last, my beauty is recognized!"

Dipo proceeded at old-lag speed over to the workshops and dumped the sack of paper. With the connivance of the lazy Kop in charge, she carried away a smoldering chip of

tinder from the small forge furnace. She retired to a se-
cluded spot and lit the crumpled butt of a tobacco cigarette.

Ah, bliss. Qualified bliss. She survived a burst of coughing. She wondered if her wild guess about developments
between Miss Cycler and her Peninsulan boy was correct.
Atoon would be shocked . . . or maybe not. Within the walls
of Jagdana palace, variations of human behavior were accepted—as long as decorum was observed.

The isolation of Ranganar bred nightmares. It was a relief
to find the world north of the causeway exactly as she had
left it at the new year: the same level of chaos, no worse, no
better. She had traveled here in a windowless box. But the
others reported no changes—though Jhonni was reticent
about the details of her journey. Whatever was happening
in Gamartha, it hadn't spread. Meanwhile, the foundering
Peninsulan Administration struggled in vain to control the
schemes of breakaway operators like Jeeby.

Ironically, the apathy and malice of the slave keepers
might have succeeded where Sepaa failed—if it weren't for
the slaves themselves. They had heard, in the mysterious
way that these things got about, of the heaven up in Timur.
They schemed and plotted and fought to get here. And
whatever Jeeby was up to, one had to give him credit for the
state of his inmates. Before they got here their health had
been no more, maybe, than a certain toughness of spirit. It
was genuine now. It was extraordinary to see what mere
food and rest could do for human beings who had been re-
duced to mindless, worn-out machines.

Derveet stubbed the last foul scrap of cigarette. She had
heard nothing more of the hospital. Gani was the only
source of that rumor. She could imagine various more or
less sinister purposes behind this place. The most benign
was that the healthy recalcitrants were destined to form a
loyal private army.

She would find out. She would talk to Jeeby when the
theatrical element had achieved its effect. She thought of

Sergeant Tomo, the shark in this quiet water. The command structure of the camp was transparent. Most of the officers were ciphers. Everybody knew that Tomo answered only to the Commander, and possibly—Derveet thought uneasily—reported to a higher authority, over Jeeby's head. He was the one to watch. But so far, she was sure, he suspected Dipo only of being insincere in his groveling.

The dormitories had white walls, glass windows, rows of iron cots. They were lit by flares of piped gas, one at either end. After the rice meal—their second rice meal of the day—the night guard sat chatting and joking with his particular cronies. Finally he turned out the gas and retired to his screened cubbyhole. Most of the slaves tugged their mattresses onto the floor, as they did every night. They didn't like sleeping above the ground. Many slept on the floor itself, finding the yielding surface of the stuffed pallets creepy and strange.

Derveet and Gani had claimed places side by side. There was plenty of choice, none of the dormitories were crowded. Gani came sneaking in about an hour after "lock-up." Derveet pretended to be asleep. She could tell from the sound of his breathing that the news was good. She wanted him to have the pleasure of giving her a surprise. The boy crouched over her. Something small and hard dropped onto her bare throat. Derveet sat up, palming the small object. His pride and joy were palpable in the dark.

"How did you do it?"

"Easy-easy. Naturally, it's sad and not romantic but we cannot undress." He giggled. "He keeps the keys fastened in his pocket. They come out of the pocket somehow, when I undo his belt. When he looked, the importantmost key was gone! I said, I think I feel something hard and lumpy when I take him in my mouth. But what do I know? Maybe Koperasi sometimes have lumps. Oh, the key is gone! What can I do? I must have swallowed it! Can't get it back, not straightaway." He snorted delightedly. "So, got another date with my teacher tomorrow. In not a very romantic spot!"

Derveet chuckled, in dutiful admiration of the boy's sleight of hand. The key felt strange. She delved under her mattress. She struck a chip of light, and peered at it. On her palm lay something like a rectangular sliver of oil. The material had a slick, fluid feel and a prismatic sheen. It moved like a film of water, as if on the edge of losing its rigid shape.

"This is the key to the Command Block?"

Gani sobered at her tone. "It's funny, isn't it? Not a Peninsulan thing. Something wrong?"

He had attached himself to her in the rice field. She did not know who he thought she was: maybe the famous Anakmati, without his eye patch. Maybe he put no name to this person who had walked into slavery but was not helpless. She had the glamour of purpose. Gani wanted some of that glamour, he asked for nothing more. How could she deny him? How could she resist using him?

"No. You did a good job. Go to sleep."

Cho came into the dormitory in the middle of the night, as she had done before. She would stay for a few hours. They would not make love or talk much. But time snatched together secretly like this, in the midst of an adventure, was very sweet. This time when she came Derveet was sitting, arms wrapped around her knees, like a dark rock in the soft waves of sleeping bodies. "What is it?" breathed Cho, kneeling at her side.

"This is the key to Jeeby's office." She didn't strike a light. Cho didn't need one.

"Ooh," whispered the doll, drawing back.

"Looks like a Rulers' thing to me," said Derveet softly.

"Yes."

The key was an artifact that had no right to be in central Timur. It had no right to be the key of Jeeby's private office, if Jeeby was what he ought to be: an emergent warlord, rising from the wreckage of the Occupying Army.

Neither of them spoke again. Derveet lay down. The doll, after a tiny hesitation, nestled against her side. Reassurance flowed from her. *Everything's going to be all right. Everything you do will turn out well.*

But Cho whispered unhappily, "Are you angry with me?"

"Angry? Why should you think that?"

"Because . . . the Rulers are like the people who made me."

"No! It's Jeeby who has the explaining to do. Go to sleep."

But Derveet lay awake for a long time, hand closed on the thing that Gani had stolen, staring into the dark. And Cho knew it.

The town was called Isolir: a place of no importance, far from the busy world. It was surrounded by hills and forest. The hills to the south were bandit country. The forest was haunted by the *orang hutan,* secretive and dangerous wild tribals. The Koperasi road was an aberration. It had arrived as part of some short-lived scheme for opening up central Timur. It gave up entirely a few *batu* north of town, fading into a brush-grown healing scar in the forest. Treaders didn't often come this way. Isolir was a Peninsulan town, a river town: but the river was a sleepy and quiet thoroughfare. Even the inevitable Occupying Army Office had succumbed to Isolir's atmosphere. The Kops didn't assert themselves. There was nothing for them to do. No one in Isolir was interested in politics. The curfew imposed over the whole Peninsula for the state of emergency was immaterial. There was no one on the streets here after sunset anyway.

The local Kops resented Hamzah's Reform Camp. Isolir itself seemed to accept the new installation with resignation. The traditional buildings on that side of town faced away from their brash neighbor, bowed low under their massively thatched roofs. There was no trouble between the townsfolk and the camp staff or the inmates. The traffic through that permeable fence was absorbed without fuss.

Jhonni, coming home from work, paused on the second-story veranda of Isolir's Grand Hotel. The day was roasting, but the streets below managed to look serene. The great cowled dark roofs promised cool shelter, and there was greenery everywhere: trees lining the streets, rising from hidden courtyards. The brown river lapped slowly between carved stone walls, where it passed through the park that had belonged to Isolir's noble family. They were gone now, vanished without a trace. It had happened to a lot of prominent families of Timur, Endang said. Sometimes the Koperasi helped them along to extinction. Sometimes they managed it themselves: murder, suicide, a whole generation of failed girls. Or simply death. People simply lay down and died.

Two of the hotel's ancient boy servants came by. As they passed they dropped into their crablike stoop without slackening their pace. Their heads must not be higher than a woman's.

"Selamat sore, bu Djonni."

It gave her a ridiculous kick to be called "mother," the traditional greeting for any woman over puberty.

In their room Endang was lying as she'd left him, in the half-dark. Shutters of split bamboo covered the unglazed windows, shifting in the breeze of late afternoon. His body seemed to melt into the palm-leaf mat. On the washstand there was an earthenware water cooler and a scoop. The pitcher was simple and shapely. The ladle had a silver handle worked into the form of a serpent (Naga of Timur) curled around a tree. The cover over the mouth of the pitcher was a square of creamy lace, weighted with garnet beads. Jhonni handled these beautiful things reverently, scooping water into a clean glass.

"Do you feel any better?"

"Much the same." His listlessness was frightening. He would not have stirred all day, except to creep along to the *mandi*, the washroom, to piss. She brought the glass of water and knelt beside him. He kept insisting that there was nothing physically wrong, that the spasm would pass. By his own reasoning, that didn't make sense. Jhonni was afraid that if she couldn't shake his despair he would die of it, with no other cause.

They hadn't mentioned what had happened in the forest since that night. But Jhonni had resolved to be bold today.

"You are thinking about the way we behaved, aren't you? That's part of it. I mean, you're thinking about that time." She couldn't bring herself to be more specific. "It's preying on your mind." She took a greater risk. She'd been rehearsing this assault on the way back from the camp, hoping to raise him from his despondency.

"It didn't feel wrong to me. I mean, when we kissed each other. What I want to say is, you can't help what you feel. We didn't *do* anything. And we won't. We can live chastely. It'll be as if nothing is wrong with us."

Endang laughed. Mere kissing, as he remembered, was not what their two bodies had been after—grappling frantically in the heart of the nightmare. What exactly did they want to do to each other, those bodies? That was more difficult to answer.

"If you like," she continued—she didn't know what the laugh meant—"we need never see each other again after we get back to Ranganar. But I hope you don't feel like that—"

The flowerdust had lost its wicked excitement. Jhonni couldn't understand why she'd been so frightened about becoming a drug runner. Carrying the stuff home would be a chore. As soon as she left the Reform Camp in the afternoon, her part in Derveet's plans became no more than a nagging distraction. Endang was all that mattered. She caught herself thinking, *This must be what they call being in love,* and was horrified.

He didn't answer, but he didn't move away.

"What's happening now?"

She couldn't take Endang to the camp. He was in the state that he'd been when she first met him. Except that he wasn't bitter and touchy, and he wasn't kept upright by the will to deceive. He'd given up. He was too ill to move.

They had woken, in the loft above the waterworks in the burned forest, to find that the nightmare was over. The other travelers washed and brushed their hair and changed into clean clothes, not looking at each other, not mentioning anything strange. Jhonni was too exhausted to think of sprucing herself up. And they'd traveled on and come quietly to Isolir. By the time Jhonni and Endang got down, they were the only Ranganar passengers. They hadn't spoken of the shared nightmare since. It was the same as that embrace in the forest. It hadn't happened!

On the day they arrived Jhonni went to Isolir's market and spotted the two forest tribals, sitting patiently behind a mat on which was spread a collection of ugly wooden objects. Obeying a sign from the smaller of the pair, she had found herself following Cho into the narrow alleys of the business part of the town. Cho pointed out the narrow, shabby-looking entrance of a general store. She handed Jhonni a shopping list and a ring. Jhonni was nonplussed. She knew that she was supposed to run errands, but she couldn't see herself dealing directly with a Peninsulan merchant.

"Aren't you coming with me?"

The doll-who-was-a-person shook her head with a grave smile. "As you know, I cannot go in there."

She was a machine. She was not welcome in the *dapur*.

A lady's robe. A musical instrument, a long, thin rubber tube. The list of items was peculiar. Jhonni presented it to the merchant's speaking boy in a dark upstairs room that was cluttered with piled boxes, baskets, jars. The premises were unimpressive. But Jhonni was a Cycler and a Samsui.

She knew from something indefinable in the manner of the robed lady that this merchant Fauziah was a very substantial person. Fauziah barely glanced at the ring. Nobody mentioned any names. Jhonni handed over a packed shoulder basket to the tribal girl, and walked away, carrying with her a strangely touching picture. She saw the scene in her mind's eye now: the people of Isolir passing by. Cho sitting humbly on the five-foot way with her head bowed. Shut out, waiting to be wanted again.

"Everything's fine," she told Endang. "I think."

He stared over her shoulder. She wondered what he was seeing. Her skin crept. She prayed not to see anything herself.

"You've *got* to let me tell Derveet."

"It felt," he said distinctly, "like the only right thing left in the world." He turned, deliberately looked her in the face . . . asking, waiting for her to decide.

Jhonni almost burst into tears. She hugged him instead. They rocked together, Jhonni whimpering, *We can still be friends* . . . They were safe from unnatural lust at present. The hug was just a hug. "We can be friends!" she insisted, feeling that this was all she needed for a lifetime of happiness. A soft thump came from the direction of the windows. Jhonni turned quickly, to see a small brown cat trot across the floor. It used a forepaw to hook open the door, paused to rake the two humans with a blue gaze of clinical, cruel interest, and was gone.

Jhonni drew in her breath sharply.

"I think that was Cho's cat! How did it get here?"

Endang twisted out of the hug and collapsed again, an arm flung over his face. It was difficult not to feel they'd been caught doing something shameful. "Why not?" His voice was muffled by his sleeve. "It follows her everywhere. Who knows how?"

Everyone who met her loved the doll-who-was-a-person. But Jhonni, like Derveet, regarded Divine Endurance as a creature of ill omen. If the cat was meant to be a toy . . . Well, the ancient-times people had funny ideas. The thought of a child being left alone with it was alarming. "It'll tell," she muttered bitterly.

Endang raised himself on one elbow.

"It doesn't matter. Cho knows."

"Knows about—us! How?" Jhonni was blushing furiously.

"In a way she knows. At the camp in Ranganar, before I met you, I told her what kind of person I am, and that I was so alone. She said she'd try to help me." He looked at Jhonni with a faint smile. "Perhaps she did."

Jhonni sat back on her heels. So he had had unnatural feelings before. This she had not suspected. The revelation didn't frighten her. Whatever kind of person Endang was, Jhonni was one too. She looked down at her hands, squeezed into tight, square fists against dark blue cotton. Figures from the Reform Camp accounts danced in front of her eyes. She hoped Derveet knew that Divine Endurance was about. Her presence seemed sinister, though what could a cat do? It couldn't tell anyone. Could it?

Jhonni was a revolutionary. She was *not* going to forget that.

"Listen," she said. "Did you hear me? *We have to tell Derveet.* You got sick when the Timur succession debate went sour, before the Year of the Three Princes. If you're right—"she knew better than to argue—"and you have *dapur* powers, you aren't lying there half-dead because of the . . . the general situation. It's a warning. And we have to take notice!"

"It's the dust. I shouldn't have touched it."

"All right, it's the dust. But suppose there's more? Something to do with the flowerdust? At the camp, when we first met, you told me that Derveet was in terrible danger. You were playing a trick on me; the danger was from *you*. But suppose you were telling the truth and didn't know it?

What if there's some terrible trap? And you and I have been warned and do nothing?"

Endang sat up. He gazed at Jhonni, frowning. She quailed, afraid he was going to hate her. How crass and commonplace her reasoning must sound. How could she ask him to tell Derveet and—worse!—Atoon that he was a freak, a kind of failed woman in reverse, a woman-man. How could she ask him to tell that?

"You may be right," he said at last. "You may be right." Suddenly there was more life in his face, more fight in his eyes, than Jhonni had seen there for days. "What shall we do?"

She jumped up. "Don't move!" she cried. "I'm going down to the dining room to get us some food. Noodle soup! Noodle soup, that's what we need. Plenty of chili! I can't think on a cold stomach!"

Divine Endurance would never forgive the human race for creating her and then deserting her—to descend into this pit of barbarity where they didn't remember anything that they had been. In her opinion, Cho was much too soft on the miserable wretches. But Cho's tenderness had a hidden sting that she herself didn't understand. Divine Endurance had stopped reproaching the child for siding with the humans. All would be well. Those other humans, out at sea, understood and accepted what it meant to possess an angel doll. The remnant on land would learn.

The cat was pleased with the way this escapade was going. She had been annoyed, since she found out what the flowerdust meant, at the obstinate way Derveet stayed put in Ranganar. She did not want the outcast woman to miss anything of the treat in store.

Outside the Grand Hotel, Divine Endurance yawned, stretched, and sought out the black shade under the rim of the five-foot way. The Samsui girl had worried her for a moment. It would have been irritating if Derveet had been put on her guard at the last moment, if the surprise had been spoiled. But you could trust humans to place immediate self-interest first. Noodle soup! Really, it would have been pitiful. If one was given to pity.

8

IN THE EARLY morning, G. B. Hamzah took a stroll. In the middle of the office complex there was a pleasant courtyard, where fountains spurted in a wide, shallow pool. It was part of the camp's elaborate cooling system. The water shot up, hissing and misting in the air, and fell back frothing against the cool blue tiles. Hamzah thought of the volume of water in the system, in the pumps that ran the sprinklers for the gardens and the lawns. What wanton extravagance in water-hungry Timur! He didn't begrudge a drop of it. Hamzah had his profit. He was happy for the recalcitrants—yes, and the Kop staff too—to have the benefit of the surplus.

The Commander was not tall for a Koperasi, but he carried himself well. His uniform was immaculate. He wore his springy red-brown hair cut short and brushed back. His pallor was not the kind that reddens in the sun. It had turned a permanent, dusky sallow like fine doeskin. It was an ageless face, unlined, unworn: the face of a person who keeps his anxieties well buried, who controls—if he feels them—the symptoms of strong emotion. The eyes were deep-set under a jutting, un-Peninsulan brow. It was hard to tell their color or read their expression.

A bird called, in the water-murmuring silence: a strangely dark and forest-scented sound among the white walls, in broad daylight. Three hollow notes on a descending scale, repeated . . .

G. B. Hamzah looked up sharply. The uncommunicative features suddenly acquired emotion. It was as startling a change as if the Commander had started shouting in panic, there alone by the pool.

. . . plonk, plonk, plonk . . .

The absurdly doleful noise repeated, repeated.

"Who's there?" shouted Hamzah. "Show yourself, damn you!"

A group of Reform Camp staff passed by the entrance to the courtyard on their way from breakfast. Four of the five managed to contain their astonishment and keep their eyes front. A face turned. Commander Hamzah did not fraternize with his men. He was a distant, benevolent figurehead, rarely seen at this end of the camp. He glared at the tactless one, who blushed and hurried on.

. . . plonk, plonk, plonk . . .

"I don't believe in ghosts," snapped Hamzah.

Movement caught his eye, beguiling, compelling. He stared down a paved open path between the buildings. A figure moved across the lawn at the end: a lady, veiled. Her robe floated behind her. She drifted, an ethereal shadow, to and fro over the grass. Hamzah swallowed hard. His head moved furtively, the unseen eyes hunting about. At any moment someone might pass. Someone other than himself might see that thing. This seemed to be his fear.

"Nothing there!" he yelled. "There's nothing, ignore it!"

No one answered. The Commander's hands were balled into fists, working at his sides. He must have realized that nobody who overheard this performance would be likely to answer. If rumors of the Commander's breakdown had already started, he would be the last to hear them. He set back his shoulders, muttered for the imagined audience. "Nothing there. A trick of the light. I'm not sleeping well . . . No, that is, I'm sleeping well. I have certain dreams. There's nothing wrong with me."

Hamzah straightened his tunic, ran a hand through his shock of hair, recovered himself.

. . . plonk, plonk, plonk . . .

"It's a kind of pigeon," a voice whispered in his ear. There was no one near, not a living soul. "It sits in the woods endlessly saying plonk, plonk, plonk, on a descending scale. It sounds so miserable they call it the dead baby bird: Anakmati."

"Anakmati!"

G. B. Hamzah swallowed the end of his own mad shriek. He stared around, his face distorted in panic. But in fact the cry had not been very loud, more of a sob than a scream. The pool courtyard stayed quiet; nobody came running. The Commander pressed his hands to the front of his tunic, dragged them downwards: maybe wiping sweat from his palms. He repeated the gesture, as if unconsciously. *"Anakmati . . . ?"*

"Sssh," murmured the dark, caressing voice. "Not so loud. I'm not far away. What do you want, Jeeby old pal?"

"I don't want anything! Go away!"

"But you called me, Jeeby. Clear as if you'd written a letter and sent it by express courier. Did you think I wouldn't come? Did you think I'd let you down?"

"You'd better get out of here. Go away!"

"And the ghost, too? I'm sure you want to get rid of the ghost. A place like this—bold, experimental—can't afford to have a ghost floating around. It looks bad. People will talk."

"All right." G. B. Hamzah licked dry lips. His hollowed, invisible eyes searched the courtyard furiously. Nothing stirred. "I understand. You win. Fine, no worries. We'll talk it over."

"Good. We'll meet in your office. At twilight. Be there."

Hamzah recovered. He returned to the Command Block without attending breakfast. The Commander often made an appearance in the clerks' mess, but he never ate there. He did not eat with his officers, either, preferring to be served

in his quarters. He was a secretive character. His staff, officers and men, had no objection to his odd ways, so long as
their easy life continued.

Entering his outer office, Hamzah tried the inner door
with a strangely fearful air. He peered inside, swiftly pock-
eting his command key, shut the door again quickly, stood
with his back to it, letting out a long, sighing breath.

"Nobody but you or I ever comes in here. Ever."

His secretary followed this performance uneasily.

"Something wrong, sir?"

The secretary was a promising young officer. He knew, as
no one else in this camp, the status and value of G. B. Hamzah's project. He didn't have to be told; he acted with perfect discretion. He had volunteered without prompting to
take one of the literacy classes, giving an example to the others. He was an ally in the gently-gently regime, a bulwark
against the awkward curiosity of Sepaa. A bulwark against
Sergeant Tomo, in some cases. So what was so painful
about the look in the secretary's eye, as his chief recoiled
from a shadow in an empty room? Why did Hamzah stare
with such hatred?

"What's up with the lights?" snarled Hamzah.

It was broad daylight. "Sorry, sir. Gas supply's a bit
crook."

"Well, fix it. Is something *wrong*, Dick?" The Commander's emphasis was sarcastic. His secretary flushed
guiltily. "Nothing, absolutely nothing. Sir."

The office was empty when Hamzah finally dared to
enter it.

Nobody, least of all his trusted secretary, would dream of
commenting on the Commander's growing eccentricities.
Nobody would gossip. G. B. Hamzah, though forbidding
and distant even among fellow officers, had a way of inspir-
ing loyalty. Privately, the secretary admitted to himself that
things were getting worse, and decided to postpone a certain confession. He hoped it wouldn't be needed, by tomorrow.

* * *

In a space trodden out behind a mass of shrubbery, up against a wall, the Commander's tormentors discussed their campaign. The outer layer of the wall had been dismantled—an easy task. The mortar was short of some vital ingredient and was crumbling into dust. A pile of gray bricks lay on the leafy ground. Metal water pipes nestled in the hollow space revealed behind.

Derveet fingered the stops on a wooden tube with a funnel mouth, a forest monkey-lure. The prince was folding the filmy *dapur* robe. Gani kept watch, peering through leaves at the quiet lawns. Hungry for the entrancing company of the adventurers, he couldn't be shut out of their activities without violence.

Atoon was frowning. "Is this the way you thought your former partner would respond to your joke, 'Veet?"

"No. I expected Jeeby to be very annoyed, and finally reasonable."

"Was Hamzah notably superstitious when you knew the person? Afraid of ghosts, easily terrified?"

Derveet shrugged. "All criminals are superstitious. I am horribly afflicted in that way myself. I would have said Jeeby was far more hard-headed than me." The Command key was in the rolled waistband of her inmate's pajamas. She had not shown it to Atoon. "But people change."

"Of course he's crazy," jabbered Gani, ecstatic with excitement. "Everyone knows it. He was crazy before we came. The Kops know it, everyone knows it, but why would they complain? This is a 'cushy number.' "

"I wonder if it's safe to keep that appointment?"

Derveet was thinking of Gani and his teacher. This morning, early, before they met to plague Hamzah, she had seen them outside the slaves' latrines. At least the little Peninsulan was outside, jumping up and down and shivering in the cool morning air, calling advice and encouragement to his anxious lover. The nightsoil was cleaned out daily to be spread on the vegetable gardens. Gani's tough gut was

proving retentive. Derveet had little sympathy with the
Kop. But there was something ominous about the boy's relish and glee. She knelt, listening to the placid sounds of the
camp getting up. The Command key—maybe she imagined
this—was unnaturally cold against her skin, through the
thin cotton.

"I want to get the business over with," she said. She
frowned. "This camp . . . It makes me think of my mother.
I've always imagined something sordid in the way of pris-
ons . . . a dank cell for bad deeds. I think that might be
wrong. I begin to think she must have been held in a place
like this. Clean, tidy . . . quiet."

Atoon controlled his surprise. Derveet did not talk about
the martyred Garuda heroine. If you were brash enough to
speak of Merpati, she had nothing to say. After all, she said,
she had never met the lady, not directly. He noticed that
Cho, who was very quiet this morning, had moved close to
Derveet. The doll's sweet face was unhappy. Atoon wanted
to ask what was wrong. But the presence of the boy made
that impossible.

"We will kill him tonight!" cried Gani, breaking an awkward silence. "We will kill the Red Pig!"

Derveet looked pained. "Nobody is going to be killed,
Gani. Commander Hamzah is my friend. We are playing a
joke on him, in return for a joke he played on me. Tonight
everything will be sorted out, and we'll all be laughing."

Gani could not control these bursts of excitement. He
cringed, big-eyed, from his wonderful friend's displeasure.
"Don't be angry, please. But he *is* a pig . . . Pigs who pretend
to do us favors are the worst."

Derveet laughed. "You could be right. *Baik*, let's have
pity on Gani's sweetheart and finish things tonight. But not
you, Gani. You must stay away. I don't want the Commander to be upset with you after we're gone. Really,
you've done enough."

It hadn't occurred to Atoon that the boy would expect

to come to the confrontation. His brows lifted. "Certainly not . . . a boy!"

Gani burst into tears.

Derveet and Atoon looked at him in consternation. Atoon put a soothing arm around his meager shoulders. "But, Gani—" In the traditional Peninsula a boy was a child for life. Most people regarded their bodies—not unkindly—as public property, to be cuddled, stroked, petted at will.

Gani flinched away. "Don't touch me! I am not a boy!"

"Not a boy?" Atoon managed not to laugh.

Gani drew himself up. He looked passionately at Derveet. "Garuda says: I am a Peninsulan!"

There was a shocked silence.

The boy looked from Atoon to Derveet. His own face fell, lost its glow, lost all animation. "You did not believe that I knew you." His mouth turned down, tears still glistening on his cheeks; he looked more than ever like a child. But he kept his dignity. "I *did* know you. We know about you, in the farm camp. We talk, in our houses, about Garuda who cares about slaves, about extra men, about failed women. We cannot help but like important people. But if any of us could, we always say we would do *anything.* I have worked for you." His shoulders dropped, he turned away. "But you don't want me. *Bagus,* I go."

She knew that he could not be trusted. She had dealt often with friends like Gani, in her career as Anakmati: starved children whose hunger to be important was satisfied by the bandit's glamour—and might equally lead them at the next moment to turn the famous bandit over to the Kops. But Gani had seen the stuff of dreams walk down and take a place beside him, planting rice under the whip of the Koperasi. He had answered the call he thought he heard. She had been waiting for answers, for emissaries of the different nations.

She avoided Atoon's eyes. "He's right," she said. "I owe him. If he wants to be with us, Gani comes too. Now"—

turning to the boy—"you'd better get off to your literacy class."

Atoon and Cho stayed in hiding. The two genuine inmates slipped from the bushes and separated: Gani to the classrooms, Derveet to the vegetable plots. As she worked, hoeing rows of brinjal vine, Derveet suddenly found a small figure with dust-pale hair beside her. They weeded companionably for a while. How comforting it was to work under the sun.

"I told her," said Cho at last.

This was unusual. If Cho had something to do, she did it, she didn't see any need to inform you of the fact. Derveet raised her eyebrows. The doll continued uneasily. "Jhonni says we may be in terrible danger. She says Endang says so."

"Endang, eh? Mmm. That's interesting."

They went to sit out of the sun to rest, under a massive acacia tree that had been here before the new camp was laid out. Derveet flexed her hands. Her first blisters had healed; she was nurturing a second generation.

"I like gardening. I've never tried it before." She leaned back. "Maybe, when all this is over and the Samsui are in charge—"

"The Samsui?"

"Oh yes, don't you think so? Who else could keep us in order? I will *greatly* enjoy presiding over Miss Butcher Handai's royal coronation—or whatever they decide to call it—as Madam President of the United States. Heheheh."

"You will tell her that, I suppose." Cho sighed. It was difficult keeping the peace between the Samsui resistance leader and Derveet, who could rarely resist a temptation to tease the earnest radical.

"I probably will. Poor Handai. But I was thinking, after the ceremonies maybe they will let me be a gardener, weeding brinjals for the common good. I should like that."

The healthy recalcitrants worked fairly willingly, for the

pleasure of it. The Kops sat in the shade and smoked. The camp guards were plain troopers, divided by very little from their charges. They made shy overtures of friendship. Some of them took a hand at the digging and the weeding, and their colleagues looked more envious than scandalized. Derveet watched them, the Command Block key burning cold against her side.

The Reform Camp was a magician's act of misdirection. The benign collapse of enmity in here was as insubstantial as Butcher Handai's coronation. What lay behind the illusion? Terrible danger. She could believe it. Yes, but what kind?

Sergeant Tomo came to visit the accountant from Ranganar.

"Thought I'd see how you're getting on, miss. Anything I can do for you?"

Jhonni felt she must be staring like a frightened rabbit at the Building Maintenance sergeant. Anything he could do? Oh yes, please. A few sacks of cement and two *kati* of brass nails . . . Derveet had warned her that Sergeant Tomo was the real power in the camp. It was an unnecessary warning: Jhonni had the figures.

She was a civilian, hired and sent here by the Sepaa staff office: *those buggers at Sep,* as they were known here. Of course the clerks in the office were uneasy. She was from Sepaa, and none of them had ever worked with a woman before. Though she was a Samsui they were nervous. But she was sure no one suspected why she was really here. Sergeant Tomo was surely only afraid of a hostile audit. He didn't know she was a drug runner waiting to make a pickup.

"Oh, thank you," she gasped. "No, thank you."

"When d'you expect to finish today? I wouldn't ask but the Commander's got a headache, wants some peace. No working late." Tomo stared at the front of Jhonni's jacket. "I hope you'll finish your job soon. Having you here, it's sending him potty. He doesn't like women. He could make trouble for you. It's just a warning."

Jhonni could feel her eyes swelling to the size of saucers. Her bag, the capacious document case she carried in and out every day—to get them used to the idea—was under Tomo's hand. It was usually empty. Today it wasn't. The sergeant idly turned, opened the flap and poked at the ledgers inside.

"Taking work home?"

Sweat broke out all over her. It could have been the dust! He didn't wait for her answer. He closed the case.

"I'm not afraid of you," he said, with a heavy sneer. "Samsui. I'm not afraid of those buggers at Sep. You can't touch us. We've got friends. You're wasting your time."

He left. Jhonni almost wept in relief.

At twilight the boy Gani, Cho, Derveet, and Atoon slipped out of an unused storeroom behind the officers' mess and crossed an empty stretch of grass to the entrance of the Command Block. Only the Commander and his secretary had keys to this small building, standing on its own, but there were usually guards on duty. No one was about. The Commander had a headache. He had canceled the guard; he wanted complete quiet and privacy. Nobody argued with Hamzah, especially not in his present mood.

The key slipped into a notched slot, changing shape like liquid. The door shifted; the oily sliver ejected itself. Atoon stared, but said nothing. Neither did Derveet. The Command Block was a single-story cube. Four doors lined a passageway that ended at the far wall. There were no windows. The shadows were deep. Gani was suddenly brought up short by a grip on his shoulders from behind. Strong hands turned him around. He had never seen Dipo so serious.

"Gani, listen to me. You will stay in the outer office. When Commander Hamzah comes, you must hide so he doesn't see you. If anybody else comes to the block, knock on the door to warn us, then hide again. Don't come in. You mustn't come into the Commander's office, no matter what you hear. Do you understand?"

"I understand." Gani's black eyes burned in the gloom. "You can trust me!"

Derveet nodded encouragingly, met Atoon's eyes with resignation. Sentiment aside, there'd been no option but to bring Gani with them. Fired up as he was, the boy was safer here than on the loose. It would be absurd to expect him not to talk. They'd have to take him with them when they left, she thought—a complication they didn't need on the journey south. There are always complications. The Peninsula breeds them out of the air.

It was the hour for new arrivals. The perimeter gates remained closed; the gravel forecourt in front of Reception was combed and empty. Hamzah stood looking through the mesh of the gates. The guards on duty knew better than to speak to him or notice him in any way. The Commander was in a very funny mood these days.

He turned to one of the men. "Soon," he said. "Soon, very soon." He laughed like a magpie.

The outer office was empty, dim, hot, and silent. Hamzah barely noticed a scrabbling from behind the tall filing cabinets. He unlocked the inner door, walked into his own room and closed it behind him. The windows were shuttered. The *dapur* lady was sitting behind his desk. She was robed and veiled: a woman shape cut out of darkness. Hamzah stood perfectly still. Without taking his eyes from the lady he groped at his belt, where he wore the regulation officer's weapon, a *stop* pistol from out at sea, a very different thing from the Kops' simple firearms. The *stop* fell to the floor. One must not bear a weapon into the *dapur*.

"Jeeby?"

The Commander started. He turned slowly, like somebody waking from a dream. His head was thrown a little
back. The red-brown eyes, exactly the same color as his hair,
seemed to have retreated under the heavy brows. Jeeby was
never good-looking, but this face was misshapen: clay, a
death mask. Gradually he appeared to focus on what was in
front of him: two inmates in their blue pajama suits beside a
stack of open drawers—turning over Commander Hamzah's most private papers.

"Anakmati," he said. But he was distracted. He twisted
around: too late, the robed figure had vanished.

"Where did she go? The *dapur* lady. Did you see her?"

Derveet considered her old friend warily. "She's over
there, Jeeby." She gestured with her sheaf of paper to where
Atoon was standing, the veil pushed back . . . Perhaps that
was a mistake. With his braids hidden by the gloom
Atoon's face was sexless, the dark robe invisible in shadow.
A golden disembodied face, looking, frankly, extremely
disapproving, hung in the gloom, staring silently at the
Commander.

"Jeeby." Derveet tried to catch Hamzah's attention.
"What *is* all this? Come on, confess. What trouble are you
in, old pal?"

"She's dead," said Hamzah, looking straight at Atoon.
"All dead. They don't die, but others will."

Derveet stepped over the pistol. "It was a joke, Jeeby.
Can't you take a joke?"

"Anakmati," said G. B. Hamzah, with a thick, unwilling
tongue. "Did you see—?" He shook his head. "No, you
didn't. The ghost isn't real. Try to remember that." He went
to the desk, sat down, turned the nameplate around. "Gordon Bennett: a mythical traitor." He pulled a folder from a
drawer and shook out a dog-eared slave-transfer form.
"Diponegoro, a mythical hero. We make a nice pair." His
hands flopped onto the desk, as if somebody had dropped
the strings. "I remember you. Black hair slick as a crow's
wing, big wild grin, nose like a dagger. Grip inside like

a . . . no, won't go into that. Ladies present. You never took anything seriously. But that was a fake. You were forever being *good*, on the sly. I tried to break your bad habits but, damn it, you were too much for me. We had to part. I've followed your career with interest, bet you didn't follow mine." He paused, chuckled at a private joke. "What do you want? Are you a dream? Sometimes they say you're dead."

Derveet shrugged. "I get called a lot of names. Dead is not the worst of them. I want the dust, of course."

Hamzah brought his head forward carefully, his hands still lying in front of him like dead things. "Ha. And now we've got you, outlaw. You have walked into our trap. Pretended heir of proscribed royalty, fomenter of sedition."

Atoon stirred, over in his corner. Derveet held him off with a glance and a gesture. "I don't think so," she said calmly. "The Peninsula Administration couldn't organize a plot like this, and why ever should they? I've no particular enemies in Sepaa. And if your bosses out at sea—" She spoke deliberately, Hamzah shuddered. "If *your bosses* out at sea wanted me dead or in custody, they've had ample opportunity. No. This is private, Jeeby. Between you and me. I understand that."

Hamzah blinked, then abruptly seemed to decide the charade was over. He nodded. "So. You want the dust? You think I'll hand it over?"

"Yes, I do. I want the dust, and I want you to tell me what you plan to do with the people you have collected here—for your bosses. I admired you, Commander. I didn't want to end your career. I've liked to think of you rising in the Admin. Doing more good than harm, I suspect, simply because you may be greedy—but you're not an idiot. I know where you came from. I know how rare it is for a farm camp slave to become an officer. I don't blame you for the life you've led. I respect your achievement. But if you don't cooperate, I will ruin you."

Derveet knew, as she spoke, that the balance had altered.

The weapon that she held matched a different situation: the wide-open Peninsula, the reputation of a Kop Commander with aspirations to warlord status. The key to the Command Block changed everything. With backers out at sea Hamzah didn't need to worry about what Anakmati could tell. But there was something here beyond threat and counterthreat, and besides treachery. Something thick in the atmosphere of this room, but unintelligible. Jeeby had nothing to fear, but Jeeby—for some reason—was *not* in control. Derveet smiled, eyes steady: bluffing with a poor hand.

"Are you ready to cooperate?"

Hamzah suddenly laughed.

"You could always talk, 'Veet." He laughed again, throwing his head back with inappropriate gusto. He stood and groped over the top of the desk, discovered a thick stumpy knife with a glass blade. "I use this as a paper knife. Confiscated from a recalcitrant: we can't have them hurting one another." He was fumbling one-handed with the fastening of his tunic. He pulled it open, tugged violently at the neck of his undershirt. "So, you're going to ruin me?" The silk parted, fell away. Commander Hamzah spread his hands, turned to show Derveet, Cho, Atoon the layered, neat cotton binding. He sawed with the glass knife.

"D'you mean these?" he asked. He was standing; he put one foot up on his chair, hands on his hips. He—*she* had cut herself slightly. A tiny trickle of blood ran down between her breasts, where the sweat glistened on pale, dead-pale skin.

"Sorry to be so crude." Hamzah giggled. "A nice pair, eh? Are *these* going to ruin me?"

Since she reached the camp, Derveet had not been close to her former partner before this evening. She leaned over the desk, peered into Hamzah's sunken eyes. The mystery was solved—some of it.

"Oh, Jeeby," she sighed. "You fool."

"I'm not a fool," said the Commander. She smoothed her

hands over her white breasts, peering down to admire them, rubbing her palms against the nipples. From the expression in her eyes, she might have been caressing herself with handfuls of ground glass. "You don't understand."

"Not a fool. Oh no. You are having a wonderful time. I can tell. We can tell, can't we, Cho?" The doll had come up beside Derveet. She gazed solemnly.

Hamzah put up a fumbling hand. "Stop her from looking at me!" She didn't mean Cho. She was looking through her fingers at the figure in the *dapur* robe. "I won't, I can't talk if *she's* looking at me. Why did you come here? It's not my fault. I won't tell you anything."

Derveet glanced over her shoulder. She saw that the *dapur* ghost had replaced the veil. She gathered that Atoon had grasped the situation and had no intention of lessening Jeeby's misery. And he was right.

"I'm afraid I have no control over your demons. You sent for me. You must have known I'd be here. You're the one who knows why. What's the matter? Changed your mind? Insofar as you still have one." Exasperation and bewilderment overwhelmed her, whatever secrets Jeeby Hamzah kept in her addled skull looked to be lost forever. "Why'd you do it, Jeeby? You've ruined your life, *why*? You knew the dust was poison to you. Just as *they*, your bosses, are poison to all of us. You know that too, however senile and harmless they seem."

The Commander stumbled from her perch and crouched in the chair, huddling her arms around herself. "You can't make me," she muttered, head rocking. "I know about you, outlaw. I can make trouble for you still . . . big . . ." Through the sobbed words, like following thunder, came the unmistakable sound of footsteps.

Atoon tossed aside the robes, freeing himself to fight. Derveet and Cho jumped away from the desk, back into the shadows. Hamzah stood up sharply, the tunic falling open.

Gani burst in. "Someone coming!"

He saw the Commander's pistol lying where it had fallen, ignored by the others. He grabbed it. Then he saw the Commander.

"Oh!" The boy broke into shocked laughter. "A woman!"

Atoon said softly, "A fertile woman, a traitor, and a dust addict."

There was one set of footsteps. The tableau froze, as if there were a chance that whoever it was might pass by. But there was nowhere to go in the Command Block except for this office. Someone came into the outer room. Knocked at the Commander's door, coughed. The door opened cautiously.

"Commander? I know you said . . ."

G. B. Hamzah's secretary had braved the interdiction and come looking for a private interview. With exactly what aim in view, no one would ever know. He stood in the door, staring. His pink face changed, from a look of wary anticipation into blank and unpleasant surprise. "You!" he said. It was Gani that he saw.

He started forward, indignantly. "The little cunt's lying, Commander. He *stole* the key. I've just discovered the theft. In fact I was coming to report. I admit, it was careless—"

Gani half turned. Hamzah stirred, moving like a stringless puppet. The secretary gaped: at his Commander sprouting breasts, an armed slave, *more* slaves, the Commander's secret documents rifled. The man's expression was such a picture, Derveet had to choke back hysterical laughter. Her mind leapt to her last conversation with Jhonni. In Koperasi-land, there's always another round of payoffs . . .

"*Bagus, bagus, masih kita saja seenak enaknya.* Let's be relaxed about this . . ." She made soothing gestures and spoke quickly but not too quickly. "Let's keep calm. We can talk things over. The fact is, you have stumbled on a treasure hunt, young man. Treasure. You understand, treasure. Plenty for everyone."

Neither Atoon nor Derveet had paid the slightest attention to the Commander's pistol. They did not believe a slave boy was capable of using it. Cho knew better. She had not been able to work out whether she should tell. Gani's joy at being armed was great, and Cho knew Derveet wanted him to be happy . . . Hamzah's secretary stared at Derveet, and then, doubtfully, at the rifled documents. He didn't say a word. He didn't get a chance. The big *stop* pistol bounced in Gani's hands. For an instant the room hummed, on an encompassing note deep below human hearing. The curly-haired Kop tumbled backwards. Derveet crossed the floor, dropped to her knees beside him, Atoon too. It was no use. He had taken the shock of the Rulers' weapon, which used vibration, not solid projectiles, straight over the heart. The great muscle was shattered. He was alive, for an extraordinary moment, his face working in breathless agony. A black stain rose, in the open neck of his tunic, under the skin of his throat.

"I feel nothing!" cried Gani, grinning and shaking, bending over them with horrible curiosity. "I feel nothing—nothing!"

It was the kind of death they say happens instantly. The instant had seemed long enough. "You stupid clown," Derveet snarled. "Naturally you feel nothing. No one has shot *you*."

And repented. Peninsulans like to think that boys don't feel things the way real people do. A boy says that he will oblige you by getting raped by a Kop. You take the favor, sure that it doesn't mean to him what it would to you. She knelt beside the corpse, closed the blue staring eyes. "Good work, Gani. You saved us. Thank you for being so brave. I'm proud of you, but I was upset. I never like to see a life cut short unprepared. I'm sorry."

Atoon was waiting to be told what he should do next. Gani, poor fool, was shaking in hideous triumph. Derveet looked up, and saw Cho there. The still presence of the child seemed to look down from very far away on Derveet's grim and chaotic world, through a window in time and space. That was how it had been at their first meeting: Cho's sweet and solemn eyes, seeing the muddle of treachery, violence, stupidity, and making everything quiet. *Ah, to be quiet.* She smiled ruefully, wondering was there *any* way out of this situation? "You don't need to say it, Cho. I know. I said I was going to give up being a bandit: I should have stuck to that. *Now* what do we do?"

"Get the body inside."

The voice was the last Derveet had expected. Sudden death had worked a miracle. Jeeby had come to life.

Between them Derveet and Jeeby hauled the dead Kop. "In here, for the moment." Jeeby opened a closet; they stuffed the body inside. "You in the fancy dress, whoever you are: go and have a discreet look outside."

Atoon opened his eyes wide: Derveet nodded fractionally. He went to have a look outside. "All quiet." He removed the *stop* pistol from Gani's rigid fingers and sat the boy on the floor against the wall. "Don't you stir," he whispered fiercely. "Don't do *anything.*"

Gani began to snivel. "I was brave," he protested. "He, Anakmati, Garuda said so." Cho crouched by him and took his hand.

Jeeby lit the gas lights. The room, which all this time had been plunged in shadow, suddenly leapt into bluish, sickly light. She returned to her desk: a strange, hybrid creature with the head of a Kop and the body of a woman. She picked up the *dapur* robe, wadded it between her hands, tossed it aside. She fastened up her tunic, sat, and opened a deep drawer. She brought out a tapering flask of golden-green liquid and a glass. She shook the flask.

"Sit, 'Veet. Let's discuss this. Care to join me? Only one glass, sorry."

Derveet sat. "No thanks. I think one of us had better stay sober."

Jeeby leaned back in her chair, studying her ex-partner,

apparently self-possessed. "I'm on no one's side—" she began.

"Because nobody's ever been on yours. I remember."

Jeeby rubbed a hand over her face. "You're right. I did send for you." She shook her head. "I wanted you to know. Cruel, really." She sighed. "So, you want the dust?"

"I do."

"It isn't here." Jeeby stroked the flask. "My last allowance. I'm trying to give it up." She laughed. "I hid the rest. I'll take you to it if you want. We'd better leave anyway. We've a dead Kop to explain, and I'm not sure when the Commander will be back. Commander Hamzah, he comes and goes. You understand the situation?"

"I'm beginning to understand."

"It won't do any good. The supply of poison is inexhaustible. But I'll take you there, for old times' sake."

Atoon stood beside Derveet. He had known, before they left Ranganar, that this expedition might be more hazardous and more serious than it seemed. But there was a depth of malice in the madwoman's eyes that chilled him, and a horrifying, hopeless appeal. It was as if a demon stretched its hands up out of hell. What kind of inexhaustible poison?

Derveet put out a hand, pushed the flask. It fell and shattered. "I want the dust," she said. "Take us there."

Endang stood on the second-floor balcony, enjoying the night air. Insects chanted in trees and courtyard gardens. Behind him in the room Jhonni was busy at her traveling desk. She had smuggled a heap of documents out of the camp. He thought she was reckless; he hoped she'd be able to get them back without being detected. Cho had told Jhonni that everything would be resolved tonight. If the meeting with G. B. Hamzah went well, it was important that Jhonni still looked innocent to the Kops.

If all went well . . . Why did he feel it didn't matter? Why was he suddenly sure the flowerdust was not important?

Endang breathed the cool scent of frangipani from the

flower-laden trees in the street below. His sickness had let him off the leash. Jhonni was happy. She interpreted this release as a sign that the *terrible danger* was less since they had started to take notice of the warning. He was fascinated by the Samsui attitude, so workaday, so businesslike. He hadn't the heart to tell her that whatever power was in him, it felt the nightmare certainty as much as before. He was too tired: that was all. The horrors would be back when he'd regained a little strength.

He turned to look into the room at Jhonni, bending earnestly over her work. She was such an optimist, he thought. But not a fool. There was so much common sense, so much energy and will bound up in that sturdy body, and strength to endure. He smiled. If he would let her, she would almost seduce him (a word that made his smile take a rueful downturn) into believing it was possible to fight.

He closed his eyes. He thought of Garuda, in the Koperasi camp tonight—fighting back. If there was anyone who could drag the Peninsula from the edge of the abyss, it would be Derveet. She never flinched from the truth, but she never compromised with the enemy, she never let despair creep in. *If she gets the dust from Hamzah,* he thought. *Though I don't think it means much. I will take that as a sign. And I will hope.*

Something stung his wrist. He reacted automatically, found he had crushed a small, delicately made insect of a kind he'd never seen before. Where he'd squeezed its abdomen, his thumb was stained red.

"Jhonni? Have a look at this."

She didn't hear him. The skills of the counting rooms were unraveling in her mind. BLOODY FLOWERS BRING DESPAIR. Horrible ideas kept coming to her from nowhere. Piles of corpses in the streets of a city, children lying on the five-foot way in pools of nasty liquid, bodies covered in little oozing sores as if they'd been caught in a rain of fire. She saw the aftermath of a disaster: had a big volcano erupted?

But no one builds a town on the slopes of a volcano. She shook her head furiously. Back to work. The figures made an ominous picture too. Behind the Reform Camp there was another installation being financed: a ghost, a shadow.

She straightened, shoving her hair up off her face.

"There's another camp!"

"Is that bad?"

Endang came in from the balcony, holding the strange insect by the wings. He laid it on the margin of a Koperasi ledger.

"What is it?" she asked.

"I don't know. I don't like it, though. It draws blood."

"Really? I thought you told me there aren't any noxious creatures on the Peninsula, not near people, anyway."

They were peering at it when someone tapped at the door. It was Cho. "Oh, thank goodness," cried Jhonni. "The plan worked. Are you all safe?" She looked for a bag or a sack, hoping this visit meant she'd escaped from the job of carrying the drug out of the camp. "Did you bring it? Where is it?"

"Not exactly." The doll-who-was-a-person proffered another shopping list. "A plan worked, I think. But it wasn't ours. You're to come with me to Fauziah straightaway. We're going on a trip to fetch the flowerdust."

9

AT DAWN THE riverside was sleepily bustling. Carts were being unloaded; small knots of people clustered at food and drink stalls or did business in the lamp-lit dark of open-mouthed sheds. Although it was hardly light, the air was warm and heavy. It was going to be one of Timur's days of brass. Laden, Jhonni and Endang struggled along the wooden boardwalk. Isolir, even bustling, could hardly muster a crowd of idlers. But such idleness as there was came clinging after the two strangers. Boys wanted to carry their bags, considered it their right; tried to drag the bundles out of Jhonni's hands. They didn't touch anything that Endang was carrying. They stared at him with big eyes and sniggered.

Every Samsui business traveler hated the slave mentality of the Peninsula boys: the boneless hands that patted and pestered you, the demands to be allowed to perform those useless little services an able-bodied Samsui did not want or need to have performed. Jhonni had never thought she would feel like that, because *she* was a revolutionary and she understood why boys were the way they were. But some of the things in these bags were seriously contraband. There were *weapons*. She was terrified. "Go away!" she shouted, disgusted at herself. How could this be the beginning of a secret journey? Sweat of fear was running down her arms and dribbling out of her sleeves.

"We're looking for a boat called the *Pisau Besar?*" No answer, of course. Jhonni slipped on a fragment of corn husk, staggered and almost lost her footing. She turned on Endang. "What's *wrong* with you? Can't you help me?"

Endang stared ahead of him, looking as if he were made of glass and about to shatter. Jhonni suddenly noticed that all the people on the quay were boys. They were boys, and they were sniggering because somehow they'd guessed that Endang was not. He was a stud, he should not be out here. And what did the boys make of his being in a public place with Jhonni? A particularly painful blush crawled up her face. "I'm sorry. I can't stop them," she told him, making it worse. "Let's hurry. Keep calm."

The riverboats were like huge double-prowed canoes: some of them no more than dugouts, some elaborate, with high sides, decking and a little engine house. Each of the prows was carved in the same stylized way. Jhonni stared at several before she realized what that knobbed cucumber thing was meant to be. She winced, and tried not to look again. Cho had said the *Pisau Besar* was the one "that didn't look respectable." Which was funny, in the light of those prows. She couldn't remember if *pisau* meant "knife" or "banana." She supposed it amounted to the same thing.

"The trouble is," she muttered, "Cho will tell you whatever you want to know, but you have to *ask*. She would have told us more; she would have explained everything. But if you don't ask the exact question . . . I really believe she doesn't know that you don't know. D'you see?"

They did not know what had happened in the camp: only that they must be here, with the provisions ordered from the merchant Fauziah in the middle of the night. The boardwalk ended above a weedy lagoon, where defunct vessels wallowed in abandonment. A crow, squatting inside the skeleton of a drowned cabin, tugged at a disgusting mess of fish entrails. The boat alongside had once been one of the most elaborate kind, but it was almost equally decrepit. The jutting prow had been stained dark blue. A name was dimly stenciled on the bow: PISAU BESAR. Jhonni slung down her heaviest bag, melting in relief.

"You want to hire?"

There were two boys, one old, one young. They looked the most complete ruffians. The old one had a red bandanna tied around his head, a filthy red shirt, and a pair of Koperasi uniform trousers. Strings of silver hair descended from his upper lip and his chin. The young one, wearing a purple sarong with a border of silver flowers, which you could barely make out through the grime, had a mass of sheeny black curls and large, contemptuous eyes. He was cutting a piece of white wood into small pegs, using a knife the size of a butcher's cleaver.

"Hire?" Jhonni could hardly bear it. "Yes, of course."

"You want to go upriver, or down?"

The river, which was called the Air Melangir, ran south from here through other little towns, to a greater confluence and eventually to the sea. Upriver there was the forest.

"Upriver, maybe two days. And back."

"Upriver costs more. Much more. Five hundred cash, one day." The old villain rubbed his fingers together. "Money for fuel. You got money, maybe we can take you."

"And your nice *boy* friend." The young one leered and licked his knife blade reflectively. Endang looked nowhere but he looked dangerous, as if he were about to take the insult out in blood.

"Five hundred! But that's outrageous!"

Sly old eyes looked through her clothes, riffled the wad in her money belt. "Last price." Something was happening at the other end of the quay. Jhonni heard the snarl and roar of a treader pulling up among the bullock carts. The Koperasi!

"Downriver, five hundred. Upriver, not so cheap. Against the stream, into bad forest. There are savages in there."

"But you just said five hundred," wailed Jhonni. BLOODY

FLOWERS BRING DESPAIR. This *could not* be part of the adventure. The treadie didn't start up again. The Kops were coming, the idler boys making way for them and avidly following to see the fun. "Let me see the—the accommodation!" She darted towards the *Pisau Besar*'s rotten gangplank, towards the only hiding place in sight. The young boy stopped her, pulling her arm in that hateful soft Peninsulan way. In his other hand, he held the knife.

"Number one, agree price with uncle. Number two, see boat."

"All right, all right, six hundred!"

Someone put a hand on Jhonni's shoulder. She swiveled around and nearly fell into the lagoon. It was a Kop: a dark man in red uniform, with an army cap pulled over his eyes. There were three Kops, one of them very undersized. "Jhonni," said the dark Kop, "I'm surprised at you, agreeing to a rate like that. What would your mama say?" Jhonni gasped, and at the same moment saw that the old boy's two hands, as they pretended to play with his scanty beard, had been sketching the Eagle's wings.

The villain beamed, and bowed till the string of his beard touched the ground. The young one leapt up in delight.

"Anakmati!"

The dark Kop was Derveet. Behind her, closely attended by a boy servant, was a darkly veiled *dapur* lady. Behind them, the two other Kops. "Did you get everything?" asked Derveet casually. "Good girl." She looked around, with a somehow furtive grin, at the figure in the dark robes. "This lady . . ." There were sounds of smothered hilarity from under the veil. "This lady—hush, please, you in there—will be accompanying us on our trip."

"The flowers, the butterflies, the dear furry animals," crowed the *dapur* lady. "Especially the flowers!"

"Oh, get her on board. Jeeby, *try* to take life seriously. This is dangerous, this is scary, I have kidnapped a Provincial Commander and I am wearing a uniform to which I am not entitled."

"Heeheehee."

As the *dapur* lady was carefully handed aboard by the disguised bandit, Jhonni tried desperately to catch Derveet's eye. But Derveet would not be caught. Derveet and the lady clambered into the palm-mat hut of a cabin. Jhonni was close behind. The lady flung back her veil. Derveet pulled off the Army cap, turned away and fumbled: turned back. She was wearing an eye patch, the rakish adornment worn by the famous bandit on the wanted posters. Jeeby and Anakmati howled with laughter and fell into each other's arms.

Jhonni stood watching this performance, definitely frightened. There was something horrible about that laughter. Atoon touched her arm. "Go up forward," he said softly. "You'll find Endang. Stay up there. Be patient, we'll explain. But you both had better stay out of the Commander's way."

Jhonni gaped. "Commander Hamzah is a woman?" He nodded. "Is he, is she *dangerous?*"

"Perhaps you are more dangerous to her. Especially you, *bu* Jhonni. But principally, I don't think you two fit in with what is supposed to be happening. And I think we have to fit in or we'll lose her altogether."

"Is she mad?"

"Go up forward."

The prince didn't give orders to women, not even renegade girls. He didn't say it as if he was giving orders, but as if he was too preoccupied to waste words. She went to find Endang.

After an hour, Atoon took Derveet's place in the cabin. Gani, the only one unaffected by the Commander's manner, was sprawled asleep on one of the benches that were fixed to the sides of the *Pisau*, his face nestled on his uniform jacket. Atoon and Commander Hamzah had become well acquainted during the night. Derveet and Gani had to go back to the dormitory, in case they were missed. Cho went into town; the prince stayed with the Commander. They had been alone together for several hours. A kind of understanding had been reached. He saw that she did not expect him to join her in the happy past. She gave him one glance and retreated into silence, sat with her legs crossed, a boot-toe swinging, leaning back against the matting. But she was watching him covertly.

In her office at the camp she'd been terribly restless. She had wanted to take the corpse out of the cupboard; she talked to it through the keyhole. She talked to Atoon. Sometimes she shouted, screamed, and begged him to help her fight the demons that were closing in. He thought she'd wake the whole camp. Sometimes she sat at her desk, took out papers and appeared to read and make notes. But the papers would fall to the floor; the pen scribbled on air. He thought that she was watching him now with sober suspicion and resentment, trying to remember what he knew. Wondering how much she could deny of that broken weeping, disjointed pleading, frantic remorse.

The cabin was very still since the engine had stopped. The motion of the water was soothing.

"What happened to the children, Hamzah?"

"Hamzah?"

Something flickered, a gleam in her sunken eyes.

"Hahaha. The soft Kop and the hard Kop."

"I think you want to tell me. I think it would do you good."

She sneered. "What children? I don't fuck with studs." The sneer became an unpleasant grin. "Ask 'Veet. Ask your friend."

Atoon was revolted, for a moment, at the thought of her with Garuda. But it was Derveet's business. He would not be put off. He'd learned too much last night.

"What happened?"

"There was a child." She turned her face away. "Once. I was only a kid, couldn't stand up for myself. It died. I didn't let that happen again." She turned back, sallow face like a leather mask under the shock of blood-colored hair. "It had to die. It would have ruined my career. The mother died too. Gone for a long while. Came back as a ghost. Nasty, nasty ghost."

"I'm sorry," he said.

Jeeby stretched out her arms, leaned her head back, considered with pursed lips as if savoring an unfamiliar taste. "No. I don't feel any better. Send me Anakmati. She doesn't ask damn stupid questions. I want to have fun."

Derveet was in the stern, making herself agreeable to Usman, their captain. He had made tea and proffered coconut cakes. He laid, shyly, a confirming hand on Anakmati's knee: yes, it was solid flesh. "They said Anakmati was dead, dead to us outside-the-hearth people. They said you would never come back to us."

The bandit sipped a beaker of acar tea, glanced at Cho, and smiled wryly. "It's true, I was dead," she agreed. "The tea is very good, my compliments. But I came back to life again. The Peninsula is a magical place. Such things can happen here."

"Excuse me, but is the officer-person quite well?" Usman was not alarmed by the uniforms. The *Pisau Besar* had taken many disreputable charters in its day: disguised bandits or genuine Kops, it was the same to Usman. But he could tell one from the other. And he was naturally alarmed at the state of the genuine article in this party. Derveet was amused by the villain's delicacy. If a Peninsulan wonders politely if someone is unwell, generally he is not worrying about organic disease.

"I'm afraid not," she admitted. "Not at all well. But don't worry. We will take every care."

"Perhaps an alcohol problem?" the old boy suggested gravely.

"More serious than that, even . . . Tell me, brother. Do you river people take other Koperasi up into the forest? From the new camp, perhaps? Perhaps not in uniform?"

"No." The old boy seemed surprised. "Never. The Kops never come beyond Isolir. Not for a long time, not since they gave up the road. They don't use the river, and the road does not go north . . ." He pondered calmly. "I have seen the bubbles, though." Atoon came out of the cabin as Usman was speaking.

"Ah. Often?"

"Oh, not very often. I don't know where they go. Perhaps it's something to do with Gamartha."

Usman plied Derveet's friend with tea and cake, and discreetly retired as far as the *Pisau* would allow. Atoon and Derveet sat shoulder to shoulder under the grossly carved Timur prow, Cho at Derveet's side.

"The strip at the camp had never been used," said Derveet.

"There must be another, somewhere nearby. Hamzah would drive out to it, get picked up and carried off into the forest. It's possible that she's never done this journey except by air. If, that is, there's anything in her story at all."

Derveet took a cigarette case from her tunic, a new case, filled by the obliging Fauziah. She proffered it with a grin of sly triumph. "Or are you still trying to give it up?" For a while they smoked in silence. The river reeled away behind them. A chocolate-and-turquoise kingfisher flung itself from a perch over the bank, creasing the surface in a spurt of silver.

Jeeby had promised to show them an inexhaustible supply of poison in the forest, up the river. Did she mean there was a giant plantation of flowerdust-acar? It might be true. The Rulers had their own powers. They might have been able to decipher and replicate the work of the old *dapurs*.

"The idea has the authentic, wrongheaded ring," remarked Derveet. "One can imagine the Kop staff officers jumping for joy at the thought of the Peninsula in chaos." She grimaced wryly. "*Dapur* ladies running mad . . ."

"It would never work. If they had dust beyond our wildest dreams it would end up rotting in a warehouse somewhere, infallibly. But this is not a Koperasi scheme."

Derveet nodded. "That's certain."

"And it is all we know for sure."

"You're right." She considered the end of her cigarette. "I don't believe in the plantation. But I think she's taking us somewhere. This isn't a meaningless whim. I don't believe she's acting on her bosses' orders now. More than that, I wouldn't like to guess."

Atoon was convinced that they were being led into a trap. But he accepted Garuda's rash determination with equanimity.

"Did you know she'd had a child?"

Derveet shook her head wearily. "No, I didn't know. I didn't know she was a dust addict, either. Otherwise I would not . . . I didn't drive Jeeby out of her mind on purpose."

"I don't think you should feel responsible—"

"Thank you. I will be the judge of that."

He nodded, accepting the rebuff.

He'd taken off the red tunic. Jeeby had made Atoon and Gani into troopers, and Derveet an officer, before she led them to the treader hangar this morning. This was the fourth disguise he had worn in a matter of days. It astonished him how easily he could play his different parts. His life had been so simple.

He remembered how Derveet first came to wear that eye patch. She had been defying his family, experimenting with homemade explosives up in the mountains with the outcasts. The Hanoman *dapur* saved her sight: the patch was for her good eye, to force the rebuilt muscle in the worse damaged one to work. Derveet had liked it. It was dashing, it was funny, it reminded her to act the bandit. But it meant for him the time when she became entirely Anakmati, and left him behind in the palace in Jagdana, and the years of suffocation began.

"Derveet, thank you. You brought me to Timur against your better judgment, I know it. I'm profoundly grateful."

He had spent the night locked up alone in the company of a corpse and a dangerous lunatic. But he spoke without irony, and she didn't smile. She began to see exactly what a torture the life of the prince of Jagdana must have been, some kind of elegant hell: expected only to perform like a prize animal, while his country died by slow torture.

"Think nothing of it," she said. "My pleasure."

The boy Yuda had stopped the engine and put up the sail when they were clear of the town and its lagoons, shoals, and obstacles. The heat was intense, but there was a breeze on the water. The *Pisau* moved slowly against the current, a hooked blue blade cutting through the wrinkled flesh of the river.

Jhonni sat up in the front of the boat, beyond the stumpy mast. She was stuck here, afraid to repeat the perilous clamber along the rail by the side of the cabin. She could feel, uncomfortably, the presence of Yuda, minding the sail. The old one had apologized for the way he'd behaved on the quay. "We had to bargain a little," he said. "Mustn't let the townspeople know we were already hired by Anakmati." Jhonni knew he'd enjoyed his fun. She was with Anakmati, but she was still a hated Samsui.

Dry farmland had given way to acacia and mallow scrub. Now the trees began to thicken on either side. Her discovery had been preempted. Derveet knew there was another camp. The Commander was taking them there, to a giant flowerdust farm. She hated the sight of Derveet with Commander Hamzah—swapping old stories, sharing brutal gossip about who had died and how since they last met. Their laughter sounded genuine to Jhonni, genuine and horrible. A bird with a chunky orange bill the size of its whole body zoomed across the water ahead. It called loudly, once, before vanishing into the shadows. This was the heart of the Peninsula, where anything could happen. But this was not romance. Jhonni felt her own heart hardening in a frightening way. What she was feeling was not humble cowardice. She had made a mistake. She did not like this place and she did not want to share its troubles. She wanted to be safe at home.

Endang crouched with his arms wrapped around his knees and his face buried. He remembered his first life. So many things that a young stud-to-be was not allowed to do: not to leave the compound, not to read secular books, not to have intimate friends. Because it would be undignified, because it would arouse base urges. He hadn't known the joke. He didn't know then that he didn't have any base urges. That there was no danger to his virtue in the glances of pretty boys and handsome older men.

Nor did he know how much worse the life of a stud could be.

The dapur *allowed me nothing*, he thought. *What I have, they can't take away.* His guts were churning; every joint ached. This time he was going to keep his agony to himself. It was useless. Pain is only a useful warning if it is in the animal's power to get away. Behind him in the palm-mat cabin, Derveet was playing along with the Koperasi Commander. He heard the toneless voice of the madwoman and Derveet's replies chiming in: dark, accepting, infinitely patient. He peered over his shoulder, feeling watched. Hamzah stared out of the doorless opening. She'd taken off the robe, her uniform tunic was open. Their eyes met. Jeeby looked away, smiling secretly. There was one person he need not tell. She knew the worst. Endang shivered. He swallowed bile.

They spent a comfortless night on the water. Around noon of the next day, Jeeby began to joke about having forgotten the landing spot. She was looking for a particular distinctive bush: no, a fallen tree, or was it a bend in the stream?

The *Pisau*, under engine power again, rounded a bend: and the blurred faint noise ahead of them became a distant roar. Yuda and Usman were nervous. They were getting near the rapids that marked the end of the navigable river. The *Pisau* couldn't go much farther. "Ah yes." The Commander grinned. *"Now* I know."

The *Pisau Besar* tied up against the east bank, which was grassy and open for some distance at this point. Other boats might have tied up here in the past, but there were no clear signs. Jhonni and Endang and Gani were left on board with the boys, while the others went looking for the track Jeeby thought she remembered. She had now confessed—if this wasn't another joke—that she had usually visited "the other camp" by air.

Jhonni sat on the side under the forward prow. There were tucks and dimples in the green surface of the river. The *Pisau* was secured to the bank by several ropes lashed to sturdy roots. It moved like a tethered animal, trying to escape back downstream. The boat boys were subdued; they kept peering into the trees.

"Does anybody live up here?"

Yuda showed the whites of his eyes. *"Orang hutan,* forest people. They are savages, hairy. They eat *orang kulit."*

That meant *skin people*: us. "What do they do when they can't get hold of any?" wondered Endang cynically. But Jhonni could believe in cannibals: scarcely human creatures, lost to civilization. Gani was wolfing down Commander Hamzah's breakfast. Occasionally he poked the banana-leaf platter of rice and fish under their noses. "You should eat! There's nothing to eat in the forest." Neither of them could respond civilly to the boy's irritating advances. They didn't speak to each other either. *If we are like this now,* thought Jhonni, *what will it be like in there?* She stared at the forbidding shadows: shadows full of hidden, hostile life. It would be like going underground. It would be like walking into the refugee camp at night.

The shore party returned. There was a kind of trail. Atoon and Cho did not look very happy about it. It was impossible to make out what Jeeby really thought. Or Derveet, who was not like Derveet at all: wheedling, giggling. "Stop clowning, Jeeby; give us a break, Jeeby." The Commander looked sly. "I *think* we're at the right place. This bloody river country all looks the same."

Usman and Yuda moved about the boat, casually tidying up. Jhonni and Endang shouldered their share of the carrying baskets. Derveet became something like herself again, briefly, observing the boat boys with narrowed eyes.

"You look busy. You are not going anywhere, are you?"

Usman was shocked. "Of course not, Anakmati!"

"Be here when we get back," Derveet told them.

The old boy began to protest again. "We would not let you down!"

"I'm not ordering you. This is advice. But it is *good* advice."

The Timurese nodded seriously. Jhonni wondered how long it would take the boys to recover from the force of Anakmati's personality. Not long, she guessed. And what would they do if they came back and the boat was gone? If they came back . . .

Derveet wanted Gani to stay. But he was terrified of the Timurese and refused to be left behind. Seven of them set off into the leaf-dappled twilight. The path was heavily overgrown. Atoon, Derveet and Jeeby went ahead, wielding the heavy machetes provided by Fauziah. The others stumbled behind as best they could (except Cho; Cho did not stumble); falling over the jagged, half-devoured stumps of young trees that lay in wait in the undergrowth. Most of the time these stumps were the only proof that a trail had ever been made. Once or twice there were scraps of better evidence: a piece of a canvas boot, a fragment of wire, a moldering ration package.

Jhonni did not know when this walk into the dark veered

over into nightmare. Maybe it had begun on the boat, or back in Isolir. She had been frightened of being a drug runner, but she had trusted Derveet. But now Derveet was gone, not herself. The flowerdust in Ranganar had been a message sent to Derveet. The drug running was no longer important and yet Endang's warning, the nightmare, was not explained. It was too much negation. No good, no good. Nothing any good.

She walked along and she walked along. Rattan creepers with huge thorns dropped onto her head and shoulders. She was afraid of wild animals. The Peninsula was so old a human land that you were always walking on the bones of ancient human use, buried cities. But this forest had been abandoned to the wild ages ago. She was afraid the *dapur* would consider that if you were out here you were fair game to be stung, poisoned, bitten, eaten. She tried to comfort herself by thinking of streets, houses, tall buildings. The behavior of her mother, the massed ranks of Samsui apathy, at last made sense. Streets, houses: the counting rooms . . . It didn't work. The comforting images changed as she tried to hold them in her mind. The streets of Ranganar were stacked with corpses. A forest invaded Aunt Kwokmei's domain. The limbs of trees burst through the walls. But they were not roots. They were human limbs, packed, sweating human flesh. Seven. There were seven of them walking through the forest. There were more than seven. She was walking in a thick crowd. She could smell the other bodies.

"Jhonni?"

She opened her eyes and found they were already open: a nasty experience. She had blundered off the trail. She vaguely remembered the sound of her own voice crying, *Don't you see them? Don't you see them?* And, shamefully: *Keep the filthy things away from me.* Atoon was pulling her out of a tangle of creepers. She put up her hand to wipe her face. It came away smeared with blood and she wailed.

"I'm bitten!"

"Only thorns," he said gently. "Try to stay on the trail."

Derveet's voice rang out ahead, incongruously cheery, raised in a sentimental bandit ballad.

"All my transgressions will find me out, you say
All those lies and hard words come back on me one day . . ."

Endang had hardly spoken or looked at anyone since they left Isolir. Atoon treated him gently, distantly. He seemed to know what Jhonni wasn't allowed to tell. She went to him after the prince had pulled her out of the bush, got hold of his hand. "I can't breathe," he muttered. "Stifling." There was no comfort in the touch for either of them. Their fingers slipped apart. Whatever was haunting them killed human feeling. They must endure alone.

Atoon and Cho walked side by side. Atoon had the third machete tucked into his sash; the trail had grown too narrow for three to work abreast. Cho held the Commander's jacket neatly folded over her arm. She talked quietly, the prince listening with his sleek braided head bowed. "She's not a bad cat. But she bears a grudge. I keep telling her, you aren't the same people as the ones who went away and left us . . . but she can't see it."

"Hamzah's playing with us," said Atoon, his voice taut with controlled anxiety. "The trail doesn't mean anything. I'm sure there are lost trails all over this forest. Where's she taking us? If there were a bubble overhead, tracking us, would we hear it?"

They watched the two children stumbling ahead of them; talking to themselves and shying from nonexistent obstacles. "And what do you think of *that?* What is happening to those two? How long before it affects the rest of us?"

"I feel quite ordinary," said Cho sadly. "But I'm not human."

Derveet and Jeeby had left the rest of the party out of sight behind them. They hacked a passage into a thicket of elephant grass, came out in a small natural clearing.

"Breather!"

Derveet collapsed against a tree trunk, wiped her sweat-drenched hair out of her eyes, lit a cigarette. Jeeby took a turn around the clearing, slashing at shadows. Her arms glistened in the half-light; the silk undershirt hung in rags. She had not slept or eaten, and had barely had anything to drink, for at least two days. Her eyes were sunken in puckered hollows. The bones of her face stood out white, the spectacular death-mask effect of acute dehydration. She must be on the edge of collapse.

"Well? Are we close enough?"

Jeeby came up, grinning. She swung the machete dangerously—a farm implement suspiciously honed and rebalanced. She nodded in approval. "Nice weapon." Derveet didn't flinch. "Good of you to trust a madwoman with this. And here we are alone. Ain't you afraid?"

"No. You're having far too much fun with me to kill me."

"You haven't any choice, in fact. You have to arm me. You could probably find the place from here, but apart from the pretty man, I'm your best coolie. The slave has never been in the woods before. The kids are useless."

"You forgot Cho."

"Hahaha. Only taking my cue from you. You don't use the doll. That dam' well puzzles my bosses." She grinned, winked, twisted her mouth as if at a bad smell. "Not me. The machine that everyone loves . . . I call it creepy."

"My love life is no longer your concern. Let's stick to the point. How much more of this? No offense—but I became a criminal to get away from manual labor."

Jeeby stared into the canopy. "How much more? Not very much more. Things are speeding up. A few hours, a few days. We're going to be run off our feet at the camp in a little while. A few more months and your troubles will be over."

Derveet felt the presence of a monster, the will to senseless destruction that she had declared to be fading and powerless. Had she ever believed the Rulers were no longer to be feared? No: only tried to hope. Hamzah stared upwards, full to bursting with horrible, uncanny knowledge. Derveet applied the end of her cigarette to an opportunistic leech that had materialized on her elbow. "Yes, but the *point*, Jeeby. The here and now."

The leech dropped to the leaf litter, squirming. Hamzah's pale-rimmed eyes glittered. "I call it disgusting," she said. "The way your religious principles desert you when the going gets tough. All life is sacred. Poor little thing. I hate suffering."

She was longing to confess. She was like an animal lured almost into taking food from a human hand.

"So do I. Especially my own. Come on, sweetheart. Give me a hint. What *have* you got tucked away up here?"

There was a crashing in the thicket. Gani appeared, panting and clutching a large stick. He whacked at the vanquished undergrowth. "Hard work, madam!"

Derveet controlled an impulse to slice his stupid head off.

Commander Hamzah gave one of her mirthless, rattling laughs. She flung away and strode on, breaking suddenly into the old song.

> *"Somewhere a lonely hour, darkness unallayed*
> *Waits for me counting up the dues I haven't paid—"*

"She's a bad person," hissed Gani. "Bad! She was saying evil things about you to the prince."

"Really? No worse than the truth, I'm sure."

"She should not be trusted with a weapon!"

Gani coveted the machetes. He didn't dare to ask for one. He knew he'd disgraced himself with the Commander's pistol. Derveet sighed. Atoon would be horrified, but— "Here. Give me a rest. And try not to cut your own arm off."

The boy's face shone. "Come, Anakmati. We must keep that Koperasi in sight. Don't be afraid, I'll protect you!"

* * *

Jhonni spread her Samsui groundsheet and palmed earth over it at the edges. Her territory marked, she got the basket between her knees and burrowed into it. There was food, what riches of food: pressed sticks of cooked rice, dried vegetables, dried fruit, parched corn. She ate savagely, shaking with fear, knowing that this good fortune couldn't last. The smell of her food would draw a pack of hungry and murderous thieves.

"Jhonni?"

She looked up and she was in a forest clearing. It was dark. There was a Samsui traveling lamp (her own lamp) hanging on a stripped branch someone had stuck in the ground. Faces that she began to recognize were staring at her.

"Oh!" she cried. She wiped the food from her mouth, cheeks burning scarlet. "Oh! I don't know what came over me!"

Commander Hamzah lay slumped with her head and shoulders against a tree root. She took a water bottle from Atoon with a look of hatred, and drank, like someone taking medicine that will only prolong the torture of dying. When he moved to take the bottle back she snatched it away, and deliberately upended it.

"That's for what 'Veet did to my golden wine."

It would be hard to starve in any Peninsulan wilderness. But fresh water was not easily come by in the forest.

Endang lay on his side, curled up with an arm over his face. He sobbed. He made pushing gestures at the empty air: "Stay away from me. Let me breathe . . . "

Jhonni went for a walk in the middle of the night, or maybe she dreamed that. She found another clearing, unless it was the same one, become part of her dream. Derveet sat alone beside a little fire. The Samsui lamp was gone. In its place was a little basket dangling from a stick that glowed bright, bright green like one of Derveet's fireworks.

As Jhonni came into the clearing, some other people had risen and left. She had the impression of blurred, fuzzy-outlined shadows.

"You lit a fire! I thought you mustn't do that. You're a failed woman. Domestic tasks belong to the *dapur*." She was always tactless, even when she was asleep.

Derveet shrugged. "I mustn't do it in Ranganar, in front of the boys. It would upset them. One must never upset the boys; we have done enough harm to them. I have tried to keep the rules. But only from nostalgia. They aren't essential." She propped her head on her hand. "I'm tired, Jhonni. This is the hardest work. Jeeby is wearing me out."

The green light in the little basket moved and separated. It was a lamp made of fireflies. "How beautiful!"

Derveet looked up with a curious expression of doubt and of *respect*. "Are you breaking the rules, Jhonni?"

The trail stayed on low ground, winding across a wide, moist valley floor. The air was warm and damp, the sky rarely visible. Even Jhonni knew that they weren't likely to find an acar plantation in this terrain. Rain fell in the afternoons; they collected rainwater, not much but enough to get by. Jhonni decided that Derveet had to be told that Endang had *dapur* powers, and spent some time trying to pick on a moment when she could make this confession. But Derveet was bound to the madwoman and the past, and when she escaped from Jeeby she treated Jhonni strangely.

There continued to be interludes in the walk that Jhonni hoped were vivid imaginings happening in her mind. But she couldn't be sure.

Once, she walked off the trail and found a little stream. The water was clear and brown. There was a plant with glossy dark leaves and little scarlet flowers shaped like water pitchers. Jhonni sat beside the stream. There were stones in the brown bed that were covered with delicate chiseled marks, but she couldn't read the writing. Atoon was there. He was combing out his hair. His body was lapped in a silky ocean. Jhonni saw how that mass of hair would handicap him in the outside world. It would snag on things; it would trip him up. He would be lashed by spurts of irrational rage from the pain of those tugs and catches. He would be a burden to himself and a danger to others. The hair meant his maleness. It showed why a stud must be enclosed.

A copper-colored butterfly settled on a scarlet flower. Jhonni looked at the butterfly for a long, long time. It was beautiful, but it grew so many eyes and such forests of legs. The sensation of overbearing, overwhelming weight was horrible. She cried to Atoon in panic. "Look, look, the flower is breaking! Have I taken flowerdust?" she asked him. "Is this what it's like?" He was the prince in the temple painting. She felt as if there were a warm flower unfolding in the crux of her belly.

"No. You have not," said the prince. Then he said, "It's no use. It's too late for me." His face blurred. The petals inside her burned and withered. She closed her eyes and found they were closed already. Red letters wrote on blackness, BLOODY FLOWERS BRING DESPAIR.

Eventually Jhonni decided that the vital conversation had already happened. Derveet knew about the warning and about Endang. *Dapur* powers didn't matter. They had been defeated. There was probably nothing at the end of this trail. The bad news was delivered by the journey itself. She kept thinking of the time she and Endang had kissed. But the memory was dead and dry, no longer a forbidden treasure. Nothing good would ever happen again.

Whether or not the interludes were dreams, there were two nights. On the third morning they came to a fence. It was very tall, a Koperasi web of slick-coated metal, and much decayed. Their trail passed through a wide gap where it had fallen down. On the other side the forest had been cleared fairly recently. There was a uniform growth of saplings and creepers and ground orchids, over lumpy, disturbed earth.

"Here we are," hummed Jeeby.

They stood looking in. Everything was very still.

"There was a town," said Endang suddenly. "A new town. It was supposed to be the roadhead of the Central Timur highway . . . that was never completed. How long have we been walking?"

"Two days," Atoon told him, showing no surprise at the question. "East about ten *batu*, then parallel to the river: that is, roughly north. Then half-east for all of yesterday. Is that right enough, Cho?"

The doll nodded. She could have been more precise, but she didn't correct humans unless they asked. It was bad manners.

"That would fit," Endang decided. "People were reset- tled here from the clearances, when the Kops put the last of the Garuda territory into plantations. It was years ago when I was at college in Sepaa. At the time, I thought it was a good idea."

Atoon said to Derveet, "At least let me go first, alone?"

"There is no ambush."

Jeeby stood watching, grinning her death-mask grin. Der- veet cast a glance over her companions. The Samsui. The Gamarthan who was also Timurese. The prince of Jagdana. A boy from somewhere in the princedoms; she'd never asked Gani where he was born. And Cho, who did not be- long anywhere in this time. A trek in the wilds cements friendships, or destroys them. But this journey had been a separation. She had been preoccupied with the madwoman, Atoon with his own fears. Jhonni and Endang had been behaving very strangely. She did not understand what was happening to those two. She noticed that Gani had got hold of a machete again and took it from him.

"We'll stay together."

The day was going to be hot and clear. The sky, suddenly visible in great swaths through the young trees, was blue. *We will not be taken,* thought Atoon. *Garuda will die in battle and I will fall beside her.* He knew it was nonsense, but he felt there was death in this clearing, the kind of destruction that draws one, like deep water.

They walked until they came to a collection of thatched huts. These could not belong to the forest people. The shy, barely human *orang hutan* didn't build permanent houses. Unlikely as it seemed, some of the settlers of the Koperasi new town must have stayed on after the project was abandoned, and somehow made a living for themselves. Some of the huts were tumbling down but they looked to be inhabited. Beyond them stood a row of pale, sleekly curved buildings that must have survived from the Koperasi times. Jhonni noticed that the air smelled foul. They were out-of-doors, but it was the air of a sickroom, of a midden, of the most disgusting stages of the gas-plant cycle at home in Ranganar. And suddenly, with the violence of a fist smashing into her face, she knew that it was here. *Here.* The thing, the terrible thing. Jeeby Hamzah had strolled away, humming "Somewhere a lonely hour." Jhonni could not move. Her head turned by itself and watched Jeeby. To Jhonni it seemed that the red figure of the Koperasi officer was joined to the shambles of the huts by streaming, spattering trails of blood.

The people who lived in the settlement had not had the time or the strength to run away into the forest when they heard strangers coming. Shortly, an old woman came out of one of the huts, accompanied by a not much younger boy. She wore a meager black robe but she was unveiled. Jhonni thought she was wearing a mask. Then she thought, This must be a settlement of Timurese *aneh.* The deformed, routinely driven out or abandoned, or sold, by traditional communities, usually ended up on the plantations if they lived. But some of them escaped and set up communities of their own. The woman was *aneh* . . . What was wrong with the boy?

Atoon drew a sharp breath. Gani wailed and bolted.

The couple bowed over their folded hands. The woman's remaining fingers were stumps of pink, flaking white. The half-naked boy had red flowers, little hot red flowers, scattered over his skin. "Ah," said Derveet, to no one in particular. "I *see*."

She bowed.

"Good morning, Mother. How are you today?"

"Not so very well." It was the boy who spoke. The leper smiled a mild apology. Her boy continued, watching her ruined face with attention. "I don't know how it is, but we don't seem to be so well. I am not so bad myself, but there are others who are rather poorly today, especially those who have the red flowers"—the boy paused, smiled self-consciously—"as this boy here has them. And those who have the sneezing that causes limbs to become useless are suffering slightly. It's the damp weather, I expect. We will be better soon."

The old woman lifted her muzzle to an unnatural angle, a gesture that seemed to find a chink of vision in her blindness. Her eyes flickered an inquiry.

"Excuse me," said the boy. "My lady wants to know. Not our usual Koperasi people?"

"We are not Koperasi. We are Peninsulans, in borrowed uniforms."

The boy and the old lady nodded wisely, unwilling, like country people everywhere, to appear taken by surprise.

"Ah. My lady would like to know your name? Sir-lady?"

"My name is Derveet."

"Derveet? Mother's name who?"

The other villagers had begun to appear. They crept out of the huts leaning on each other, hobbling, limping. None of them were very young. Some were blind, some cadaverous with fever, some had weeping sores or the rain-of-fire marks of the disease called "red flowers." Derveet watched them come, eyes steady with understanding. She stepped forward, took the leper's hands, embraced her. It seemed the only thing to do.

"I am Derveet Merpati."

10

THE KOPERASI BUILDINGS were smooth egg shapes, rising seamlessly from the ground cover of weeds. At each end there was a ridged screen that moved easily. Within that there were double doors, set with windows of meshed glass. Atoon peered through. The bunker inside was windowless, but brightly lit. He could see no source for the light. There was a pallid room, lined on either side with tanks or cages of fine black suspended powder. The powder moved: insects. In the other buildings there were rats, tanks of water, other small animals.

"I wonder what they're for? Something nasty, I've no doubt."

He had recognized the leper. There was a picture of a leper in a book of horror stories which had been an object of secret, shuddering pleasure when he was a child. He knew little more than the name. Derveet had been the one who ferreted into the past. Serious study was not encouraged in princes. It was not elegant, not manly. "Do you know what they are?"

Cho nodded. "Yes."

If he asked her to explain, she would. But he wouldn't understand a word. She had such an impenetrably oblique way of looking at the human world. Then she'd be more unhappy: he hadn't the heart. They were all stunned almost beyond emotion by Jeeby's village. But the doll-who-was-a-person seemed most forlorn. Derveet would know. He hefted the trumpery chain, a couple of machete blows would sever it.

"Can you help these people?"

Cho's tender, childish mouth trembled. "They're not unhappy," she said. "The creatures infesting them don't hurt them. They've been given medicine for the pain. They don't know why they're like this. They don't know what they are for, so they're not upset."

"Can you make them well?"

He discovered the source of her special misery.

"Derveet doesn't want me to."

Atoon looked around. "Did Gani come back?"

"Not yet," she said. "But he won't get lost."

"Yellow jack. Leprosy, elephantiasis, poliomyelitis, smallpox, dengue, viral meningitis . . . malaria, of course. Typhoid and variants, cholera, measles, tuberculosis."

Commander Hamzah was reciting the catalogue of her wares. She paced between the settlement and the edge of the clearing, never quite reaching the huts or the trees. She'd been doing the same thing for hours. When she passed close to the open-air kitchen, where Jhonni was working with the women and boys, the chant resolved into these words. Jhonni didn't know what they meant, but they sounded evil. The villagers didn't have much food. They'd been waiting anxiously for an overdue ration-drop. What they had was being prepared for a feast.

Did Jhonni eat meat? What a shame, there was none to give her. Unfortunately the men had not been able to hunt for a while. Did Jhonni have children? Not yet. Ah, that was wise. Take life slowly, relaxedly, that's the best . . . Woodsmoke and cooking smells only partly masked the stench of sickness. The women spoke haltingly aloud, making up the gaps with smiles. Bu Tiah, their leader, was the only one who knew eye-talk. They had none of them been raised as *dapur* ladies. They were patchily informed, though, about the world outside. They were overwhelmed and delighted to have Merpati's daughter here. They had heard of Derveet. But Ranganar they knew as the pleasure island in the south. Great ladies kept seaside houses there. Was it beautiful? None of them had seen the sea.

Derveet was in the huts, visiting the bedridden ones. *Dear Mother Sky*, prayed Jhonni, *don't let me have to go in there.* The Commander looked as if she were strolling idly. When she wase close you saw her mouth working, fists clenching, shoulders twitching in an agony of restlessness. *Poor devil*, thought Jhonni. And then wondered how on earth she could feel pity.

Someone touched her arm. Jhonni flinched away, but it was Gani who had appeared at her elbow. His eyes were popping-huge, his teeth chattering. "What have you come back for?" she snapped.

"Ttt—there might be tigers." He cowered, shuddering, hugging himself in the oversized Kop tunic. "Please, Bu Jhonni. Give me some job. Or I will go crazy."

Poor beast, he couldn't help being the way he was. "Since you're here, you can wash the rice." He took the crude wooden vessel from her, awkwardly.

"What's wrong with you?"

"I—I don't know how."

He was a camp slave. He'd never seen a kitchen utensil. Big and small, petty and terrible, there was no *end* to the miseries of these people. Finally it made you angry. It made you hate them.

Jhonni saw the clumsy hands of the sick boys and women, struggling over the domestic tasks of the *dapur*: the ghastly faces raised to smile. She realized, blindingly, that she had been accepted and welcomed into the sacred hearth of a traditional Peninsulan homestead. It was a dream come true, but in such a cruel distortion! Savagely, she swiped the back of her hand across her eyes, licked the tears from her mouth. "Oh, *Mother*. Peninsulans! Put it down. I'll find you something else."

The villagers feasted their guests beside the open space that would have been their market if this were a real place. Everyone who wasn't too sick to move joined the party. It was difficult to eat, impossible not to try. Cho was right. They didn't know. Their innocence was eerie and terrifying.

"Bu Tiah, how did you come to live here?"

Derveet, failed woman, was given the place of greatest honor that she could be allowed, right beside the tattered *dapur* screen that hung before the small huddle of women. "The Koperasi," Tiah's speaking boy answered readily. "It is a plan called *transmigrasi*. They brought us here to make a new town. That was several rainy seasons ago."

Tiah's slight embarrassed laugh came through the screen.

"Living in the country," explained the boy with smallpox elegantly, "one loses track of time. Things didn't work out for the town, but we stayed. Our job is to care for the insects and other creatures in the egg-buildings. The Commander who is a secret lady looks after us. The Koperasi pay us in rice and goods. It's easy work." He smiled. Behind the screen, Tiah held up her blunted hands. "Luckily for us!"

"How did you become ill?"

"I don't know. We simply became sick, all of us." The boy sighed. "My lady says I should tell you, we honor the *dapur* here for the sake of decorum. All of us here were taken or were sold by our families so that others might live better. It's a choice," he explained with dignity, "that country people must make. In fact, none of our ladies have been blessed: we have no children. We have become families anyway." He lowered his voice. "But perhaps, my lady says, I may mention this to Merpati's daughter. You will know what this means. There are things our ladies cannot do."

"It happens in the best of families," murmured Derveet. The boy nodded diffidently, eyes lowered.

"Could you not leave here?"

Bu Tiah sighed.

"My lady says, country people get by as best they can. You don't blame us for taking work with the Koperasi. We know that without asking." He added, speaking for himself for once: "I've often thought if only I could get home to my mother, she would restore the feeling to my lady's hands. But I don't know the way. And the Koperasi have fed us when we were sick, and given us medicine. Who would feed their little creatures? It is a problem, what to do."

The villagers jostled quietly, each eager to get as close as possible to Merpati's daughter. Tiah nudged the boy. "Now that you have come, of course all will be well . . ." He leaned forward, out of the lamplight. A tall, stumbling figure had blundered by. "Could I ask something on my own account, sir-lady? Is something wrong with the Commander? She is not usually like this."

After the feast a younger boy led them to a shelter that had been prepared while they were eating: a framework of green stakes roofed with fresh leaves. The earth inside had been swept clean and beaten flat. There was a tiny charcoal fire, clay lamps hanging from the supports, a wickerwork-covered pitcher of water, and a dipper. The boy, Arun, crept about lighting the lamps, keeping his head below the heads of the honored guests.

"We are sorry, it is very humble. *Selamat malam . . .*"

The heat of his fever and the smell of his sick body wafted out into the dark. They sat in the firelight, breathing cleaner air with relief. "I don't understand!" cried Jhonni, plunging into the silence. "You people told me that *dapur* magic protects the Peninsula from sickness!"

"It does. It protects them." It was Commander Hamzah who answered. "We've tried to cause an epidemic up here. We can't. The Timurese haven't had contact with these diseases for hundreds of years. They should be completely vulnerable, but they are not. It isn't conscious. It's something in the air, something in the women's piss, even in this benighted backcountry. We don't know what's going on. But it works."

She stood leaning against one of the shelter supports, a bulky ghost. Her profile in the lamplight was stern and still. Gani jumped up. "Kill her!" He looked around wildly, hunting for a weapon. No one else moved, except that Derveet took out a cigarette and lit it. The boy subsided.

"What happens when the villagers die?" Jhonni answered her own question. "Oh. That's what the camp at Isolir is for. Replacements."

Jeeby slid her an oblique glance. "They don't die."

"You're experimenting with extinct diseases," said Endang. "You've re-created some hideous forms of mass destruction of human life. So that was the great secret. *Why?* For God's sake, why? What's the use of ruling a country full of corpses?"

"Don't ask me," said the empty, detached voice. "I only work here. Did I say *diphtheria?* I think I forgot diphtheria. It's not only the old diseases. We tried inventing new ones, they don't have names, just numbers. It didn't make any difference."

It's the Rulers who are doing this, realized Jhonni, with a shock. She had not thought about that. Jhonni never thought about the Rulers. They were the Koperasi's bosses: but it was the Kops you had to deal with. The Rulers were dim, neutral figures, almost faded from the world. *The Rulers have abandoned us. They don't care anymore.* That was what Derveet used to say. But it turned out that wasn't true. The truth was much worse. She found that she'd begun to shiver, and couldn't stop.

"We've tried investigating the phenomenon. It's hard to keep full women alive in captivity, and when they die—you may as well know, the legend is true. *They destroy themselves.* I mean, literally. Nasty. Useless. Pool of goop, as I understand it."

"Have your bosses tried taking a live one apart?" Derveet wondered mildly.

Jeeby looked across the firelight. "They tried. Once. Didn't find out anything useful, and they dropped the idea. You know, the fuck about working for those people is the way they drop things. This village, for instance. They forgot about it for years because what's the use? We can keep the subjects sick, but we can't make them infectious on the Peninsula."

"I could have told you that—"

"And they *don't die.* They don't, don't die. They just don't die. They lie there in their shit and don't die!"

Derveet studied the tip of her cigarette. Atoon and Cho were on either side of her: all three very still.

Jhonni saw that they were not shocked by Jeeby Hamzah's revelations. She had the feeling of some extra, *more terrible* knowledge that she and Endang didn't share.

"Well, 'Veet? How broad-minded do you feel? Are you going to forgive me? Aren't you wishing you'd never touched me? Don't you feel dirty all over?" No response. Jeeby persisted. "The Kops are normal selfish pigs. If it weren't the poor bastards of Peninsulans it would be us, that's their rationale. I suppose you could say I've had a hard life. I was bound to grow up twisted. My bosses, though, how d'you explain them? Who ever harmed them? What d'you make of their choices? No, seriously. I'm curious."

"Genocide." Endang stared at the fire. "You taught me that word, Derveet, years ago. I tried not to believe you. But the dreams are true. This foul village is only a confirmation. It doesn't matter. Our Rulers want us dead, and somehow they'll find a way. That's what matters." He looked up at Hamzah. Jhonni, beside him, was shocked by the likeness between the two faces: the scars of an unbearable clairvoyance. "I know how you feel," he said. "These others, they don't know. But I do: exactly. I don't want you dead. *I wish you a long life.*"

Twigs in the fire crackled and wept sizzling moisture. Derveet asked, in an ordinary tone, "How long have we got?"

"A few days." The Commander stepped out of the light. They heard her crashing away through the young trees. How long for what? Jhonni wondered. The exchange seemed meaningless; what did time matter? No one spoke for a long while.

"How strange that Gani remembered to be afraid," murmured Atoon at last. "That's what happened when the Rulers first arrived, hundreds of years ago. They had machines, gadgets. People associated those things with evils that the *dapur* had banished. No one *envied* them. People ran because they were white and had lumpy faces. They looked like lepers, which is to say, like monsters out of our legends. How strange that Gani remembered to be afraid."

"I did not remember," whispered the boy. "I was just afraid."

Derveet stirred. She leaned to toss her cigarette end into the fire. "I hoped I'd get some news while I was up here. I suppose I have . . ." She was caught there, as if paralyzed, staring into the red heart.

"Derveet?" said Atoon. "Garuda?"

She sighed, came back to life. "You're wrong, Endang. This village is important. Not the most important thing we've learned, but . . ." She pushed her hair back with both hands. "I don't know about the rest of you, but I've had enough amateur dramatics to last me several lifetimes. I am exhausted. Let's sleep. We have work to do in the morning."

"Work?" cried Jhonni, bewildered. "But what can we do?"

Derveet was surprised. "What my poor friend is begging us to do. Why else did she bring us here? Destroy this place."

* * *

Forest birds called in the night. Jhonni woke in daylight, empty of dreams, and found that someone had tucked one of the villagers' blankets over her while she slept. Probably Atoon, who did not believe in infectious illness. She shoved it away and sat up. Derveet and Atoon were examining a pile of carrying baskets that had materialized overnight, in a heap a few paces from the shelter. The baskets were made of green leaves, with necks like pitchers. Jhonni had not seen anything quite like them before. You could see they were to be used only once; there was no way to empty them except by ripping them apart. Atoon tore one up; out rolled about twenty pumpkin-sized gourds. He pulled a stopper of raw rubber: an unmistakable stink blossomed.

"*Hatcha,*" exclaimed Jhonni, who had left her bed and come over to investigate. "Where on earth did it spring from?"

"Engine fuel is a plant extract," said Derveet. "You know that. There's no need to look so surprised. There are no plantations in the forest. But everything the *dapur* ever made for us can be found here, if you look."

"But who?"

"I was going to use it to burn the flowerdust plantation. I didn't believe it existed, but I thought we should be prepared."

"But who? Who brought it here?"

"Don't ask," said Derveet. "Friends of mine who live in the forest. That's all they'd like you to know."

Jhonni helped to carry heaps of the gourds to the egg-shaped buildings. Atoon hacked the chained doors open. They shared the fuel impartially. Derveet laid crude soaked fuses. There were five eggs, in two rows. By the time the second had burst into an orange quivering bell, the flames were unstoppable. They ran, yelling and shouting, and stood a safe distance away. Fierce waves of heat billowed through the air. The alien building material burned like firecrackers, flaring and crackling.

"It'll spread to the huts."

"There's a deep ditch in between, full of damp green stuff. That'll slow it down."

But the eggs burned out very quickly. The fire began to die without spreading. Atoon sighed in grim satisfaction. "All life is sacred. However, I cannot mourn those things with the fuzzy headgear."

"Mosquitoes," said Derveet. "I didn't like them either." In the trees birds called, perhaps alarmed by the fire. Derveet turned and headed back for the huts.

"What was in the other eggs?" asked Jhonni.

Atoon shrugged. "Strange containers. Gadgets, invisible insects. Who knows? Who cares?"

Jhonni imagined Bu Tiah and the others, carefully opening those doors and standing docilely inside while weird insects sucked their blood. "Atoon, could *we* get sick?" She was almost ashamed to ask. Except for Gani, the others had shown not the slightest fear for themselves.

"You heard Hamzah," Atoon reassured her. "If it could be done, Timur would be seething with bizarre sickness by now. I think it's safe to assume we are protected."

Jhonni rubbed her arms through the sleeves of her grubby jacket. It was a great relief to set fire to things. But the will behind this plan was newly terrifying by daylight. "And we thought the Rulers were a spent force. Atoon . . . what chance have we got against people who would do something like this? For no reason. *We haven't done them any harm.* How can we fight this?"

The last egg was a blackened puffball. As they watched, it collapsed into papery fragments. A gray pall drifted over the ground. "By tackling what is in front of us," he said quietly. "By never giving up." He became businesslike. "At present, by getting everyone away from here before Jeeby's bosses smell the smoke." He frowned. "Hamzah has disappeared. I suspect—I rather hope—she's gone off to hang herself, but we can't be sure. There could be another twist to her plot."

* * *

Atoon had wanted to send Hamzah's victims south, to Jagdana, where they could be passed from hand to hand until
they came into the care of his own family. Derveet had
thought of sending them, by the same route, to Bu Awan.
The people of the *aneh* sanctuary in the caldera of the
Mother Mountain had been Derveet's first allies. But they'd
decided that both courses were impractical, Atoon explained, as he and Jhonni walked back. The distances were
too great, and there was too much Koperasi presence in between.

"So where are they going? Who's going to look after
them?"

The village was full of activity. The docile villagers were
collecting together, clutching bundles of belongings and
smiling their sweet, dazed smiles. Bu Tiah's speaking boy
was offering flowers and rice to their Naga shrine for the
last time. The basket in which he would carry the living
coals of the last hearth stood beside him, wreathed in green
leaves. Jhonni counted thirty-eight people, including the six
who lay patiently helpless on newly made litters. Who
made those? she wondered.

She hung back, wishing there were something else that
she could burn. It was much harder to face the victims, smiling in their living death. "Who's going to look after them?"
she asked again, hoping cravenly that it wasn't going to be
her.

"Gani."

"*Gani?*"

"We've found out that he comes from Kambing Negara,
the little princedom north of Jagdana. It's a quiet place, very
remote. The Kops rarely trouble about it. He will reach the
border of that country, if he travels west, in about ten days'
very easy walking. He'll be well guided as long as the forest
cover lasts; and he won't take them all so far. West of here
there are other waterways. There are real villages in the for-

est. He will find refuge for these poor souls, a family here and a family there."

"But who's going to guide him—?"

Jhonni looked at the woven litters. She thought she recognized the same handiwork as in those baskets. Involuntarily, she looked towards the forest. Was there movement in there: a group of almost-human shadows? Atoon saw the direction of her glance and deliberately looked away.

"Don't ask." She said it for him. "All right, I won't." She drew a breath. "I can't believe it's so easy. I thought—I felt we had discovered a hopeless disaster."

"Possibly we have," he said. "But it isn't happening here."

He was looking at her strangely.

"Don't you know?" he said. "No, you *don't* know. How odd."

Gani was with Derveet, looking frightened and brave and proud. He had taken off the Koperasi uniform and was dressed in clothes borrowed from the villagers. His machete was stuck in his sash at the back, like a prince's dagger. He watched his flock. His urchin face had grown adult with pity. Bu Tiah came with her speaking boy to announce that everyone was ready.

"Our poor little homes," mourned the boy. Bu Tiah sighed wistfully.

"I am sorry, *bu,* but it must be done. As I told you, Commander Hamzah brought me here because she was worried about you, because you are sick and don't get well. I'm afraid the only cure is for you to leave."

"The Commander, our secret lady, she agrees?"

"Yes," Derveet assured her. "The Commander agrees."

Bu Tiah reached up. With great simplicity, she embraced Derveet. "God go with you, dear daughter," said her speaking boy. "God prosper you. Your visit has been a great pleasure."

Jhonni walked away. She couldn't stand anymore. And

there was Endang. "I've been fire-setting as well," he said. "Isn't it fun?"

They had walked through a cloud of evil dreams, back into the normal world. They tasted cautiously, exchanging wary glances, the sense of return.

"Years ago," said Endang, "when I met Derveet at the succession debate, she was in the middle of an argument about the Rulers' medicine. A bunch of Timur bandits were peddling some useless Ruler stuff to the *aneh*. Derveet said it was a deliberate plot. They were trying to wean us from the *dapur*'s protection because they wanted us to die. No one believed her, of course."

"I don't understand why they hate us. What did we *do*?"

"We don't need them, you see. And we ought to need them. It seems so *wrong* that we should be self-sufficient. We don't do anything to deserve it. Subsistence farming, handicrafts: that's all we achieve. The rest of the time we sit around giving puppet shows, dancing, playing games."

"That's why the Samsui hate Peninsulans, too."

Endang laughed. He stretched his arms. "I'm better," he announced. "I feel *well*. The horror is in the world, not in my soul. So I'm free." He sobered. "I'm well because those people are suffering." Jhonni thought of the way Atoon had looked at her, and felt a breath of misgiving: what did that grave stare mean? But she answered cheerfully, so happy that he was happy.

"I feel it too—ashamed, but *glad*."

They stood, obscurely united by something that felt like a new guilty secret: the will to live.

Bu Tiah and her people moved off slowly, Gani in the front, shouldering the first of the litters with one of the more able-bodied of the villagers. The forest and its secrets closed around the halting procession. Then they torched the huts. The palm matting was damp, but *hatcha* fuel would burn with almost anything.

"And it's over and we can go home," declared Jhonni, as

they watched the smoky flames. "Pity about the flower-dust," she joked.

"Not quite over," Derveet corrected her. "There were two camps, remember."

Derveet, Atoon, and Cho looked at the two young people. "You don't know," said Derveet.

"Know what?" quavered Jhonni. "What's wrong?"

Derveet thought of the night when she had left the others sleeping, to go and parley with the *orang hutan*. When she looked up and saw Jhonni standing there. Jhonni, *but you could see the trees behind her* . . . They had walked back to the first clearing together, and Derveet had seen this ethereal Jhonni slide like a trickle of water back into the body lying sleeping on the ground.

The hairs stood on her nape as she remembered. She had never seen such a thing before; there was nothing so extreme in the dancers' repertoire. Atoon had had the reverse experience. He said Jhonni had walked into his dream and shown him things . . . He didn't want to go into details. But they all three, Atoon, Derveet, Cho, had seen Jhonni and Endang acting out their visions on the trail . . . seen rise around the young people on the forest path the shadows of a terrible future: the future that might be.

But Jhonni was a Samsui girl, and Endang a full male.

She became aware that Jhonni was waiting for an answer. Jhonni looking not in the least like an emergent goddess, but frightened and resentful. Jhonni obviously wishing desperately that she'd never come away, that she was safe in Ranganar.

Safe!

"Hamzah couldn't start an epidemic up here," Derveet said. "But there's a place that would present a soft target to this secret weaponry. Her bosses must have realized that, but it didn't suit them to attack Ranganar before. Not until now."

"Ranganar!" cried Jhonni.

"Don't be frightened. It is not going to happen. But

there's the camp at Isolir. When we left, the Kops were waiting for an influx of new arrivals. There's an old saying: how do you hide a leaf? In a forest. The plan was to deliver the disease carriers from this village to Ranganar, hidden in a flood of refugees. The first wave is already there. The infection, we've dealt with. But another massive influx of *healthy* refugees would be bad enough for the city. We still have to stop that."

"But . . ." Jhonni gaped. "But how did you—? Who told you all this? Was it Hamzah?"

"You told us, Jhonni. You and Endang."

Jhonni began to shake. She knew what Derveet was telling her. This was the meaning of her waking nightmares. *Me?* she thought. *No! It isn't true! I'm not a* dapur *lady!* She understood that she and Endang felt released not because the danger had passed, but because the warning had been delivered.

"Ranganar!" she wailed. "It's gone! I can't go home!"

"Not yet," said Derveet, with a small, grim smile. "We aren't beaten yet. Let's go."

Someone followed them as they moved quickly down the trail. They didn't have to slash their way and were not distracted by visions. They were keeping up a fierce pace, but their shadow stayed close behind them. Hamzah had not been seen since she left them after the conversation in their guest hut. Jhonni hoped Atoon was right and she was dead. She thought the following shadow must be one of the same guardians who were watching over the sick villagers. At the first halt she discovered she was wrong.

The Provincial Commander's uniform was stained and dirty; it was no longer red but a blotchy dried-blood brown. She kept her distance, peering from between the branches. She had something in her arms. They couldn't make out what. She rocked it; they heard a faint crooning. When Atoon tried to approach her, she ran away.

The sun had been high before they left the clearing. When

the early dusk of the forest overtook them they went on walking, by the light of torches dipped in *hatcha*. A smoky screen of light moved beside them; the rest of the forest vanished behind it. A puppet shadow stumbled sometimes across the screen, nursing its bundle. When they stopped to sleep, Hamzah stopped too. Atoon again tried to reach her, with a lure of food.

"Leave her," advised Derveet. "There's nothing you can do. Don't worry, it isn't a real baby."

"She must be eating something," he said. "Or she'd be dead by now." They left a portion of pressed rice, some fruit, and a half-full water bottle by a gap in the trees.

Jhonni lay down, tired to death. She thought of Commander Hamzah, rocking a tiny mummified corpse. There had been a child, Atoon said so.

She was awake, suddenly, and aware—as you sometimes are in the middle of the night, when grief and anxiety are pressing you hard—that she could not possibly sleep again. They had halted in a clearing made by an uprooted stump. The half-moon looked down through the splayed giant fingers of the dead tree's roots. She sat up and saw Derveet and Cho sitting close together against a frieze of black and silver. They weren't touching, but she felt she'd interrupted something private. She lay down again quickly, but too late.

"Go back to sleep, Jhonni." Now Derveet was alone.

"I can't sleep. I'm worried about Hamzah." Jhonni wondered where Cho had gone.

"Jeeby won't harm you. And I don't think you can help her."

Derveet's tone was cool but unforbidding. Jhonni crept around the sleeping bodies to join her. "Why is she following us?"

"Why not? Where else is she going to go?"

"Does she think that's a live baby?"

"I don't know." Derveet stretched out her legs and tipped her head back to gaze at the moon.

Jhonni swallowed. "The *dapur*," she whispered. "Why didn't they *do* something?"

"D'you mean the women of central Timur? I don't suppose they knew that the place existed." She gave Jhonni a quizzical look, a crooked smile. "Or do you mean the *dapur* which is a matrix of strange emergent powers, belonging to fertile women? In which case, you did do something, Jhonni."

The experience of waking nightmare flooded back. That other reality which Jhonni had visited imposed itself on the night: the teeming bodies, the fear, the fighting for food and space and breath. She doubled over, shuddering.

It passed. She sat up. Derveet was gazing at the moon.

This is dapur *power*, thought Jhonni. *This terrible, vulnerable knowing. This is how it feels to have magic-that-works. It is not infallible; it is not a weapon. I know why the women who have this power, or know what it is, were afraid to listen to Derveet.* Dapur *power used to be a secret, but now it isn't. The Rulers must know: and partly because of Derveet. The people who made that village know about our only hope.*

Jhonni felt, unbearably, pity for her idol. Derveet kept gazing at the moon.

"I can't imagine it," whispered Jhonni humbly. "What goes through people's minds when they're deliberately, slowly torturing people who've never done them any harm? The worst was, those people didn't know. They were grateful for being poisoned. That's hideous. Oh, Derveet, what if they try again?"

"People can get sick on the Peninsula, sicken and die in all kinds of strange or commonplace ways. To protect life doesn't mean denying natural death. The Rulers should have known better. Killer infections still exist in our world, or did: on the Black Islands, for instance. On the Peninsula infections become—not *harmless*, but not dangerous either. If they tried again—" Derveet shook her head. "We're getting weaker all the time. The *dapur*'s protection is not infallible. I don't know how long it would last, now, against determined assault."

"I can accept greed, stupidity, selfishness. I know Samsui who'd do absolutely anything for a profit. But how can anyone do things like that, plan things like that, when they're not *getting* anything for it?"

"You can't imagine. Be thankful you can't. Don't try."

"Derveet, please? If someone doesn't talk about it, I think I'll go crazy as Hamzah."

"You want to talk about the problem of evil." Derveet sighed resignedly. "I have often," she said, "wanted someone dead: *out of my way.* Sometimes for honest gain. Sometimes simply because I hated the sight of them. I've felt that way about—oh, whole groups of people, briefly, or for longer periods. The Koperasi, the Rulers. Atoon's hideously complacent family. Miss Butcher Handai, on occasion. It's a question of . . . being lucky enough not to have the power to make our vicious whims effective. Or, having that power, being lucky enough not to use it. And being careful."

"Careful?"

"Not to wish too hard, just in case."

She was silent then. Jhonni decided that she'd gone to sleep sitting up. She tiptoed back to her own hollow among the roots and slept peacefully until morning.

The river had changed since they left it. The *Pisau Besar* was riding high against the bank, the water churning ocher-yellow instead of dimpled glass-green. There must have been some heavy rain up above. The boys had dismantled their cabin and rebuilt it under the eaves of the trees, with a sail stretched for an awning. They came out of this gracious pavilion, in a fine-grained afternoon downpour, to greet the returning explorers.

"I hope you have had a pleasant rest," said Anakmati. "Not too lonely? No idea of going off without us?"

"Oh no." Usman grinned self-consciously. "No idea of

that! There are the birds and animals. One particular bird was very attentive. It kept us company."

"What kind of call? Was it like this?" She cupped her fist over her mouth. ". . . plonk plonk, plonk . . ."

A bird in the trees answered: *plonk, plonk, plonk.* "How odd," remarked the bandit innocently. "I didn't think one found that kind of bird in these parts." The boys grinned and shivered. It was very flattering and very satisfactory that the great bandit had been able to set a watch on them, up here in the trackless forest. They were longing to get home and tell the story.

Derveet performed the role of Anakmati for a while. It was near to sunset when she walked out along the grassy riverbank. The *Pisau* was being reconstructed. She was not desperate about the delay, and if she *were* desperate, fury and panic would achieve nothing. It was inevitable; it was the Peninsula. When she was out of sight of the others the shadow that had been following just inside the forest emerged from hiding. They met in silence. Jeeby rocked her bundle.

"I like your little girlfriend," she remarked at last. "She's sweet. Sorry I said that about her, before."

"Everybody loves Cho."

"You know the Rulers have got one?"

"I know."

They sat under a tree. The rain had stopped; late sun burned up the moisture. White wraiths of mist rose from the water. Jeeby laid down her blanket-wrapped bundle tenderly.

"A doll that makes dreams come true. I can see why you feel nervous of her. Everything beautiful is tainted." She sighed. "I loved you, 'Veet."

Derveet raised her eyebrows. "Preserve me from my enemies!"

"I said *loved*. I don't have feelings now." She pushed her hands into her tunic pockets, gave a whistling sigh through her teeth. "It's horrible, when you're in a state like this, how one clings to life . . ."

She became thoughtful. "The village was a wasted effort. It was forgotten. They'd abandoned the idea. I was given charge of it, like being told to look after a deformed child that's been kept in secret: everyone hopes it will die, but it doesn't die. Shit, the way they *didn't die.* That was the worst. Your precious *dapur* has a lot to answer for. But you've got the bosses rattled, 'Veet. I'm not flattering you—it's the truth. So then, someone remembered the village. What a party all those myriads of tiny monsters would have had in Ranganar. The water supply running out, the Physician clan running around making bad worse. What a mess you'd have been in." Jeeby laughed aloud, and suddenly, guiltily, swallowed her laughter.

"Course I didn't like the idea. But orders is orders. I hope you noticed there were no children. Grant me that. And they didn't suffer, nobody suffered."

"What finally changed your mind?"

"The dust." She pulled a rueful face, strange grimace on that death's-head. "I don't know why I started taking it. It was a whim. Could be I was missing you and the old life, or something. I started drinking so I'd be able to go on with the work. Then the golden wine took over and . . . oh, nightmares."

"What d'you think they'll do when they find out?"

Jeeby shrugged: uninterested. "They know already. I was supposed to have been picked up by a big bubble today, to go in and organize the special consignment back to Isolir by air for the transfer south. I expect they'll do nothing. Or think of something worse. Who knows? Things are getting very . . . very *random,* out at sea." She leaned back, dreamily gazing. "Don't you think those mist things on the water look like hands? Too pale, too blurred . . . They could be lepers' hands. I've seen the future, 'Veet. Your future. Do you believe that?"

"You've seen a future that could be. It can be changed."

Jeeby chuckled and fell silent. After a pause she turned to Derveet earnestly, taking hold of the front of the Kop tunic with grimy and skeletal fingers. "I've always wanted to be good. Not good the way you mean it, but *the best*. To be respected. They gave me that. Correction, they gave me nothing. I earned it."

The hands dropped. "I could fill my pockets with stones and jump in the river. I don't think I will. Something that young man said . . ." She broke off. "What the fuck are you *doing*, 'Veet, traveling around with an en-too-rage of pretty studs! I call it decadent!" She cackled, stopped herself with a smirk, began again. "Something that young man said: he wished me a long life. Well. Maybe I wish that too. Bu Tiah and her folks didn't die. I won't die." She raised her head, which had dropped almost to Derveet's shoulder, raised her voice. "I've decided I'm not coming back to Isolir. I'm going to take a walk in the forest." She gestured vaguely. "Upstream. Somewhere."

She stood, stumbled against the dead-baby bundle. "Oh, that's yours, by the way. Sorry about that part. Not good, we're supposed to be pals." She lifted her shoulders, pulled a funny grin, scratched in the shock of red-brown hair: lost gestures, memories.

"What can I say, 'Veet? It seemed like a good idea at the time."

A little later Cho came up the bank. She knelt by Derveet's side, looking upstream, where the Commander had disappeared into the mist and the wet green thickets.

"She doesn't want me to help her."

Derveet shook her head. "Nor me. Nothing to be done. Dust addiction does permanent harm, they say, beyond the *dapur*'s powers. Addicts don't recover. She can't come back from wherever it is she's going. The dust must finish what it began."

"There's never anything that I can do," sighed Cho. And then, cautiously, "Did you love her very much?"

"Me?" Derveet was startled into silence: stared at the

river, laughed shortly. "Oh, I love a lot of people. It's part of my job." She turned. "But I have never been *in love* with anyone except you." She drew a solemn cross over her heart. "True."

She pulled Cho into her arms, into a long and quiet embrace. Derveet possessed a secret. The Rulers didn't know what she knew: she had seen the way they treated an angel doll. The Samsui and the dancers in Ranganar had been kind to Cho when they thought she was a human stranger. Since they had learned the truth their attitude had changed. They called her the doll-who-is-a-person, but they didn't believe it. No one else knew . . . except perhaps Atoon. *Cho is a person.* The marvelous toy is a human being who can think and feel.

Magic unravels. Look too closely, touch the web, and it disappears. Maybe those who have the mysterious power only dream dreams that are acute, intuitive judgments of likelihood. And if *dapur* power truly shows the future of a particular moment: that future changes as you know it; you change it by knowing it. She was not afraid of Hamzah's veiled threats of hopeless doom. Isn't it inevitable that lost souls should have bad dreams?

Derveet held the doll-who-was-a-person in her arms and wondered about this other, alien magic of the past. Perhaps it would unravel in the same way. What did Cho *do?* What did her brother do for the Rulers? If you believe that your toys have the power to grant your most secret, guilty wishes—that they *must* grant these wishes—is the belief enough? Wouldn't that belief make it possible for you to do terrible things and feel no shame?

But supposing it's true, and the angel doll will grant your most secret wishes? Then your only recourse is to strive to have a pure heart. *Let thy thought be for the good of all,* as it said in Scripture, *and do thy work in peace.* You must not ask her to do any of the marvelous things that she can do. The risk is too great. No matter how sad it makes her that you don't ask for her help. You must not *use* her, machine though she is, and only happy when she is working.

Derveet shuddered, returned to the commonplace—and remembered Jeeby's casual revelation. The airship that had failed to rendezvous with the Commander might have gone on and discovered the burned-out village already. The Kops would have reported back. Would they search the forest? There was nothing Derveet could do for Gani and his charges. They were as well guarded, as safely hidden as they could be.

That was another crime to add to the catalogue: to have enlisted the service of the gentle *orang hutan*. Those innocents should have nothing to do with war. But over and over again, Derveet had to do what was expedient. She released Cho, sat back on her heels. "Do you recall, I said I was never going to play Anakmati again?"

Cho nodded hopefully, catching the gleam of amusement in Derveet's eyes. Cho liked Anakmati.

"Well . . . one *last* time. This is *definitely* the bandit's farewell. Cho, could you run another errand for me? I could go myself but I don't think I should. Anakmati in person would be too exciting for their weak nerves."

Someone—Jhonni—was calling them. Derveet stood and picked up Jeeby's dead baby. The blanket wrapping fell apart. Eight plump little sacks of black oiled silk rolled out. Derveet lifted one and loosened the doubled stitching at its mouth. A sweet, compelling scent blossomed in the air.

The *Pisau* rode downstream swiftly and silently through the darkness. Usman and Yuda moved about like monkeys, with swinging lights, using the steering oars and the sail to control the boat's passage through the well-known hazards of the Melangir by night. The passengers kept out of the way: Endang and Jhonni in the cramped space in front of the mast, the other three behind the engine well. There wasn't much conversation. Derveet was dozing, head dropped on her arm. Atoon cast a discreet glance through the open shed of the cabin. The young people were wide awake, silent, not touching, but clearly engrossed in each other.

"Derveet . . . this is a very strange question, but have you wondered about those two?"

He was not referring to the supernatural experiences they'd witnessed in the forest. Atoon, Derveet knew, had said all he was going to say about that. It was very hard for him to accept what he'd seen and felt: *dapur* power outside the *dapur!* He was wondering about something more mundane, but startling.

"Yes, I have," she answered, without lifting her head. "Semar told me about Endang. I didn't believe him, but I said something to Endang, back at Dove House, and his reaction left me in no doubt. Are you shocked? I think they're sweet together."

"Well!" said the prince, astonished. "Well—"

Cho left the boat quay as the *Pisau* was being moored, left Atoon struggling with a wildly changing world, left the quiet streets of Isolir. She continued south over earth-banked paddy fields, through a narrow cultivated band of coconut palms, into the red rocks, the thorn scrub, the foot-hills of Timur's bandit country.

In the dawn light every shadow was painted black as the mouth of a well. Every tall boulder was as clear-cut, distinctive as a word in a large red language. She trotted briskly, checking off the landmarks Derveet had listed without breaking her stride. She was surprisingly close to town when, after scrambling up a narrow gully, she ducked under an overhang and found the entrance to a short, sandy passage. It ended in a lamp-lit cavern. There was a smell of smoke from the lamps, and a good smell of boiling rice. Cho coughed politely. The bandits jumped up in alarm. Flustered, though they were grown men and hardened in their outcast life, they all tried to stand between the stranger and the pot on the charcoal brazier. Cho was thrilled to be once more in the presence of real live bandits, like a story. But the bandits were unnerved by her candid gaze.

"We are only poor extras!" protested the leader. "We have no mothers, no sisters to do *dapur* tasks. We must live!"

At thirteen or fourteen these extras would have been turned out to fend for themselves, along with the failed women. In the pure tradition they should have committed suicide. Most of them, given the option, preferred a life of crime and shame.

"I came past your sentries," she apologized. "I was afraid they would keep me talking: and this is urgent. I've come from Anakmati."

The bandits hissed and gasped. "So it's true, then!" someone cried. "He's come back to us!"

She took something out of her pocket and held it out, with a little bow. It was a seashell. The leader of the band, a veteran of about twenty-five, took it from her hand. It was a small conch shell, far too small to produce a sound, but whimsically he put it to his lips and blew.

Awake. Arise. To work, to your duty, children of earth . . .

The bandits leapt to their feet, eyes glowing, as the inaudible summons echoed around the cave. "Our day has come!" declared their chief. "A day of death and glory."

Cho tried to calm them. "Not *exactly* . . ."

They subsided. The chief, Tjakil, settled cross-legged. The others gathered around. "Not yet," he said. "Not *yet*."

Cho didn't contradict him. She explained what Anakmati wanted.

11

THE DORMITORIES WERE awash with humanity. The neat
bed rows of the Reform Camp regime were drowned in the
flood, became irrelevant. Bodies crowded between them,
over them: boys, children, women, studs. Intact family
groups protected little citadels of floor space. People picked
their way up and down, holding lost children by the hand.
The experience was so new to them that people were still
being kind to each other: sharing food, commiserating,
swapping horror stories.

Two Kops shoved open the doors and poked their heads
inside. "See what I mean, Sarge. *Cukup*: we're packed out.
Any more come in and we have to have them camping on
the lawns."

"Then let them camp, Trooper. We're required to help
these people."

The other Kop nodded. "Course. Assisting-and-facilitat-
ing-voluntary-movement-of-population. Movement caused
by unrest inspired by bad elements that don't have the support of the people or the royalty of Gamartha. But . . ." He
looked anxious.

"What's wrong with you?"

"It's going to rain, Sarge. They'll ruin the grass."

"I wouldn't worry about that."

The trooper pulled nervously at the open door. There was

an ominous grating sound; he quickly desisted. The bottom hinge was coming away from the wood. The refugees, who had previously seemed unaware of the Kops, turned to look: a swarm of eyes.

"What will the Commander say? He's murder about his lawns."

The sergeant gave the young man a quelling look.

"They won't be here long."

Commander Hamzah had disappeared. His secretary had gone missing the same morning, which had caused some gossip, until it transpired that the lieutenant had taken official leave, and the fact hadn't got into the usual channels due to a clerical error. But for the Commander's absence no explanation was forthcoming.

Sergeant Tomo made a note on his clipboard about the dormitory door, and left the trooper to his crowd-minding. There was suddenly a dreadful amount of work for Building Maintenance. It was shocking how things fell apart: the white paint staining, the cooling system flooding, the mortar in the walls crumbling. The sergeant headed back to Reception, mentally composing reports that laid the blame on Timurese contractors, on local corruption, and, more cautiously, on obstruction and possible misconduct within the regular Timur Administration. Or at Sepaa. He didn't expect he'd need this cover, but old habits die hard. When he reached the graveled forecourt the treadies were lining up. This was a big relief. There'd been some genuinely antsy moments in the last day or two. The delivery of refugees had happened smoothly. A proportion had turned up by themselves, a copycat effect predicted and allowed for. But transport onwards was a different phase of the operation.

Hamzah had vanished. Tomo had found the evidence of what you might call a lovers' tiff . . . He'd covered up, not from any feeling of loyalty to his CO, but because the timing was disastrous. Tomo saw a great future ahead of him in the refugee movement business. But with Hamzah gone, he'd discovered arrangements that hadn't been made, fixing that hadn't been fixed. He wasn't surprised. He'd seen the signs. He wasn't surprised, either, that the Commander had cracked up completely and done a bunk. But he was determined not to let anything go wrong with this first completed operation. This refugee business had a great future, and Tomo was going to be right there raking in the profit.

Luckily, Tomo knew what to do. These days the Occupying Army was a loose confederation of private gangs, run by so many petty warlords in uniform. So long as you understood that, everything was *bagus.* Tomo grinned. Some of the drivers in those cabs didn't look much like regulars. But they were in uniform, more or less. Paper would be exchanged, to satisfy those who were living in the past. All would be well. The office leapt into action as he walked through the doors. He liked to see that, and for a change, today there was actually plenty to do.

"No trace of the special consignment, Sarge."

The "special consignment" was Hamzah's baby, and unlikely to turn up now. "Can't be helped. We've got to move these people on, get the throughput going. The specials can go in a later delivery. Right. Let's have those treadies filled and on their way." He tossed his clipboard to a clerical officer. "Building faults. Get onto it. Any response from Sepaa on the Commander?"

"Nothing yet, Sarge."

The Reform Camp's official second-in-command, a fool by the name of Major Andi Durno, had wanted Sepaa informed instantly of Hamzah's disappearance. He was such a dimwit, he didn't even know that Sepaa was their deadly enemy. But Tomo had the Officers' Block well trained. He'd persuaded them the information was too sensitive for wave communication. He reminded them there were bandits in the hills with illegal equipment, monitoring all Koperasi transmissions. Which was nonsense, but officers always believed it. Finally, a sealed report had been sent by hand via the regular Administration Office in Isolir. The obstructive buggers in town could be trusted to slow that down. Especially since they'd have had difficulty securing motorized transport of any kind at present. Tomo glanced out of the window beside him at the ranks of treadies, *his* treadies. The news about Hamzah was probably traveling to Sepaa on foot.

A white-faced youth with floppy black hair, Tomo's personal assistant, came up and murmured, "*What if Jeeby doesn't come back?*"

"What if he don't? We'll get ourselves a new CO. Things might change around here, but they were going to change anyway. No more gardening, no more schoolrooms. We're moving into phase two." Tomo's eyes glistened. "There'll be other camps like this, a whole network. To be built, maintained, supplied . . ."

"Processing the involuntary movement?"

"What's that? Voluntary, you mean."

Boldly, the youth grinned and pointed to the topmost form on a pile. "It says here, *in*voluntary. Must be a misprint."

Tomo laughed. "Involuntary voluntary refugees. I like it."

The white-faced youth leaned closer.

"But Sarge, what about the stuff?"

This tactless question earned him a disgusted look. "Business before pleasure, my son. And this is *big* business."

Tomo had never been taken in by Hamzah's formidable reputation. He knew the man was the sort who would crack under pressure. He believed the Commander would turn up, in a day or two, when he'd had his binge. And then Tomo would have him on a string. You don't murder a fellow officer and get away with it, not without a lot of help and support. Not even these days. Tomo would prefer that outcome; therefore, he would do nothing in a hurry. But if time went by . . . The sergeant had a very good idea where the flowerdust was hidden. He could go and fetch it himself.

No. Tomo's mouth moved in unspoken, unspeakable denial. He would not go *up there*. There were things he didn't know and didn't want to know. If Hamzah never came back, another Hamzah would arrive. There would be a new CO with contacts above his purported rank, burdened with privileges to which Sergeant Tomo did not aspire. Let the CO deal with the bosses and the *up there*.

But it would be a pity to lose the treasure. He considered his assistant. The lad would never be an empire-builder. He was convinced that the big secret behind this operation was a piddling bit of drug smuggling. Tomo never touched drugs himself. Let the kid, who enjoyed the pleasure, take the risk.

The white-faced youth, feeling that glance, bent earnestly over his paperwork. The hairs on his nape were prickling. *It's not wrong,* he thought, *everybody smokes. It's not evil. We're helping these people . . .*

Tomo went to watch the contents of dormitories one (faulty lower left hinge on outer doors, blocked gas pipe) and two (leaking roof, subsidence) loading up. The refugees were cooperative; they practically did the work themselves. They didn't know how far they were going. They had no grasp of distances, no knowledge of the country beyond their own fields. Or maybe they'd have protested at being packed so tight. Djordj Tomo could foresee a time when things wouldn't be so nice and easy. He made a mental note to try to keep hold of these drivers. Old-fashioned discipline, obedience for the sake of it, was something you could no longer expect. But they did not seem the sort who would object if they were asked to get rough.

"Involuntary voluntary movement," he muttered. "That's good."

* * *

At the Grand Hotel, Isolir, on that same day, there was a strange meeting. It took place in the room of the young Samsui accountant. Also present were the accountant's Peninsulan clerk; Nyonya Fauziah, a highly respected merchant and member of the Isolir *pancasila*, the town council; her speaking boy; another unnamed *dapur* lady; and a lanky, flashily dressed person who called himself Fauziah's bodyguard.

The Town Liaison Officer from the Administration Office, who'd been asked to come here by Fauziah's speaking boy, examined a folder of closely written papers. The ladies and the Samsui waited. The Peninsulan women's faces were invisible, of course. The Samsui girl looked grave and nervous—as well she might. The brigand walked up and down the room, being a distraction.

The Koperasi officer, kneeling on the floor in the manner prescribed by Peninsulan etiquette, itched to order that man-woman to wait outside. He didn't dare. He had a strong feeling that Fauziah—and he knew the merchant as well as any Koperasi could hope to know a *dapur* lady—was *afraid* of this supposed bodyguard. Knowing Fauziah, he was impressed.

"Madam really had no need to employ an armed escort."

Fauziah's speaking boy answered without glancing at his employer. "Madam says, these days one cannot be too careful."

He gave the officer a meaningful look. Captain Djason, the Koperasi officer, realized that the presence of the bandit was far from incidental. Fauziah wasn't interested in corruption at the Koperasi installation. She'd become involved with this on the orders of that lawless constituency up in the hills. It was a sobering thought.

"I didn't know who to turn to," explained Miss Cycler. "I haven't been qualified for long. This is my first real job. And you'll see. The way things are, I couldn't be sure *who* to trust at the camp." The young woman had a round, honest face, at the moment scarlet with embarrassment. "So I went to Nyonya Fauziah, and *she* said we should take it to you. The problem, I mean."

He wondered how she'd picked on Fauziah. It was unlikely that a heretic from the south had been welcomed into the traditional society of Isolir. He'd worked with Fauziah for years, never heard her voice or seen her face. This young woman, alone in an alien country, had had the initiative to find out where the reins of power were held in this town. He saluted her.

She did not know, of course, that Hamzah had disappeared. As far as Miss Cycler was concerned she was the one who'd absconded. She hadn't returned to the camp, he gathered, since she'd decided to tell tales. He wondered if Fauziah knew. He wouldn't be surprised. He wouldn't be surprised—he suddenly decided—if Fauziah and this gawky bandit turned out to know quite a lot about the Commander's disappearance.

"We would like your assurance," said the speaking boy, with a diffident air that was entirely assumed. "We would like to know that something will be done, urgently."

The bandit came up and took the papers out of Captain Djason's hands. Djason was too startled to react. The bandit turned his back on them all, turned his back on the ladies, which was a shocking breach of Peninsulan etiquette. The Liaison Officer studied those disdainful slouching shoulders, controlling his irritation. Could the ruffian read? It seemed unlikely. But the insolence confirmed his guess as to where the power lay.

The Peninsular Administration Office in Isolir hated the Reform Camp. The project drained supplies; it devoured water. It made no sense in relation to the increasingly frightening events in Gamartha. There was corruption in there? Of course there was—the whole operation was corrupt! The Isolir office didn't need a callow Samsui to tell them that. But it had been known (word gets about) that

Hamzah could not be touched. So nothing could be done. However, if the hypocritical profiteer Commander had seriously fallen foul of the Timur bandits, then he was finished up here, no matter who his friends were.

Captain Djason's impatience dissolved.

"There'll have to be an investigation."

Fauziah's dark robes stirred. Caution, he decided, was rank ingratitude. "In view of certain events at the camp, quite separate events, I think we'll be justified in taking over. We'll have the place closed down pending investigation."

Things are falling apart, he thought. No one knows where final authority rests anymore. Sometimes this ought to work on the side of the righteous.

"That will be satisfactory," allowed the speaking boy.

They were packed into the treadie like sacks of rice, like bundles of firewood. The roof panel was open; otherwise they would have suffocated. When the rain began the people underneath it got wet. One baby cried and cried. Other children wept and complained. Everyone defended his space. People who had larger bundles of belongings began to be the object of hostile shifting and muttering. A chicken wrapped in someone's arms squawked and kicked. Old boys and the studs, who tended to have poor bladder control, suffered the first real humiliation. They wormed their way into the corners to relieve themselves, crept back to their families pursued by a stink that made them feel like penned animals. After about the first hour nobody talked at all.

Then the treadie stopped. The silence and stillness was such a relief that they merely sat and enjoyed it. Nobody even hoped that they'd be allowed out for a meal break or to stretch their legs. The tailgate fell away with a rattle and a crash. Air and light flooded in. The people waited for permission to get down. When nothing happened, they began to climb out anyway in ones and twos. Finally everybody was standing around in the rainy sunlight of . . . somewhere.

They were at a crossroads. There was another treadie drawn up beside theirs, and another group of people—a mass that surely couldn't possibly have been contained in that squat metal box—stood beside it. The graded road with its spattered verges was crossed by a red-brown country path. There were rice fields, as yet unplanted. There were coconut groves with blue steep slopes beyond. There was a brown, hurrying stream that disappeared into a tunnel of whispering bamboo. The people stared at this deeply familiar scenery, very confused.

One of the women prodded a boy into action. He approached the Koperasi. The Kops were stretching and yawning, shedding tunics and settling for a smoke. "Excuse me, sir." The boy bobbed and smiled ingratiatingly—you had to be careful with Kops. "Is this Ranganar?"

The driver he'd addressed took off his cap and shook out a luxuriant, splendidly masculine fall of hair. "No, it's not Ranganar. This is Timur." He jerked his thumb towards the red path, spoke loudly and clearly. "Now hop it. The lot of you. Get home. And try not to be so fucking stupid in future, peasant."

The boy stared. He looked back towards his family.

"But, the unrest?"

"Forget the unrest." The driver thrust out his chest. His uniform tunic fell open, revealing the folds of a purple sash and the ornate hilt of a dagger. He gestured with a lordly hand over the lovely countryside of the Timur hills and the grinning group of his companions. "From now on you're under the protection of the acar-growers' mutual friendly society. Now get lost."

Derveet pored over Jhonni's evidence, moving her lips laboriously as she spelled down the pages, while the Kop's nervous attention reached a pitch of unease. It did no harm to let the man feel how far the balance had shifted. She shuffled the papers, closed the folder, feeling admiration and respect for Cycler Jhonni, then strolled onto the balcony, taking the folder with her.

Cho and the cat were out there. They were not exactly hiding from the Kop. He wouldn't notice them if he saw them. But Cho thought it was better to keep out of the way. Divine Endurance sat precisely, tail twitching. She was trying not to show it, but she was very annoyed. Cho could not resist teasing her.

"What a good idea it was to come up-country. You told me it would make Derveet happy, and it has."

"You wait," snapped Divine Endurance. "The sick ones were a decoration. The Rulers' plan will work without them. You wait."

Cho giggled.

Derveet gazed over the roofs of Isolir to the road down which a stream of treadies had passed this morning. The Reform Camp was empty. *Selamat jalan,* she murmured. Safe journey, my friends. The cat was staring up at her. She looked down at the dainty animal mask, alive with such eerie, cold intelligence: such inimical purpose . . . Cho had told her that the cat had *known* what was happening in Timur: known and triumphed in the knowledge. Was it possible? She laughed. "Better luck next time, monster."

EPILOGUE

JHONNI THOUGHT DERVEET would throw the flowerdust into the Straits. Derveet had other ideas.

Nightfall on the West Bank. There was no street lighting this side of the river, and hardly a lamp visible in the maze of courtyards, palm shacks, ramshackle wooden shelters. When an inner door opened or a screen shifted, the secret glow of a cooking hearth would shoot out. For the most part the West Bank accepted the deepening twilight without resistance.

Under the great trees around the old water palace of the Garudas, darkness fell quickly. But in the square pool, the last glow of sunset was overtaken by glittering fire. Lights burned through the shutters along the upper room, scattering gold over the water. Dove House was entertaining.

The boys had set up a long table. The company sat around it on antique straight-backed chairs, no two the same. Hanging lamps of glass and gold filigree shed brilliant light on linen painted sumptuously in a design of clouds and eagles' wings. The tableware was equally impressive: greeny old gold and cobalt-shadowed silver, bronze table knives, gold-inlaid crystal, massive, ancient blue-and-white china platters.

It was a varied gathering. There were Samsui women. There were robed Ranganarese and Timur refugees, attended by their speaking boys. There were West Bank boys without a trace of servile diffidence, who were here on their own account. There were failed women from Hungry Tiger Street, gaudy as parrots. There were two Koperasi officers from the Admin Compound, wearing Samsui blue and looking surprisingly at home—they were among familiar friends. Everyone who was anyone in the underworld of Ranganar was here—with the exception of one notorious brothel-keeper, who had never reconciled herself to the upstart in Dove House and who had business out of town.

Some of the company were shocked to find a Peninsulan gentleman at the table, even such a poised and elegant gentleman as Mr. Ardjuna from Jagdana. But not shocked enough to walk out on the sharing of the spoils.

"So, for the purpose of this recovery the pr—ah, Mr. Ardjuna—was disguised as a woman and you were dressed as a man!" The big Samsui on Derveet's right laughed. "It sounds like something out of an opera. As good as the old *Blue Schoolroom!*"

Derveet inclined her head, smiled benignly.

The woman was a union leader. She wasn't personally interested in drugs. But she made things happen in Ranganar in any matter that involved unskilled labor—the minor clans. She could produce a mob for any purpose, or keep the streets quiet. She surveyed the clutter with admiration.

"You've got some lovely things. I wonder why you've brought them out just for us. There's some funny customers here tonight, if you don't mind me saying so."

Atoon, rather differently impressed, had wanted to know where all the outrageous junk came from. Derveet had no idea. The boys had gone out into the West Bank "to borrow a dish or two," and here was the result. Some of the stuff was old enough to have been looted from this very house a hundred years ago.

"It's all right," she said. "Most of it isn't mine."

The big woman chuckled delightedly.

Serious discussion broke out halfway down the table. A bullet-headed Samsui matron was on her feet, shouting.

"Don't you talk to me like that, red monkey! I can make you very sorry—"

The Admin Officer addressed yelled in return. "And don't you threaten me, Mrs. Pig. I have girls of yours in the Assistance, remember. Depending on my tender care—"

Pigs eat rubbish. Mrs. Pig was an affectionate nickname for someone whose business was in the disposal of two-legged refuse. The Assistance was Ranganar's prison.

"Gentlemen, ladies." Derveet tapped her glass, the crystal sang. "Please. Mrs Babi; sir. This is a friendly meeting. No talking shop." She beckoned Petruk. The Dove House boys were suffering emotional contortions, delighted to be entertaining, appalled at the company. "I believe it's time to sample my vintage."

"Ah—"

"Ah—" The Samsui and the Koperasi settled into their elegant, unfamiliar seats with identical murmurs. Each of them gazed with the same tenderness at the golden tincture that bubbled from Petruk's flask.

The rest of the dust, still wrapped in its oiled silk, lay in front of Derveet's place. Its visible presence was a risk worth taking. The Timurese and Ranganarese, probably the most important people here for Derveet's purposes, wouldn't touch the golden wine. But they could see the treasure. It lay between the hands of the puppeteer: proof of her skill.

Obviously, she decided wryly, it had been a mistake to turn her back on the world of Anakmati. When she had tried to be respectable, nobody came to her parties. It was appropriate. Property is theft, didn't someone say that? She thought of the original Garudas: women who'd carved an empire for themselves out of another chaos, long ago. They'd be amused, perhaps, at the range of interests around this table.

There were no political activists here, none of the dancers, none of the Samsui radicals. Few of Derveet's guests would have stayed in the room if they'd heard the word *rebellion*. They hated politics. But by Derveet's side sat the child-in-white. Everyone looked that way from time to time, with wary respect, wondering how much of the rumor was true. And at the foot of Derveet's table was the gentleman from Jagdana, in formal dress—wonderfully regal, his hair dressed high on a silver frame, his golden breast and shoulders bare. The message was clear. Names would not be named. No open acknowledgment of Derveet's separate pretensions would be required. But if they wanted the dust the gangsters must accept, tacitly, Garuda.

Derveet sat back in her chair and watched the show, traced the rim of her glass with a fingertip and felt the airy sweetness of the dust rise through her mind. Atoon had asked her: "Do you think the Isolir camp is the only one?" "No," she had said. Things would fall apart. They had stemmed a fake flood of refugees; what about when the real flood began? She could see a time coming soon when the Clan Council and the Admin Compound would be completely helpless. The flowerdust was Derveet's means to get a hold on the *other* government of Ranganar.

She did not know if she was right to use the dust. As always, it was a choice of evils. They were not gentle people here, nor wise. But in the worst case, these organized, seasoned cutthroats were the best hope the city had, and she might need them yet: to defend her stronghold, her citadel of Ranganar.

Derveet rehearsed disaster, still daring to wonder if there could be a different end. If she could bring this horrible crew to talk together . . . She imagined the whole of the Peninsula gathered like this, recognizing their common interest, sitting down to do business with goodwill. Was it possible?

Atoon watched Garuda's face. The Ranganar crime world

would be pacified for a while and that was good. But he was celebrating a different occasion. If no one else had noticed it, Atoon remembered that in that deathly place in the Timur forest, Derveet had for the first time claimed her mother's name. In recovering the dust they had made terrible discoveries. But he felt himself answering her call to arms with his whole soul. *We have a place to stand*, he thought. *Battle is joined.* He raised his glass to her in a silent toast.

She returned the gesture gravely. *He is mine*, she thought, and was chilled for a moment. *Mine to use* . . . Oh, Atoon, what will I do to you? But brightness rose and walked about her mind. They will never give up. They will never leave us in peace. The tide will rise again, something more that I love will be swept away. The tide will rise . . . *But this time, I win.*

If you demand a righteous victory, she told herself, you'll be disappointed. If you look for justice or reparation for all the wrong in the world, you will never be satisfied. But if you look for consolation, you will find it. Consolation and mercy.

And she thought of Jhonni and Endang: the strange promise of *dapur* power outside the *dapur*. *Something will survive* . . . She lifted Cho's hand from the tabletop and kissed it.

"Whatever happens—" she whispered, defying fate.

"Whatever happens," answered Cho.

In the doll's sad crescent eyes Derveet read the future that she'd refused to hear from Jeeby Hamzah. But her blood was singing with gold and even that future looked beautiful: a precious silence, an alluring darkness, the end of desire.

Endang and Jhonni were in the courtyard outside Semar's kitchen, without a lamp, backs against the matting wall, legs stretched on the scoured bare boards of the veranda. They had watched, slightly horrified, the arrival of the dinner guests. They had not been invited to the party. They were having their own small victory celebration down here. There was a green bottle with a cork stopper, which Jhonni had provided. It did not contain flowerdust wine, but a Samsui concoction called "natural medicine." Honey was part of it. Endang, being a Peninsulan, didn't drink. But he had tried a swig or two.

"The problem about Derveet," declared Jhonni wisely, "is that the Peninsula, what *she* thinks of as the real, true Peninsula, can't be saved. We can't return to *dapur* rule and enclosed princes, and slave boys doing the chores. Can you imagine shutting Atoon up again, sending him back to the playroom? *I* can't. You say there was good in the old ways. *Bagus* . . . If you say so. But how are you going to disentangle the good old Peninsula from the rottenness? You can't destroy one part of a bad situation and save the rest. It all has to go." She passed the bottle. "I'm talking such rubbish."

"I don't mind." He was smiling the same superior *you-don't-know-you're-born-Samsui* smile that she'd known in the old *Blue Schoolroom* coffee shop, a lifetime ago. She loved to see it. It gave her a sense of continuity, something she was seriously short of at present.

"Another thing. If Derveet admits—and she *does* admit it, though it goes against her every instinct—that the old system won't work anymore, if men aren't enclosed and there are no more boys, then . . ." She spread her hands. "There have to be more people like us."

Here in Semar's yard, where the boys might come by any minute, they did not touch each other, though the twilight was deep. But they had touched. They were getting acquainted with their unnatural urges—slowly, by degrees of daring.

Jhonni looked in the mirror at home and saw a face that couldn't be totally commonplace. She began to be satisfied with words that she'd hated: *well built, sturdy.* It was like being in love. Even her family had noticed the change in her. Fortunately they put it down to character-forming experiences up in Timur.

She was working in Aunt Kwokmei's counting rooms again. Life was back to normal, the frenetic normality of the state-of-emergency. But Aunt seemed older; she was quieter. She did not talk about the past, or complain about the present. And often it seemed to Jhonni that the "normal life" around her was thin as paper. One day, one day very soon, reality would break through.

She looked at the bottle. The level was getting low. "Endang, what would you do if it was the end of the world?"

He smiled that annoying *what-do-you-know-about-it* smile. A bat skipped through the deep blue air.

"Look! A bat! That's good luck."

"There must be hundreds of thousands of bats on the island. Are people here so remarkably fortunate?"

"Well, there's you and me. We're lucky to be alive."

The adventure in Timur was like a shadow play: unreal, impossible. The Reform Camp, the river trip, that trek through the forest. And Commander Hamzah moving through the story like a tragic demon . . . Jhonni was going to say something about good coming from evil. She stopped herself in time.

"There are no happy endings," she pronounced. "There are only happy beginnings. Like in the *Blue Schoolroom*, when you leave them starting a hopeful new life."

Endang snorted. "You mean, when the stud has been graciously allowed to settle down in a chicken coop, in his rich Samsui girlfriend's backyard?"

"It's not a *chicken coop*," protested Jhonni. "It's the *school*. He's become the family's schoolteacher, a respected person." Endang was laughing. Jhonni sat up. "I have to go." She had come across the river to see the spectacle of the gangsters arriving. Endang was staying at Dove House. They did not want to be closer, or together more often. Not yet. It was something they both understood.

He touched her wrist delicately. "You've missed the ferry."

"It doesn't matter. I can get someone to take me."

Along the river, rows of dark go-downs loomed. Furtive yellow lights glimmered. A Samsui should be afraid just to be here. Jhonni braked on the ferry path, using her feet; her bike needed attention. The place where Endang had touched her wrist felt the cool pressure still. Once, in Timur, she had believed that Ranganar no longer existed, that she had no home to go to. That moment didn't fade. It grew; it became more real than the streets. She looked up at the star-dusted sky. In the north, in Gamartha, Peninsulans were fighting for freedom. *"Soon,"* she whispered, saying goodbye. "Soon."